CAMILLE

Also by Bob Marshall-Andrews

The Palace of Wisdom

A Man Without Guilt

Off Message

CAMILLE

AND THE LOST DIARIES OF SAMUEL PEPYS

A NOVEL

by

BOB MARSHALL-ANDREWS

First published in the United Kingdom in 2016 by
Whitefox Publishing Ltd.
39 Roderick Road
London NW3 2NP

Set in Minion Pro

Designed and typeset by K.DESIGN, Winscombe, Somerset
Printed and bound by Clays Ltd, St Ives plc.

ISBN 978-1-911195-12-2

For Gill

• CONTENTS •

I discovered Camille Lefebre's manuscript in the basement of the Radcliffe Science Library, Oxford in July 2010. My pass to the Bodleian Library was to research "Corruption at Chatham Dockyard during the Restoration". Inevitably this included the work of Samuel Pepys as Secretary to the Navy. At Oxford, the Pepys library was in temporary accommodation in the basement of the Radcliffe during refurbishment of the Bodleian itself. Many of the manuscripts had been transferred in boxes and the otherwise excellent indexes were more difficult to locate. On a rainy Friday morning, I had requested documents relating to the purchase of thin rope at Chatham and Deptford in the 1690s. I received a cardboard storage box containing numerous Bodleian folders bearing archive tags linking them to the master index. The documents were largely financial accounts with little by way of manuscript notes. I became increasingly bored and was contemplating an end to the week's work with lunch at the Randolph in the company of a friendly and delightful don. I was repacking the box (half-read), when I noticed two bundles held together with red tape. They did not have archive tags and I assumed that they had become parted from their folder. Mainly through idle curiosity, I retrieved them onto my desk. The larger was bound in heavily waxed paper, cracked and bent with age. The smaller was a thin leather folder closed by a drop flap, the hinge of which was worn to the point of disintegration. I could find neither item described in the index. How they had arrived in the Pepys library was an immediate mystery. I had an hour till lunch and gently opened the larger bundle, hoping that it contained something other than detailed accounting. I was not disappointed. Inside was a block of fine paper, browning with age. I estimated something over 100 sheets. They contained, on both sides, uniform confident handwriting. Occasionally there were deletions and corrections, which indicated that they were certainly not the work of a copy clerk to the Navy. Furthermore, the entire manuscript was in French. In that language I possessed a working visitor's knowledge and I applied myself to the text.

The heading was simple and revealed why it had been consigned to the Pepys library.

Camille Lefebre. Récit de mes voyages avec Monsieur Pepys. 31 Décembre 1702.

I experienced something of a shock. The date revealed that it was written within months of Pepys's death. I was not a Pepys scholar but I was confident that this document was unknown. The fact that it had obviously been barely visited and certainly never copied confirmed that view. Shock became excitement, increased by the opening sentence on the first page:

C'est effarant de tuer un admirateur.

I stopped reading and sat back assembling my thoughts. I was due at lunch so I read no further but opened the second smaller packet by its leather hinge. I extracted the entire contents, some thirty pages of manuscript written on finer paper of considerable weight and quality. The writing was again in French and the hand undoubtedly the same. There was no title but the first words revealed its purpose. It was a diary.

Nouveau Journal de SP.

4 Mai 1670.

To Whitehall.

At lunch I shared my discovery with my guest. She listened, eyes wide with disbelief. We ate, drank a bottle of Meursault, and formed a plan. At two-thirty, I returned to the library, retrieved the bundles and approached the temporary desk. Would it be possible, I asked, to copy original documents within the boxes?

I was informed that it was indeed possible unless the folders were marked indicating that special permission was necessary from the head librarian. Was the folder so marked? This provided an immediate problem. The bundles were not found within a folder. I said that I would check. I returned to the box and selected the largest folder containing reams of naval accounts. I removed the accounts, inserted the pages from the packets and returned to the desk. The assistant assessed the volume and shook her head. That number of pages could not be copied until the following day and would be ready, on payment of 25p per page, by twelve noon on Saturday.

I returned at eleven-thirty, gripped by anxiety and half expecting the full library committee to be waiting. In the event I paid £128.50, and retrieved the copies and originals, which I replaced perfectly within the box. Two days later I delivered the copies to my friend Catherine Poinso. When I showed her my discoveries over lunch in Richmond, she reacted with Gallic sangfroid and said she would contact me that evening. When she did so, she asked questions in a tone of repressed excitement. What was the source? Were there other related documents? Were they genuine? Who knew of their existence? I answered them all as best I could. At the end there was a long pause in which I thought she made notes. Finally she came to practicalities. The French was 300 years old. The vast majority was legible but some required interpretation. It would take her three months, during which we would need to meet regularly for lunch. That, she said, would amply repay the work. Finally she came to publication. Was it to be an academic tract? If so she would apply literal translation. If not she would apply the liberal modern vernacular. I had anticipated the question. Let us, I said, give Camille the voice she would want. *D'accord*, she said, *d'accord*.

All that was five years ago. Now, on the eve of publication, I ask myself again if I have behaved *properly*. Should I have revealed my discoveries to the library, to the university, to the academic world? Was I guilty of some form of theft, some deceit? These questions and their consequences have occupied sleepless churnings in the darkness before dawn. In the end, I have no doubts. Had I revealed the manuscripts they would have been seized upon by querulous and conflicting academics. Camille's voice would have been drowned before it was heard. Doubts would have been cast on its very authenticity. Her spirit would be submerged by scholarship. Finally, in the early hours, I asked myself how Pepys himself would have advised: "Publish and be buggered," he would have said. And so I have.

One thing still causes me concern. Three months ago Catherine phoned to tell me that their wine cellar in Twickenham had been flooded. The wine had all been salvaged subject to the labels.

Unfortunately the cellar had been used for the storage of non-essential documents, which included the copies of Camille's manuscript. All had been ruined beyond salvage. I immediately contacted my Oxford friend, now happily sitting on a Chair of Nineteenth-Century Literature. I carefully described the box into which I had placed the original bundles and she undertook to use her Bodleian ticket to retrieve them. The Pepys library had now been returned to the Bodleian itself and was the subject of a new computerised index. Despite thorough digital searches and physical investigation carried out by her willing undergraduates, no trace has been found.

B M-A

• CHAPTER 1 •

It is an awesome thing to kill an admirer; the more so if he is of noble birth and from a family capable of terrible revenge.

The murder (which it was not but which it came to be called) took place in rue d'Essaye, where it bisects the rue des Verriers. It occurred a few hours before on the morning of 1st of May 1670. I was on my way to my lodgings. The weather was warm and close and the tight corset that I wore to flatten my bosom caused some minor discomfort, as did the redundant leather codpiece strapped over a void. I was also a little drunk, the result of my amazing success. I carried the fruits of that success, a sum of money equivalent to five years' work and advanced as a single extraordinary sum. I was happy, newly rich and professionally fulfilled.

Murderous I was not.

I heard them before they came into view and, surprisingly, I recognised the noise from the theatre a few hours before. Even there the raucous drunken babble had risen above the near-deafening applause. I remember now the grip of apprehension. I was alone and the street was deserted. Dawn was in the sky but it remained quite dark. The torches, lit to discourage the congregation of tarts, had guttered to their extreme end and the only other light fell from a pair of open shutters beyond which candelabra burned upon a raised table. From the approaching noise I instantly calculated four or five voices and as many expletives shouted in chorus. It carried the atmosphere of threat and challenge which always has attended the revels of drunken men. I contemplated retreat but the junction was very close and the rue d'Essaye runs dead straight. Any increased distance would have negligible effect and would have involved the turning of my back. The rue d'Essaye has no doorways or arbours. I could see a small alleyway, the Passage Dorse, on my left, but it was closer to the junction and, before I reached it, they came into view, five in all and walking abreast. I immediately took their attention and they paused before one, the smallest as I recollect, barely two inches taller than myself gave the first shout.

"Aye, aye, now what have we here? I think we know who this is, don't we my boys? This is someone famous. Someone fucking famous and wandering around without any company."

As he spoke they moved towards me, appearing to fan out across the road. Instinctively I clasped at the hilt of my sword. It was noticed.

"Aye, aye, a fight is it then? A fight?"

He adopted a grotesque swagger with his hips thrust forward and grasped his own sword, as did his companions.

"No, I don't think so," he continued. "Because we know who you are, don't we my boys? Robert Lefebre. *Monsieur* Lefebre, the greatest female impersonator in the whole of Paris, France, the *World* on his way home from the Théâtre du Marais all alone."

They were now, all of them, close, within a sword's length. The smallest, unmistakably the leader, had his face within two feet of my own: a plump, handsome, cruel face. The eyes were hard but swimming in a sea of alcoholic milk. He was drunk but he was steady enough and he reeked of brandy.

"Robert Lefebre. Robert Lefebre. *Monsieur* Robert Lefebre.

We have spent a lot of this evening watching you on the stage. Haven't we my boys? Haven't we?"

As they nodded I said: "You are right I am Robert Lefebre and now, if you don't mind, I am tired and on my way home."

It appeared to amuse him:

"Tired is it? Tired is it? After two hours dressed as a tart it would be, wouldn't it? Yes, it would."

Unexpectedly he thrust his face forward to within inches of my own.

"You know what?" he said. "You know what? You were fucking magnificent."

*   *   *

Considering I was to kill him scarce minutes later, I find it difficult to confess now to a moment of passing pleasure. A feeling I acknowledge reflects badly in the circumstances. But then I was a thespian, and a thespian to my boots.

Magnificent! Yes, I had been magnificent. The Théâtre du Marais would never forget it and Paris would talk of it for months.

As I had delivered my final lines, still, poignant, full of exquisite irony, I heard from the packed and silent audience an audible and collective sigh. What followed as the performance drew to a close was a torrent, a tumult. Universal applause was followed by cheering. It spread throughout the packed auditorium as though orchestrated by a baton. I curtseyed and curtseyed again. I lifted my bowed head and turned. Behind me I saw the entire cast, now assembled on the stage, were also applauding. I raised my arms towards them, then spun as though in character towards the auditorium and raised my arms again *les embrassant tous du regard.* The roar became a transportation, coherent but uncontrolled and then *they rose,* the entire audience rose and extended their arms. The curtain fell, rose and fell, rose again and finally, as it fell, I swept my hand decisively towards the engineers in the wings and we, the cast, remained frozen, a tableau facing the red velours. The anti-climax became unbearable. We left the stage; exchanges were whispered between us, quiet and exhausted.

I had nearly reached my dressing room when Paul Detain caught me by the arm.

"Camille . . . Robert! You must come back! They are screaming for you."

I shook my head.

"No, no, no."

"You must. You *must.*"

I did. I stood in the centre of the stage alone. A muffled, indistinguishable roar came from beyond the drapes. The curtain rose again and this time it rained flowers, sweets, parcels and money. Coins, gold and silver beat an uneven discord on the boards. I bowed once more, raised my eyes and then I saw them. They occupied the first tier box nearest the stage. The most expensive, the most regal, the most eye-catching of them all. Rich and lurid, they chanted together. Simultaneously they thrust their right arms towards the stage, fingers extended, in apparent mockery. The chant I did not hear but I saw those in the boxes around and beneath react with anger and contempt. And finally, as the curtain fell, from that very box a missile struck the stage, bounced beneath the curtain and finished at my feet. A bird, a capon perhaps, stuffed, half eaten with the head retained as a curious decoration. As the carcass rolled the head rose and fell in a parody of nervous flight.

I was shocked, but not much. I stepped across the bird and stooped to gather a small posy of the finest flowers. I left the stage and, on the way to my dressing room, directed our stage manager to share the money with the crew. As I opened my dressing room door, the small exclamation I gave was not entirely theatrical. I had anticipated the possibility of visitors and, indeed, the very man who rose from my seat and gathered me in his arms.

"Camille," he said into my ear, "*Robert*, you were magnificent."

"I know," I replied, withdrawing and patting his cheek. "And I see you have bought champagne."

On my dressing table, a bucket, one of the props of the play, revealed at its lip three bottles of Pérignon, one already open.

"I have," he said. "I bought them before the performance as a celebration and I was right."

"I did not see you in the auditorium."

"I was in the gods, the only place I could find in my own theatre. Here . . ."

He handed me a glass and began to pour the wine.

"Let us drink to your magnificent success."

"It is not just me Paul," I said. "It is a fine cast and a great play, a great play."

Paul did not answer me but a voice came from behind the partition, which separated the two dressing tables in my room. As he spoke the concealed gentleman stepped forward, smiled and briefly bowed his head.

"Yes," he said. "You were magnificent. It is true that it is a great play and that Racine is a fine playwright but it was you that they applauded. I can say with certainty that I have never seen an audience applaud like that."

With a movement of his glass he acknowledged my surprise.

"I am sorry to have been hiding in your room. Paul wanted to congratulate you first without my interference. As he owns most of the theatre and the rights to the play, not to mention you, he may do as he pleases."

Paul Detain, who was indeed the director of the Marais, replaced the bottle in the bucket and said:

"I think that you know Jean Molière?"

"I have spoken his words on many occasions but we have never met. I am honoured monsieur."

Detain indicated the three chairs, which were placed in the cubicles.

"That is enough of the performance. We all know what it was and we all know what it means. The Théâtre du Marais will be full for months. We will attract society. Who knows, the King himself may attend his own box if he can be coaxed from Versailles."

"Speaking of society," I said, "there was one part of the audience which did not appear in tune."

"Ah," said Paul. "The first tier box on the right? The dead bird? Yes, I saw it. The Marquis de Pertaine, his brother Michel and their gang. Nasty, dangerous and very rich, the sons of the Duc de Pertaine and even nastier than their father. They were very drunk but I am afraid that we could not deny them a box. The theatre would have been attacked."

"Dramatic art," said Molière, "has few friends in the aristocracy. I know. I myself have been attacked. The King is an exception. He provided me with my first theatre and, even now, stages my work at Versailles."

Paul Detain raised his hand. "Do not let us worry. They will not come again and are best forgotten. Let us to business. I, we, have a proposition."

"For me?" I asked.

"Indeed, for you. Jean wishes to return to Paris. He has a play but two more are already in gestation. He wishes to write them for you."

In my dressing mirror I saw my eyes widen.

"For me?"

"Indeed, for you, around you," Molière smiled. "I want you as a muse and as my dramatic interpreter. You have precisely what I want. Your beauty is, of course, a byword but your timing, ah your timing, is beyond compare. I can give you words that can make you history. I can give you parts that will make you legend. One play is ready. I have called it *Les Femmes Savantes*. It suits you perfectly."

I looked, and was, stunned. Beneath the stage powder my colour rose.

"But my contract . . .?"

"Your contract terminates," said Paul, "with the end of this play. I will renew it for a series of three plays. Tomorrow we will announce that *Bérénice* will run for four or five months. An end date will ensure that our performances are packed. After tonight and the inevitable reviews, tickets will fetch a premium from which we can all benefit."

In the pause I said: "I am committed."

"I know," Paul interrupted, "committed to return home. Also, I know that your present *arrangements* are intolerable. But I have discovered something from Jean which you should know. The edict will shortly be repealed."

Both men looked at me whilst my thoughts spun. I knew, of course, the edict to which he referred. For eight months, by municipal decree, women under thirty had been banned from the stages of Paris, a city which contained the greatest French theatres of the age. Female public performances were to be equated with organised prostitution, punished by fines and, if repeated, by incarceration and even branding. The edict had not been tested. The artifice which I employed enjoyed a measure of toleration but artifice it undoubtedly was. I was Robert Lefebre, female impersonator extraordinaire. Outside the theatre, my public appearances, my journeys to and from my address in the rue Feuillette, were as Robert Lefebre, a man of striking, effeminate good looks who, notwithstanding his fame, declined all invitations in society.

When not working I adopted yet another disguise. The stage beauty known increasingly throughout Paris became a woman of indeterminate age and modest demeanour who frequented the shops and occasionally the bars of the rue d'Essaye but otherwise kept no company at all.

These circumstances were, indeed, intolerable. As Molière said, I was beautiful. Not perfect but beautiful. And I was young; a young and beautiful woman with a young and beautiful woman's needs. To have your bosom crushed by whalebone and to display a ridiculous codpiece was, to say the least, an inhibition. In 1670, Paris was the artistic centre of the world. I wanted to be part of it. I *was* part of it but only as an actor on a stage.

"When it is to be repealed?"

Paul gestured towards Molière who said:

"Soon, within three months. The King himself has indicated his opposition. The edict is a municipal edict only. It cannot withstand the royal displeasure."

"I have my family in Périgord . . ."

"And your brother," said Paul. "Yes, I know and I know how important that is. You have told me more than once. There is, however, a solution. If you did not return to Périgord why should your brother not come to Paris?"

"He needs me."

"Precisely, then he can come to Paris."

"But I have no accommodation. No suitable facilities."

Paul smiled, refilled the glasses and said:

"That can be cured. Let us talk about terms. I will tell you what I have in mind. Let us assume, as we must, that Jean's three plays enjoy their traditional success, magnified greatly by your own contribution. Allowing six months for the present production I would propose a contract term for two years."

He raised a hand to stop my interruption.

"I know that such contracts are unheard of in the French theatre, but in your case an exception must be made. I would not expect you to commit yourself to such an undertaking unless the terms were exceptional."

He paused. Both men watched me intently waiting for my next reaction.

"The terms I have in mind," Paul said quickly, "are 500 *livres* a year."

Any theatrical reaction was unnecessary. I gasped and my hand rose to my bosom and then to my mouth.

"*Five hundred livres?*"

"Indeed, 500 *livres* for two years. 1,000 *livres* in all. With such a sum you may take lodgings in the Bois de Boulogne, Les Halles, wherever you wish. You will have a salon. Your family may visit as often and as long as they wish. Accommodation will be no problem and, for your brother, of course, suitable care and facilities can be provided without difficulty. Here, have some more champagne."

In the pause that followed, I looked from one to the other, literally struck dumb.

"Finally," said Paul, "if you are prepared to accept, I am proposing to advance six months – 250 *livres* in gold and payable *now*."

Paul was a theatre manager, the best in Paris, and probably in France, but he was no thespian. However, there was no mistaking the drama with which he produced the leather sac from behind the champagne bucket. He put it on the edge of my dressing table and smiled.

"Two-hundred-and-fifty *livres* in gold, to begin to pursue your life's ambitions. What do you say?"

What was there to say? Nothing. I rose silently, executed a full pirouette and sunk into a stage curtsey of acrobatic élan. I straightened, took my glass of champagne and said:

"Well, Monsieur Molière, tell me about these plays."

We drank. We spoke for three hours and drank as many more

bottles of champagne. When they left me I was more than a little drunk, which accounted for my decision to carry 250 *livres* into the Parisian night. I removed my make-up and my costume and stood naked before my mirror. I was reflected on three sides and I allowed myself a variety of poses from demure to erotic and then, with a sigh, became Robert Lefebre. The whalebone flattened my finest features, while the breeches and the boots completed my transition. Finally the male wig was placed firmly upon woman's hair, gathered into a severe bun. I applied the belt buckle and sword and crossed the deserted stage and wings to the stage door. It was opened by André, the doorman, a role he had enjoyed for thirty years, and I stepped onto the cobbles. The night was clear and the dawn was beginning to light the shuttered street. I strode to the avenue Fause, crossed, entered the rue d'Essaye and walked towards the junction where I would meet my nemesis and Michel de Pertaine would meet his premature death.

CHAPTER 2

Who am I? I am Camille Lefebre; now a woman of a certain age and much experience. How did this memoir come to exist? How was it *provoked*? It happened on the last day of 1702. From my windows I could see rain driving across the Bois de Boulogne obscuring the Pas de Marche where, more than thirty years ago, I had fought to the death. I was impatient and listening for sounds of arrival. After nine years of slaughter France was at peace and my son, freed from the army, was to visit his mother to celebrate the New Year. I was surprised by the knock on my door. Jacques knows it is always open. A messenger stood at the entrance, removing a package from his satchel. His riding clothes were drenched and his boots covered in mud. When he spoke it was in English, a language now heard again in Paris five years after the war: "Was I Camille Lefebre, otherwise known as Catherine Browne?" At the mention of my second name he watched my eyes widen with shock and smiled as he handed me the parcel, covered in oilskin.

"I have been told," he said, "to give this to you and no one else."

I weighed it in my hand and asked the obvious questions: "What is it and who sent it?"

He smiled again. "I do not know the contents but I was given it in Clapham by a man called Will Hewer. He asked me to tell you that your friend is very unwell and wished, above all that you should have it. There is no other message. My charges have been paid."

I knew, of course, what it was. I felt my heart pound and my colour rise. As the messenger turned to go I said, "Will you not come in? You are wet through and must be cold."

He shook his head. "I have taken lodgings very close and I must be ready to return tomorrow. But thank you."

I returned to my study overlooking the Bois and placed the package on my desk. I poured myself a glass of brandy and sat before it. My stomach was tense and my throat knotted. I felt, already, tears smart in my eyes. The brandy calmed me. After ten minutes I fetched a paring knife from the kitchen, breathed deeply, steadied my hands, and cut through the binding and the outer skin. There was an inner lining, not bound, which parted easily. It revealed a black leather folder which I had last seen in Paris thirty-two years before.

I did not immediately open it but sat stroking the leather. It had obviously been guarded well and its condition appeared unchanged. Only the worn hinge indicated that it had been opened on many occasions. I took another deep breath and a large swallow of brandy, opened the flap and drew out the papers inside.

They were exactly as I had left them, unaltered and meticulously in order. The diary sheets of the finest quality paper bore signs of wear. They had been frequently read and replaced. Otherwise they were undamaged. My handwriting has changed over the years but remained unmistakable. The diary entries, fourteen in all, were in French save for some of the opening words. I took up the first sheet and, through blurred eyes read the first line in English: *To Whitehall.*

It was too much. Memory flowed into my brain, clear and rising like a boy's song. Uncontrollably, I wept and read at the same time. The tears I kept from the paper by holding it before me in the light of the candles.

In barely an hour I reached the last lines of the last entry:

And so, finally tonight we will celebrate with the instruments and the bottle. We have achieved the means for a great government and that, for now, is enough.

I was able to stop weeping and reflect. On the day after I wrote those words I had been flayed by the rapier in the very woods I now saw disappearing into the Paris night. The man who dictated them to me saved my life.

With a new resolve I poured another brandy and sat at my spinet. Absorbed at the keyboard I did not hear Jacques arrive behind me. When I paused I was startled by his applause. As I embraced him he said, "Bravo, *Vertes Manches*, I have not heard you play it for years." He pulled away from me and said, "Maman, you are crying. You have been crying before, I can see. What is it?"

In reply I could only gesture at the documents on my desk. He crossed the room, picked them up and began to read by the candle. I heard him exclaim as he turned to me, his eyes wide with disbelief, "Are these . . . Are these the diaries?"

When I nodded he said, "Pepys? These have come from Pepys?"

I nodded again and he crossed the room to hold me. "Maman, this is wonderful. They came today? That is why you were playing *Vertes Manches*. Of course. Of course."

His pleasure was infectious and I began to laugh. He heard the slight hysteria and took control: "More brandy for you and for me. I must read these notorious writings. Then let us eat before we celebrate and discuss them."

And we did. The writings were notorious, of course, only to my family and children, who had been told of them from infancy. Jacques was, he said, not disappointed. His imagination had carried them accurately all his life. Towards the end of our meal, over champagne, he became serious. "Would Pepys," he asked, "now publish the diaries?"

I shook my head: "I have heard that he still has many enemies in Parliament. Twice they have had him committed to the Tower. Some would say that the diaries reveal high treason. Perhaps they do. They cannot be published until he is dead."

Jacques looked at me over his glass: "And then?"

"I don't know."

He rose, took a chair, and sat by my side. "Maman," he said, "You must write it. Not just the diaries but the whole story: you, him, the Kings and the Treaty, the politics, the murder, the revenge, the duels, all of it. The diaries will be part of it, real and in context. You *must* do it."

We went to bed, a little drunk, shortly after one. I could not sleep. Jacques's words and those of the diary would not leave my brain. Splinters of memory, some painful, could not be ignored. Finally, after seven, I returned to my desk and watched the light appear between the trees.

I made myself coffee, a taste I had acquired in England. I retrieved a supply of paper from the drawer. It was not the best but good enough. I carefully laid out the pile of diaries, selected a nib, opened the ink and began.

Shortly after eight, Jacques found me writing by the light of a clear winter's day. He prepared more coffee for us both, stood by the desk and selected the first of the newly written pages before saying, "May I?" As I smiled and nodded he began to read:

It is an awesome thing to kill an admirer; the more so if he is of noble birth and from a family capable of terrible revenge.

He made no comment and within the hour was ready to leave. He came to stand behind me and gently restrained me from rising, "Don't stop," he said. "Don't stop."

* * *

I was born on the 25th of May, 1645, twenty minutes earlier than my twin brother Robert Lefebre, whose identity I was to assume with such terrible consequences. We were born in my mother's bedroom in the Mas Lefebre whose shuttered windows overlooked our considerable estates close to the village of Tocanne in the region of Périgord.

My mother's maiden name was Catherine Browne and she was, as she sounds, English. Four years before we were born she had met my father, Jean Lefebre, in London. She was playing Ophelia at the Fortune Theatre. Despite the political turmoil that marked the coming Civil War, the theatres of London glittered with performances of Shakespeare, Marlowe, Kyd, Deker, Suckling and a hundred more. The theatres were full to overflowing as though the public, themselves, could anticipate the eighteen years of darkness enforced by a Puritan age. The last theatre closed in 1642. The genius of Shakespeare branded as sin and silenced as the grave.

My father, then twenty-eight, attended the very last performance and watched my mother (twenty-five) bow with her resurrected Hamlet to an ovation extended inevitably by the universal knowledge of impending censor. My father that night was in company that was well known to my mother and her family. He was, therefore, spared the clichéd indignity of camping at the stage door of The Fortune and, within days, had obtained an introduction to his future wife at one of the remaining salons in Piccadilly. Here they fell in love and, within six months, had married and decamped to France. The marriage enjoyed the blessing of my mother's family, four of whom – her father and three brothers – were to die on the same day in the Royalist cause at Naseby. My father had been sent by his family to study English agriculture at the great college in the town of Wickham. The English had created a husbandry that was the envy of Europe, and certainly the envy of the landed classes of France. It was historical and genetic accident that the Lefebres' estates had retained both their size and the substantial living which was their yield. My father was the only surviving son of an only son and, in the preceding generation, the plague had accounted for all but one of seven other children.

In his two years at Wickham my father had acquired an eccentric use of English and also a raft of friends whose lands extended throughout England and to the borders of Wales. In the Civil War that followed, the majority of them took the Royalist cause but not all. Several fought on opposing sides and many died. It was during a gathering of these friends in London, the last as it transpired, that my father was taken to observe his first Shakespeare play and my mother.

My mother had no further children after the birth of her twins. This was deliberate and agreed with my father, who had perceived in England the advantages of defined inheritance. She was unable to return to her profession. In England for eighteen years there was no stage and the growing theatres of Paris and Lyon were distant. These were beginning to employ the greatest playwrights of their age but their dialogues and repartee required a native tongue. She was content. She was the mistress of the Mas, kind, calm, well liked by the staff and contractors who fell within her domestic rule. Her education was remarkable for an English woman of her time and her reading was eclectic and vast. She accumulated a substantial library containing English, French and Italian literature, which occupied three rooms on the first landing where I obtained much of my education.

My father, by contrast, read little but applied his English-taught husbandry with a strenuous zeal. In all he nurtured and farmed ten thousand acres of Périgord. We grew cereals, barley and corn. Our livestock contained three herds of cattle, two hundred pigs, yards of scratching hens and fine horses for carriage, plough and pleasure. We produced a substantial quantity of indifferent wine. Two thousand acres were kept as rolling woodland, dropping majestically to the shores of the Dordogne. In them, he and his neighbours hunted for boar and allowed the hunting of truffles with minimal taxation in kind.

By reason of his inheritance he held a prefect's rank and, as a result, travelled to Paris a dozen times a year, sometimes with my mother but more frequently alone. He was, I was later to discover, a considerable philanthropist and philanderer. Neither activity affected the serenity of our lives although both, I believed, taxed my mother's patience as housekeeper and a wife.

So it was perfection, an idyll? Not quite.

We were identical twins, Robert and I. Identical in appearance but that was all. I arrived in the world as I continued, noisy, energetic, already running a furious race, legs pumping and fists clenched hard as steel. They say the prehensile grip of a child is sufficient to take its full weight and to ensure survival beneath the canopy of primeval forest. With my grip I could have hung for days shrieking angry defiance at imaginary wolves. My eyes were my mother's eyes, wide open at birth. The minute they left the pubic girdle, they gazed unblinking at a wondrous world.

Twenty minutes later a different child arrived, inert, listless and, at first horrified assessment, dead. Energetic battering and massage caused tentative movement and finally a whimpering and mewling noise close to a sigh with eyes tight shut against a terrifying reality. All of this my mother told me, and told me again. I had, apparently, in my rush towards life absorbed his oxygen causing the brain to seize. And, thereafter, we grew side by side, manifest and faithful representations of our birth.

The identical beauty we both possessed seemed, in its very sameness, to be a mockery. This, in near entirety, was owed to my mother. From my early childhood I walked with her in the streets of Tocanne and saw men's heads snap round as though compelled by the same force. Her English features had a careless pale symmetry. She possessed an abundance of blonde hair and startling blue eyes, enhanced as she grew older by deepening creases of good humour. Her mouth, like ours, was too big, her nose pointedly too long and her chin a little heavy. The ensemble was stunning as it was with us all.

My father was an ox of a man, handsome in a way that spoke of the earth and its usage. He was immensely strong, a characteristic which he endowed in me but not, unhappily, in Robert. For my brother it was as though the struggles to breathe had exhausted the very sinews and muscles which propelled him into life. We were, at first sight, identical in build but the first sign of movement portrayed the difference. I was agile, quick, possessed of near-perfect physical timing and, by way of accompaniment, near-perfect pitch. Robert moved without apparent coordination. There was no spasm or palsy but a physical dysfunction as though cerebral commands were passed through long chains of different lengths and timing. His awkwardness and the obvious inability either to fight or flee imparted a natural nervousness. His eyes were either wide or flickered with nervous anticipation. It was in marked sad contrast to my own steady, increasingly ironical stare.

From an early age, tutored by my mother, I could speak both French and English with a fluid facility and could effortlessly mix both to find precisely the right nuance and intonation. I could, my mother observed theatrically, time a line at a hundred paces. Robert stuttered. Words, either French or English, found their early syllables hopelessly snared at the point of delivery, repeated with agonizing, toneless repetition until, inevitably, the frustrated listener supplied the word and, in doing so, another small humiliation.

Despite, or because of this, I loved him beyond all imaginings. Every frail disability increased my adoration. Behind it lay not guilt but an awesome responsibility. If I had taken his oxygen then I would give it back and I did everything in my power to fill the gulf between our abilities and aspirations.

We were educated at the Mas and had tutors that were the best Périgord could provide or that anyone could afford.

There were five in all. Literature, French, English and a little German was provided by a tall, bespectacled gentleman, originally from the University at Bordeaux but now firmly settled in the village of Duchapt, three miles to the west. The classics, Greek and Latin, were taught by one half of a diminutive couple from Rouen. The other half, a stern humourless woman, provided mathematics and the basic sciences, skills learnt from her father, a professor at the University of Lyon. Music – the lute, the spinet – and some grounding in fine art was left to a gentleman who sold musical instruments in Périgueux itself, a perilous living he augmented by enjoyable but inexpert tutorship. Finally, at the insistence of my mother (and to a great extent, myself), a young man was obtained for ten hours a week with a broad brief to cover the dramatic arts and athletic pursuits of every unspecified nature, which included the use of the rapier and the broadsword.

His name was Jacques Delaine, the son of a master builder from Rheims. At the age of nineteen he joined the army, obtained a commission and was wounded at the Battle of Arras in 1654, when a musket ball passed clean through his neck. He made a full recovery but his commission was not renewed. He was granted a pension that gave him a measure of independence and allowed him to travel to Paris. He possessed no formal skills other than the use of the rapier, at which he was exceptional.

In Paris he rented rooms in the Place de Nîmes and embarked on a career as a writer, for which he had no talent whatsoever. He did, however, keep bohemian company in the *demi monde*. It was through the recommendation of one of his lovers that he attended the Théâtre du Petit Bourbon to audition for the role of Jodelet in Molière's first masterpiece *Les Précieuses ridicules*. It was immediately obvious that he possessed a rare and extraordinary talent and the production was a famous success. Lead roles followed one upon the other and, at the age of thirty, he became, briefly, one of the acknowledged stars of Paris society. He was rakish, handsome, liberated and, then, totally without scruple. His fame and theatrical fortune lasted for three years. Disaster arrived in the beautiful form of Annette Dubarry, the teenage wife of Paul Dubarry, a man of immense wealth. In his mid-sixties he was the main patron of the Hôtel de Bourgogne, later to become the Comédie Française. The affair between Annette and Jacques Delaine became the talk of Paris and was finally discovered by her husband during a production of *Monde*'s translation of *Othello*, in which Jacques Delaine played the Moor. Dubarry, unwisely, paid an unexpected visit to Jacques's dressing room to find his young wife playing her part in Iago's 'beast with two backs', gazing breathlessly into the mirror with the blackened face of Jacques Delaine immediately above her. By reasons of his immense wealth there were few more powerful men in Paris than Paul Dubarry. Jacques Delaine wisely departed the capital and arrived six months' later in Périgord, desperately in need of a job. He applied for and obtained the post of tutor to the twin children of Jean Lefebre, a post which included accommodation in the annex joining the Mas.

His task was to teach us the rudiments of dramatic arts, the secrets of deportment, timing, gesture, pace and repartee and also the basics of swordsmanship, essential then and now to a theatrical career. I was fifteen and, so he informed my mother within a week, possessed of extraordinary thespian talents. In addition to an impeccable sense of timing and natural grace of movement, I could mimic any accent, impersonate any acquaintance, male or female after the briefest of meeting, throw my voice the complete length of our barn, pitched at barely a whisper and, by adopting the subtlest movement and contortion, appear as man or woman of any age or class.

"She is," said Jacques Delaine to my mother, "simply a genius."

"Yes," replied the former actress and doyenne of the English stage, "I know, Jacques, but, for God's sake, don't let her know."

Perceiving, rightfully, that there was little he could teach me, Jacques concentrated on Robert with my assistance. He was a gifted and patient teacher and, through the recitation of text and careful and repeated dialogue, Robert's stammer improved. Over months, with intense concentration and slow delivery, most diction became possible.

Three times a week we spent two hours with the rapier. For Robert this was quite impossible and would have been dangerous if not suicidal. So he sat and watched, smiling and occasionally laughing as I learnt the business of thrust and parry, cut and feint at the hands of a master with whom I was rapidly falling in love. The basic elements I swiftly mastered. Within three months, the mock duels that we fought had moved well beyond demonstration and emulation. After six months, although I could not beat him, it became exceptionally difficult for him to beat me. By the time I was sixteen he had long ceased even to call the passes.

"Thrust, cut, parry, parry, cut, slash, parry."

And so the months passed and the years. Other tutors came and went but Jacques became part of the family. By the time I approached eighteen, formal lessons were no more. I was deemed fit and ready for marriage. There was no shortage of suitors. It was widely known that Robert's disabilities would ensure that I would effectively inherit the Mas and I was as eligible as any woman in France. My father took rooms in Paris, in Les Halles, and I was encouraged to enter Paris society. Here more young men, some on the borders of French aristocracy, provided attention and extravagant gifts, all of which I politely refused. I liked some of my suitors but to most I was indifferent. I was already in love in Tocanne with a man against whom I duelled on a daily basis.

When not engaged in swordsmanship, we increasingly walked together through the estate and the woods, rehearsing all manner of drama, whilst Robert limped behind us.

Some of the texts we had used in tutorials we now had word perfect. The new works of Racine, Molière and Corneille were randomly mixed with Shakespeare, Marlowe and Middleton into a multi-lingual *mélange*. Sometimes we fenced with our swords or used branches to improvise imaginary duels. The death of Mercutio and then the death of Tybalt were enacted furiously in translation before Robert, his eyes wide with wonder, his mouth open in silent applause. Sometimes we just talked. The army had given Jacques a taste for politics. The Civil War in England, which had brought the death of the majority of my mother's family, had now given way to the Commonwealth. We argued lightly, without conviction. I was a natural Monarchist. In Versailles, the Sun King presided over peace and, for us in Périgord, prosperity and plenty. Jacques professed himself a Parliamentarian. History, he said, rendered inevitable a return to the abandoned democracies of Greece. On one occasion he stopped and selected a pebble from the stream by which we walked. He gave it to me.

"*Psephos*," he said, "the vote. It is inevitable."

"But for whom?" I argued. "What class, what section of the people possesses the collective wisdom to govern?"

He smiled. "One day it will be universal."

As my eyes widened, he laughed.

"But not, Camille, in your lifetime or mine. Much blood must be shed. More kings and princes will die on the block."

I shook my head and we launched without deliberation into the balcony scene, for which I climbed into the fork of the nearest oak.

"Roméo," I said, improvising and murdering the text, "Où es-tu? Lève toi! Monte tout de suite!"

He did as he was bidden. Within seconds he was sitting beside me. The lower branches and the leaves shielded us from Robert, who scuffed the ground looking for truffles. He kissed me, more than once. He touched my breasts. His hand moved towards my waist. I removed it.

"No," I said, "not now."

We descended and walked to the Mas in silence. We parted with barely a word and in my room, as the night disappeared behind the shutters, I counted the minutes and the hours until our next duel.

I was up at seven and by eight changed into my best boots and doublet. I was waiting for him in our barn, the rapier already in my hand. I had a plan.

One of the gifts that I possessed, no doubt at the expense of my poor brother, was to be ambidextrous. Robert was clumsy and ill-coordinated in either hand. I possessed equal power and dexterity in both. I had a plan. When Jacques arrived he smiled with surprise to see me poised and ready. He selected his rapier. We presented arms and went at the game with extraordinary and renewed passion. Thrust, parry, thrust, cut, slash, parry. We moved backwards, forwards, circling, then, as he came forward at the lunge I spun, a perfect pirouette. As I did so I changed the sword between my gloved hands. When I faced him a split second later I thrust with the right and he parried against nothing, the air. Before he could recover the button of my sword, clasped in my left hand, was against his throat.

"Touché, mon cher," I said, "touché."

We remained so for moments while Robert applauded wildly. I tossed the rapier onto the rack and we moved silently and alone to the path we had taken before and to the Juliet tree. Robert, still in the house, would miss us soon but not before we had made love beneath its branches. I was eighteen years and three months. This was my first passion and in the years, the travels and the adventures to come, it was never equalled.

We lay together afterwards and spoke of the future. Every word I spoke was on the assumption of imminent marriage. The stewardship of the Mas, what role he would play and how he would, in time, assume the responsibilities and management of our mighty estate. He said little, nodding occasionally, caressing my face and then, mindful of my brother, we rose, dressed and reached the Mas as our steward, Jean-Pierre emerged with the bread and wine for breakfast.

Jacques was to go to Ribérac that day to purchase books. That evening I was due with my parents for dinner with a relative at a neighbouring Mas. By agreement I said nothing to my parents about my new plans with my tutor and, when we returned shortly before midnight, I contemplated storming the annex in which he lived. I did not. Time enough in a future of wonders, drama, duels and delights.

The following day he was gone. No word, no message, no gift. I searched everywhere, of course, an exercise in utter futility. His clothes, his books, his weapons were all gone. Eventually I found one thing. Inserted in the hilt of my rapier, on the rack in the barn, a pebble, smooth from years of running water. Now, after thirty years, I have it still.

CHAPTER 3

I was not the only member of my family who had attachments to Jacques Delaine. He had lived with us, effectively as part of us, for three years. Each of us, in our own way, had developed our affections for this handsome, talented buccaneer. Robert, of course, adored him, attributing rightly to his tutorials the improvement in his speech, his confidence and his coordination. My father, who had himself served peacefully in the army, enjoyed the exchange of soldier's tales, and my mother, denied participation in the momentous events in England, spent hours at our dining table discussing the politics of a republic yet to be born. Where Jacques had obtained his knowledge of politics or his dedication to the *cause populaire* I never knew but he carried as part of his portmanteau letters from Walwyn, Rainsborough, and other obscure radicals of whom, then, I had never heard.

When it was discovered that he had literally disappeared there was, of course, a family inquest. My own pain was observable enough in the signs of dashed and unrequited love. I pined, became solitary, ate little and slept less, none of which was lost to my mother. Three days after the event she took me to her private dressing room and spoke English as an added precaution.

"Was there anything between you?" she asked, employing the understated nuance of her mother tongue. For this I was prepared and I simply inclined my head. My pain was, of course, increased by the risk that I would become pregnant. I resisted the temptation, great though it was, to confide that in my mother.

Following my affirmation my mother's tone became gentle.

"Tell me," she said, "what occurred and for how long?"

I told her much of the truth. I rehearsed our daily activity and the growing closeness between us based on our own theatre and the refined beauty of the rapier. Then I lied. Jacques, I said, came to me two days before he left. He had professed his love and a passion which he had hidden for many months. Friendship, alone, he had said, was no longer possible. He proposed love, marriage, a life dedicated to the service of my family and to the estate.

All of this was spoken directly in English under my mother's clear and penetrating gaze. She did not believe me I know, but it did not matter. I told her I had rejected him firmly and with kindness. I acknowledged a deep friendship likely to endure for the rest of our lives but denied the existence of passion or love. I said he had taken it well but was obviously much distressed. When he left, I added, at the full pitch of mendacity, I was not altogether surprised.

At the end of my account there was a long silence between us. She then demonstrated clearly the level of her sceptical intuition.

"Did anything," she said, "occur?"

Again I shook my head and lied.

"He wanted to," I said, "but I denied him."

My mother was still, twenty-five years after leaving the stage, an accomplished actor. The willing suspension of disbelief was, after all, her stock-in-trade. She lifted her eyes to the ceiling then recommended a number of potions, elixirs and tonics which, she said, she took regularly to avoid the risk of childbirth. She also listed a number of strange exercises and postures which seemed, to me, both uncomfortable and futile.

I took the pills and the potions and, within a week, endured my always regular monthly period. Whether my mother's nostrums had the slightest effect I will never know but I retained the knowledge nonetheless and, on occasions in the following years, have used it with the same results.

A month later I was summoned to the presence of both my parents in the salon which overlooked our estate and, beyond it, the great sweep of the Périgord. It was time, they said, seriously to consider my marriage. I was close to my nineteenth birthday and, by the standards of the time and my class, already assuming spinster status. The time had come for a selection. For this purpose they had prepared a list of a number of worthy candidates, some of whom I noted with alarm, were well beyond forty. At the end of my father's short and prepared statement, they both waited for my reaction and approbation but I declined. Notwithstanding the obvious merit of the selective list, I said, I had no intention of marrying anyone. Mutual exasperation followed.

What, my mother demanded, was I to do with my life and, in particular, with the extraordinary and obvious talents with which I had been endowed?

She then made a mistake and drew attention to the view expressed many times that my prodigious talents had been at the expense of my beloved brother.

"Precisely," I said, and it was for that very reason that I had no intention of entering into a marriage or leaving the Mas. I intended to devote my life to Robert's care. I was aware of raising my hand against objection. Robert needed me and I was determined, I repeated yet again, to provide the oxygen in life that I had apparently denied him at birth.

Argument, inducements, even pleading followed based, as I well knew, on the deepest concerns both for myself and the family. I was unbending and intransigent. I would devote myself to Robert and to my studies. I would become an intellectual, perhaps a writer, but certainly not a wife.

And so it was.

For the next three years as I grew from girl to woman, I cared for my brother and immersed myself in the studies of literature and drama. I found a routine which was, by no means, disagreeable. We walked together, Robert and I, through the woods and meadows of the estate. These were walks which we had begun and explored, with Jacques and, at first, the pain of loss was intense. However, within six months it became bearable and within a year it seemed of less consequence. The passing of the seasons, the softness and strength and the majesty of the Périgord, acted as a therapy. After Jacques left, Robert's stammer became worse and, even with me, conversation was limited and sporadic. I recited poetry aloud and took both parts in theatrical dialogue. On occasions I invoked the crowd and the chorus itself, declaiming wildly beneath the trees. All of this was done to Robert's immeasurable joy. He watched as I enacted the death of Desdemona and when the light was finally put out, notwithstanding his partial comprehension, tears welled in his eyes. As a result of repetition, he developed a repertoire of snatches and sayings. Between Jacques and myself he had witnessed the death of Mercutio on so many occasions that he made it his own. While I enacted the waspish dialogues of the Misanthrope, he would suddenly exclaim:

"A pl ... pl ... plague on ... bo ... bo ... both your h ... h ... houses" and we would dissolve into wild laughter echoing among the poplars and the limes.

Every six weeks I would travel to Paris, a journey taking, in all, six days. I stayed in rooms at the top of a house in the rue Feuillette, owned by Paul Challon, who had, for twenty years, been the second steward on the Lefebre estates but moved to Paris when the death of his father provided him with a fine *maison*. There he continued to administer the affairs of the urban bourgeoisie as he had my father's lands. When in Paris I visited friends, occasionally attended soirées and parties and provided repeatedly the false justification for my lack of a husband (no suitable candidates). I replenished from the Left Bank my growing stock of English, French and, occasionally, German or Russian literature. I was, let us say, not unhappy but I was manifestly unfulfilled. I continued to fence against shadows and hanging sacks in the barn. I developed methods of passé that at least served to retain the skills that I had. Often, in the evenings, I turned the barn into my own theatre, acting a vast range of parts and dialogues, mounting bales of hay to declaim comedy and tragedy alike. On several occasions I knew that my mother quietly entered through the wicket gate and watched my performances, tears smarting in her eyes.

After three years, this existence came to an end. In October 1669, I had come to Paris and was staying in the rue Feuillette. Unusually, I had been accompanied by my mother. After thirty years she retained friends in the theatre, many of whom had fled to Paris when the renaissance of English theatre was eclipsed in 1642. On the second night of our stay we dined together in the Champs Elysées. My mother arrived late in a state of considerable excitement.

"I hope this will be of importance to you," she said, beckoning a waiter and mouthing unmistakably "vin blanc". "Paul Detain has become the owner and director of the Théâtre du Marais. He has commissioned a season of Racine which will commence with *Les Plaideurs* on the 1st of November. He is auditioning from next week. I knew him well in London when he was invited to direct at the Swan. He never directed me but he saw my work often enough. Yesterday he tried to persuade me to audition for one of the 'mature' roles which is, of course, impossible for many reasons."

She paused as our drinks arrived and then fixed me with her most urgent gaze.

"I told him about you. I told him you have a talent vastly better than mine. Please don't interrupt. I told him that you are a genius. He wishes you to audition. There are three minor parts left and it would be a beginning."

As soon as she finished I sighed in protest with something close to exasperation. Secretly I felt a surge of anticipation.

"I cannot live in Paris. What of Robert?"

"You cannot live your life for Robert. It is bad for you and dangerous for him. Poor and disabled he may be, but he must be allowed a measure of his own independence. I say this without wishing to hurt or offend you but, in the last years, you have not given him oxygen. You have smothered him with love. I know perfectly well what happened with Jacques. No, he did not tell me but I am a woman, a mother and also I am *your mother*. I observed the haste with which you swallowed the concoctions that I gave you which were, incidentally, as you may have suspected, harmless and useless. Of course you will not be happy married, even well married in the Périgord or any other region of France but you will never be happy or fulfilled without the stage. I know, neither was I."

When she finished I was unable to speak. My throat constricted and tears rose to my eyes. It was simple but it was right. When I recovered I said:

"I cannot leave him for months or years. That is simply impossible."

My mother waved impatiently with her wine glass.

"That would require enormous luck as well as skill. Most actors, even the best, rest for weeks and months on end, neither the theatre nor the public are ours to control. Even if you enjoyed monstrous success, even if you are retained for weeks or years, no manager, no director will deny you time between or during productions. This is your future. You must take it."

In reality there was no choice. I smiled, she smiled and our glasses met across the table. "Touché."

She was suddenly businesslike.

"Audition nine o'clock on Monday. Stage door Théâtre du Marais. Paul is expecting you and will know who you are. I have told him you are me twenty-six years ago."

"Oh," she said, as if in afterthought, "there is one small matter. You must become a man. Don't look so shocked. There has been a wretched edict just passed in Paris prohibiting young women performing on the public stage without attracting

34

penalties identical to common prostitution. It won't last long. It has never been a prohibition in French theatre but for the moment it is in force. It will not be necessary for the audition but, if you are lucky enough to succeed, your public life outside the theatre must be that of a man. It is absurd but it is necessary and nobody could do it better than you. If the edict required it you could, if necessary, impersonate an elephant and, in a sense, there is a poetic symmetry. In order to avoid leaving Robert you must *become him*. The edict cannot last long and then you may reveal that Robert Lefebre is indeed the woman he appears to be. But for the time being you must crush those bosoms and affect an unnecessary male appendage. You can release them only when they are revealed to an enraptured audience."

I was laughing without control as I frequently did when my mother entered such a discourse. Had she and I known of the terrible events that would follow upon this seemingly harmless artifice, we would have strangled the enterprise at birth. But we did not know and the future was now set.

On the Monday I presented myself at the Théâtre du Marais and auditioned for the part of *L'Intime*. I was awarded it without difficulty and, indeed, heard surprised exclamations from the darkened theatre as my audition came to an end. The production was a success but, after four weeks, Mme Lassalles fell from her coach after a soirée and broke both her ankles. I was her understudy and had four hours notice to take the lead role. I did not leave it. The production ran until March when the theatre closed until April for rehearsals. I spent two weeks in Tocanne, joyfully reunited with Robert who I noted (with perhaps a little disappointment) appeared, despite my absence, to be happy, fit and well.

I returned to Paris to take the lead when *Bérénice* opened on the 1st of May, 1670, the fatal date on which the murder (which it was not but which it came to be called) took place in rue d'Essaye. In the following days as a fugitive I would assist the secret machinations of kings, seek to inflict a terrible revenge and become, somewhat unwillingly, the amanuensis of Mr Samuel Pepys.

Events for which I was wholly unprepared.

CHAPTER 4

"You were fucking magnificent," said Michel de Pertaine, his face barely a hand's breadth from my own and the brandy on his breath sufficient to water the eyes.

"Thank you," I said, "now, please, I must go, I am on my way home."

He glanced at his companions.

"Oh no, I don't think so. I don't think that would be a good idea at all. The night is still young and I have got an idea. Do you know where we are going? We are going to the Société Bleue. You have heard of us? Yes, I see that you have. We have a little meeting at our rooms in the rue des Singars. Now I suspect you have got your girlie clothes in there," he said pointing to the valise, which did, in fact, contain both my costume and my money.

"So why don't you come with us and give us a little private show? Nothing too fancy, just get those lovely fake tits out and sing us a song. Then we will have a collection and you may even make some money."

"Thank you," I said, "that is very kind but I must go home, I have another performance tomorrow."

"Tomorrow," he said, "tomorrow, tomorrow is already today and today . . ."

I had begun to move to my left towards the Passage d'Orse. As I did so, the man immediately to the right of Pertaine altered his position towards me. I moved to the right and was blocked by Pertaine himself, who, whether through drink or intention lunged forward and pushed me backwards. Instinctively I dropped my valise from my left hand and grasped the hilt of my sword.

"Ho, ho," he said, "it's a fight you want, is it? A little duel here, well come along then Monsieur Lefebre, let's see what you poofters can do with a real rapier. Spread out boys, take a corner each. Let's not be disturbed."

As his companions moved to the four corners of the rue d'Essaye and the rue des Verriers I said, "I don't wish to fight you. I mean you no harm."

"No harm!" he said, "no harm? You mean me no harm? Well, well, well. I think you need at least a good spanking my friend with flat steel."

He backed away three or four paces and drew. Still I demurred.

"This is not necessary," I said, "not necessary."

Voices had been raised and I was aware, as we spoke, that lights were beginning to appear behind shutters in the upper apartments immediately adjacent to the junction. That would, I hoped, restrain him but it did not.

"More light," he cried, "more light, yes, let's see how this boy can take his medicine."

He took a step forward and slashed with his sword intending, no doubt, to flay my left arm. This, I had anticipated and I moved to the right, lent back and instinctively and without choice, drew my sword. We set to. He was drunk but he was obviously good. I subsequently discovered that he possessed a fearsome reputation as an aggressive swordsman and had fought three duels. All of which had seriously maimed his opponents, one of whom had subsequently died. At first his intent had obviously been to inflict a flogging with his sword. The upward and downward slashes I could contain without difficulty by movement or parry. He became angry.

"Well, well, well," he said standing during a short pause, "they've taught you something haven't they, my pretty boy? So let's see how you deal with a real whipping."

He came now in earnest. Thrust, lunge, thrust, cut. I moved, parried and backed in a circle offering no response except defence. He began to tire and, with the frustration, his temper rose.

"Right," he said, "let us have you then."

Drunken or otherwise, there was no doubt as to his real intent. He was intent on the central target, the unprotected left side and the head. He executed the classic cut, lunge and feint aimed at a decisive thrust. I was moving as fast as I had ever done in our practice duels in Tocanne and, despite the danger and the inevitable disaster, felt my own blood rise. I changed tack, retreated no longer, feinted myself and aimed at his sword arm above the wrist. He withdrew in time but I felt my blade cut into the top of his sleeve drawing a curse of anger and pain.

The fury of his next onslaught could only have had one purpose. I was fighting for my life and, I confess, felt a surge of excitement and blood. I was weaker than him but I had a trick. It had only been employed once and that four years before against an opponent whom I loved. I waited for his next lunge, feinted and spun in a perfect pirouette. As I did so, I passed the sword between my hands and, in the split second when we faced each other again, thrust with my empty right. As Jacques had done years before, he parried into thin air. The point of my rapier, now in my left hand, was at his throat.

"Yield," I said, "disarm now."

Whether he was aware of the extent of his risk no one will know but his sword arm reacted with a slash aimed straight at my head. Left without choice, I thrust and felt the blade pass clean through his neck. I immediately withdrew and, amazingly, he stood barely swaying before me, his mouth moving in silent speech. I did not pause. Without sheathing the sword, I snatched up my coat and my valise and ran to the Passage d'Orse. His companions, still standing guard, did not react. The fact that he remained on his feet must have caused them to pause. I was near fifty yards down the Passage when I heard the first cries and then, quite distinctly, heard the sound of a body falling heavily on the cobbled streets. Before I heard any sound of pursuit I was a hundred yards distant and had turned through two of the conduits which linked the wider passages. I knew my way well. I had frequently explored this small maze looking for a shorter and less conspicuous route to my lodgings. Barely three minutes later I arrived at my street door. My key turned without difficulty and I fell into the darkness of the house. The door closed behind me in near silence. I mounted the stairs and reached my rooms on the third floor. I stood by the shutters and listened for the sound of alarm or approach. Nothing. Once I thought I heard distant shouting and running feet but I could not be clear. Thereafter, nothing but silence.

I had, remarkably, formed a plan. As I moved about my room, it took clear shape. Flight, at least, for the immediate future was inevitable. The option of public protestation and appeals for justice I barely considered. These were powerful men from powerful families, among the most notorious in Paris. They possessed all the witnesses and all the power. If I was to assemble a case it had to be done at a safe distance and after suitable support had been obtained, a process which might take months or years. I had immediate advantages. I had money in substantial quantity and my professional ability to adopt alternative identities. At the theatre only Paul Detain was aware of my Paris address. He, I knew, would have already left Paris in the early morning to travel with Molière to Versailles. He would not return until the following day. The chance of discovery by random search was negligible. Thus I had time, perhaps forty-eight hours, in which to make my escape.

I began to pack. Unsurprisingly, I possessed more women's clothes than men's. I laid out a dress, bodice, bonnet and cloak which I had to my recollection never worn on stage. They were the clothes of a Parisienne. I would have wished them to be more demure but I had no choice. I selected three alternative costumes in all. Two female and one male. The male garments were only in part those which had recently been worn by Robert Lefebre in the rue d'Essaye. I packed the clothes, the money and what basic toiletries I required. My sword I detached and folded within my cloak. I wrote a message for my landlord, which told him little, and a letter to be dispatched to my parents, which told them little more. By what code I could I explained that there had been a misadventure and I was wholly innocent of any wrongdoing but that in the immediate future I must disappear. I said that I knew a place where I could be well and safe. Before expressions of love, I employed the exclamation *tant d'horreur*! I assumed and hoped that my mother would understand the double entendre. Her only remaining English relative, my aunt, lived in London. We had never met but we had corresponded and she had expressed the wish that I should spend time with her in that city. This would now come to pass in circumstances she could not conceivably have imagined. By the time I had finished my preparations it was gone seven o'clock. Beyond my shutters I could hear the commerce of Paris begin and I knew I must wait until it was in full flow before I could risk leaving the house. Overladen I struggled down the stairs, hoping that my landlord's family would not be disturbed. I was disappointed. As I passed his rooms on the first floor, I met him not yet fully dressed. His eyes widened in surprise.

"Camille, what are you doing? Where are you going?"

I told him everything except my plan. In due course he would inevitably be questioned and any knowledge would be a contagion. He protested.

"But the Magistrate, you must go . . ."

I interrupted.

"Paul, now I would stand no chance at all before the law. Think. They have all the witnesses, powerful witnesses, and I have an obvious secret to hide. There will be time to formulate a defence but it is not now."

He agreed with obvious reluctance. "But where are you going now, immediately?"

I told him that it was my intention to go to the Quai d'Orléans to board a carriage. I did not tell him the destination.

He waved his hand and impatiently said: "No, no, no. You cannot do it. It is likely, even now, that the major terminals will be watched. I have a friend nearby who has two carriages which he rents. Tell me at least the length of the journey that you propose and I will send to him immediately, requesting a suitable coach and driver." I paused, nodded, and said the journey itself would take one day so the carriage would be required for two. He called immediately for his houseboy, Maxim, gave him a sealed note and the address. After he had gone I told Paul that they would be likely to trace me within forty-eight hours. I said that there was a letter in my room already written which told him of my departure but which otherwise provided no other details. He must say that I had already gone when the family awoke. Any other account would render him an accomplice. On this we were agreed.

"I am truly sorry," I said, "that you have become involved in this matter."

He held up his hand: "Your father provided me with the best job and living I have ever had. It is a small repayment and, in reality, the risk is not great."

Within the hour a single carriage arrived, as instructed, in the mews at the rear of the building. My packed belongings were loaded. With brief goodbyes and *bonne chance*, we parted. The driver had been informed that the destination would not be revealed until we were outside the gates of Paris. I directed him to the West Gate and then told him my destination was Calais. He made no enquires and, apart from requests for brief stoppages, no conversation occurred until we arrived at the great port. I offered him the fare which was declined. It had, he said, already been settled. I was put down at the quay and made enquires as to the Dover packet. I was fortunate. A boat was to leave in the early morning on which there was available accommodation. The booking clerk was inquisitive and I told him that I was on family business. I paid for the passage, one *livre*, and spent the night in the Hôtel Bretagne, an omen of a kind. I boarded the boat when it was barely light. I was gripped by all manner of apprehension as I scanned the crowds already forming at the quay. My luggage was embarked. My accommodation was good. Five hours later, with a fair wind, I disembarked at the Port of Dover, a foreigner and a fugitive. As a result of my mother's persistent tutelage, I spoke perfect, unaccented English and, employing my mother's tongue, I booked a carriage to London due to depart the following morning. I found lodgings, bathed and sat at the window of my inn watching with growing curiosity the strange customs of a strange land. When I thought of the Théâtre du Marais a heavy sadness fell upon me. The audience would, by now, with angry disappointment, have watched my understudy falter through the lines. Paul Detain, my friend and mentor would be distraught. A future that held more promise than I had imagined possible was reduced to a bagatelle. Then for a fleeting moment, despite the awfulness of my position and the inevitable sadness, I felt a frisson of wild anticipation. I was young, I was beautiful, I was, for the moment, relatively rich. I was alone and in that moment I experienced the freedom of the fugitive, more precious and valuable than any other. The future I contemplated was dark but alive with fearful adventure.

I was not to be disappointed.

CHAPTER 5

I boarded the London coach at six-thirty. The day was fine. The north quayside of the port was already alive with commerce and lines of travellers awaiting the morning packet to France. Two porters from the inn carried my valise and my portmanteau. It was unseasonably warm and it was necessary to remove my travelling cloak and carry it across my arm. I wore the same clothes in which I had left Paris. My luggage was loaded. The coachman assisted me into the rear of the carriage with a look of undisguised approval, which I learnt to be the stock-in-trade of those who drive carriages in England. He told me that I was initially the only passenger. The coach, he said, would stop at Chatham at the entrance of the Great Dockyard, thereafter, briefly at Rochester, Deptford and New Cross before driving post-haste to London. The horses, he told me, had rested the day before and, given fine weather and good passage, we should be in New Cross by five and at Charing Cross by seven. He anticipated two further passengers at Chatham but, otherwise, the coach would be half empty allowing even greater speed. I settled myself in the rear corner and watched the countryside pass before me.

My mood of the previous night had not entirely disappeared. Despite the awfulness of the events in Paris, I felt a curious sense of liberation. This was heightened by my impressions of the English landscape which I had never seen. I had always fondly believed that it would resemble the sweep of the Périgord or the intense horticulture of the land beyond Paris. What I saw was in marked contrast. The land was interlaced with hedgerows, sprinkled with coppice, which settled against broad-leafed woodland clinging to the hills with the softness of folded linen. The meadows had been newly harvested and stacks of corn stood in regular and orderly intervals providing contrast to the hedgerows in which they were contained. After an hour the landscape changed. Meadows gave way to orchards, often extending beyond the eyes' horizon. The first fruit harvest had already started for the day. Industrious figures carried ladders between the trees and carts. Barrows of fruit, from dark green to the deepest red, were already piled to the brim. To my foreign eye it appeared serene and I was entranced. I had heard my mother speak of England as a garden but I had not anticipated so clear a metaphor.

As we approached Chatham, the coach road ran directly along the banks of the River Medway. Here the English Navy was everywhere to be seen. As we passed the mouth of the Dockyard I saw several warships waiting for the tide. Surrounding these were small boats selling produce hauled onto the deck by rope and baskets which also carried payment in coin or in kind.

Finally the coach came to rest outside the Dockyard gates around which a furious commerce was taking place. I declined the coachman's offer to descend and exercise my legs. I sat in the corner of the coach awaiting, with interest, the identity of my fellow passengers. I heard their luggage being loaded before they entered the carriage on the far side; two men, very different in appearance. My impression of the first was faintly repellent. Without being gross, he was fleshy. Unusually the lips were the first feature that took my attention; very full, slightly protruding and glistening as though he had recently eaten a succulent meat broth. In sympathy with the flesh below them, the nose was not big but bulbous. At first I could not see his eyes because his wig had been knocked sideways by the lintel of the carriage door. When I did see them it became apparent why he had unnecessarily struck his head. Although wide-set and even handsome, they were drawn into the tight squint which signifies a serious myopia. Because of the wig he did not see me and practically landed upon me, muttering a carnal oath while he readjusted his hairpiece. He fell into the seat opposite and, his wig reassembled, noticed me for the first time. When he did so the squint increased and he jerked his face forward in order to better focus on me or, I suspect, my cleavage, over which, instinctively, I placed a gloved hand.

"Ah," he said, "ah."

His companion had entered the carriage with considerably greater elegance. He was strikingly and darkly handsome. His face was long, his cheekbones high and his eyes set a great distance apart from an aquiline nose. His wig was fine and richly textured and fell upon a silk jacket and shirt opened fashionably three buttons below his chin. On seeing me his reaction was similar but more restrained than that of his companion. I heard a distinctly *sotto voce*, "s'blud" as he took his seat next to the first. As he did so, the other reached into the inside of his waistcoat and produced a pair of spectacles which he carefully arranged on his considerable nose. The strength of the lenses was immediately apparent and his eyes magnified like giant shellfish, once more fastened themselves upon me, this time at a rather higher level. When he spoke his voice had a pleasant unusual resonance. My thespian training sensed a man given to song and skilful at it.

"Dear lady," he said, "how delightful to have you as our travelling companion. May I introduce both of us? My name is Pepys, Samuel Pepys, and this gentleman is John Wilmot, the Earl of Rochester, gentleman of the bedchamber and," he added with a slight change of tone, "probably England's finest poet."

As he said this, his companion gave something between a modest acknowledgement and a stage grimace.

An expectant silence fell before he said, "May we enquire as to your own . . ."

I had already decided upon the wisest course of action. I sat there nodding with a smile of complete incomprehension. When he finished, or did not finish, the sentence which related to my own identity, I simply deepened my smile and gently shook my head. For a moment he appeared perplexed and then he said:

"Ah, I see. Pardon, vous êtes française, n'est pas?"

I graciously inclined my head.

"Ah, mille pardons, je recommence. Je m'appelle Pepys. S-A-M-U-E-L Pepys. Et mon companion est John Wilmot, Comte de Rochester, lyricist extraordinaire, peut-être le meilleur d'Angleterre."

In the pause that followed I reflected on his accent. Tutored, basic French. He continued.

"Et vous Mademoiselle," he continued, "vous êtes . . ."

"Je m'appelle Camille," I said smiling brightly. "Camille Lefebre."

"Enchanté. Et vous êtes d'où?"

"De Paris Monsieur," I answered. "Originaire du Périgord."

"Périgord!" he said, smiling broadly. "Très joli."

He continued to smile but turned to the Earl of Rochester.

"French," he explained, "recently from Paris but a native of Périgord. Never been there myself. Apparently she speaks no English."

The Earl of Rochester smiled and nodded directly at me.

"Yes," he said. "Pity. Magnificent tits."

"And eyes too. Do not overlook the eyes."

The Earl continued to smile at me.

"Yes," he said, without taking his gaze from mine. "The eyes certainly, but the tits, magnificent. You are an artist, Samuel, I am a voluptuary."

I continued, with some difficulty, to maintain a smile devoid of understanding. To my relief I was abandoned as the immediate subject of conversation.

"Ah well," Wilmot continued, "I must leave you at Deptford and I dare say you will make what headway you can with our young French friend but not for me I fear. Let us make the most of this journey. How are you and how is the King? You have seen him since I have. You may have heard that I have been banished from the Court."

Pepys shook his head as though in mock bewilderment.

"Indeed I had. Banished again? Is this the third time?"

"Fourth," said Wilmot with a flicker of ill humour. "He will have me back, of course, on some pretext but, for the moment, it is hideous."

"Just so," Pepys removed his spectacles and carefully polished them on his sleeve. "Just so. I gather that he disapproved of your new poetry."

"So he did. I find it difficult to believe. I dedicated the first edition to him, calf bound. It cost me a fortune. Next thing I know I am banished, cast out like one of his tarts. And, though I say it myself, they are my best work. Have you read them?"

When Pepys nodded, he continued.

"Some of them are particularly fine. Have you read 'A Ramble in St James's Park'?"

"Oh yes," said Pepys, replacing his spectacles and glancing in my direction with a smile. "I read it quite carefully."

"What did you think?"

"May I be candid?"

"Of course. Be as candid as you wish. I respect your view more than any. What was your first impression?"

Pepys gave a small sigh.

"Over extensive use of cunt."

"What, what?" the Earl of Rochester exclaimed.

"I counted the word ten times in forty lines. And that takes no account of the friggings and fuckings and various similar."

"Oh come Samuel, you, of all people, cannot possible object to that."

"I have no moral objection, it just becomes a bit repetitive."

"But Samuel . . ." Wilmot, I observed, was genuinely distraught.

"But Samuel, it is art, Samuel. *Art.* It reflects the spirit of the age."

"Is that what you told the King? Frigging in St James's Park reflected the spirit of the Restoration?"

"Well, not in so many words but . . ."

"I am beginning to see why you have been banished."

"But that wasn't the one that he objected to. The one he threw at me was 'Signor Dildo.'"

"Ah," said Pepys, smiling beyond his spectacles. "Not much vagina but a lot of prophylactic."

"Yes, yes, or rather no. He said it reflected badly on the ladies of the Court. It is impossible, Samuel, to reflect badly on the ladies of the Court. If one invoked the worst carnalities of Caligula, it would barely tickle the ladies of the Court. He just doesn't see it. He walks around with his nose in the air when it is not in Nell Gwynne's . . ."

"Yes, yes," said Pepys, "I have the point but I am afraid you are going to have to live with it. At least in the short term but tell me, what are you doing with your time?"

As though this was some form of cue both of them turned simultaneously and smiled at me.

"Oh dear," said the Earl of Rochester, "they really are quite painful to look at, aren't they? What I do with my time? I have taken to using some of it in Parliament."

Pepys turned and stared at his companion. "Really? How extraordinary. Tell me, what do the Members think of your poetry?" Before Wilmot answered he said, "Ah, Rochester."

The coach had been passing through streets of timbered houses and now came to a halt. Through the window I could see the doors of a great church or cathedral. The surrounding stonework contained fine and ornate carvings already worn smooth by age and weather. The coachman announced a delay for the loading of the post and I decided to leave the carriage. Despite the heat and, in order to assume the necessary decorum, I removed my cloak from the luggage rack, careful as I did so, to leave my rapier in its far recess. I stood and admired the cathedral. By French standards it was small and dwarfed by the castle, which it faced barely fifty yards distant. The outer walls of the castle had been badly damaged, the result, I assumed, of the recent war, but the keep still stood massive and formidable against the blue sky. I entered the cathedral by the wicket gate and was struck, immediately, by its serene simplicity. The contrast with my own cathedral in Périgueux could not have been more marked. Here all religious ornament had been removed and the bare stones were the colour of honey in the morning light. The only decoration was provided by flags hanging along the nave and decorated organ pipes, which rose above the carved screen. I found it sublimely beautiful and, as I watched, a distant choir began its morning practice, singing, unaccompanied, in the English vernacular. Half of my blood was English and, as I listened I felt, for the first time, that I had come home. Unwanted tears had started to my eyes when I heard the voice of Samuel Pepys barely a foot behind me.

"Magnifique, eh?" he said. "Petite mais parfaite."

I nodded and smiled my now familiar acquiescence. An unpleasant noise intruded and, turning to face him, I saw that he had bitten the top from a strange vegetable, a process that involved strong mastication. His mouth still full he gestured towards the remaining stalk.

"Fennel," he said, "délicieux et fortifiant."

He offered a bag that contained two similar plants, which I graciously declined. He gave a small shrug and turned back towards the cathedral doors.

Whether through vanity or otherwise, he had removed his spectacles and, as a result, struck his head a substantial blow on the top of the wicket gate dropping, in the process, the bag which contained the remaining vegetables. I hurried behind him, picked it up and when we were outside the cathedral doors helped to rearrange his wig. As I did so I unconsciously brushed aside a small speck of blood, which had appeared on his upper forehead.

"Thank you, thank you," he said, "merci."

His smile contained unmistakable invitation and quite changed the bulbous contours of his face. He appeared, for a moment, if not handsome at least *présentable*. I was, I confess, a little disturbed. My experience of older men, besides my father, was largely confined to the theatrical world of Paris. Most of these thespians had little interest in me, or any other female for that matter. The attentions of others were friendly, lewd and easily repelled.

We returned to the coach, where I resumed my seat before indicating in a universal language of the head that I intended to sleep. Pepys nodded.

"Dormez bien," he said.

I closed my eyes and rested my head against the leather facing of the coach wall and paid close attention to the conversation that followed. I was in a strange land and I needed to learn its customs.

"So," said Pepys as the movement of the coach began. "You are intending to become a Parliamentarian as well as a courtier. Be careful, the two do not necessarily mix."

The Earl of Rochester sighed.

"For the moment I have no choice. I am banished. Many of my best friends, even the poets, will not acknowledge me when I am in this condition. Writing further poetry, certainly like

'Signor Dildo', would be distinctly unwise, and so I am driven into politics. Do you know I made a speech last week on the provision of drainage after the Great Fire?"

Pepys's eyes — now, once more, bespectacled — widened with disbelief.

"My dear John, what do you know of civil engineering and drainage?"

"Absolutely nothing. It really went rather well. I had been paid to give it by Richard Bayliss who, as you know, runs the Swan Theatre. It is ruining his production of *The Alchemist*. No, don't laugh. It may do no good but it paid well."

Wilmot removed an envelope from inside his jacket and, I heard, rather than saw, waved it gently in the air. "All for a twenty-five minute speech. Better than poetry and you can't get banished."

Pepys, I could hear laughing, "Well, my good Earl, you will become a successful Parliamentarian. I would never have imagined."

After a pause Wilmot's voice dropped an octave but remained perfectly audible.

"Seriously Samuel, how long do you think this Parliament can last?"

"It will last a long time. The King cannot disband or prorogue it. He needs the money and Parliament is his only source, at present. There is no need to drop your voice. She is fast asleep and, in any event, cannot understand you. Doesn't she look quite beautiful?"

"Indeed," said Wilmot, sounding a little impatient. "Seriously why does the King require money? He has enough for the Court, which contains a sufficient number of whores and charlatans, particularly now that it is devoid of poets. His designs for a new London have been accepted and paid for. Why does he need the money and why does he need Parliament?"

Pepys's voice dropped an octave.

"He wishes," he said softly, "to make war."

"War!" said Rochester in a voice which, had I been asleep would, undoubtedly, have woken me.

"War?" he repeated, "War against whom?"

"The Dutch."

"The Dutch?! Ha!" Wilmot's voice cracked with disbelief. "*The Dutch*?"

There was a pause before he said, in a voice rich with irony:

"My dear Samuel, remind me. Have we not just had a war against the Dutch?"

"Indeed."

Through my near-closed eyelids I saw that Pepys now affected to stare fixedly out of the window. Wilmot, now patently enjoying himself continued.

"Now remind me, Samuel, didn't the war go rather badly? Indeed, so badly I think that, without putting a poetic gloss upon it, we lost."

I heard Pepys sigh.

"Yes, indeed, go on, enjoy yourself."

Wilmot plainly was. "And remind me Samuel, before we lost, did not they, the Dutch, under a gentleman called Admiral de Ruyter, sail to your very own Chatham Dockyard with a broom attached to the Admiral's mast?"

The poet's tone was infectious and Pepys, himself, was now laughing.

"No, they sent fire ships into Chatham. They landed at Rochester and, as you well know, they briefly occupied the city."

"I had not heard that," said Wilmot. "No, that had escaped me. How extraordinary. What happened?"

"I am sorry to say that they behaved impeccably. They put four crews ashore. There was no resistance to speak of. They took over the city and, instead of the anticipated looting and raping, distributed barrels of gin, sweetmeats for the children and handkerchiefs for the women, *lace handkerchiefs* to the women of Rochester, who normally blow their noses on their petticoats. Then they got back in their boats and sailed up the estuary, waved off by a grateful population. It was deeply embarrassing. Of course we tried to find some incident of violence, however little, or sexual activity, however consensual. The women of Rochester are used to entertaining the Royal Navy. They would have fucked a few Dutchmen with no trouble at all. There was nothing. Absolutely nothing. And as there was nothing we could hardly exaggerate it. There was a meeting of Privy Counsel and it was suggested that we might put some elaborate spin on it, pretend it was some kind of cunning trap but even Montague baulked at that. The King was speechless with rage, blamed it all on the Parliamentary Committee for destroying the Navy. That allegation was totally unjust but at least it took the heat from me. There were sackings in Parliament, all manner of enquiries and we made a peace with the Dutch. It was proclaimed as a victory that absolutely nobody believed."

Throughout this declamation, Wilmot had been snorting with laughter. At the end he said, "Well, Samuel, I am delighted that you survived."

Pepys smiled.

"I did rather better than that in the end. I retained my job, charged with rebuilding the Navy. Parliament could scarcely withhold the funds and so I am indebted to Mr de Ruyter. But the King remains incandescent with rage. He believes that he has been personally humiliated and he is probably right. He is obsessed with his relationship with Louis. Any mention of the French King is as bad as mentioning the Dutch. He goes into a steep decline and ends up in bed with Nell. He was a guest of the French Court for nine years and now he craves what he calls 'a special relationship'."

I saw that Pepys was energetically polishing his spectacles, a nervous gesture which, I subsequently learnt, accompanied moments of deep frustration of almost any kind.

"I am amazed," said Wilmot in the ensuing pause, "truly amazed. None of this has reached the Court, not even by rumour, nor Parliament."

"That is not entirely true," said Pepys, replacing his eyeglasses. "There are forces in Parliament that wish nothing more than another royal head on the block, closely followed by mine. They know that another Dutch War will reinforce the King's authority. Make no mistake, they are dangerous and powerful."

After a short pause I heard Wilmot exclaim, "My God, another war! For nothing! When will these princes learn?"

"Never," said Pepys emphatically. "Why? God knows. It is made worse by the existence of the British Navy. It is the perfect instrument of divine delusion. They want to fight with it *because they can*. There will always be princes and politicians like that. They will cause many deaths."

"My God, Samuel," said Wilmot, "if this is true why do you, you of all people, do his bidding, build his Navy? Why? You are not even Catholic." Wilmot paused suddenly. "Are you?"

"Of course not. There are those that say I am but, of course, I am not. Why do I work for him and do what I do? You have seen what Parliament can do. You have observed this country under Puritan censorship. Give me plague and fire and war before we return to that. And they are still there, the Puritan rump. You know well who they are: Shaftesbury and his gang. They are the new Templars and every bit as nasty. They are fond of the block but, in truth, they prefer the stake. I would not burn well."

There was a long silence during which I deemed it to be expedient to stir a little and mutter some words of French in my "sleep".

I heard Wilmot say, "Pretty. Very, very pretty. When I leave you, Samuel, you must see if you can work your famous magic in French. You make this pilgrimage to Chatham and Deptford many times. It must be tedious."

"Not really, yesterday I spent a pleasant afternoon frigging Mrs Barraclough so there are compensations."

I heard Wilmot laugh. "Remind me who she is."

"She is the wife of Mr Barraclough."

"Who is he?"

"He provides half the yardage of thin rope for the entire Navy. I give him the orders and he gives me Mrs Barraclough among other things. Oh, don't look at me like that, John. Yes, occasionally, I have felt guilty, particularly when Lizzie was alive, but she does what her husband tells her, sleeps in my bed and appears to enjoy it. She has rejected one or two of my more inventive suggestions, not unreasonable of her in the circumstances."

For nearly half-an-hour there was silence. The carriage was making good progress on smooth tracks and, on occasions, I came close to the sleep that I pretended. I was at the point of "waking" when I heard Pepys continue, his voice soft with conspiracy.

"I should tell you, John, that your parliamentary career may not, in fact, extend far into the future."

I heard Wilmot turn on the leather seats.

"What do you mean?"

"I think dissolution may not be very long delayed. Possibly within a year."

"But the money? You tell me the King requires his money and only Parliament can give it to him. How can he dissolve us in these circumstances?"

"There may be . . . other ways."

"*Other ways without Parliament?*"

"As I said earlier, the King maintains that he has a 'special relationship'. I am sceptical as to its reach or, indeed, its very existence. The King maintains that he has it and hints that it may be turned into lucre."

"My God, my God, you mean Louis?"

Pepys was silent but I sensed apprehension.

"I think," he said, "I have spoken too much."

"But for the French to provide money to *govern Britain* . . .?"

"Only in part to govern Britain, although that part would require conditions. The other part is to wage war."

"The Dutch? My God, an English Navy paid for by French money to wage a war based on personal humiliation? Is this real?"

"I am very much afraid that it is."

Now there was no mockery in Wilmot's tone.

"Charles has not been to Versailles for five years. If this is real, who has been part of the negotiation? Was it here or in France?"

I heard Pepys's sleeve rustle as he raised his hand. "I cannot answer these questions. I have been told only of the idea and I am one of a small number, five maybe, no more. Why me? I think it is obvious. The King needs a Navy and he knows that I will provide it if requested. He is also aware of my total loyalty and, for what it is worth, my views on Puritans and Parliament."

Wilmot exhaled a long breath.

"My God, Samuel, I am sorry that you told me."

"No you are not. What I have told you could be the greatest secret of the age. Guard it well for one day you may write it in your incomparable verse."

As he spoke the carriage began to slow and, taking advantage of the change in momentum, I feigned a return to consciousness. I stretched elaborately to the evident admiration of my travelling companions and resumed my fixed smile. Pepys inclined his head gracefully.

"Nous arrivons à Deptford, Mademoiselle."

I nodded and gazed pointedly out of the window.

"C'est joli," I said, which was, in fact, anything but the truth.

Pepys frowned slightly and turned to the Earl of Rochester.

"So you will be leaving us, John. It has been, as always, a great pleasure. We have covered much ground I think and now you must leave me with my charming and delightful companion. I will see what I can achieve."

"I think the phrase," said Wilmot, "is *bonne chance*."

He was in the process of gathering his travelling cloak about him and, as the carriage came to a halt, he lifted the inner latch and pushed open the door. As he stood, he said, "Now I am banished, Samuel, may I take it that you are at home for me in London?"

"Of course, my friend," said Pepys. "You will never be banished from my house and I hope your temporary disposal will mean that we see you more often, when," he added with raised eyebrows, "you are not gainfully employed in Parliament."

The men shook hands. Wilmot departed and the door was shut. I was alone with a man whose life and secrets now resided securely in my breast, a fact of which he was in total ignorance. We sat in silence, both anticipating the renewed movement of the coach. Instead, after barely ten minutes, Wilmot's face reappeared beyond the window.

"Samuel," he said, "may I speak with you a moment over here?"

Surprised, Pepys rose and, taking extravagant care to avoid the upper side of the opening, extended his head to within a foot of his friend's face. The conversation was muffled but, from my position at the other side of the coach, I was able to hear perfectly what was said.

"I have been talking to a post-rider who has come on a single errand from Dover. He has overtaken us here and is continuing to the terminus at Charing Cross. Apparently there has been a formal *rogatoire* from Paris. I could not get all the details but there has, apparently, been a political slaying of a powerful aristocrat. A name was mentioned which I did not catch. There is a directive to the Company to be alert for any strange or unexpected travellers from France and to pass any intelligence immediately back to Dover and then to Calais. I thought you should know in view of our fellow passenger."

I saw Pepys's shoulders shrug.

"Really, John, she is a young girl visiting her relatives. A fugitive she most certainly is not. I will not give it another thought."

John Wilmot drew a little closer before he said, "You are almost certainly right but I should point out something which your poor eyesight may have missed. On the rack beneath her cloak there is a rapier. It is possible to see the handle, from which it appears to be of fine quality. It may be that she doesn't trust her English uncles but it does not entirely fit with the image that we have seen. I will do nothing but I leave it with you."

The coach at this stage was beginning slowly to move and I heard Pepys's reply.

"I had not seen this. Perhaps you are right. I will consider bringing it to the attention of the Company when we arrive."

He straightened and, given the movement of the coach, made his way carefully to his seat immediately opposite my own. When he did so, he arranged his spectacles and assumed an expression close to inquiry. Before he could speak I said, in my perfect English: "I think, Mr Pepys, that would be very unwise."

He started with such force that his bottom, I swear, left the seat by a full six inches.

"My God," he said, "you are English."

"No," I replied, "I am not English, I am French."

"But you told us you spoke no English."

"No, I said nothing. It was you who said I spoke no English, although I can see the assumption may have been reasonable."

He continued to stare at me.

"My mother is English. I can speak my mother's tongue."

"You have been spying on us."

"That is quite wrong. Before your introduction I had never heard of you or your noble friend. I did not know you before you boarded this coach. It was neither anticipated nor desired. I suppose I should have stopped you but there did not seem to be an appropriate moment. I assumed the role that I did because of the obvious . . . attentions that you both paid me."

At that point he removed his spectacles and began to polish them furiously.

"Have you been, as you seemed . . . asleep?"

"No, although it was not for want of trying. I am afraid I heard everything that passed between you in all its, shall we say, varied content."

"My God," he said, "this is terrible, terrible."

As I watched him I was possessed of a feeling difficult to describe. Here was a man near old enough to be my father, obviously enjoying status and power and rank. I felt something close to maternal. It was a feeling not unlike that which I had for Robert. Perhaps it was stimulated by the spectacles and the myopia, which enlarged the panic and agitation.

"Now," I said, "Mr Pepys, I advise you to calm down, you are getting very excited. I know little of English politics and I have no interest in your King or your Parliament or, for that matter, your poetry."

A moment's discomfiture caused him to blink.

"But, please, who are you?"

"I am here to visit my family, the only family on my mother's side."

My manner and my information appeared to calm him. After a deep breath he settled further into his seat.

"Very well," he said. "I think before we have further revelations apologies are in order. The language that we employed must . . ."

I interrupted.

"Monsieur Pepys," I said, "I am an actor. I live and work among actors. I am painfully aware of my own appearance. If I was shocked by the conversation between yourself and the Earl of Rochester, I would be in a permanently deranged state. Give it no further thought."

Despite the concern which still, obviously, gripped him, a smile of understanding flickered across his face.

"Just so," he murmured, "just so."

And then, with renewed alarm, "You heard our conversation about Parliament and France?"

"Yes, I did, but do not distress yourself, Monsieur, I am as unmoved by the corruption of princes as I am by the doings of the Dutch (which, incidentally, I found remarkable). No one will assume that I carry such secrets and I certainly will reveal them to nobody except, of course, under some form of torture. But that, I hope, is some way off."

As I spoke those words my confidence suddenly began to ebb. My own dangers had, remarkably, receded from my thoughts. Now, with the mention of pain, they suddenly invaded my mind causing a spasm of sickness in my throat. It was not unnoticed.

"Mademoiselle," he said, reaching forward and taking my arm, "you are unwell?"

"No, Monsieur, I am not unwell. I am very fit but our conversation suddenly reminded me of my own position and the true reason why I am in your carriage causing you such alarm."

"Is it," he said, "connected with the information I have just received from John Wilmot? Are you, indeed, pursued? And, whilst on that subject, is it correct that there is a rapier concealed in your luggage?"

I had recovered enough balance to respond.

"Yes, Monsieur, I do indeed possess a rapier and I also possess the ability to use it."

Pepys regarded me intently for perhaps a minute and when he spoke his voice changed. It contained a tone of calm authority. I immediately knew (as I was intended to know) that this was a man of power and influence, accustomed to risk and danger.

"So, is it you about whom these enquiries are made?"

I nodded. "It may well be, I do not know."

"Have you been involved in murder?"

"No, no, I have not. But some may call it so."

His fixed gaze did not waiver.

"I see or, at least, I think I see. If I reveal your identity at Charing Cross or earlier then you will reveal the . . . indiscretions which you have just heard. That is it? Silence for silence."

I returned his gaze steady, I hoped, as rock.

"No, Mr Pepys, that is not it. Despite my English mother, I am not English so it may surprise you to know that I also possess principles of honour. They extend to knowledge that I possess as a result of misadventure in part of my own making. As I have already indicated your *indiscretions* are entirely safe. As an actor I have a facility to remember words. I also have a facility to forget them. That has already occurred. Of course, as I have said, they might be drawn by torture but there is no reason to suppose that anyone would seek such information from me." I shuddered before I said, "Any pain which may be inflicted on me as a result of my recent actions would be of a gratuitous nature. Revelations, however important, would not relieve it."

He removed his spectacles, polished them and frowned in the process.

"That is the truth. I am possessed of many skills and proclivities, Mr Pepys. They do not include blackmail. I was, to employ the English expression, properly brought up."

For the second time since I spoke English I saw Pepys smile. Despite the nature of what passed between us I observed that his face, faintly repellent in repose, much improved with animation. An uncomfortable silence fell between us for perhaps an hour during which the coach continued its good progress and both of us stared fixedly at the increasingly populated countryside which passed the windows. I noticed, however, that from time to time his gaze shifted to the rack above my head searching, no doubt, for the rapier which John Wilmot had reported. My spirits inevitably sank. Pepys was, I knew, an official and a powerful one. He owed me no favours and, indeed had legitimate reason for indignation that I had received his confidence as I had. Whether I would be apprehended at our destination I did not know but certain it was I would be immediately and successfully pursued. No formal undertakings existed between England and France as to fugitive felons but the power of wealth and noble blood extended between them like a fine and invisible net. The family that I had bereaved were powerful indeed, notoriously so. The Pertaine I had killed, I learnt from Paul Challon before I had left Paris, was not the Marquis. He was the younger son, wayward, dissolute and violent. In these respects, however, I was told he was a pale shadow of his elder brother, the Marquis. Édouard de Pertaine was his name and he was, Paul told me, about to inherit the fabulous family estates which extended from Bordeaux to the ports of Cherbourg and Honfleur. I could not have picked upon a more dangerous and lawless family. Set against them, my own father, strong, respected and distinguished though he undoubtedly was, would be extinguished like a candle in a storm. The thought of my family, their anxieties and their pain increased my despondency and I fell into a dark mood, barely conscious of the continuing journey. My senses returned quite suddenly as the coach drew rapidly to a halt and I was aware that we had arrived at the centre of a town. The time, I suspected, was about five in the afternoon. I turned towards my only fellow passenger and we contemplated one another in silence.

"New Cross," said Pepys. "I should stay in the coach."

He, himself, crossed the coach and, carefully avoiding the lintel of the door, descended into the street and disappeared. I could see post being loaded and unloaded, passing through a doorway on which was a crest which I took, rightly, to be that of the Royal Mail. Several horses were tethered outside the doorway and, as I watched, I saw Pepys reappear and enter the building. I contemplated leaving the coach and disappearing into the crowd. It was a brief contemplation. Even with the use of my travelling cloak, my clothing would have marked me as though I was carrying a flag. My belongings, including clothes and the majority of my money, were in the portmanteau strapped to the carriage above my head. The rapier, it is true, lay in the rack above me but I had no wish to use it. The fatal thrust that I had inflicted upon Pertaine represented the only injury, however slight, that I had deliberately inflicted in my life. It was enough. I, therefore, closed my eyes and entered a state of enforced calm which I employed before any theatrical performance. So I waited. Minutes passed. The shaking of the coach that accompanied the loading and unloading of mail came to an end. Immediately thereafter the coach door opened and closed and I heard and felt the occupation of the seat in the far corner of the carriage. I kept my eyes closed and controlled my breathing as best I could. Above me I heard my coachman whistle. Slowly we moved forward and, within minutes, the rocking of the coach commenced. I opened my eyes. Pepys had moved across the coach to his former position, immediately opposite mine. He smiled.

"I am surprised you are able to sleep but I should have known by now that your unconscious state is not all it seems. I made some tentative enquiries. It appears that they are pursuing a man rather than a woman and I did not quite catch the name. The Postmaster asked me if I had seen or heard anything suspicious or unusual on my journey and I told him that I had not. He asked one of his men to check the passengers in the coach but I forestalled him by saying that it contained only myself and a charming young lady with whom I had spent several hours in conversation, speaking what was clearly her mother tongue."

His smile broadened and rippled across his face and lines of laughter creased his weak eyes.

"So you see," he said, "I have become a conspirator. Some say I have a gift for it. The King, indeed, accuses me of it every week. No," he raised his hand, "do not say anything about it. I will simply say this. Had you threatened me, I most certainly would have reported your presence to the Carriage Office and, indeed, would have alerted the local constable, useless though he undoubtedly is. You would have little trouble running him through like a pincushion but I strongly fancy that is not your stock-in-trade."

I shook my head. My depression lifted and, despite my circumstances, I broke into a smile which, uncontrolled, became laughter in which he shared.

"I really don't know," he said, mopping his eyes behind his spectacles, "what we are laughing at and, indeed, the nature of the criminal venality that I have just conspired to conceal. At this speed and at this time, we have over two hours to Charing Cross. Would that be time for you to tell me who you are and what you have done? And," he said, reaching for the bag behind him, "can I interest you in a stick of fennel?"

CHAPTER 6

I told him everything, substantially as I have, thus far, recorded. Jacques I mentioned insofar as it was necessary to explain my skill with the rapier. Otherwise he appeared as a tutor and as a friend. Observing Pepys's face as I concluded my description of Jacques, I saw a flicker of disbelief but it was the only such moment. Otherwise he watched me intently, stopping only to wipe his spectacles with increasing frequency as we entered the outskirts of London and, despite the closed and drawn blinds, dust settled on every surface.

When I spoke of my family and, in particular, of Robert, my voice faltered, tears rose and I felt his hand instinctively covering my own. I did not actually cry but I did not remove it. When my narrative reached our present position, I shrugged and shook my head, indicating a tale unfinished and to be completed.

As though on cue, he said, "A remarkable story, remarkable. There is one aspect which I do not entirely accept but that is of no importance and can wait. But tell me, what do you intend to do in London besides finding your aunt?"

I said that I had made no plans. I had priorities; safety, security, contact with my family and the few good friends that I possessed in Paris. Now many years later when I consider the account that I gave between New Cross and London and the answers regarding my present position and concerns, I am, yet again, amazed and mortified that I omitted (or perhaps avoided) the one terrible and obvious calculation as to the consequences in France. Subsequently, when these dreadful consequences were revealed, Pepys was to inform me that he had, himself, perceived the dire possibilities from the detail of my story. He had made no mention of it. His next question took me by surprise.

What, he asked, did I know about the political state of England?

I told him, truthfully, that my knowledge was limited. I was, of course, aware of the Civil War, the regicide and the subsequent Commonwealth. From my narrative he knew of my family's persuasions and that my grandfather and three uncles had died at the Battle of Naseby. My aunt, I added, had adopted the Parliamentarian cause, dictated in part by her loyalty to her husband, a staunch Republican. Notwithstanding their political differences, the sisters had remained in contact, albeit living in different countries and in very different circumstances. My mother's single visit had not been repeated and she spoke little of it. I had found this a little surprising but made no enquiry.

Having digressed into my family background and sensing a mild irritation in my companion, now examining his spectacles critically against the light, I returned to his question. My knowledge of the details of British politics was limited to that which had been imparted by my mother and in long conversations with Jacques, whose Republican beliefs I have already recorded.

"And," I concluded, smiling a little, "to that knowledge could be added substantial information that I have obtained whilst sleeping on this very journey."

Still examining his spectacles, Pepys laughed and shrugged.

"Despite my reputation I can be remarkably indiscreet but you heard the views that I expressed. You are now aware of my views on King and Parliament. In the last forty years England has seen the best and worst of both. For the present I accept what we have. Its benefits can be seen from that very window and they are benefits that will lighten your heart."

I followed his indication and saw that the carriage was in a wide and handsome road, which I subsequently learnt to be Haymarket. It was a warm, early evening and, as a result, the walkways were full of colour. Street stalls were everywhere and we passed several theatres. At their doors queues were forming, before which musicians played solo and in concert, and collection boxes passed. Undeniably, it was a collective scene of happy and even raucous good humour, comparable to anything that the boulevards of Paris could create.

"It was not always so," said my companion, rightly assessing my thoughts. "During the Commonwealth this was a miserable place, dark and dour. My aversion to that world and my unashamed affection for all this including," he said, pointing to a group of young women on the Piccadilly corner, "*that*, has caused people to brand me a Catholic. It is a strange argument that those who reject Puritan conformities must, ipso facto, embrace another form of religious zealotry."

Aware that he had been musing, he abruptly returned to the business of my knowledge and education.

"So," he said, "enough of politics. Tell me, is your written English as good as that which you speak?"

"Probably better," I replied. "My mother insisted that I master both the vernacular and the written language. I may be a little rusty but I can write well enough in both tongues."

These were to be my last observations as the conversation drew to a close and the carriage to a halt in an assembly of many vehicles of different sizes and the coachman announced that we had reached the end of our journey at Charing Cross.

Pepys looked directly at me.

"There may be enquiries here. Stay with me and keep that damned sword out of sight."

Instinctively I did as I was told and gathered up my cloak. We were on a raised pavement that separated the long-distance post-coaches from the Hackney carriages ready for business ten yards away. A number of Hackney drivers were standing before their cabs and, as I stepped off the pavement, I excited the same attention to which I have already referred. An official of the Post Company was checking the vehicle and the mail boxes with reference to our driver, who stood beside him. He then turned and spoke to Pepys.

"Mr Pepys, sir, you will be pleased to hear that you are a full half-hour before your expected time." After Pepys nodded approval, he added, "We have had some requests, sir, some enquiries to be made."

"Really?" said Pepys. "Before you do that can I introduce you? My new secretary, Catherine Browne, who will be relieving my poor eyes from the burden of writing. Catherine, this gentleman is Mr Burlington, William Burlington, the manager of this excellent company, who has taken it upon himself to welcome us personally at the end of a most enjoyable journey." Burlington looked at me and smiled a little more than politely.

"How delightful. I am very pleased to meet you Miss Browne. I am sure you will find Samuel a . . . diligent employer."

I am, as I have observed, a thespian to my boots but this tested my reaction, timing and gesture.

"Thank you, Mr Burlington," I said, assuming the accent of the dutiful gentlewoman. "I am indeed looking forward to the post."

"Well, Samuel," said Burlington, "I am instructed to ask whether you have observed anything untoward or suspicious during your time at Dover or, indeed, on the journey? Whether you observed any strange or suspicious passengers?"

"Oh yes," said Pepys, "I most certainly did. Between Chatham and Deptford we were accompanied by a most extraordinary fellow who writes, it appears, dirty verses."

"Really!" said Mr Burlington, reaching for a notepad, "how interesting. He was French?"

"No, I fear not, he was not French at all, although some of his *habits* I suspect may be. No, I'm very sorry to say that he purported to be an English aristocrat."

"Really?" said Mr Burlington again, removing a pencil from his waistcoat pocket.

"Yes, he maintained he was the Earl of Rochester."

Burlington laughed and replaced his pencil.

"Mr Pepys, you jest with me. I confess that I am or have been an admirer of John Wilmot's poetry. I have purchased his latest edition. In view of what you say, I will ensure that neither my wife nor my servants have access to it."

As we walked towards the Hackneys, Pepys observed:

"Excellent man, Burlington. He has got me to Chatham and back on a number of occasions when it appeared impossible for one reason or another. I am sorry to observe that he neglects his duties when it comes to apprehending French spies. In the circumstances it is understandable. Please keep that sword out of sight. Now we are both going in the same direction. Indeed we are both going to Spitalfields. It would be a pleasure to guide you to your aunt's house at Bishopsgate, which is a short stop before my own."

We entered the Hackney and waited whilst our respective luggage was loaded onto the tailgate. I looked at him squarely.

"You said that I was your secretary."

"No, I said that you were my new secretary and that you have not yet started to work for me. It is true that I require a secretary. I have, for the past ten years, kept a diary. My eyesight is rapidly failing, something which you have obviously observed. I have a pair of spectacles which irritate me enormously. So I have stopped the diary but I miss it as though I would miss a child. I want someone to write it for me. I need an amanuensis. That much is true but I fear you would be most unsuitable for the job even if you wanted it."

"So why did you help me by telling a lie?"

"Because I believe what you have told me and believed that you needed the help." He paused, his enlarged eyes narrowed in thought. "Also I know your aunt and her husband, quite well. They also know me."

I began to speak but he raised his hand to stop me.

"You will discover soon enough what I mean."

We travelled for several minutes in silence. He stared from the window in obvious contemplation. Finally he turned to me and spoke as though in confidence. "It may be that you will feel unable to stay with your aunt. I base that on an assessment of you both. London is a wonderful but lawless place. I will give you the address of an inn well known to me where you will be safe at least for a while. If you take my satchel from the rack you will find a travelling box which contains paper, quill and ink. When we stop I will dictate the information and a message."

As he spoke the Hackney came to a halt beside a row of half-timbered, mullioned houses with doors giving immediately onto the street. As I rose to retrieve his satchel he said, "We are here. Your aunt's house is, I think, the second on the left."

I resumed my seat, opened the travelling box, took out the paper and writing instruments, dipped the pen and waited. So it was that I took my first dictation from Samuel Pepys:

To John Mellor, keeper of The Goose Inn, Fenchurch Lane.

Seething Lane. 3rd of May, 1670.

Dear John,

  Catherine Browne, the young lady who carries this letter is a friend of mine. I can vouch for her character and her means. She lives in France and has recently come to this country to visit relatives in London, Norwich and Exeter. Please provide her with good accommodation and such assistance as you can.
Sincerely . . .

I wrote easily in English with a fluent pen. When the note was finished he held out his hands for the paper and quill. Before passing them to him I said,

"Norwich and Exeter?"

"Ah yes, both a considerable distance from London and in opposite directions. If you are pursued it will provide an interesting goose chase."

Seeing the surprise on my face, he smiled with obvious complicity as he signed the paper. He continued, "Do not thank me, it is quite unnecessary. Now go and give my best wishes to your aunt."

I smiled back and said nothing except to murmur adieu. I gathered my cloak, carefully concealing the sword, directed the setting down of the portmanteau and, as the Hackney departed, approached *la porte de chez ma tante.*

CHAPTER 7

When the door opened, we both — from our different sides of the porch — confronted my mother. My aunt Julie was three years older than my mother and I twenty-five years younger, but we both possessed her features and I observed in Julie immediately her particular beauty. There was one obvious difference. She lacked the etchings of humour that surrounded my mother's eyes. Our mutual recognition rendered introduction unnecessary.

"Camille," she cried, "dear God, it is you."

As she embraced me and I her, she said:

"Why did we not know you were coming? How long have you been in England?"

My joy and relief at seeing her was now mingled with disappointment. Obviously she had heard nothing from my family. I had hoped despite the impossible timing that some message might have reached her.

"My dear girl," she continued, "come in at once. John will fetch those," she said, gesturing towards my valise and portmanteau. "Leave them and come in. You must be tired, thirsty, hungry. What a surprise. The last I heard . . ." she stopped with a look of sudden concern, "you were playing the lead, my dear, the lead in the Théâtre du Marais. Your mother was beside herself with joy. The letter was practically on fire! My dear, what have I said, what have I done?"

The mention of my mother and the life that I had left behind, now in ruins, had proved too much to bear. It was, if anything, made worse by the feeling of relief that I was with part of my own family in a house which was secure and welcoming. We had arrived at the kitchen and I slumped on the nearest chair and wept. At intervals I attempted to gather myself with deep breaths and much drying of the eyes before another convulsion overwhelmed me. It is a cliché that soldiers weep after battle and neither before nor during conflict, and it is not difficult to understand why. Minutes passed before I could reassemble my face and my voice and confront the agonised face of my mother/aunt through a bleary vision of tears. I had, in some part, rehearsed my words:

"Aunt Julie, this is not, I fear, a happy visit as it should be. I have a desperate tale to tell. I only wish you had been prepared for this arrival."

I breathed from the bottom of my lungs and cleared my throat. Aunt Julie immediately took control.

"Sit there," she said, "do not move and say nothing for the moment. I will fetch you some water, some bread and some cheese. We have not yet had dinner. When I say we, it is only myself and John who eats with me. My husband, Paul, is away in Oxford and will be gone until late tonight. I will tell John to eat in the pantry so we will be alone and undisturbed. You are safe and welcome here. You have the love of your family even if you lack friends."

Her words I remember struck a strange chord. I did have a friend. By the most extraordinary circumstance I had created a friendship and, amazingly, some unsolicited help. I was about to impart this to my aunt when John entered the kitchen. He was, I was told, Paul's second cousin who was serving a guild apprenticeship in Holborn. He was an ill-favoured boy, sullen, fat and heavy-chinned. His greeting was unsmiling and his handshake inert. He observed my clothing with evident distaste before seizing the portmanteau with an audible sigh. My family position was briefly explained to him. I was said to be visiting London on a vacation for an indeterminate time, information he received with apparent indifference.

Without further conversation I was shown to the spare room where my aunt said I could sleep and read without interference. It was a small room with mullioned windows overlooking a garden at the rear of the property. It possessed a bed, a desk with two chairs and a wooden chest. My luggage was deposited on the floor. I did not unpack. My travelling cloak, which still concealed my sword, I laid carefully upon the chest. Within minutes I presented myself in the small front dining room, where Julie had produced a tureen of hot soup. Cold meats, beetroot in vinegar and sliced brown bread were laid out upon the table. I sat opposite my aunt suddenly drained by fatigue.

"Now," she said, having served soup, "eat that and when you are ready, tell me everything. We have never met but I think we know each other very well. If secrets are involved they are safe with me." And so, for the second time in five hours, I embarked upon my tale. The recital of my childhood was unnecessary, save for the introduction of Jacques and my apprenticeship with the rapier. When this was mentioned and when I came to my performances in the Théâtre du Marais, I noticed flickers of brief distaste cross my listener's face. At the time, engrossed in my own story, I thought nothing of them. When I reached the duel and its fatal conclusion, my aunt gasped and placed two hands over her open mouth. By the time I reached Dover, she was repeatedly shaking her head. The journey to London I barely mentioned, true to the undertakings I had given to Pepys. As I omitted these parts, I briefly reflected that, even then, I was becoming a conspirator with my silence, almost a spy. I also omitted to mention the continued possession of the rapier. I did tell her that I had fellow passengers and that I had overheard talk of enquiries after French travellers.

At this point her eyes widened with apprehension.

"You were pursued? Have been pursued?"

"Perhaps, but we may never know."

During the entire narrative I had referred to Pepys and the Earl of Rochester simply as "gentlemen" who had joined me at Chatham. I did add, by way of postscript, that I was much indebted to the second gentleman, who had brought me to this house in his own cab, and that I felt I had made a valuable friend.

"Perhaps," said my aunt. "I do indeed hope so. Did you discover his identity and his address?"

I nodded emphatically. "His name," I said, with a note of triumph, "was Pepys, Samuel Pepys."

At that moment the smile on my face was in marked contrast to the look of unfeigned horror which passed across that of my aunt.

"My dear," she said, in hushed exclamation. "My dear, you are not serious? You cannot be serious! Praise God, oh praise God, you have told me. You must have nothing to do with this man. Nothing. Samuel Pepys is a devil. Indeed he is close to being *the* Devil."

My look of astonishment and horror must have matched my aunt's.

"Wait for a moment, I must go and find John to direct him to leave us undisturbed. Help yourself to the biscuits while I am away."

When she left the room I reflected on what she had said and the manner in which she had delivered her denunciation. In doing so I found myself reassessing the house in which I sat. In the tumult of my arrival I had failed to notice the complete absence of decoration from the walls or surfaces of the rooms. This stark simplicity was broken only by a stern Erastian crucifix, identical copies of which hung prominently in every chamber. My aunt wore a simple, high-necked, grey dress, gathered at the waist but, otherwise, shapeless. Surprisingly I had not noticed the marked, indeed, violent contrast between that and my own *mode parisienne*. The boy, John, I recollected, had also been dressed in severe grey. His surly manner now assumed a religious air. With some prescience I began to anticipate what was to occur. Indeed it happened soon enough. My aunt re-entered the room carrying before her a black bound book, which I rightly anticipated to be holy scripture. No immediate reference was made to it.

"My dear, you ask why I had that reaction to Mr Pepys. Please listen carefully to what I say. Now you have met this man you must be fully armed should he attempt again to enter your life." She raised both hands and, for a moment, I thought she was about to sink into prayer. Instead she turned and spread her left palm so that her fingers could be used as counting points.

"First," she said energetically, seizing a thumb, "he is a Papist, yes, *a Papist*. If he were asked he would, doubtless, tell you he is not but the truth is widely known. He practices Mass, which provides one of the reasons why he has . . ." she moved to her index finger, "been committed to the Tower. His release was obtained only by his fellow Papists and . . ." she positively pulled her third finger, "*the King*. He is the King's Man and he does the King's bidding. The fact that he does so brands him *a traitor*. When Parliament succeeded in the war, he was Parliament's man. Those he now despises and derides were his colleagues as Members of Parliament or as parliamentary officials among whom is my own husband, Paul, who you have probably been told is a clerk to the Commons' Procedure Committee. Finally," she concluded, seizing her little finger and bending it backwards with a slight wince of pain, "he is a notorious lecher, drunkard and *bon viveur* – you are obviously acquainted with the expression. He regularly frequents coffee houses and taverns, where he indulges in drinking, music and song and consorts with those who are known to write the most vulgar and lewd works, which masquerade as poetry or drama. He is an habitué of theatres of the Haymarket and Piccadilly, where he has the most sordid relations with a number of women who purport to be actors." She broke off at this point having clearly seen my expression.

"I am sorry, my dear. I am not, of course, acquainted with the theatres of France, which may be very different from those in London, as witnessed by the praiseworthy edict to which you have referred. But in London it is well known that the ladies who are permitted to perform upon the stage in what is referred to as 'Restoration' theatre are little better than common whores."

As she uttered the last word, her hands covered her mouth, the unmistakable gesture of one who has just delivered a profanity.

"That," she said, lowering her hands and placing them upon the Bible, "is Mr Samuel Pepys. Papist, criminal, traitor, conspirator and lecher. Thank God and praise God you have informed me in time."

"Now," she said, opening the cover of the Bible and producing several sheets of blank paper and a pencil from the cuff of her left sleeve, "I want you to think carefully about what Pepys said to you or to his companion (who sounds suspiciously like one of his fellow lechers). I appreciate that you know nothing of English politics but any detail or opinion which may have appeared of no consequence could be of great significance if I bring it to the attention of Paul, who can inform the real Members who he serves."

It is frequently said in idle prose that the mind is *in turmoil*. Often this is mere hyperbole for passing confusion. I can say, however, with perfect and detailed accuracy that my mind was *in turmoil*. The speed of the indictment had left me speechless and I found myself open-mouthed regarding my aunt as though she had appeared from a pillar of dust.

Of course, by artifice and accident I was possessed of information that could have kept my aunt counting her fingers for hours. In a matter of minutes I could have filled her notebook with graphic details of royal plots to disband Parliament, mortgage the government of England for the tainted largesse of the French and make renewed war on the Protestant Dutch. Even this would have made no mention of the corrupt procurement of the contracts for rope, the admiration of Haymarket and whores and the analysis of frigging in St James's Park. I do distinctly remember as my thoughts reassembled that I began, remarkably, to take instant decisions. In doing so I reflected that I had travelled a very long way in every circumstance since my conversation with Molière in the Théâtre du Marais. I must have remained silent for an uncomfortable period, for my aunt adopted a gentler tone.

"Well, my dear, did he say anything which may assist us?"

I was now, amazingly, quite calm. I was, once more, an actor with a selection of roles to play. I distinctly remember reasserting control over the muscles of my face. I had also made the first of a number of important decisions. I managed a worried and bewildered smile, shaking my head as though concentrating on the smallest of recollections. My aunt, pencil in hand, leaned expectantly across the Bible.

"I do remember," I said, "a conversation about St James's Park."

My aunt began to scribble on the first sheet of paper. I saw her write *St James's Park* and underline the result three times.

"Can you remember," she said, coaxing gently, "anything about the park? Were there to be meetings? Were there any names, descriptions? Anything which might be a code?"

I deliberately furrowed my brow. "I was partly asleep," I said, "but I distinctly remember a word beginning with 'c.'"

"Ah," said my aunt and I saw her carefully write the letter 'c' beneath St James's Park and underscore with three heavy dashes.

"A 'c' word," she said, her gaze intent with helpful persuasion. Her left hand, above the Bible, made beckoning gestures as though drawing out a recalcitrant child. "Anything else, anything at all?"

I gave a hopeless shrug, my hands outstretched.

"I am afraid that is it for the moment but I am sure more will come. All these terrible events have left me totally confused. After some sleep I am sure that I will remember more. I think, perhaps, I must sleep now and make further efforts tomorrow. I have much to think about."

"Of course, my dear," she said, carefully replacing the paper with its limited writing in the black Bible. "Of course, you must sleep now. There is no need for you to rise early but when you do I am afraid I will be gone. So much has been said that I have not begun to tell you of my present occupation. I am working in a bookshop at Lincoln's Inn. We specialise in law and scripture. During the Great Fire the entire stock was moved. In the process it became hopelessly mixed and confused. I am rebuilding the archive. It is a job that may take years but it must be done. John has gone to stay with his Guild Master in Holborn. In view of the matters that we must deal with, I have asked him to stay there for a few days. He intends to return tomorrow morning at eleven to collect the remainder of his belongings. I will return by two o'clock then we may revisit your journey and make detailed plans for your stay in London. You will be quite safe in this house but do not consider leaving. You may still be pursued by agents from France and, worse, you are still in the same vicinity as Mr Pepys. There is food in the kitchen, simple but plenty of it and the fresh water will last for several days. It is now nearly ten o'clock and I will see you to your room. You have only to sleep."

At the foot of the stairs I paused.

"I would like some fresh air. So much has happened I need to clear my head. May I spend a little time in the garden before I take to my bed?"

"Of course," said my aunt, "I will provide you with a candle and a tinder box. Bolt the door behind you. You must be tired, do not be too long."

I stood in the small garden and looked at the night sky. I knew that I should be overwhelmed by the magnitude of circumstance, chance and misadventure. I knew as I stood, taking my deep thespian breaths, that I should be crushed by feelings of helpless inadequacy in the face of dangers perceived and barely imagined. I felt none of these things. What I felt was exhilaration with a curious mixture of guilt and pleasure. Unimaginable circumstance had forced upon me decisions and actions for which I was wholly unprepared and totally ill-equipped. The first irrevocable decision would be taken in the morning light and I anticipated little sleep.

I re-entered the house, bolted the door, lit my candle, took a pitcher of water and mounted the stairs. I entered my bedroom, lit two further candles, opened my portmanteau, changed into my nightclothes, checked my rapier and, after the briefest toilette fell into my bed and the deepest sleep.

When I awoke my room was in darkness. A pale light came from the night sky which I could see from my window. I did not know what had awoken me until, within minutes, I heard raised voices from the room below. I left my bed, ascertained a part of the floor by the edge of the carpet, lowered myself and laid my ear against the bare boards. As I did so I reflected that I had become a persistent and unwilling eavesdropper.

I immediately heard a male voice, thin, querulous and rising intermittently to a high pitch, which much improved its audibility.

"But," said the voice, "she is a murderess. She has committed a mortal sin."

I heard my aunt's voice, softer and cautious with submission.

"She says she has not . . ."

"She would say that, would she not? If she has not committed murder why is she here? Why is she not before a magistrate in Paris pleading her innocence? Why is she a fugitive in our house?"

"She says she would not be believed."

"Not believed! Of course she would not be believed. She is an *actor*, a *woman* on the stage. She is little better than a whore like her mother."

"She is my sister."

"Oh yes, your sister whom you have seen *once* in the last fifteen years. *Once*. Where was she during the war against the tyrant King? Where was she during the great Parliamentary Commonwealth? She was *in France* with our fornicating King. She was probably in his bed."

"She has a husband in the Dordogne. A man of wealth and stature."

"Really. 'A man of wealth and stature'. So why is she not there? Why is she not with her parents? Why is she here? An outlaw in this house!"

I did not hear my aunt's reply but the volume and tone were unmistakable. It was a voice of surrender. The man's voice continued.

"She cannot stay here. Not in this house."

"She has nowhere to go."

"She must return to France. She must *be returned* to France as soon as it can be arranged."

After a further inaudible reply, the man's voice rose to a falsetto.

"Of course it can be arranged. There are channels in Parliament direct to the French authorities. They have agents here in London. She can be *persuaded* to return. If not persuaded she may be taken."

I heard my aunt sigh before she replied.

"When can this be done?"

"Tomorrow. Instantly. The morning should be sufficient. She must be kept here until the afternoon whilst arrangements are made. I will leave early. You must ensure that she is secure. Bolt her in."

"If I do not leave for my employment, she will be suspicious. I have told already that I will do so."

"Very well. Do not make her suspicious but *bolt her in.*"

"I can lock and bolt the doors but what of the windows? The mullions open above the street."

"She is a *woman.* Women in dresses cannot leap from mullioned windows. What would she do in the street dressed like a French whore? If her removal cannot be arranged by the afternoon, we will take steps to secure her further. In the meantime, lock the doors from the outside and keep the key."

The voices fell to a murmur and within minutes I heard the door to the kitchen below my room close before footsteps on the stair. I swiftly returned to my bed and feigned sleep in case I was observed. I heard further doors closing and then silence. I lay in my bed staring at the ceiling. As best I could, I formulated my plans for the following day for escape. Despite the danger I remained exhausted from my travels and before the daylight entered my room I had fallen into a light sleep. It did not last long.

CHAPTER 8

When I woke morning sunlight was falling upon the floor, which I had only recently vacated. I had been awoken by knocking on my door, which was now repeated. I rose and, making a fine pretence of semi-consciousness, opened the door to my aunt. What she said had clearly been rehearsed and she spoke without meeting my eyes.

"It is time," she said, "for me to leave for Lincoln's Inn. I have set out your breakfast in the kitchen. You will be quite safe here today but you should not attempt to leave the house. We are making discreet enquires as to any news from France. For your safety I will lock the street door from the outside. The side door I will also bolt inside and out. It is possible to reach that door from the street so do not touch the inner bolts under any circumstances. This means you will be unable to go to the garden but fresh air can be obtained by opening the mullions upstairs in your room."

I nodded my head and indicated that I was grateful indeed for the precautions which were being taken for my safety. She smiled and, for the first time, looked me in the face. Her eyes narrowed with fatigue and something approaching concern.

"You are," she said, "so like your mother."

Shortly afterwards I heard the front door close and the key turn in the lock. From my window I heard footsteps sound along the side of the house and bolts being drawn across the side door.

The footsteps receded, no doubt in the direction of Lincoln's Inn and the house, my prison, returned to silence.

I immediately inspected every window to which I had access. All of them were barred. The upper casements could be opened but the space allowed by the bars would not accommodate either Camille Lefebre or, as I had hoped, Robert Lefebre and his whalebone corset. The two doors that gave onto the street and to the side of the house were both substantial and secured from the outside. In desperation I climbed to the attic rooms and found that there was no access to the roof space. I was trapped. One room that gave onto the landing was locked. There was little enough furniture in the house and my searches of shelves and drawers revealed no key. I assumed this room to be occupied by cousin John, whom I had encountered upon my arrival. Thinking of him awakened a memory of my aunt's conversation: "John has gone to his schoolmaster in Holborn. He will return for his belongings at eleven tomorrow."

Would he still come? Would he have been informed that I was a prisoner in the house and not to be released? There had been no mention of this in the conversation I had overheard but then I had heard only a part. I had no choice but to hope. I repacked my portmanteau and, with considerable difficulty, wrestled it to the ground floor. I dressed in my full Parisienne splendour, drank a little water, opened my valise and applied myself to drafting a note to my aunt:

Dear Aunt Julie,
   I have now had time to consider our conversation and your wise advice. I was not aware that your husband, Paul, was in

the Government's employ. I am a fugitive from a powerful and influential family. I have reached the conclusion that I can no longer place you and your own family at risk. In time they will doubtless discover your identity and soon that I have sought refuge in your house. I cannot place you and your husband or your reputation at risk. I have other contacts in England and sufficient funds to reach them. I am most grateful to you for the care you have shown towards me. I hope and pray that in the future justice may be done and we will be reunited in happier times.

Your loving and affectionate niece, Camille.

I placed the note on the kitchen table. The clock in the spartan dining room (the only ornamentation other than a crucifix) showed the time to be ten minutes before eleven. I sat on my portmanteau, gathered my cloak and concealed rapier to me, clasped my valise and waited with dark apprehension. Nothing happened. Every ten minutes I rose, paced the rooms and gazed irresistibly into the street. It contained few people and little traffic which added to my sense of isolation. Twelve o'clock came and went and desperate thoughts entered my mind. One was to fire the house and call out for help from whatever services were available. I would undoubtedly be apprehended in the enterprise and despite my present dangers had no wish to ignite a further Great Fire to add to the growing indictment against me. A little after one I heard a noise immediately beyond the street door. As I stared at the dark oak I distinctly heard a key turning in the lock. The door opened and fat John stood before me. His eyes widened with surprise. As he opened his mouth I spoke first.

"Ah, John. Thank goodness you have come. Aunt Julie said that you would be arriving to assist me with my departure."

He blinked rapidly, started at the portmanteau and said: "I was not informed."

"Really? How strange. She was quite clear that you would arrive. You are a little late – as you see, I have been waiting. Aunt Julie told me that you would get me a Hackney to carry me to Charing Cross. I am going back on my travels."

Still he did not move. "I think," he said slowly, "that I must check with her at Lincoln's Inn."

For this I had already formulated a plan. I left the portmanteau and advanced upon him causing him to step back smartly into the street.

"That really will not be necessary. I think you should know that you are one of the reasons why I am leaving."

As he blinked, I continued. "Aunt Julie thought it inappropriate for us to remain living under the same roof with the obvious danger of mutual attraction between us and the risk of sinful thought and action."

His face went through a number of contortions: surprise, followed by a flicker of suspicion and, finally, an unpleasant leer. It was repellent but it had worked. He straightened, adopted something approaching a swagger and announced that he would obtain a Hackney from the station at Fenchurch Place. Whilst he was gone I firmly placed my portmanteau on the street and, by way of double precaution, visited the side door and threw the outside bolts. When I returned to the street the Hackney had arrived. The driver loaded my luggage and, with a final farewell wave to the leering John, we set out to Charing Cross. As we reached the end of the street I tapped smartly on the screen. When the coach stopped I lent from the window and informed the driver that my destination had changed.

"Do you know it?" I asked hopefully.

"The Goose at Fenchurch Street? Of course I know it. Best inn in London. Best landlord too. You staying long?"

"That rather depends," I said, "on a number of things," and sat back reflecting on that obvious truth.

The Hackney made good speed and within ten minutes we stopped before a handsome half-timbered building. A sign attached to the upper beams displayed a splendid and colourful goose, quite dead and awaiting the pot. The driver unloaded my luggage, which he carried into the front room and set down beside an unnecessary fire burning in a large grate. He acknowledged his fare and tip and then nodded to a burly red-faced man who appeared behind a dark wooden counter.

"Here you are John," he said, "I have brought you a welcome guest."

As the driver left I asked for John Mellor.

"That's me," said the florid man, observing my Parisian clothes with obvious approval. "And you, I think, are a young lady from France called something like February." He smiled at my surprise and added: "Yes, Samuel Pepys told me that you might be arriving and you have a letter. Perhaps you would let me see it?"

I handed him my note, which he read before saying: "Just so. Well, Miss February, I think we must find you a good room. One that Samuel himself has stayed in from time to time. I will not mention the circumstances."

With that he summoned two servants and my portmanteau

was carried to a generous room in which a large, handsome bed took pride of place. I had spoken barely a word since my arrival. As I thanked my host he nodded and smiled.

"It is a pleasure. Until he was given the job of rebuilding the Navy, Mr Pepys was one of my best customers. He is a musician, you know, as well as much else."

He left me alone and I sat on the splendid bed and contemplated action. One thing was immediately clear. I could not remain long at the Goose Inn. I knew that agents were being employed to secure my arrest and detention. Whoever they were they would have little difficulty in locating me at the Goose. Fat John would lead them to the Hackney he had obtained and I had no doubt that the driver, whatever the inducement, would direct them to my present lodgings. I needed another place of safety and, if possible, some form of employment. In truth I had little choice. I did not unpack. My portmanteau I placed against the wall and carefully concealed my rapier behind it. I took my travelling cloak, locked the room and descended to the dining room below me. The clock told me that it was now half past one in the afternoon and I presented myself again at the counter beside the main door to the street. I rang a bell which was immediately answered by John Mellor, who smiled with something between enquiry and understanding.

"How far," I asked, "is Seething Lane?"

"Walking," he said, "twenty minutes, perhaps more. By Hackney, ten minutes."

I asked for a Hackney to be summoned, which arrived instantly and, before two o'clock, I arrived at Seething Lane and, for the first time, pulled the bell beside the door of Mr Samuel

Pepys. It was opened by a tall, genial man in his thirties with a wide face and steady eyes. I enquired whether this was, indeed, Mr Pepys's house, adding, "I am…"

"You are, I suspect," he interrupted, "a lady from France who recently shared Samuel's carriage from Chatham. Do not be surprised. Samuel tells me everything. My name is William Hewer. I lived in Samuel's house since I was a boy. Now that his wife has died I visit regularly. He is not here at present. He is at the Navy Office but he has left instructions. If you arrived I was to let you in, make you welcome and leave you here until he arrives which will be, I think, in about two hours."

There was little to say and I followed him into a house which I can recall in meticulous detail to this day, thirty years on. He offered me food which I declined then took me to a drawing room whose windows overlooked the street.

"I am instructed," he said, "to tell you that you are quite safe here. I must go about my own business. By all means explore the house. Pepys said that you were likely to do so. Apart from what is locked in drawers, there are no secrets to be kept from French ladies. You will find food laid out in the kitchen when you are ready."

He left almost immediately. For a short while I sat in the drawing room doing something to assemble my thoughts then, inevitably and irresistibly, I began to explore the house which, as I write these words, comes alive again in my old brain.

• CHAPTER 9 •

It was a handsome town house, larger and more imposing than my aunt's and that was not the only distinction. In every room, even those which were unoccupied, pictures and tapestries hung on the wall and good rush matting and turkey rugs covered most of the stained floors. The paintings revealed an eclectic taste. There were some portraits, which appeared to be contemporary in the bold empathetic style of the Restoration. The dining and living rooms contained fine examples of still life from the Flemish school. These displayed silver plates laden with fruit and meat set out on damask with the unlikely addition of dead rabbits, pigeons and thrushes, unskinned and unplucked hanging from invisible wires or piled around the fruit bowls awaiting their part in a future feast. They were intended to stimulate a lusty appetite for the food itself and a wider sybaritism imagined without difficulty. Several of the paintings also contained pitchers of wine, glasses half-full set beside them and surrounded by a litter of paring knives, half-consumed bread, cheese, quinces, and figs split open to reveal pink and glowing flesh. My aunt, I fantasised, would have burnt them all on a great pyre with the unrepentant artist thrown upon it. The upper rooms were mainly decorated with tapestries, some of considerable age. There were also landscapes reflecting the British countryside through which I had recently passed for the first time. Every room contained fine furniture polished to the point of reflection. In the dining room silver candelabra, jugs and plates were displayed prominently on the table, dresser and chests.

I located a drawing room, in which was a fine desk with paper, quill and ink. I sat and wrote a brief letter to my family. My exact location and circumstances I omitted but inserted sufficient code for them to learn that I no longer stayed with my aunt but was in the same town and in safe hands. I told them, which was true, that I longed for news from them and from Paris.

I did not say how this news could be directly provided but added *tant mieux* reflecting, as I did so, that it was a code as flimsy as a Dutch veil. I placed the letter in an envelope, which I sealed and addressed. How it would be delivered I did not know but the Secretary to the British Navy would find a way.

As I recall these things, I am, again, amazed and no little ashamed that I did not make the terrible and obvious calculation as to the consequences of my flight from Paris and my presumed identity. Why I failed to see these things I do not know. The most obvious explanation, that I subconsciously erased so terrible a possibility, I have considered but rejected. I am, by nature, impulsive and, as will become apparent, foolhardy but I do not lack physical courage in the face of threat to myself and my family. Had I contemplated what was to occur I would never have left Paris. The consequences would haunt my life and drive my actions to a suicidal pitch. All that was in the future.

I left the desk and went in search of food. As I descended the stairs I passed a still life that depicted two hanging pheasants, a dead hare and a flagon of Flemish wine. I realised that I was again very hungry. I found the kitchen without difficulty. On the scrubbed table before the range I found plates of cold meat, most of a pie, braised leeks, a chutney and several eggs, boiled and peeled. There was a basket of fruit, apples, pears and early damsons beside two covered earthen pitchers which contained water and a dark ale. There was one place setting. I helped myself liberally to the food which I enjoyed with a small tankard of the ale. It was strong stuff after a sleepless night and a momentous morning and even at the table I felt my eyes begin to close. I returned to the drawing room, selected a deep, buttoned chaise, fell upon it and, immediately, into a deep sleep.

I awoke without immediate recollection of the room in which I was sleeping. The present realities assembled themselves like pieces of a strange puzzle. The single wall clock told me it was three-thirty in the afternoon. I had slept for barely an hour but I was alert, prepared and curiously without apprehension. The house still appeared to be empty. I moved from room to room and, on one occasion, gave a muted "allo". There was silence save for the ticking of a pendulum swinging below a large and painted clock at the end of the dining table. I climbed to the first floor and explored the other rooms. The first was a chamber dedicated to music. Barely four paces square, the walls were hung with portraits including a handsome young woman whose décolletage revealed an ample and generous bosom. The artist had captured a half smile, part pleasure and part invitation. Next to it and obviously by the same hand was a picture of Pepys himself. It might be said that it did him no justice. Equally it may be said that it was a frank, unadorned depiction of the man himself. Below the picture was a spinet open and ready for use. In addition to this instrument, there were two lutes and a flageolet. There was also a violin, a gypsy instrument I had never played, recently made popular by Mr Corelli. I sat at the spinet, flexed my fingers and began a tentative melody. I was rusty but many years of consistent practice had embedded the tune in my brain. My hands remained supple, stage work always involved the flexing of palm and fingers as did practice with the sword. After barely ten minutes I was playing with some confidence and began, softly, to sing the words of *Vertes Manches*. As the song progressed I allowed myself more volume and as a result did not hear the door open behind me. How long he had been there I do not know but as I finished with something of a flourish on the keyboard he applauded warmly from a seat he had taken on the far side of the room.

"Bravo," he said, "très, très joli."

I affected rather than felt some confusion.

"I am sorry," I said, "I should have . . ."

"Not at all. I came from the street into a house of music. That has happened but rarely since Lizzie died and it gave me immense pleasure. You may already have seen her. She is over there."

He indicated the painting which I had already concluded to be his wife.

"They are a pair," he said unnecessarily, "it is a fine likeness of her and also, I am sorry to say, of myself."

The analysis was neither false nor contrived and, when he smiled, I experienced the same feeling which surprised me during our conversation in the coach. Ridiculous, I thought, physically unappetizing and old enough to be my father. Aloud I said, "Did your wife play the spinet?"

"No, she played the lute rather badly but, on occasions, we played together. She would sit and listen to me play. She enjoyed repetition. I would finish a song and she would stand behind me and demand it again. 'Play it again Samuel,' she would say, 'play it again.'"

His tone changed when he said, "That song, it is an English tune."

"No," I said, "it is a French tune, played in the Périgord for a hundred years."

"I think you are wrong," he said. "That tune was composed by an English King as a dedication to his wife. It is very beautiful and speaks of a great love. Subsequently he cut her head off. Music can be deceptive. Play it again and sing it in French and then, if you like, I will sing it in English."

I affected a measure of resignation and turned, once again, to the keyboard. As I began to play I heard the lute behind me. He played with great skill and, encouraged by the accompaniment, I played and sang with greater élan. For the first time since I left Paul Detain and Jean Molière in the Théâtre du Marais, I experienced a surge of real and excited pleasure. The song came to an end, both instruments rising and falling precisely together into a rapt silence which we both enjoyed.

"Now," he said, "let me at the keyboard and I will sing it in English in its original setting."

I smiled, shook my head and vacated the chair. He began to sing and then stopped with an exclamation of surprise when he heard the lute begin behind him. He turned abruptly.

"You play the lute?"

"Yes, I do, rather better than I play that."

And so we began again. I preferred the French but he sang it well and with confidence. His voice, as I anticipated, had a deep resonance entirely fitted to the ballad itself. When we finished for the second time, after a pause, I said:

"Play it again, Samuel."

"English or French?"

"We are in England so let us sing the King's words."

And so we began. He did not stop playing or singing but his shoulders jerked with surprise when he heard my own voice above the sound of the lute singing the English words. When we concluded for the third time he spun round on the chair laughing aloud.

"You are playing with me again," he said. "First, you pretend you cannot speak English. Now you pretend you did not know the words."

"No," I said, "wrong on both counts. I did not maintain my lack of English, you assumed it. And I did not know the words of this charming song but, Mr Pepys, you forget I am an actor. One of the skills that come with the trade is an ability to learn verse and prose practically as it is spoken. Some of us are better than others and we tend to lose the knack as we grow old but, for the moment, I have it. Also, it is not a particularly difficult song and even its composer would admit to the repetition."

"Well," he said, "let us to it once more. You on the keyboard, myself I will return to the lute."

It was probably our worst rendition. We were both taken by a measure of over-confidence and it began to be a little noisy. It was, however, good enough and both of us on this occasion failed to hear the door open and close and were thus both surprised when more applause rang out behind us. Will Hewer had entered the room and was clapping enthusiastically above his head.

"Bravo," he cried, "encore."

"I think not," said Pepys, "it is not for the moment getting any better and it is time to pause."

Turning to me, he said, jerking a thumb towards Hewer:

"Don't worry, he doesn't play anything so we are not going to turn ourselves into an orchestra but we must find other songs to sing. We have music to teach each other. I know a little of French song, some of it, I fear, not entirely proper. I have heard some rather gloomy and tuneless stuff from the Auvergne which we should avoid if possible. Now I need some broth and then there are matters which we must discuss. I suggest that we do that in the dining room while Will asks Deborah to prepare our supper."

"Deborah?"

"She is my housekeeper who ensures my survival."

We descended to the kitchen, where I met Deborah, and then both he and I carried cups of broth into the dining room, where we sat on either side of the polished table and discussed the future.

He subjected me to a full minute's survey, his head inclined and his magnified eyes narrowed in amused contemplation. Eventually he spoke: "Well Miss Browne, I saw your cloak in the hall. It appears that you have abandoned your aunt." When I nodded he continued, "Tell me, did you also meet her husband?"

"I have not met him but I heard him."

"That is probably enough. Let me guess. He found you an unwelcome visitor?"

I nodded and he smiled: "And, if he knows your story, no doubt he is, even now, arranging his 'agents' to return you to France."

I nodded again, my eyes widening with surprise.

"It is not a difficult assumption if you know the man, odious shit that he is. You are lucky to have escaped. Did you go to the Goose?"

"I did. I have just come from there. I left my luggage in my room."

He nodded briefly. "I anticipated as much and how did you get there?"

As I told him the story of my escape and the hire of the Hackney he frowned.

"In these circumstances it will not be long before you are followed. Whatever you do now we must retrieve your luggage from The Goose."

He rose, left the room and returned immediately.

"I have asked Will to fetch your things, which, I suspect, includes the rapier. Did you leave my note with John Mellor?"

When I nodded he said, "Good. John will give it to whoever follows you and it will set them off on a tour of England." He resumed his seat, removed his spectacles and polished them on his cuff.

"Well Miss Browne, what are we to do with you? Do you have any other Puritan aunts or indeed anywhere more amusing where you may hide?"

I held his gaze and I shook my head. "That is why I am here."

"I thought as much. Well, you will be safe here for a day or so while I make enquiries. I have friends in the country that may assist. Huntingdon. It is a beautiful place and a long way from Paris."

I took a deep breath. "I had hoped," holding his gaze, "that I might stay here and do you some service."

The eyes, now back behind his spectacles, widened and I continued.

"You said in the coach that you needed a scribe. I am fluent in three languages and know a little Latin. I can write all four with a fair hand. I may be able to earn my keep."

I had rehearsed the speech all morning but now felt the blood rise to my face.

He sat awhile in silence and then slowly shook his head.

"It is an attractive proposition Miss Browne, in many ways, but I can think of many reasons to refuse. Most of all, you are a danger to me. Your pretence in our coach has left you in possession of terrible secrets. You will not have forgotten. I may soon be involved in schemes that many would call treason. Information in the wrong hands could lead me directly to the Tower. I have endured enough pain from surgeons and can imagine the worst without difficulty. I am afraid I must send you to Huntingdon, where you will dazzle the rural squires."

I held his gaze and continued the role I had rehearsed.

"Mr Pepys, may I ask you, implore you, to think again. I have not engaged in matters of state but you are as much a danger to me as I am to you. One word from you and I would be returned to Paris and to the mercies of the most powerful family in France. The agonies you would endure in the Tower would, I assure you, be nothing compared to those I would suffer. We are both custodians of each other's secrets and so we are already *entwined*. It could be a matter of fate. My fluency in French and Italian may well do you service. Your knowledge of my past assures you of my future silence. Furthermore, if your diaries were transcribed into French would it not provide some protection for your secret thoughts?"

As I spoke he began to smile. He rose and walked to the window, from which he could see the roofs of London already glowing in the evening sun. He remained silent for several minutes then returned to his seat and tapped a slow tune on the surface of the table. When he stopped he spoke directly to me but also, I fancied, to himself.

"Fate, fate indeed. It is something to which I have given much thought as I grow steadily blind. I had reflected on the possibility of a second sight. Another voice to stir the imagination."

He suddenly changed and looked directly into my eyes.

"Very well Miss Browne. Let us see if this can work. As soon as Will returns I will have him show you your room. Indeed I fancy that I hear him at the door. You are now Catherine Browne and Camille Lefebre is, for the moment, disappeared. For as long as we are *entwined* you are as safe as I am from arrest and pain. That may not be much comfort. As we say in England, you have stepped from the pan into the fire. Let us hope we remain unconsumed."

As he spoke Will Hewer reappeared in the doorway.

"Ah Will, Miss Catherine Browne will be our guest for some time and will take over duties as my scribe. She may have your old room overlooking the lane and, indeed, your old bed to which you can introduce her now if you would. Have you brought all her belongings? Ah, I see from your face that you are aware that Miss Browne carries an armoury. Do not be alarmed. She has, I think, only impaled one nobleman, which will not be repeated while she lives in Seething Lane."

I rose and stood above my new master who remained sitting.

"Thank you," I said. "Bien, merci."

He smiled and nodded. "Dinner," he said, "in two hours and then to business and the diary."

CHAPTER 10

I was led to a long, generous room with two windows, one of which gave a handsome prospect across neighbouring roofs to a river, undoubtedly the Thames, glinting in the sun. The room contained a bed, already made, two linen chests, a hanging rack and a good desk, leather inlaid. I had a small sofa and two leather chairs, one of which was drawn up to the desk beneath the larger of the windows. On one wall there was a large tapestry depicting the inevitable hunt; landscapes occupied the other two. As I unpacked my belongings Will brought me three lamps. One he placed beside the bed. The others were put on the desk and the linen chest not required for the disposal of my clothes. I hung my travelling cloak on the back of the door. My rapier was suspended beneath it and the hilt banged gently against the woodwork whenever it was opened. I found it reassuring. I tried the strong lock set into the frame. It was well oiled and the key turned smoothly and silently without effort. Fresh water had been provided and a quantity of brushes and toiletries, the property I assumed of the late Madame Pepys. I prepared as best I could and set out for the dining room. As I passed the drawing room I was intercepted by Pepys who ushered me inside. He indicated a chair and we sat on either side of the desk.

"It is only a matter of time," he said, "before your aunt discovers you are working with me. Unless you are to become a hermit in this old house that is quite inevitable."

Anticipating my concerns, he held up his hand.

"I understand. What is important is that she should not do so until you have had communication from your family. Let us hope that is within a matter of days. We will take steps to send a message to your home in France so we can establish a direct line of communication. For the time being stay in the house as much as possible. You have already discovered the library and the music room, which can afford some diversion. I have arranged for Lizzie's dressmaker to come next week and provide you with suitably shapeless clothes. At the moment you are a little conspicuous for Spitalfields, although you will pass unnoticed in the Haymarket. As a precaution I will plot the route that your aunt would take to Lincoln's Inn in order that you may avoid it whatever you are wearing. Her ghastly husband works at Westminster but I understand he has never met you and he never gets his head out of his ledgers. Food and drink, beer and some wine, are always available in the kitchen and the cold larder. Help yourself. Deborah cooks in the evening when that is necessary and cleans three days a week. You will like her. I am not proposing to entertain until next . . ." He consulted a small black diary, "Wednesday, which should be an agreeable dinner that you are very welcome to attend. I think that is all apart from this . . ."

He took up a case and removed from it a black leather-bound folder, which he pushed across the table. I opened it and he said:

"As you can see, it is blank paper, good enough quality to last a few hundred years if necessary. It is my new diary kept at dictation by Miss Catherine Browne, amanuensis extraordinaire."

He removed his spectacles and squinted at me while he polished them on his cuff. "Have I missed anything? I hope not."

When he replaced his spectacles I held his eyes and said:

"Just this, if I am pursued by agents of the Pertaine family and if my whereabouts are discovered then it is likely that they will attempt to capture or kill me. They are unlikely to respect your rank or your office, however celebrated and distinguished. Have you thought of any precautions for yourself?"

This appeared to amuse him.

"My dear Catherine, absolutely not. We have no shortage of our own villains, some of whom, incidentally, are also celebrated and distinguished. In England, in my lifetime, plotting in one form or another, regicide, fratricide, matricide or even plain homicide, has become a national recreation. Quite a lot of these plots have and, no doubt will, concern me. If I 'took precautions' against all of them I would live like a mole."

As I looked at him across the table I realised how apposite the description was. His spectacles greatly magnified his eyes and the bulbous upturned nose appeared to my sudden imagination to be ideal for tunnelling. I smiled to conceal my thoughts and said:

"Not a life that would suit you I think."

He smiled in turn. "That exhausts my agenda. Now let me know, if you wish, what happened with your aunt."

My immediate future was now fully decided and settled and I had no reason to dissemble. I told him of my initial welcome by my aunt and described the interior of her house which had him nodding with suspicions confirmed. I told him that I had reported the meeting with two men on the coach from Dover. I emphasised that I had provided her with no details of the conversations that occurred between them. Finally, I said, I had revealed to her that one of my companions was Samuel Pepys.

"Ah," he said, "so you did. What did she say I wonder?"

"She was horrified that I had fallen into such company."

"Was she indeed? I am not surprised. She thinks I am a devil."

"She does," I said. "She actually said you were *the* Devil."

"Really, how elevating. I must tell my friend John Milton. He could turn me into a gloomy poem. 'Paradise Doomed Again'. Did she provide any reasons for her view?"

"Yes indeed," I said, elevating the fingers of my left hand precisely as my aunt had done. "Papist, King's Man, conspirator, traitor to the Parliamentarian cause, dissipated lecher and a habitué of prostitutes and lewd entertainments – pretending to be plays – performed in the Haymarket."

Pepys's shoulders were shaking with silent laughter. His spectacles came off before he said:

"Really? That is quite an indictment and all on one hand. Some of it is not entirely fair. I don't often go to the Haymarket theatres. I prefer the new ones in Piccadilly." He was laughing but then abruptly his mood changed. He gave an exaggerated sigh.

"It really is not a laughing matter. It is easy to see how these allegations may begin. In all of them there is a kernel of truth. It is hard to understand how they are maintained and by apparently intelligent people. It is a form of conspiracy, almost impossible to control. It is like spinning a web. You tether it to a set of doubtful facts and then you spin those facts together into an invisible mesh to catch fools and wrap them in deceit." He sighed again. "Fortunately there are some wider truths outside this sticky mess. The Navy is a truth. Intellectual toleration is a truth even if it is anchored to the myth of the King's divinity."

It was a soliloquy to which no answer was required and I said nothing. Noises from the kitchen brought him to the mundane.

"Good. Let us dine and speak no more of your aunt. If you give me the letter for your parents I will see it is entrusted to safe hands. After dinner we will begin the first page of the diary."

He left me sitting at the desk, the diary sheets open before me. Before I followed I carefully inscribed the date *4 Mai 1670* on the first blank page of the folder and wrote beneath it in French, "The new diary of SP". I then joined my employer in the dining room. We ate alone as Will, I was told, was keeping company in Pall Mall. We ate the remainder of the pie with salted beef and what appeared to be mashed swede. This was followed by warm bread with a good cheese and wine, which SP told me was from Cahors, a region of France I had never visited but which, judging from the wine, possessed a climate not dissimilar to Périgord. After dinner we took the jug and the pewter cups to the library, where we assumed facing seats across the central table. He appeared awkward and confessed that he had never given dictation on anything other than naval matters. He indicated that he would speak slowly in order to allow the simultaneous translation into French. I found this unnecessary. I was completely bilingual and, subject to the translation of the vernacular, was able to maintain a steady pace. I sat with my pen poised, ink glistening at the tip.

Silence.

I raised my eyes and saw he was staring fixedly out of the window. He transferred his gaze to me and said, "Block. I think I have a block. It is a new experience."

Fully a minute then passed during which I shook the nib

against my saucer and immersed it again in the well. At this point he lifted his head, squared his shoulders and cleared his throat. I waited until he said: "*To Whitehall.*"

"I am sorry," I said, "could you say that again?"

His face twitched with impatience before he repeated: "*To Whitehall.*"

"What exactly does that mean?"

"It means," said Pepys with a note of irritation, "*to Whitehall.* I have gone to Whitehall."

"I see," I said, "when exactly did this happen?"

"I don't know," said Pepys, "I don't usually put that in unless it has some other relevance."

"Does it?" I asked.

"No, not on this occasion. Given what is coming it matters not a Dutch fanny when I go or have gone. It is a convention. I just say '*to Whitehall*'. Is that so difficult?"

"It is just," I said, "that it means nothing in French. If I write '*vers Whitehall*' it will get you some but not all of the way. If I just write '*à Whitehall*' it means you are there already."

Pepys shook his head and said, "Do you think we had better do this in English?"

"No," I replied, "I think we must do it in both. If it means nothing in French but something in English then I will write '*To Whitehall*' and then when you are at Whitehall I will lapse into French."

"Very well, let us start again."

To Whitehall and then to the Navy Office. I learn that word has been sent from the Council although I expect the hand of Le Roy lies behind it.

"That is," I said, "French."

"Of course it is French," said SP emphatically cleaning his spectacles, "of course it is French. It is the code that I use for the King."

"As I am writing in French would you like me to transcribe it in English?"

"No, let us stay with the French."

As he replaced his spectacles, his eyes swam across the table.

"Do you think," he said, "you could just write what I say? It may make no sense to you and, indeed, it may make no sense at all. Perhaps in hundreds of years' time clever people will spend their lives examining what I say, unravelling codes and the like, and it may all mean nothing even then but, just for the moment, do you think you could transcribe exactly what I say whether it means anything or not?"

"Fine," I said, feeling myself become a little heated, "if that is what you want me to do I will do it. I was simply attempting to be helpful."

His eyes lowered for a moment to my bosom and then resumed their customary good humour.

"You may not be as entirely qualified for this as for your other work. However, for the moment, let us persevere as best we can."

"Very well," I said, "shall I read you what I have written so far?"

"Yes please, that would be helpful."

To Whitehall (in English) and then to the Navy Office. I learn that word has been sent from the Council although I expect the hand of Le Roy lies behind it.

"Excellent," said Pepys, "This is going well." He continued:

I spend some time checking the accuracy of the figures we are to provide. The result will please Le Roy. The majority of the Channel Fleet can sail within a week. What value this may have at this time is bound to cause conjecture. Then to Gray's Inn to visit R to discuss the new erections in Chancery Lane. I am with her awhile in excellent conversation by which I was much fulfilled. Then to Seething Lane to find CB already at the lute.

"Spinet," I said, "I assume CB is me? I was at the spinet."

"No, you were at the lute, I took the spinet."

"Wrong," I said, "it was because I was at the keyboard that I did not hear you enter the room. Had I been at the lute I would have seen you immediately."

"Please write *at the lute*."

"I find this very difficult as I know it was the spinet."

We looked straight at each other and his eyelids fluttered with blinking.

"Very well," he said at length, "just put 'I find CB already at the instruments.'"

"Fine," I said.

"*And singing an English melody in French.*"

"I believe that the melody is French."

"The melody is not French. The words are French but the melody is English and composed by an English King."

After a short silence I said:

"Can I suggest we just say, 'sweet melody' to avoid the argument?"

"This is not an argument. This is my diary. What is in my diary accords with my knowledge and recollection."

"Even if it is false?"

"It is not false and it doesn't matter if it is." His spectacles had come off yet again but when he replaced them he smiled.

"Very well. 'Sweet melody'. And then add:

It was my pleasure to join her at the instruments and we played well and sweetly together until the arrival of WH. I have expectations of CB who will, I know, fulfil her roles with great skill and care having already expressed concerns for my own wellbeing.

Startled, I looked up.

"Did I . . .?"

I saw that he was laughing and, with that response, I emphatically laid down the quill and joined him without restraint.

"I think," he said, "that we have been rather better at the instruments than the recording of historical fact."

I continued to smile.

"Melody," I said, "may be sung in many ways; history, I fancy, is no different."

We parted shortly after and I made my way to my toilette and to my room. I carefully locked the door, removed my rapier and placed it under my bed. My first day, *chez* Pepys, had left me tired. My head ached but when I closed my eyes I found myself smiling into sleep, the melody of *Vertes Manches* insistently filling my head with, unaccountably, English words.

CHAPTER 11

When I awoke the morning sun flowed through the window and Pepys's voice could be heard through the door.

"Catherine, it is seven o'clock and there is some business."

I rose, washed briefly, dressed and was in the library within twenty minutes. Pepys sat at the table, which was occupied by several charts and what appeared to be ledgers. These contained small and indecipherable banks of figures. He nodded a friendly welcome.

"Good morning Catherine. I am sorry you have been dragged from your bed. I wanted to speak to you before I left."

"Left?" I said with some alarm, expressing a now familiar insecurity.

He smiled. "Yes, but don't worry. I am directed again to Deptford and Chatham. The messenger arrived shortly after six and the coach is waiting. As it bears the King's Arms we should make fast progress. That is to say the coach and myself not you. I strongly suspect you have no immediate desire to retrace your steps towards France. I see I am right. Something came with the messenger which may occupy your time."

He passed me a folded document on which the wax seal had been broken.

"It is in French, a language the King believes me to speak fluently, which I now do with your assistance."

Talking of the document he appeared agitated. This brought

on the energetic cleansing of spectacles, passing them between his open, exhaling mouth and the handkerchief attached to his cuff.

"Do not," he said, "allow this to be taken from the room and do not commit the translation to paper. I understand the gist of it, for the detail I look to you. We can consider it together when I return. Given the size of today's business I will, inevitably, be detained at the Dockyard tonight. The coach is at my disposal and, all being well, I will return by midday tomorrow. Now go and get a proper breakfast while I fish what I need from this sea of paper."

As I left the room, he said: "Oh, two things. First, this," he held up a small leather pouch, "is a key to this library, the only key apart from my own. Neither Deborah nor Will possess one. Keep the room locked and when you have considered this document leave it in the drawer of this desk, which also has a key. Take that as well. You will then have two keys, which may be put in the same pouch. Keep them with you at all times. How you conceal them is a matter entirely for you, although I can make the obvious suggestion. Second," he said, "on the subject of clothes and bodices, I have arranged for Lizzie's dressmaker to attend you this morning at eleven o'clock."

"How," I said, "am I to pay this lady?"

Pepys shrugged with impatience. "It is my idea and I will pay for it. I cannot have you walking the streets in those clothes. Even in this newly liberated age they will provoke disorderly behaviour."

As he resumed his work his head descended within a foot of the desk and his wig brushed the chart he studied. He flicked it away with irritation and then, finally, removed it and threw it into the open case beside the desk. Observing that I was still in the room he smiled with resignation.

"I have sent for new spectacles with stronger lenses. Soon they will be like telescopes."

I did not see him again before he left. In the kitchen I joined Hewer for breakfast and, with slight diffidence, discussed our respective roles in the Pepys residence. I learnt that he had been a part of Pepys household since 1660, when he came, aged eighteen as a manservant and clerk but mainly, he said, "to have his ears boxed". Seeing my surprise he laughed. "I was," he said, "a ruffian and deserved what I got. Also," he added, "I was big enough to knock him down if I wanted but the ear boxing was so hopeless I rather enjoyed it." He had become a clerk in the Navy Office, where he remained as a "convenient source of information". Five years before he had moved to his own lodgings in Spitalfields but kept a room at Seething Lane. "I have spent much time here," he said, "since Lizzie died." Considering his next words he looked straight at me, "Samuel has more friends and keeps more society than any man in London but loneliness afflicts him like a pox."

Briefly I described my own background, omitting almost entirely the events of the previous week. He nodded politely whilst I did so. The description was so brief that I anticipated questions. There were none and I assumed, rightly, that he had been instructed to refrain from enquiry. During my days at Seething Lane I saw little of this clever and amusing man. With Pepys, the avuncular relationship was obvious, but there was more – a sense of shared hope and expectation, close to conspiracy perhaps.

After breakfast I returned to the library. The document with the broken seal was on the mantel above the fireplace. I took it to the desk and flattened it against the leather. It was a folder containing two sheets of fine paper densely covered in writing. The fastidious conformity of the script indicated, immediately, its official nature and importance. There was little by way of preamble and what followed was detailed enquiry. It related entirely to ships in different categories. Warships, supply vessels and merchantmen. Thereafter there were sub-divided enquiries as to tonnage, size, displacements and the requirements of crews whether at sea or in dock. The largest section and the main enquiries related to warships, the number of guns which they could carry and the numbers which were actually available. Information was sought as to the number of vessels at sea, their location, whether in British or European waters or, specifically, the Americas. The document required the number and status of vessels in various dockyards, their state of repair and the readiness of the crews. In some cases, the requirements, expressed in French, were technical. Ironically, these were the easier passages to translate. The maritime and nautical world has its own tongue, which is both universal and precise.

In two hours I had assured myself that I could, if required, faithfully transcribe the entire document, both its direct meaning and nuance. I reassembled the folder and placed it in the desk drawer, which I locked. The key I placed into the leather pouch containing the library key, now lying on a chest by the door. I crossed the library and stared at my own reflection in the mirror above the mantel. I placed both hands on its marble surface and noticed with concern that they were shaking. As a sensation for me it was not new. It frequently occurred before the curtain rose on the first act or at the moment of imminent appearance from the wings. I knew, from experience, that the tremor would disappear immediately my performance began and thought was turned into action. The similarities appeared obvious; knowledge and the nervous anticipation of its consequences. The manner of my arrival in Pepys's house and receiving the knowledge I now possessed was by any standards, remarkable. Equally remarkable was the fact that the events of the past four days had assumed an inevitable quality, the one proceeding upon the other as though set to a distant music. Within this score danger had been laid upon danger as though building towards a symphonic climax, anticipated but unknown. I stared at myself seeking confidence in my own features. The document I had considered and concealed represented, I had not the slightest doubt, the politics of princes on an epic scale. If the requirements of the document were met the recipient would possess an intimate knowledge of the British Navy, its capabilities at sea and on land and its readiness for war. I was working for a man I barely knew but who possessed this information to an extent and detail none other could provide. The first and most obvious question concerned my own selection. I was now possessed of a terrible secret, incomplete and possibly inconclusive, but sufficient to damage or destroy the power of princes.

Why had I been entrusted with this document and its content? I was young, totally ignorant of the affairs of state or their machinations. I had no training other than in a profession with an awesome reputation for the instability of its members.

I was, to boot, a possible fugitive from strong forces, unjust forces but of terrifying power. As I made these reflections my eyes widened with yet another wave of dire comprehension. *I was French.* These communications, revealing potential treason, were between the Kings of England and of France. Given my nationality I was not only a harmless translator of treasonable documents, I was a spy. That is why Samuel Pepys could travel to Chatham with total confidence. The woman he left behind with documents of deadly importance and the access to keys secured in her bosom would no more contemplate revelation and confession than impaling herself upon a spike.

For a short while I gripped the edge of the mantel, as a feeling of giddy nausea receded and I came, once more, at least to resemble my thespian self. I straightened, shrugged and rehearsed in the mirror a number of facial expressions, all exhibiting confidence, savoir faire and even a measure of sangfroid. Through dreadful turns of fate I had arrived at a position devoid of choice but with the prospect of playing in a drama of which, until days before, I had barely conceived. I left the library and mounted the stairs to my room.

The house, again, was empty. Hewer was on a day's errand to Whitehall and Deborah was not due until six o'clock to prepare dinner for us both. I sat at my desk and composed another letter to my brother Robert. I told him that my return home would be delayed "perhaps for a month or so" and that I had been given a number of "unexpected opportunities", which bore some semblance of truth. I sealed the letter and placed it with the message that I had written to my parents the day before. When and how these documents would get to Périgord was still unknown and subject to the assurance I had received from Pepys. I descended to the music room where I spent half an hour at the lute. My finger work had improved and would, I thought, have satisfied my old tutors.

I returned to the library. On one of the chests I found a manuscript containing two plays by Ben Jonson. I read them with a professional's eye and rehearsed out loud a scene from *Volpone,* taking both the part of Volpone and Nano in full noisy dialogue. This was my calling and my vocation and the mere recitation of the lines calmed the anxieties of the morning. The painted library clock showed two o'clock. I had four hours without immediate occupation. The house was my security but it was rapidly becoming my prison. I felt trapped. The fugitive, I learnt, instinctively seeks not sanctuary but the capability of flight. Mentally I rehearsed my movements if the house was attacked. One of my windows gave onto a parapet, two feet wide, which extended to the neighbouring houses. It was intended, I have no doubt, for boxes of lavender or herbs to combat the unmistakable smell of excrement that rose from the central drain. It was perhaps twenty feet to the street below. To fall onto the cobbles might not be fatal but would certainly do some substantial damage. To reach the neighbouring windows was a distance of about three yards, possible but perilous. Moreover, it would be quite impossible in the dress and petticoat that I was wearing. This was an escape to be made by Robert and not Camille Lefebre.

The sense of imprisonment deepened and I resolved, whatever the risk, to take to the streets. I felt the need to be armed. I opened the second linen chest and from it extracted the clothes of Robert

Lefebre, including the whalebone corsetry which compressed my woman's body. I changed, selected one of two wigs, took my sword belt from the door and buckled it at my waist. The belt supported a small leather satchel into which I placed the keys to both the library and the drawer. I made use of the stairs and the hallway to adopt a male stride then passed into the street, secured the door behind me and added the key to the contents of my satchel. Pepys had provided an advance payment of my stipend and I possessed some English coin in addition to four gold *livres*, which I placed in the pocket of my leather waistcoat. Pepys, as promised, had also provided me with a map. This plotted the likely movements of my aunt between Spitalfields and Lincoln's Inn. I had committed the main parts to memory, including the whereabouts of churches whose spires I could see from my window. Armed with this information I was confident that I could follow my planned route. This passed through the Old Gate then followed the Fleet until it met the River Thames. Thereafter a bridge provided access to the embankment before turning right to Temple Church. Then I planned a direct line to Holborn, Fenchurch and Seething Lane. From the map I anticipated a journey of some two miles, which could be accomplished well before I was due, as Catherine Browne, at the kitchen table.

The foolhardy nature of the expedition is all too obvious with hindsight. The most obvious flaw concerned the date of the map which, I subsequently discovered, was 1662, two years after the restoration of Charles II and four years before the Great Fire. As soon as I crossed into the Old Gate I saw that many of the streets and thoroughfares had ceased to exist in whole or in part.

Building works were everywhere. Cranes and pulleys, some fifty feet high, stood on flattened areas of land like giant instruments of siege. Some buildings appeared already to be occupied, others were mere shells. Water required for construction was carried in culverts and pipes. Many of these had overflowed or burst and what passages existed were often ankle deep in mud. I made slow progress and enquiries for directions received answers which often appeared contradictory. At ground level the cranes, the machinery and the growing buildings themselves obscured the landmarks I had mapped from my room. It was well over an hour before I arrived at the Fleet. Here the works had a greater sense of order. A great cathedral or church was in the process of construction. Its perimeter was fenced and roped, allowing spaces at which small crowds had gathered to view this mighty monument rising, literally, from the ashes.

I realised that my journey must be shortened. Having reached the banks of the Thames itself I turned to retrace my steps as best I could. It was because of the volte-face that I found I was being followed. I saw them immediately. Two men, both dressed in black, not a uniform but a conformity. As I turned they appeared, in unison, to hesitate. They then continued. I remained stationary and they passed close beside me. At this point they both jerked their faces away as though simultaneously drawn by an identical sound. Still walking they maintained this fixed contortion, gazing at a pile of rubble and mud as though it had suddenly erupted into life. For one of the men the consequences were immediately unpleasant and painful. Staring fixedly to the left he failed to notice a deep excavation designed to receive the excess water and slurry running down the narrow street of unfinished buildings. The hole was partly surrounded by a canvas sheet intended no doubt to allow its use by the many workmen and artisans in the absence of any other rudimentary sanitation. It was, in effect, an open sewer a full six feet deep. The man who arrived first at the pit felt, rather than saw, his foot fall into open air. There was a short scream and oath as he disappeared from the footpath. The sound of his landing at least indicated that the consequences would be less than fatal. I turned and continued as swiftly as I could in the direction of Old Gate. Twice I lost my way and by the time I reached Seething Lane and entered the hall it was close to five-thirty by the library clock. I climbed to my room and once again assumed the character of Catherine Browne. I took my boots to the kitchen and used the washing water to clean them as best I could. I replaced them in my room and set about recording a description of the two men whilst they remained fresh in my recollection. At dinner I barely spoke and then retired to my room and firmly locked the door.

The following day I described the men to Pepys when he returned a little past midday from Chatham. He listened carefully, requested repetition and then said:

"Can you be sure from this that they followed you?"

I nodded emphatically.

"Oh yes. Nothing else could account for their behaviour."

Pepys looked at me through his spectacles.

"Well, that does seem conclusive but it makes little sense. If these were your friends from France it is unlikely that they would have sought to avoid a confrontation with you, certainly not to the extent of falling into a sewer."

"They were not French," I said, "I have no doubt of that. As the man disappeared into the pit he cried out in English. It was an oath but also, I suspect, a description of the contents."

Pepys smiled, "I see. How very satisfactory. It still makes little sense but let us record it in our diary, which we will do when I return from the Navy Office this afternoon."

His evident sangfroid provided me with some comfort but uncertainty preyed on my mind. The night before I had risen twice to test the lock on my door and, on both occasions, had stood at my window scanning the dark doorways for signs of movement. For the immediate future I decided that neither Robert nor Camille Lefebre would travel abroad alone into uncharted streets.

CHAPTER 12

When Pepys returned from the Navy Office he asked me to join him in the library. I gave him the key to the drawer, from which he extracted the French document. He opened it and spread it upon the desk.

"Have you had time to consider it?" he asked.

"I have. It is very detailed and it took some time."

"Does it present any problems?"

It was a question that invited misunderstanding so I demurred.

"Problems? In what sense?"

He looked at me sharply.

"I meant, of course, the translation. Some of it is of a technical nature."

"That," I said, "did not cause me any problems. Many of the technical terms are common in both French and English. That is not a problem."

He continued to look directly into my eyes.

"Do you have any other concerns? If so you must tell me."

It was impossible to dissemble. I took a deep breath.

"I know little of your English politics although I am learning very fast but it is impossible not to conclude that the information required by that document would be invaluable to an enemy of England should they obtain it."

"That causes you concern? This information is required by

France, your own country and with whom there has been no conflict for forty years."

"I am not concerned for England. I am concerned for you or, more accurately, for us. Knowledge, as I well know, can be a contagion."

There was an uncomfortable period of silence before he said:

"Do you wish to reconsider your position in this house? Even after so short a time I would be very sorry to see you go. If you decide to do so I can make arrangements for your safe accommodation without having to return to the Puritan mercies of your aunt. You have no obligations to me and the knowledge you possess will never be revealed."

"I was followed."

"Perhaps. But even if that occurred it was not, fortunately, Camille Lefebre who was followed. Your wanderings can have taught them nothing apart from the perils of the open sewer." He paused, then after evident reflection continued, "You are right to this extent, dangerous conflicts still exist in England notwithstanding the glorious restoration of our monarch. The Civil War and the Commonwealth have left many open wounds. In the last thirty years England has experienced two very different forms of government. Both were far from perfect. Both employed their own form of tyranny. There are many that have seen both but embraced neither. I am one of them."

As he continued I was aware that dialogue had become a meditation. Spectacles removed, he gazed through the window at the roofs and chimneys of London slowly dissolving into dusk.

"You may embrace neither," he continued, "but total rejection of both is not available. Governed we must be and those of us who play a small part must take our decisions. Often, what is best is that which is least abhorred. What we have learnt above all is that power and religious sanctimony do not create Utopia. What results is dangerous to the state and nasty for its citizens. Kings purport to rule by divine right but everyone knows that is nonsense including the kings themselves. It is a device that ensures the order of the state and, at its best, creates a measure of responsibility. Infinitely more dangerous are men who believe they are right, who govern from their own moral precept and recruit the Almighty to their purposes. In thirty years we have had both and have rejected both at their extremes. That itself is cause for hope. We are groping our way, thank God, towards an age of reason."

He turned from the window and addressed me directly. "You will have learnt something from your unsuccessful pilgrimage yesterday. The buildings that are rising from the ashes of the fire are, for the most part, built with skills, materials and designs that will ensure they stand for a thousand years. New architecture is based on new science and science is now on the verge of a new renaissance. New art and literature is no longer simply tolerated. It *demands* the freedom to exist. This age of reason cannot be extinguished and the divine right of kings will not survive it. Soon it will seem little better than witchcraft. That is inevitable and does not require the assistance of political drudges like myself. What I fear are the moral bigots who believe that they own the moral compass and have unique access to its directions. They are the enemies of political reason. If they are not controlled they cause, and will cause, great pain and much destruction. For the present, this fragile, self-regarding, pampered monarchy forms the best hope that we have. One day perhaps there will be a settlement, a form of royal republic where real power ultimately resides in the people – Athens without slaves. It is my judgement that it will only be achieved by sustaining, for the moment, this infuriating King. The worst elements in Parliament (and they are very bad) would deny him the money to play a part in government. They do so only in order to provoke. They seek to drive him, like his father, to levy direct and unlawful taxation. If they succeed, there will, inevitably, be another Civil War more terrible than the first. What would emerge, God knows. One thing is certain, whatever it is, it will be infinitely worse than what we possess. This brief renaissance would stand no chance against the tyrannies that will come."

He paused, rose from the desk, smiled, stretched his back and crossed the room to pay exaggerated care to a bookcase. Without turning to me he said:

"So now you know the secrets of my mind and my motivations. I have little power but some influence. I have one considerable strength. Those who loathe and fear me endow me with far greater powers and far greater influence than I could ever possess. Indeed your aunt apparently believes me to be demonic. That, in itself, provides a considerable political advantage. Those that oppose will exhaust themselves meeting a threat which does not exist. So," he said, turning from the books, "would you like me to make alternative arrangements? I assure you they will be comfortable, safe and agreeable. The arrangements for discreet contact with your family will remain unaltered and I hope that our acquaintanceship will not entirely disappear. If you remain here I cannot pretend that it will not involve some risk but that is part of the territory on which we stand." He paused again, this time with obvious expectation.

"I think," I said, "that I need to reflect upon what you have said and its consequences. For the present, let us continue as we have begun. You have said that you can rely upon my confidence. You are right, whatever my decision may be."

He resumed his seat at the desk and smiled. "Right, of course, take your time but not too much." He looked at the library clock. "We will eat within the hour. Deborah, I think, is cooking mutton, which you will find delicious. We have no time for the diary before dinner. Can I, instead, interest you in a little music? I have found scores for some English songs I suspect may translate immediately into French. I will take the lute and let you dominate the keyboard."

We played and sang with something approaching harmony. The melodies he had selected were, indeed, universal. We played a madrigal and then a French lullaby, humming rather than singing a snatch my mother taught me as a child. To have sung the words would have brought tears, perhaps to us both. When I finished I sensed from the lack of movement that he was silently contemplating my back. I was right. When I turned I saw that his head was laid on one side, almost against his shoulder. The lenses magnified his eyes to an extent which made definition impossible. It was a moment before he removed his spectacles and affected to dab at the irritation they had caused.

"Mutton," he said, "then diary."

We dined together with Will. Pepys was noisy and messy with his food. There was much random chopping as he chased the mutton across his plate. Partly this was caused by his eyesight or lack of it. He was unwilling to wear spectacles at the table. At times the energetic pursuit of the meat gave the impression that it remained elusively alive. He spoke little and conversation between Hewer and myself was limited to the mundane. I told him of my journey to the Thames, omitting detail of my pursuers. We discussed the building of the great cathedral and debated the likely expense and the benefit to commerce and trade. After a good cheese and fresh figs, Pepys and I returned to the library and took our places at the desk. I had the diary with me which I opened at the next blank page on which I carefully inscribed yesterday's date, *5 Mai 1670*. He saw me do so and nodded with approval.

"Let us start with yesterday."

"Indeed," I said smiling brightly.

To Chatham. Le Roy has sent a small coach which bears his arms on both doors. There is also a rider in livery, who proceeds our passage. Because of this we make good progress. For the horses we stop at New Cross, Deptford, and, briefly, at Rochester. The rider provides advanced notice and warning and small crowds gather at each stop. Some are hostile but the majority are pleased enough and, from these, there is even some cheering and clapping as I grope my way back from the inns. Several petitions, no doubt hastily constructed, are thrust into my hand and one is thrown through the window of the coach. I indicate that I will, indeed, present them to the King which leads to more sounds of approval. Here, at least, the King has many friends. Pray God they do not have to prove it again. We are at the Dockyard by midday. My bags are carried from the gate and I walk by choice to the Admiral's house.

I see much that pleases. The yard is busy everywhere. I count twenty ships at anchor, all fully rigged. Three new frigates are in the slips. I think again of this sad place five years ago and I have much joy in the change. The Commander is ready to see me and, after a good meal, he provides me with a new report and much detail. These I now need as I have requests from the Committee and others as to the readiness of the Fleet.

He paused and I met his gaze across the table. I allowed myself the barest movement of an eyebrow, a gesture he returned before turning again to the narrative.

After much talk we inspect the works. I am offered a sedan which I decline although the ground is rough and the distances considerable as the Yard now extends a full mile on the Medway. I count thirty masts in the soaking pits. In the ropery the beams are full and, as we return to the Gate, cannon arrives on the Arsenal carts. It is now past five o'clock. I am offered accommodation which I refused as I will stay with Mr B. I arrive after six and we eat a good beef. I am early to bed and Mrs B comes to me as usual.

I sense that he is now watching me as I transcribe. I do not lift my head but refill my nib and my pen remains poised above the paper.

She is attentive as ever but I decline which causes her great alarm. She makes offers of a kind which normally would stir my thing mightily. Still I decline. She enquires for my health. Am I unwell? Do I have a 'condition'? I tell her that I have neither the pox nor the palsy at which she is much relieved as it is but four days since we were at it. I am kind in my refusal for she is much distressed. I tell her that she pleases me as much as ever and add, for good measure, that I have today signed the new purchase orders that will employ Mr B for many months. She is relieved but still questions my refusal saying, which is true, that this is the first such occasion in our meetings that have seen much energy and coupling. Again she offers certain attentions which I confess had me stirring which she sees. Her distress is such that I believe she should be provided with a reason. 'I have,' I said, 'formed an attachment to another which, for the moment, has me adverse to general rutting'. She says that this attachment must be very recent and of considerable strength. I tell her that it is very recent, within days, and indeed, a consuming matter. She suggests that we might, at least, make some noises of the customary nature that her husband's concerns may be laid at rest. Reluctantly I agree and we fall to much banging and panting and sudden cries which come so close to the actual business that I am almost moved to unwanted tumescence. Finally it is over and she returns to Mr B's own couch where no doubt she will make personal amends.

Throughout these passages I had maintained fast attention to the diary, occasionally dipping my pen and scratching more noisily to my task. The long pause that followed at this stage was no doubt intended to attract my attention. I continued to stare at the point of my pen and, at last, he continued in a voice tinged with disappointment:

In the morning Mr B appears much pleased, whether through the news of his contracts or the administrations of his wife or both – I do not enquire. As I step to my carriage he strikes me heartily on the back, an unnecessary gesture which dislodges my spectacles. It is some time until they can be located by Mrs B on her knees beside the door of the coach. Watching her thus I confess to a moment of regret accompanied by a small surge. When our journey resumes I discover his customary parcel on the seat of the coach. At least one part of our relationship remains unchanged.

"I think," he said, "that we should pause there."

I laid down my pen and met his eyes, now without spectacles and squinting a little across the desk. It was best, I thought, to affect complete indifference to the contents of his dictation, which I did.

"We have," I said, "extended the diary to this morning. Would you wish me to enter a separate date?"

This appeared to cause him disproportionate concern.

"Ah yes," he said, "you see I have never kept my diary in this manner. It is very different and I find that I am running on without thought and beyond my usual custom."

After a further moment's thought, he said: "Just put today's date in the margin, otherwise the narrative will be flawed. Let us take a short break." He looked at the library clock. "It is half past eight. Let us start again on the hour."

CHAPTER 13

I reached my room in a state of considerable confusion. In order to reassemble my thoughts I decided to analyse the nature and extent of my present predicament. The events of the past five days were all too clear. As I rehearsed them in my mind I felt a strange sense of disbelief. A mere five days ago I had walked from the Théâtre du Marais, crowned with success and rewarded with acclamation, not to mention largesse. At that time, beyond practice and training, I had never been involved in violence and my life had been dedicated to art in one form or another. Now, having killed a man of noble blood, I was a fugitive from revenge and a distortion of justice. I was in a strange country in a strange house, employed by a man I had met three days earlier on a coach journey that contained unwanted introductions into high politics and low verse. I was now embroiled in the same politics. I was running the risk of impeachment and a painful death for acts of treason and espionage against a government I had barely heard of. I had undoubtedly been tracked and followed by agents of some unknown person or power. I had discovered that my aunt was involved by marriage in political activity and had become a religious zealot. Now it appeared that the man on whose guardianship I relied was simultaneously engaged in subversive plans, the plotting of princes and the building of the British Navy ready for war. This same man had now, by a method unknown in all my knowledge of romantic literature, announced that I was the object of his passion. So great was his adoration that he had rejected the advances of a woman whose carnal activity had been lavished upon him as a corrupt inducement for the award of contract.

I sat on my bed and gazed fixedly at the hilt of my rapier hanging beneath my cloak. I supposed it were possible, with some ingenuity, to run myself through. As I made that contemplation I realised that, despite my dire circumstances, I had no wish whatsoever to do so. On the contrary, if truth were told, I felt something close to exhilaration, an extraordinary derangement which, in itself, required some careful analysis. As part of the process I read, again, the dictated words of the diary from the point of arrival at the Dockyard. Having done so, I took my lantern to the window and stared at the dark London sky. Despite conscious efforts to avoid it my thoughts kept returning to a single unwanted conclusion. I was *attracted to Samuel Pepys*. What conceivable, rational process, I asked myself, could have impelled me to this emotional disaster? It was incomprehensible in both languages. He was, I reflected, an ugly, purblind, corrupt lecher, as my aunt had clearly indicated. Certainly he was clever; very clever indeed. His mastery of the lute and the spinet had attractions as did his obvious love of the theatre and the intellectual freedom to produce it. He was also, I suddenly realised, undoubtedly brave. However reprehensible his political actions, whatever the treason or trickery that he contemplated, the risks he ran were beyond calculation. I knew little of the law, particularly English law or its prescribed punishments, but in the case of treason they were not difficult to imagine.

Leaving the window I took up a seat on my sofa facing the door and, again, sought some comfort from the weapon hanging against it. Apprehension, dread and a delirious sense of excitement struggled within me. Without conscious thought I murmured the lines of the agonised and desperate Hamlet:

"The native hue of resolution, sickly o'er by the pale cast of thought."

Where it would lead I had no idea but I would certainly "take up arms" against this sea of troubles. Whether they could be terminated or, at least, mitigated remained to be seen.

My travel clock told me that I had five minutes before the resumption of the diary. I needed some action. I removed the rapier from its scabbard, slipped out of my dress and petticoats and affected my practice regime against an imaginary Jacques: lunge, cut, lunge, thrust, parry, lunge, cut. And then, on the stroke of nine, I executed my pirouette, changed hands, and with my left hand thrust the rapier through an imaginary throat. Minutes later, a little out of breath and gleaming with perspiration, I resumed my seat in the library opposite the man who had occupied my mind for the past half hour. I had resolved to show nothing of my confusion, dilemma or, indeed, the sense of excitement I consciously attempted to suppress.

I opened the diary, picked up my pen, and smiled brightly with anticipation. Pepys must, himself, have contemplated the final passages of the dictation and the revelations they contained. Much later he was to tell me that the words had sprung from him without premeditation. It was, he said, an outburst without control. I didn't believe him then and I do not believe him now. In the travels and the dangers that were to come, he did little or nothing without thought or regard for consequence. I was aware, however, that my eyes searched his face and his visible upper body. I was looking for features that, in themselves, provided the basis for approval if not attraction. Apart from the eyes, either squinting or magnified like oysters, there were none. Incomprehensible, I thought, in any language.

All of this was for the future. At five past nine on the evening of the 6th of May he spoke his language and I transcribed into mine:

With no rider to lead us the journey to London is slower. It is dry and there is much dust which enters even the best appointed coach. At home I have time to eat, change and wash away the worst of the journey. Then to the Navy office to record my findings and my observations. At the very door I am intercepted by a messenger who tells me that I am summonsed to the presence of Le Roy. I leave my papers, cancel the afternoon meetings with M and B, present my apologies and, by the same coach, arrive at Court. I am asked to wait and it is after five before I am admitted to the presence. He is with a secretary discussing the new architecture at Holborn. Plans are on his desk and he holds a model, rotating it between both hands, as he inspects its dimensions. As I arrive the secretary is dismissed and leaves with the charts and plans. Le Roy places the model on a chest where it joins others of different sizes, one has a great dome of a cathedral as yet to be identified. He returns to his desk and, as often, removes his wig and indicates that I should do likewise. He looks tired but his eyes are sharp.

'Well Samuel,' he says, 'do I have a Navy?'

'Yes sir,' I reply, 'you have a Navy and it is in good heart.'

Good heart,' he says, 'I like that. That is well said but is it ready Samuel? Is it rigged and manned and gunned?'

'Yes sir, it is ready. Indeed some question the reason why it is so, why we have men and officers on full pay.'

'I know Samuel, I know.'

He tells me that he knows of these murmurings but for the moment, he says, Parliament will provide the money.

'They accept the demands of the Privy Council, if not mine, and the Council wants no more humiliations. So, for the moment, we have a Navy and it is ready. Can it beat the Dutch, Samuel?'

'Sir, I attempt to build navies I do not command them.'

He becomes impatient with me and then says, 'Yes, yes Samuel, I know that so let us make assumptions. Let us assume that I have commanders who know one end of a frigate from another and crews that have not been pressed into mutiny. Let us not assume genius but assume competence and apply our knowledge of the Dutch Fleet. Can they be beaten? I ask for your view with all its limitations.'

'The Navy is capable now of victory over any other at sea. It is capable, provided of course, that is ordered to do so by your Majesty and Parliament.'

When I mention Parliament he becomes irritable.

'Samuel,' he says, 'as you know Parliament would not give me the money for a washbasin let alone a war. I am kept bereft of funds beyond that necessary for my Court. Those funds they provide so that I may appear, as they wish me to appear, rich, excessive and opulent. They seek to force decadence upon me. I know full well they provoke me. They want me to behave like my father. They want me to march into the Commons, arrest their Speaker and dissolve them. They want me to behave like my father, to raise taxes for which I have no legal entitlement. They want another war Samuel. Not all of them but you know who they are and I do

*not need to spell their names. They are powerful in Parliament
and their power grows. The more I appear to have no function
other than fornication, it is not difficult to plot against me. We
must avoid a war Samuel, not for me but for my people'.*

*He was silent for a while and I did not add to the conversation.
Then his mood changed.*

*'Not that there is anything wrong with fornication, Samuel. It is
what ultimately motives all men and women. Doing it, wanting it
or exercising their authority to deny it to others. Great wars have
been fought over fornication, Samuel, but we should not attempt
to fight the Dutch for that reason. As you know they couldn't even
fuck anyone in Rochester.'*

*I left him in good humour but as I left he stopped me in the
doorway and asked me to return.*

*'I think,' he said, 'I may have found a way in which I can become
a King without unlawfully robbing my subjects. Even now I am
awaiting news which may provide that answer.'*

*Then, as though on the same subject, he said, 'I have never asked
you before Samuel but I do now for a reason. Are you a Catholic?'*

'No sir,' I said, 'I am not a Catholic.'

*'From what I know of you Samuel,' he continued, 'you are not a
Puritan or a Protestant either. Yes? I see I am right. Now tell me.
Do you believe in God?'*

*'I believe,' I said, 'that an almighty wisdom will guide your
Majesty's decisions.'*

*He laughed out loud and then said, 'Well said, Samuel. You
are a casuist. A hundred years ago that answer would have saved
you from the stake. I do not, for one moment, believe it but it was
well said. Let us be serious for a moment. There is a reason for*

my enquiry other than vulgar interest in your faith. Assuming, as you tell me, you are not a servant of Rome do we believe the Catholics should be tolerated and that their practices should be allowed? Should we tolerate the Mass in private and without a public pulpit? You can tell me Samuel, it will be a confidence.'

'I believe,' I said, 'in toleration and that toleration should be tolerated.'

Le Roy returned to his desk, took up a pen and carefully wrote the words I had just spoken.

'Don't worry,' he said as he wrote, 'this is not for publication. It will never be attributed to you but it is a good answer Samuel; a good answer. Now tell me, if I proclaim that to be my solemn position that the Papists should be tolerated, a Declaration of Toleration extending across all faiths, what will be the consequences? Think a little before you answer.'

I did so and said: 'I think sir it would provoke many who still hold to the Puritan cause and the Commonwealth. They will undoubtedly say that you are motivated by your own faith. That you seek to tolerate your own sins.'

'Yes, indeed it will,' he said, 'it will provoke but how many Samuel, how many? Will this provocation amount to an act of war?'

I answered readily enough: 'In my opinion, it will not. Undoubtedly there are zealots who will seek to ignite or reignite conflict on that alone. I do not think they will succeed. Their numbers diminish with every passing year of your reign. Commerce has returned. The taverns and the theatres are full. That, in itself, is a toleration embraced by the people. In my view it will extend without difficulty to acts of faith.'

'Ah,' he said, 'you comfort me Samuel. You comfort me indeed.'

As I stood by the door for a second time and waited for the clerk to return, he said, 'The matters of which I have spoken may need immediate action by yourself and others. I will know more by tomorrow. The Court has a reception at the Banqueting House at two in the afternoon. I should like you to attend and bring, if you would, your new amanuensis. Don't appear so surprised. This decadent Court is not without intelligence.'

I had stopped writing and was staring at Pepys across the desk. He looked at me.

"Surprised? Yes, so was I. Very surprised but I have given it some thought and I think I know the source of this entirely accurate information. We will find out tomorrow."

"Am I to come to . . .?"

"Yes, I am afraid it is quite unavoidable. The power of kings is not what it was but you cannot refuse their invitations. He holds these receptions in the Banqueting House in order to annoy his Parliamentarian enemies. It is the chamber from which his father walked to the scaffold and he frequently stands by the window with one of his mistresses. It is tasteless but it makes a point. I have now heard that your new clothes will arrive tomorrow morning but I don't think you will need them. The Court, you will find, vibrates with bosoms. Come let us finish this business then I have a new song before bed."

I return home to find CB has taken to the London streets despite my best advice. Fortunately it was Robert Lefebre who did so as she, as he, was followed. For what reason remains a mystery which, I suspect, will not be long in solving. Then to dinner and to the instruments and a growing collection of songs sung sweetly in French and English with growing harmony.

"That's it," he said, "we have done well and have recorded our lives to the very moment. I will take the keyboard. The tune I think you will know, the words we can mix. I have a new word for the mixture. We will call it *Franglais*. Rather good isn't it?"

We managed barely half an hour before weariness took both of us to bed. As I undressed I was amazed at my own lack of excitement or fear. I realised that I had ceased to wonder at the epic drama which had become my life. In its context it appeared almost inevitable that I should be presented to the King of England as a scribe rather than the fugitive criminal I was. I reflected as I lay on the verge of sleep that this king knew how to be a fugitive better than most, though I did not contemplate any other affinity between us.

CHAPTER 14

When I woke the calm acceptance of a benign destiny had quite disappeared. It was replaced by profound anxieties. If all went to plan, the afternoon promised my first meeting with a King of England – or of anywhere else for that matter. The worst apprehensions arose from Pepys's revelations dutifully transcribed into his diary. This monarch was, apparently, aware of my identity and my role from a source unknown. Who could have provided this information if not Pepys himself? Who else had access to the royal ear and knowledge of my existence? How much information had been revealed? In the absence of knowledge my fertile and fevered imagination reached the realms of fantasy. Was this a trap? In France the Pertaine family possessed great influence and power. How far did it reach? In my imaginings they had befriended Charles, the exiled monarch, when he lived in France, and provided him with all manner of assistance from which obligation flowed. I would be arrested in the Banqueting Hall at the very point where the King's father had walked to the block. In my unfolding drama I was transported to Paris in chains, facing excruciating torments at worst, the scaffold at best.

Pepys and Will had left the house early and I sat before my morning meal, for which I had no appetite whatsoever. I drank a little water and picked at a slice of quince. Gradually my resolve strengthened with a welcome onset of common sense. Kings of

England do not spring elaborate traps for French actors, whatever their felonies and misdemeanours. Pepys must, himself, absently, have described his new assistant, possibly with reference to the finer aspects of my appearance. This King possessed a reputation for such things, a fine notoriety even when set against the royal houses of Europe. This contemplation of the royal libido was strangely comforting. It provided an explanation far more likely than epic revenge.

At ten precisely my new dressmaker arrived at the door and I spent two hours being tucked and pinned into dresses, demure and plain enough to avoid any form of arousal. These, I decided with prim satisfaction, would suit my vocation as a scribe. I would deport myself accordingly. The dressmaker had brought an assistant and a quantity of buttons, material and thread. The clothes were finished as they were fitted and by the time Pepys arrived at half past twelve, the size of my wardrobe had doubled. I presented myself in the plainest of the new garments complete with a shy smile and a deliberately awkward pirouette. He nodded briefly with approval.

"Excellent for the house and street but, I fear, wholly inappropriate for the Court. I will advise the dress in which you first made my acquaintance, which will, I expect, find immediate favour with the King of England. My coach remains in repair so we have a Hackney in half an hour."

We disappeared into our respective rooms to meet the royal desires whatever they might be and arrived together at the street door, beyond which a single Hackney was already waiting. The drain that served one of the adjacent houses had blocked and I was forced to lift the hem of my dress to an indecent height and achieved the open door of the cab in one athletic bound. Pepys, who did not possess my training, was forced to wade myopically through the effluent, cursing his neighbours who, he told me, could provide "enough shit to dam the Medway". Much of it still clung to his boots requiring the windows of the Hackney to remain open admitting a fine dust but allowing the escape of the foul air which rose from his footwear.

The building works with which I was now familiar obstructed several streets leading towards Westminster and we arrived at the Banqueting House fully twenty minutes late. As he paid the fare the driver looked disapprovingly at the floor of the cab. To this look he added a prolonged sniff and exhalation of breath.

"Not many passengers are going to want to get in there, are they?" slamming the door and slowly counting the change.

"Oh keep it for God's sake," said Pepys, "and, on the subject of shit, you might get a bum sack for that horse."

"That," said the driver, "is natural. That is manure. That is digested vegetable matter. That," he said indicating Pepys's boots, "is human shit and smells like it."

As we passed from Whitehall into the street entrance I saw Pepys squinting at the hangings and drapes for an opportunity to clean his boots. None was apparent and we entered, conscious that we carried with us the pungent evacuations of Mr Pepys's neighbours. The hall was crowded and the King was yet to arrive. The Court was assembled containing, even to my Parisienne eye, an extraordinary display of excess. Many male heads carried wigs that towered fully ten inches above their painted eyes, peering out from between vast curls. These, apparently light as air, settled on their shoulders like driven snow.

As to the ladies, Pepys had been right. Protruding bosoms were everywhere measured, it seemed, in feet rather than inches. The cantilevers necessary to create the upward thrust could be seen secured against the outer bodice and straining beneath heavily embroidered silk. The pressure must have been nigh unbearable and, before the King arrived, I saw one of the larger ladies slide gently down a woven tapestry to sit, unconscious and apparently unnoticed, on the polished floor. The King arrived with the Queen upon his arm, whereupon they parted and attended separately to the Court and its guests. As they preceded the press of bodies opened before them, wigs and bosoms swaying as though rocked on the same tide. Occasionally I saw the King pause and incline his head to conversations of differing volume. On rare occasions he laughed out loud before moving forward in a serene and interrupted passage. It appeared to be without conscious direction but as I watched he scanned the chamber with predicted purpose. On Pepys's advice we remained stationary, side by side. As we did so Pepys attracted a limited number of acquaintances who pressed his hand and smiled at my introduction with polite approval. Several, I noticed, audibly sniffed and frowned before continuing onwards, hands raised above their silk cuffs in permanent salutation. It was a matter of minutes before the King's gaze fastened upon Pepys. This we both observed as Pepys acknowledged the royal wave indicating, beyond doubt, that we should remain stationary to receive later attention. As he approached I noticed a familiar figure moving, as though bidden deliberately, in the King's wake. I turned to Pepys with silent enquiry, which he returned with a nod of comprehension:

"I see," he murmured towards me, "that the Earl of Rochester once more attends the King. Now we have an explanation for your own presence."

When the King was barely five paces distant he raised his hand in formal acknowledgement: "Welcome, again to the Court, Samuel. And this," he directed, his eyes towards mine, "is, I suspect, your new and beautiful scribe. Camille n'est pas?" His eyes danced and creased with real amusement. "Camille. Vous connaissez déjà John Wilmot, le Duc de Rochester?"

John Wilmot's face appeared at the Royal shoulder, wearing the smile of a conspirator unmasked. The King turned to Pepys: "Elle est vraiment très jolie." Turning back to me he said: "Et pour nous, Mademoiselle, il faut parler en français?"

I met the King's gaze and delivered my own surprise. Speaking English I replied:

"As your Majesty wishes. I am delighted to speak to your Royal Highness in French or in English, which is, indeed, my mother's tongue."

Behind the King's shoulder I saw Wilmot start. The smile disappeared and his eyes widened in disbelief followed by a heavy frown of consternation.

The King turned towards him.

"Well John," he said, "you have misled me. You told me Samuel had met a beautiful new assistant who spoke only French, yet she appears to speak perfect English. I hope you have not said anything in her presence that you regret."

Laughing aloud at his own joke, the King turned again to Pepys. The conversation had lasted longer than the usual Court formality and a small attentive group now attended on his words.

"Well, Samuel, you see that the Earl of Rochester is once more with us. I think you know that he was banished from our presence but now he is returned to be at my right hand. Tell me Samuel, does that meet with your approval?"

Pepys inclined his head.

"Of course sir. So fine a mind should not be absent from your Majesty's Court."

"Fine mind Samuel? *Fine mind*? My dear Samuel, he has a mind like a Dutch sewer. Have you read his latest poetry? I see that you have. Have you read 'A Ramble in St James's Park'? He gave it to me as a gift, bound in calf's skin. I am surprised it didn't break out in boils. I read it several times Samuel. Do you know that the female *part* appears ten times in forty lines? Ten times! Not to mention frigging and fucking and that is not the worst of them. The ladies of the Court were horrified. They thought it reflected on them, I can't think why. So he had to go. He was banished, banished for the third time was it not John?"

"Fourth," said the Earl of Rochester.

"Fourth, indeed, fourth. Banished four times and four times forgiven. Do you know why I forgave him? As I read it again I realised Samuel that it is art. *Art* Samuel. The sexual images are graphic but they are metaphors, artistic metaphors for the spirit of the age. It conveys the opening of minds Samuel, the spreading wide of science and literature. It is the spirit of the Restoration itself."

The King paused and, beyond his back, I saw John Wilmot quickly raise his elegant eyes to the plaster ceiling. In the pause, the King had been watching Pepys closely. "I see that you do not entirely agree with me, Samuel. No, don't deny it. Disagreement is entirely permissible and, on this subject, understandable. You are not an artist Samuel, you are a civil servant and there is no reason why these things should concern you."

The King lowered his voice and, as though at a signal, those listening turned their backs: "You are a fine civil servant Samuel, one of my best. It is for that reason that I have asked you here with your charming new friend. I will be finished within the half hour and will then go to the antechamber on the next floor. I wish to see you there. I wish to speak to you and I have already made arrangements for you to be escorted for that purpose. I need to speak with you alone so you must abandon your lovely companion. I will leave the Earl of Rochester to protect her, which may be necessary. The Court is alarmingly full of artists of one kind or another."

With that he resumed the regal smile, cold as fish and proceeded forward into the parting throng. His entourage followed with the exception of John Wilmot, who moved to my side and bowed with an exaggerated courtesy.

"Well, well," he said, "Camille Lefebre, *bilingual* Camille Lefebre. You tricked us both."

I said: "No, your grace . . ." before Pepys interrupted.

"No John. She did not trick us, we tricked ourselves and she allowed us to do so and frankly I do not blame her. As a result she is possessed of confidences which I have no doubt she will keep. You may also remember a number of personal observations which a gentleman might regret?"

Wilmot raised his arms in the air.

"I regret, I repent, I apologise without reservation. I have hopes of redemption. If the King of England can forgive frigging in St James's Park, Camille may forgive my reference to her magnificent tits. And eyes – let us not forget the eyes. I confess, however, that they were sentiments I do not entirely regret."

Pepys turned to me. "There," he said, "I think that will do, don't you? Apologies from poets and politicians are rare and should be accepted and treasured in the bosom."

We all laughed together, which caused some attention from beneath a number of neighbouring wigs.

"Well," said Wilmot, "I feel redeemed. Now, if you are Samuel's scribe then you must also be his confidante, so you may hear what I have to say."

His mood had changed abruptly and his lowered voice became serious.

"There are things, Samuel, you must know before you see the King. I know what he will say and what he will require. Before you accept you should know the dangers."

He scanned the room for private space then pointed across the chamber: "Let us go over there, by that awful tapestry."

We crossed the room passing, as we did so, the large lady of the Court still sitting apparently unconscious on the floor. He indicated the sitting figure.

"She is dead to the world. Happens quite frequently I am afraid. Even fully conscious she would not understand. I think she is Welsh. Before I begin, what is that awful smell?"

Pepys and I exchanged glances before he said: "I think it is probably her." He pointed at the sleeping form. Wilmot nodded.

"Yes probably, well let's try to ignore it. What I have to say will not take long."

His eyes moved once more across the room before he continued.

"When I was banished from the Court it was assumed by my colleagues who sit in Parliament that I had turned against the King as he had turned against me. I acquired a number of new and unwanted friends. It was not entirely of their making. I was angry and humiliated. These friends included John Connault, Peter Wormold and Robert Crespi. I was invited to dine with them on two occasions, awful meals devoid of wit, warmth or wine, but I listened and even appeared sympathetic. Much of it came as no surprise, the usual vituperations about the Court, its extravagance and the royal rutting. It is no secret that they want him gone, preferably in the same manner as his father. They speak of the Commonwealth as though it had been a Utopia. No mention is made of the censorship and the ghastly morbid conformity. Of course they know my views and were aware of my poetry (fortunately none of them had read it in detail). Perversely they assumed my banishment entailed some form of Puritan repentance and I did not discourage them. I suppose I was inquisitive and I became something of a spy. They began to trust me but the full danger was not revealed until I was approached by Roger Rawle. He, as you know, is a member of their group but he is a snivelling little shit and they know it. He is tolerated in memory of his father, who was shot at Aylesbury. He espouses their cause and their manners but he is desperate for a little decadence. He saw me, quite rightly, as the man to provide it. He made repeated references to 'St James's Park', which showed, at least, that he can read. Finally I took him to the Haymarket. We visited the salon run by

Marie Lorgnette, which is not her real name, nor is she French. Despite his protestations he spent much of the afternoon with one of Marie's less-discerning and more-obliging girls. After this experience his guilt was such, with little encouragement, he drank three bottles of porter at the Dancing Bear. When utterly pissed, *as the French say*, he became very indiscreet and told me of the plans and plots that are in hand. There is a new Parliamentarian group that contains all who you may suspect. They were called the Commonwealth Group but they have changed their name to 'The New Puritans'. How they are to be distinguished from the Old Puritans he tried to explain. By the 'new' image it was hoped to persuade the people that they no longer have a penchant for gloomy persecutions."

At this point Pepys interrupted with a shrug.

"All of this John," he said, "is amusing as you tell it but well known. I had heard of the 'New Puritans'. If they use the name to create a new faction it will cause nothing but derision."

Wilmot raised his hand in agreement. "Just so but if our friend Rawle is to be believed, before he fell from the table, this has gone deeper. They campaign, as we know on a daily basis, against the King. Because of the nature of the Court and its reputation they have achieved some success among those that would not otherwise follow their zealotry. As we know, this has denied the King money and, as we know, it is intended to provoke him into suicidal action. All of this," said Wilmot, again raising his hand against interruption, "all of this we know but new and more dangerous allegations are to be made. They concern the King's Catholicism, or alleged Catholicism, and his relationship with the King of France."

Beside me I felt Pepys stiffen with attention. "What do they say of this relationship?"

"They claim to have intelligence that Charles will declare himself a Catholic, dissolve Parliament and join Louis in a war against the Dutch."

"And who would pay for this war?"

"That is unclear. The allegation will be that Charles intends to raise direct and illegal taxes."

Pepys gave an audible sigh. "That is quite impossible."

"Just so, and that is their problem. At present all of these allegations amount to nothing more than suspicion. I will continue with my story of Rawle's Haymarket apostasy. After he passed out I took the disgusting little squirt to his house in a Hackney. On the journey to Putney he woke up and was violently sick, revealing large quantities of porter and pickled goose. It did not amuse the driver, who delivered a long and boring invective on the behaviour of Members of Parliament. When I got into the house he became embarrassing and professed to have fallen in love with me 'man to man'. He announced that we were part of a new brotherhood and attempted to hug me, which was not difficult to avoid. He did, however, provide further information. Although they suspect the King's intentions, they have 'as yet no evidence'. Even today such allegations against the King without evidence would amount to treason. They believe they have a way of obtaining the evidence and it concerns you."

"Me?" said Pepys.

"Yes, I am afraid so. They know what you have already told me in our coach from Chatham. The King trusts you completely, partly as a result of your work on his Navy. They believe you will be, or may be, his chosen instrument. How, it is unclear. They believe they can expose the King through you. Sooner or later they believe that your actions, or the possession of documents, will betray you and through you the King."

Pepys was shaking his head in disbelief when Wilmot added: "Do not underestimate these men. They intend to destroy the monarchy and re-establish the Commonwealth. They are powerful and their friends are rich. Some regard the return of the Commonwealth as inevitable. When that occurs they wish to retain both their wealth and their influence. Rawle did not specify the sources but he estimated the sums involved. Allowing for drunken exaggeration they are still huge. The New Puritans may not be the joke we first believed them to be. As to what they are doing with the money, he had limited information. But I can tell you, Samuel, that you are certainly being followed and that may well extend to your household."

Saying this he glanced at me and recognised immediately the surprise on my face.

"From the look on Camille's face it appears that you may know this already. That is all the information that I have. The following day, yesterday, I received the royal summons and now, once more, I am a pampered recipient of the royal favour. That may not last but certainly it will come as a shock to Rawle who will, no doubt, withdraw his declarations of passionate love. For precisely that reason I have no doubt that he will remain silent as to the information he has provided to me. His Puritan colleagues may not take kindly to his activities in the Haymarket and the Dancing Bear and copious vomiting in the London cab.

I took the number of the vehicle as a precaution, should I need a witness to this disgusting behaviour."

Pepys interrupted. "What do you think they will do?"

"The answer to that is almost anything. Do not, I repeat, underestimate this danger. They believe you possess the keys although they are uncertain what they are. To obtain them they will undoubtedly kill you if necessary and will, in the resulting chaos, place the blame on anyone they choose. If the King himself is revealed as a Papist plotter there will be thousands who will believe whatever is spun. And they may include those who are now our friends. Ah, I see she is waking up. Excuse me Samuel, I must assist her, she is, after all, a member of the Court, even if Welsh."

As he left us a uniformed footman appeared at our side. Softly he indicated that he was to escort Pepys to the Royal Antechamber. Before he departed John Wilmot returned: "She is quite recovered," he said. "She has the constitution of a Welsh heifer." Seeing the footman, he said: "You must go, Samuel. I know what the King will require of you and weigh carefully what I have said. I will undertake the care of Mademoiselle Lefebre until you return."

As Pepys departed towards the door of the chamber, Wilmot turned to me: "Well, Camille, we must not let these affairs of state interfere with your first experience of the Court. I hope it will not be your last. If you wish I will volunteer as your personal guide and mentor. I am now well placed. The King regards me as an artist although for this monarch, that is a wide definition."

I was about to speak when he placed his hand gently upon my lips. The impertinence caused my eyes to widen as he said:

"Don't reject me immediately. From what I know the next two days may change your circumstances and my offer may become more attractive. Now," he said, scanning the nearby groups, "let us make some introductions. Ah, over here . . ." Taking my arm he propelled me towards a small gathering, some of whom were obscured by a pillar. As they came into view, Wilmot abruptly changed direction: "No, I think not, they are listening to John Dryden, England's second greatest poet, and biggest bore. Ah, there is a more worthy target."

He crossed to a window overlooking the Strand approaching from behind a tall figure in clothes that were, by contrast to his surroundings, somewhat restrained. Wilmot called his name, which I immediately recognised. Wilmot introduced us: "Camille Lefebre," he said, "you may have heard of John Blagden?"

"Indeed," I said, "I am honoured, monsieur."

The great actor politely extended his hand. "Camille Lefebre," he said. "Camille Lefebre? You are French?" He frowned, then said, "Please forgive me but your face is so familiar. I feel that we know each other and know each other well. Were you ever on the stage?"

"Yes, I have been on the stage but only for a short while and not in England. My mother, however, was on the English stage."

"Ah," he said, tapping his forehead in recognition, "your mother. Your mother was Catherine Browne, am I right?" When I nodded he continued. "Catherine Browne, the most beautiful actress of the English renaissance. She was Ophelia to my Hamlet in 1642. It was our last play before the Great Darkness."

I turned to see Wilmot regarding me with evident reappraisal.

"Catherine Browne," he repeated. "You are Catherine Browne's daughter? I never saw her on stage but she was a legend. Well deserved, I think, John."

"Oh yes," said Blagden, "Cromwell deprived us of many things but no greater talent. Perhaps that is unjust. By the time of the Great Darkness your mother was already in love, a not unhappy coincidence. It has provided us with another great beauty."

I felt myself colouring and he laughed. "Forgive me that was impertinent. I am an old man and I felt for a moment that I was actually talking to your mother. So Catherine Browne has returned to the stage as Camille Lefebre and in Paris. Let us sit over there and talk of our Business. You can tell me about Corneille and Molière and other giants. Johnny will forgive us, he probably has a poem coming on." Wilmot shook his head in exaggerated resignation, shrugged, winked at me, and disappeared into the wigs and bosoms.

As we sat side by side Blagden nodded at the retreating back, "He is a better man than he thinks he is and a better poet but a life so spent is likely to be a short one."

We sat for an hour absorbed in our craft and my present employment and would have continued as long again. We were interrupted by Pepys's return. They were old friends but did not speak for long. We descended to Whitehall and took a carriage precisely below the window where the King's father lost his head.

CHAPTER 15

In the coach home Pepys was silent and much preoccupied with the needless examination of his spectacles. By contrast I was unusually voluble. My long conversation with John Blagden had left a sense of exhilaration. His knowledge of my mother and the profession which we all shared contributed to a sense of wellbeing. There was a world beyond murder, vengeance and politics. This sense of belonging encouraged an entirely false feeling of confidence. As the coach passed through Whitehall into Piccadilly I was animated, chattering and observant. It was not until we reached the Old Gate that Pepys gave a snort of irritation.

"Please, Catherine," he said. "Please could you desist? I need to think without the whole of London being explained as the view from a Hackney carriage."

A little hurt I relapsed into silence for the remainder of our journey. As the coach stopped he replaced his spectacles and stared at me then smiled.

"Catherine, please don't sulk. What I have been told and what I must consider is serious beyond measure. It is also potentially very dangerous. I needed to concentrate."

I apologised in return. "May I," I added, "assist in any way?"

"Perhaps, perhaps not. Wait for the diary and all will be revealed."

By the time I returned to my room it was gone four o'clock. I changed, sat at my desk, and composed letters to my family and to John Blagden. To the latter I expressed my happiness at our meeting and made tentative enquiries as to the state of the London stage. My present employment was, to say the least, precarious and I needed, if possible, some alternative security. I sealed both letters, placed them in my escritoire and, by half past six, presented myself in the music room. Before we had left for Court, Pepys had shown me the score of a short cantata written by Tomaso Albinoni; a duet, he said, would relax the mind before dinner. It did nothing of the sort. The copy which had been made for the spinet was poor and sometimes quite inaccurate. While I struggled with the keyboard, his playing of the lute steadily deteriorated. After ten minutes we finished in near-perfect discord. When I turned on the stool I saw that his eyes were tight shut as though in pain.

"I am sorry," I said before he interrupted.

"No, no. You were bad but I was awful. I have no concentration. Mood and melody, I am afraid, cannot be divorced."

He opened his eyes, smiled and said: "Beef and then diary. My mind needs committing to paper."

Over dinner and several cups of French wine his mood improved. He spoke of the great cellars and tables of London which, he said, had reappeared after the Commonwealth as though they had been in a period of deep and successful hibernation. Discussion of food and wine led him, unhappily, to the subject of his own health and the removal of a bladder stone ten years previously. As he poured me a glass of wine he said that the details were distressing. This was entirely accurate.

It was necessary, he said, to insert a long silver instrument through the penis. The size of this instrument he demonstrated by gripping a silver meat skewer and inspecting its tip with one eye through his spectacles. The purpose of this insertion, he said, was to locate the stone in the bladder and to 'nudge it' towards the scrotum. There is then, he said, an incision at the base of the scrotum through which the stone may be located with an instrument similar to "these", he said, indicating the nutcracker which lay in a pile of walnuts.

I sensed that this account had been provided on previous occasions as a mild provocation. I, therefore, adopted a fixed and polite smile, nodding occasionally with academic interest. At the end of this description I thought some observation was necessary.

"It must," I said, "have been a painful experience."

Catching the irony, he replied, "Hardly at all. Throughout the entire operation I reflected on the immense value of the male member and was overcome by a sense of gratitude. Would you like a walnut?"

"Certainly," I said seizing the nutcracker before he could reach it. Employing my father's grip I demolished the shells of two of the larger nuts. I sorted the kernels onto a separate plate, which I held towards him. He selected two picces and chewed them whilst watching my smiling eyes.

"Délicieux. Now diary."

By the time we reached the library the levity had disappeared. We took our accustomed seats. I opened the leather folder, took up my pen, dipped the ink and wrote *7 Mai* at the head of a new page. He had brought with him a silver decanter and two cups. He poured wine into both, sipped, swallowed and began.

To Whitehall at the bidding of Le Roy. My carriage is still under repair and it is necessary to take a Hackney. It is uncomfortable and the driver disagreeable. The reception is very grand and the chamber is quite full. The Court appears, I think, precisely as Parliament would wish, excessive and idle. CB looks very well in her Paris clothes and is a full match for the ladies of the Court. The King is late but spends some time with us. He is obviously much taken with CB whose presence as my assistant had already been reported to him. The Earl of Rochester now returned to the Court and in close attendance. His pornographic poems have been forgiven in the name of Art and the Spirit of the Age. The King requires me alone in his antechamber. Before I am summoned Wilmot provides alarming news. The New Puritans, Shaftesbury's faction, believe that there are secret negotiations with Paris. I am thought to be involved. If this is true we are in danger of impeachment or murder or both. How Shaftesbury has obtained this information is unknown but it is undoubtedly close to the truth. Also, with Wilmot back in favour, we have lost our only spy. CB was present during this talk and the revelations. I now trust her implicitly after so short a time.

He paused, anticipating, I suspect, some reaction from myself. I laid down my pen, stretched my hand, and met his gaze across the desk. I said nothing but raised both eyebrows and inclined my head. It was a gesture conveying, I hope, both complicity and resignation. He smiled and nodded towards my pen, which I took in hand, dipped and held above the page. With a small sigh he continued.

I am summoned to the antechamber where I find Le Roy has already discarded his wig and taken up a dog. This animal is said to be a favourite of Nell Gwynne's and, indeed, has some of her features. In particular the eyes roll aimlessly around the head as the royal hand strokes its bottom. He ordered me to sit.

'Well, Samuel,' he said, gently patting the furry rump, 'did you enjoy our reception? No, do not answer that. I know you find them tedious and the company dull. You are right, you are right. I repay favours that were owed to my father and to my restoration. In return they fawn and they flatter me but when it comes to money and to wisdom they are, as John Wilmot would say, frigging useless. That is why I have him back in Court. He is intellectual diversion, a dirty devil though he is. Also he told me of your new assistant whom you both met on the Chatham coach. His description did not do her justice. He concentrated entirely on her tits. He omitted the fact that she has the clearest and cleverest eyes I have seen in a long while. You would have thought a poet could do better than that. But quite lovely, she must be a comfort to you.'

When I did not reply, he continued.

'And French, too. A knowledge of French can be very useful, Samuel, very useful indeed.'

It was a cue which I accepted. 'She is indeed, sir, of great assistance to me in many ways, French among them.'

The royal eyes, full of irony, were fixed on mine and, with a shrug, he said, 'That brings us conveniently to our business . . . I have been, as you know, in negotiations with Louis. Those negotiations are now close to agreement. Much of what I will say you already know. Louis, my kinsman, will provide me with

French gold. In return he requires Toleration of the Catholics. He also requires my assistance in a new war against the Dutch.'

He removed his right hand from beneath the dog's bottom and held it in the air against any interruption. I noticed that the royal cuff had become slightly stained.

'Our contribution will be provided entirely by the Royal Navy. That contribution will be limited to fifty men of war. Do not look surprised Samuel. This Fleet is within our capability. I know because you have told me. Before we continue Samuel, I wish you would desist from polishing your spectacles. It is quite unnecessary. The air in here is very pure.'

As he waved his right hand in demonstration, Le Roy noticed the stain on his cuff and threw the dog onto the floor.

'Fifty ships at a maximum. I do not suggest that they should be assembled in one armada. Some will provide the necessary blockade while others engage the Dutch Fleet to prevent support of the armies set against the French. Without their Navy the Dutch are no match for the French, so I have been informed. Now, Samuel, I have finished for the moment. Let me have your questions and your views.'

I began with a question. 'Your Majesty says that the sum involved will enable the payment of the Court and the administration of the State. That is a very substantial sum.'

Le Roy nodded. 'It is indeed.'

'It would replace the Parliamentary vote?'

The King nodded. 'It would. It would indeed.'

'And what of Parliament?'

He leaned forward and fixed me with a single stare.

'It will be dissolved. I will dissolve Parliament.'

'And that dissolution will be for how long?'

He did not take his eyes from mine when he said, 'Indefinitely.'

'Indefinitely?'

'Yes Samuel, indefinitely. This is not a Parliament, Samuel. This is a den, a hotbed of conspiracy. They plot against me and you know it. They plot against you, too, believing that you make my cause. I suspect you have spoken to the Earl of Rochester? Yes, I see that you have. He has told you about the attentions of Roger Rawle, disgusting little bum sniffer that he is. We killed his father at Aylesbury. It is a pity that we did't do it many years earlier but then we would not have had this helpful informant. These men are dangerous. They are not Libertarians. They are fundamental zealots. They would kill me and you and destroy my country with another Civil War. Then what will follow? What about education? Learning will become a black Bible business, devoid of anything but the scrutiny of scripture. I know John Milton was a Puritan and a fine poet but I will take "St James's Park" over "Paradise Lost" and so would you. Yes, indefinitely. Let us spread them out into the countryside and the constituencies they are supposed to represent. In order to plot they will have to travel the length and the breadth of England, taking their unwelcome pious presence from town to town, preaching as they go. Yes, that is the plan Samuel and its execution. For God's sake, stop playing with those bloody spectacles.'

I replaced my spectacles and watched as he narrowed his eyes.

'There Samuel, that answers your question. Now let me have the benefit of your views.'

'I cannot disguise from you, sir, that this troubles me greatly. You know that I share many of your views and much of your *aversion to the Puritan element of the Parliamentary cause but the English Parliament has existed for five hundred years. And now your Majesty proposes its termination.'*

'Not termination, Samuel, dissolution. They can continue their functions in the fields and the fens of Britain but not here in Westminster, yards away from where they murdered my father. And when I say indefinitely, I do not mean it literally. They may appear every five years or so in order to pass a vote or two and then go back to their business. What is your view of that?'

'I fear your Majesty is embarking on two courses which will prove deeply unpopular with the people. War with the Dutch and the emasculation of Parliament by whatever name it is called. If Parliamentarians are scattered throughout the country they will be among the people. If your Majesty's actions are unpopular then they may stir up discontent, even rebellion.'

The King paused, transferred his gaze to the dog, which could be seen chewing the bottom of a silk tapestry. He returned it to me with a smile, partly weary and with a sigh of resignation.

'I respect your views Samuel more than any other but what you have said is utter rubbish. There is only one kind of war that is unpopular and that is civil war, a war in which families kill and slaughter each other. Foreign war is always popular and it creates the popularity of princes. It doesn't matter whether it is the Dutch, the French, the Spanish or the Irish. Provided there is an enemy to be mocked, derided, pilloried and lampooned, it will be popular. The enemy can be accused of brutality on a massive scale. What stands between us and that brutality is the King and his Navy. Furthermore, it is a war which will be fought entirely by the Navy. No conscription, no land army, no press gangs or recruiting

sergeants. The British countryside will be at peace. In fear, yes, but in peace and cheering its King ...'

He stopped and held up his left cuff to indicate a pause. He rose, crossed the room and removed the dog from the tapestry, which involved striking it smartly across the nose. After an initial whimper the animal began to snarl as the King opened the door and tossed it into the corridor beyond. He resumed his seat and said, 'Nell's dog. I would have it castrated and fitted with a bumsack but she loves that dog. Says it reminds her of me, but I do not piss on the floor or eat the tapestries. I must indulge her a little. Where were we? Ah yes, unpopular action. You say that dissolving Parliament will be unpopular. Let me tell you something, Samuel. The people love Parliament but they hate politicians. It is a strange paradox but true. My father never understood that and it cost him his head so we must be careful.

'This must be carefully spun. I am not terminating Parliament. I am terminating politicians and I am doing so because they have failed Parliament. The Parliament which is loved by the people and the King has been failed and betrayed by the politicians that were elected to it. This is not a difficult message. I have the funds and wherewithal to post it in every town and village and the people want to believe it. How have they failed Parliament? It doesn't matter. High living, debauchery, failure to attend for debates and votes, drunkenness, brothel keeping and, thanks to Mr Roger Rawle, attempted sodomy on the Earl of Rochester. That will go down very badly in the Puritan heartlands. Furthermore, he couldn't have picked a worse target. Wilmot may be a dirty devil but he is a fine and popular poet. Some blank verse on the subject of Rawle's behaviour will do more for the Royalist cause than divine right.'

169

At the conclusion of the declamation, I confess that we were both laughing. I was expected to reply and I said: 'Your Majesty makes many compelling and wise arguments against me. Also, as I have already said to your Majesty, I do not consider that the toleration of the Catholics will, in itself, be unpopular. It will, of course, be very popular with Catholics whose numbers are, I suspect, greater than we think but I cannot pretend that I am not troubled.'

What then occurred surprised me greatly. The King rose and crossed to the side of the desk where I was sitting. He lifted the hem of his coat and sat on the desk itself. He picked up the royal seal and used it to punctuate his sentences.

'I know you are troubled Samuel and I know why. At heart you are a Parliamentarian. You are a complex man. You are not a Republican and I think not a Catholic. I doubt if you believe in my divine right,' he lowered his voice to a whisper, 'anymore than I do. But you do believe that one day we will have a proper Parliament. One day we will have an assembly that does not consist of placemen, Puritans and zealots. One day we will have a proper Parliament in partnership with a proper King; a glorious peaceful revolution. You may be surprised to know Samuel that I believe it too. But with this Parliament it is not possible and you know it. There are factions in this Parliament that would see another regicide and the countless homicides that would follow. That is why it must be dissolved. "Indefinitely" means until the constituent parts are no longer a threat. Then, perhaps, with another King we will have another constitution. Until then, it must go.'

He returned to his seat, replaced the royal seal, and continued with a new tone that signified official business.

'I have a commission for you. Because of its nature I would not order you to undertake it but I would be disappointed if you did not do so. As I told you, negotiations are close to agreement but there is still important work to be done. In particular, those that advise Louis and speak for him need confirmation as to the strength and availability of the British Navy. They need to know precisely when it can be put to sea and in what strength. Much of this request has already been provided to you in the document you were given two days ago. This cannot be done by correspondence, however substantial and however secure. This must be done in person and face-to-face. It can only be done by a man who has total, unequalled knowledge of his subject. The French are aware of your work in Chatham and Deptford – they have spies everywhere – and they know your value and your status. They will speak to you. Next question, obviously, is where should this conversation and this meeting take place? One thing is certain. It cannot take place in England. Shaftesbury has agents everywhere and spies everywhere else. I know there have been attempts to follow you and those that live with you. It is difficult to avoid these attentions in England. The meeting must take place in France and in a city where it may be concealed. Versailles is not a candidate, which leaves only Paris. Furthermore it must be done quickly. As you know from Wilmot, the enemy in Parliament already suspect something close to what I have told you. The longer it is left the greater their knowledge will be.

'Provisional arrangements have been made for you to be taken to Paris in two days' time, the day after tomorrow. You will not be alone. Two of my best men will escort you. A larger entourage would cause nothing but attention. A suitably nondescript carriage will take you to the Channel ports. You will be met at Calais, after which you should be safe. The whole journey should take no longer than six days. Having received your information, the treaty can then be drawn up and signed. Arrangements are being made for it being signed in secret at Dover.'

He paused again and his eyes examined the tapestry somewhere behind my head.

'As I have said, this "request" goes well beyond your duties, that which I am entitled to require. I do not expect your answer now unless you feel that you can give it.'

In the silence that followed I fixed my gaze on the royal seal. The request was not entirely a surprise. During his discourse my mind had shifted and, until his final arguments, I had been set upon refusal. Now I found myself changing.

I said, 'I do not need time. I shall be ready to go when I am required. I will anticipate the details tomorrow. It would be unwise to carry unnecessary documents and, unless your Majesty wishes me to do so, I will take only the French dossier which I have safe in my house. It has been read by my assistant and I know I can answer its requests.'

At the mention of CB the King's eyes widened into a smile.

'Ah, so the beautiful amanuensis has become a conspirator. Is this wise Samuel? Are you sure?'

When I nodded, he said: 'I think you are right. I have only had the pleasure of seeing her once and a very great pleasure it was. I was in Paris and Versailles for nine years Samuel and remember her dress and others very like it, worn on many fine ladies whom I knew well. She may be capable of many things but betrayal into the arms of religious zealots is very unlikely.'

As he walked with me to the door I turned to him and said, 'On that subject, your Majesty, I have one request.'

As he raised the royal eyebrows, I said, 'I know that your Majesty believes me to be fluent in the French tongue. I am not. Without assistance any negotiations would be slow and tedious indeed. I have the perfect amanuensis and, if she would agree, the perfect translator. Would there be objection to Camille Lefebre or Catherine Browne returning with me to Paris?'

'On the contrary, Samuel, I think it is an admirable idea, perhaps the best that you have had this afternoon. Whether she will consent, of course, is another matter.'

I waited with my nib poised above the paper and a substantial pause ensued. My nib dried and I did not replenish the ink. After a full minute I lifted my head and looked him squarely in the eyes.

"No," I said.

CHAPTER 16

If he was disappointed it was not apparent. His face was impassive when he said: "Is it possible that you may change your mind?"

I shook my head: "I cannot return to France, it will be a death sentence for me and probably those that travelled with me." As I spoke the words I felt a great sadness descend upon me as though a physical weight had been placed upon my shoulders. I was an exile from my own country; from my family, my home, from my theatres and my vocation. I felt tears in my eyes. To conceal them I rose, crossed to the fire and placed both hands on the mantel. Behind me I heard him say:

"Catherine, think for a moment, it appears that they were looking for a man."

Again I shook my head. By now the truth would have been revealed. The theatre would have been their first point of enquiry. My true identity was known to the entire cast and all who worked there. Camille Lefebre could not return whatever clothing she wore and neither could Catherine Browne.

Now, as I recall that scene, I am again distraught that I failed, even then, to contemplate the dreadful consequences of my disappearance. Did my mind consciously or unconsciously reject so awful a contemplation? Was it there but like passing shadow without substance and wilfully ignored? The thought torments me still and no comfort is derived from its recording or repetition. At the desk I heard him sigh with resignation.

"Perhaps you are right. I would not wish to place you in greater danger. Here you will be safe whatever your identity. I will do my best to keep a brief record of my journey. When I return we will have six days of diary to complete." I heard him rise from the desk and a minute later, he stood beside me at the fireplace. He carried two silver cups, one of which he placed on the mantel before my face: "Brandy," he said, "my best. If you cannot go to France you can still drink it."

We drank the brandy and then another before spending an hour at the spinet and the flageolet. We sang well and in gentle harmony. Pepys had discovered a new score in a bookshop by Middle Temple Hall. It was a sonorous ballad, well suited to his baritone and my counterpoint soprano. It was a little before midnight that I climbed into my bed reflecting, as I did so, that I had ceased to lock my bedroom door. It was not an invitation but it reflected a growing sense of security and wellbeing. I lay awake in the dark room contemplating my travelling cloak, black against the oak door. Behind it hung my rapier, which would not now be employed on a journey to France. I felt an inexplicable sense of guilt. This in turn gave way to irritation. Why was I guilty? Why did I feel (which I did) a sense of obligation, duty towards my purblind employer and fellow musician? The deep affairs of state and the attendant dangers were not my concern and were none of my making. I had trouble enough without inviting new perils over which I had no control or influence. Guilt, I decided, was entirely inappropriate. Of course I was grateful for my protection and my safety but I was providing service enough in the writing of the diary and the contribution of voice and music. Returning to France and untold dangers were not part of the bargain. These thoughts and reflections were entirely sensible and rational. They could not be faulted and yet, and yet, the irritating guilt persisted, causing me to turn and turn between the sheets, seeking a position that would bring sleep and mental relief. Neither came and I found myself rehearsing again and again the rational arguments for my decision. Finally I left my bed, crossed to the desk, struck the tinder and lit two candles. By their light I opened the last page of the diary and added a passage of false but rational dictation.

> *CB tells me that she will not accompany me to France. In all the circumstances this is a sensible and rational decision that I fully accept. On reflection it is unthinkable that she should place herself in such danger on an enterprise which is not of her making. I told her that she was undoubtedly right. We spoke no more of it but drank some good French brandy and spent a most pleasant hour at the instruments. CB sings exceedingly well and we complement each other in perfect harmony.*

Having completed my small forgery I read it again to achieve some comfort from the false but reasonable artifice. It did not work and I contemplated destroying the page. I did not do so and the passage remains there still. Whether it has come to the myopic attention of the apparent author I do not know. I returned to bed and finally fell into a troubled sleep. I awoke to hear Will's knock upon the door and his voice announcing the time to be near nine o'clock.

To my relief the morning brought a new sense of resolve. I would not and could not go to France and that was it.

I arrived at the library to find Pepys at his desk reading the French request regarding the Navy. He beckoned me to his side and I provided translations at his request. These he noted on a separate document which he attached to the original.

We remained at this work until gone twelve, when Pepys announced it to be finished.

"The difficult work is done, the rest I can translate myself. I do wish, however, that you were with me." He raised his hand against possible protest. "That is not intended to persuade you. You are quite right. You may well be in danger and my needs will be provided by our friends in France." He assembled and folded the French papers. "These," he said, "must be made secure. If it were discovered by Shaftesbury and his gang we would all be on the scaffold after an unpleasant stay in the Tower."

Will had placed a travelling trunk in the library, which was already half full of clothes and leather boxes. Pepys took the folded documents and crossed to the trunk, which he opened, revealing the underside of the lid. He searched briefly with his fingers before finding a catch concealed at the very corner of the recess. The catch released a slide within the lid itself. This provided a narrow access, barely an inch wide, into a concealed compartment. He attempted to insert the papers, failed, and held out the package towards me.

"Catherine, if you would, this little trick was not made for the blind."

I inserted the papers, closed the slide, and snapped the catch into its hidden slot.

"How," I said, "will you retrieve them?"

"That is not so difficult and once they have been used they can be destroyed. Now, enough conspiracies for this beautiful summer's day. Let us lunch at The Lamb and hear some music."

He had already made arrangements. His fine carriage, newly repaired, was waiting. The road had been cleared with new rushes laid and we arrived in The Lamb at Fenchurch before one o'clock. We found a table close to the window and he ordered broiled leg of pork, buttered eggs, anchovies and wine. An alcove next to the bar had been set aside for music and was occupied by three men playing the flute and two flageolets. The music was fast, animated and punctuated with error, which caused good-natured booing from part of the audience, plainly well known to the musicians themselves. Pepys, it appeared, was known to them all. After we had eaten, one of the musicians held out his instrument to Pepys, which he accepted to general applause. He indicated that I should take another instrument and a lute was produced from the back room. I made some show of reluctance but was piped across the floor by the flute to a further round of cheering. We now had a small repertoire. The instruments were poor and barely tuned but we applied a mutual enthusiasm, which brought us further, prolonged clapping and another jug of wine. Several customers began to dance and two – a man and a young woman – climbed onto a table, where they stamped and twisted to the fast jig. In half an hour we had exhausted our finer songs, ending with *Vertes Manches*. We rose together, returned our instruments, declined several offers of further liquor and regained the coach twenty yards beyond the courtyard. The weather had turned and by the time we reached Seething Lane a light rain was falling. As we entered the house Will announced that we had a visitor and, as we entered the library, the Earl of Rochester rose to greet us. He had already obtained a jug of wine and three cups, one of which he waved in the air as we entered the room: "Samuel, Catherine, welcome. As you can see I have made myself quite at home. I have news and I thought we would need some of this excellent claret." Pepys took a cup and passed one to me.

"Is it that bad, the news, or is it a celebration?"

"In a way, both. The news itself is not good but the fact that I have it is a cause for celebration. It concerns affairs of state but as Catherine has now become a fully fledged accomplice there is no reason why she should not know. Let us sit comfortably."

He arranged himself on one of the leather chairs beside the fireplace and his tone became serious: "The news concerns your momentous trip to France. The King knows that I am here and also what I will tell you. It comes from the odious Roger Rawle, the poxy Puritan I took frigging in the Haymarket. I had assumed that his affections would come to an end when he learnt that I was, once again, in the royal favour. Happily this was not the case. Yesterday evening, this aspiring sodomite presented himself at the door of my lodgings. I was going to The Bear and had no wish for his company, let alone his sexual advances. I was about to slam the door in his face when I had a sudden reflection. He had already provided information and possibly could provide more. I therefore invited him in, sat him firmly on one side of the dining table, gave him a glass of wine and took a chair at the far end of the table ready, if necessary, to lay him out with the fire tongs."

"I hope," said Pepys smiling, "that the King appreciates the lengths to which you will go to obtain this intelligence?"

"He does, although there are strict limits on the extent to which I will engage the attentions of Mr Rawle. Anyway, I am a poet but I find it difficult to describe how awful he was. He was obviously half pissed and sat there gazing at me like an infatuated toad. Finally, he started on a lot of rehearsed rubbish about my poetry and the 'beauty of my own person'. I had, he said, made him realise that spiritual truth could not be obtained without carnality. He had discovered the relationship between faith and flesh which he kept on repeating, faith and flesh, flesh and faith. He repeated it so often I began to quite like it. He now realised, he said, this was the true road to salvation. I actually got quite enthusiastic and gave the little weasel another drink before he revealed the second reason for his visit. He had, he said, told Shaftesbury and Coventry about 'our relationship'. As a result they had asked him to investigate my present standing with the King. Now that I, once more, received the King's affection, did I return it? I thought this opportunity too good to miss. Certainly, I replied, I had returned to the royal favour but this had not changed my view. I had been publicly humiliated before the entire Court and could barely tolerate the daily decadence of my existence. For me, I said, it was a spiritual awakening as profound as his own. It was, I said, a revelation. With this he appeared to undergo a spiritual tumescence. He closed his eyes, raised his clenched hands over his head and remained silent for all of a minute. Worse was to come. He opened his eyes, fixed me with a gaze of transparent rapture, raised his cup of wine as though it was Holy Communion and drained it in one ecstatic gulp. You have been *sent*, he said, for this purpose and I am your vessel. He rose from his chair and I took a firm grasp on the fire tongs behind me. This was unnecessary. He thrust both arms into the air. Hallelujah, he said, hallelujah. He resumed his seat, poured another glass of wine and fixed me with pious adoration. We have, he said, information. It concerns the King and high treason. Really, I said, releasing the tongs behind me. Is it of great importance? It is of the *greatest* importance, he said. We now know for certain that Charles is close to agreement with the French King. In return for vast sums of money he will give toleration to the papists, dissolve Parliament and permit England to make war on the Dutch. He paused for effect and I said again, 'Really are you sure?' He had, of course, told me this before but what followed was more important. 'We believe a negotiator at the highest level is about to travel to Paris.'"

On the chair beside me I saw Pepys start forward with an exclamation: "He said exactly that!"

"Exactly that. I asked him, of course, where the information came from, but he would not or could not tell me. He claimed not to know but said it was from the 'highest source'. I asked him, when will this journey take place and who will be sent? At this stage he became quite conspiratorial. We knew *who*, he said, but we do not know exactly *when*. The man involved is undoubtedly Samuel Pepys although others will be sent with him as guards. The King could trust no one else and no one else has his knowledge. We believe, he said, that it is certainly Pepys but we do not know when. It is *thought* to be at the end of this week, Friday or Saturday."

I heard Pepys draw breath sharply and then give an audible sigh.

"They are two days behind. Their information is good but flawed. That alone may help us to discover its source."

Wilmot nodded and continued. "Of course I asked for the source of this material and, again, it was refused. I also asked how they proposed to use the intelligence they possessed. Presumably, I said, Pepys was being followed? He said no, he was not being followed. Originally two men had been employed for that purpose but there had been an accident. One of them had apparently fallen into an open latrine and had developed a variety of pox. As a result, future surveillance had been abandoned. It was for this reason, among others, that he had come to my house."

Wilmot paused, rose from his chair, retrieved the jug of wine and filled our glasses.

"The next part is really quite amusing. Was it true, he asked, that I was acquainted with Samuel Pepys? Certainly, I said, and furthermore I believe him to be a royal lackey of the most unprincipled and unscrupulous kind. Good, he said, that is exactly as we hoped. They required information as to the timing of the journey. Could I possibly obtain it? Using my knowledge of Samuel Pepys, could I obtain his confidence and the details that were required? This information would greatly assist and would ensure that Pepys's journey to France could be intercepted or ambushed."

Wilmot leaned forward and looked directly at me: "And so you see Catherine, I have agreed to play the spy. I am an agent of the New Puritan cause. My hatred of the King has led me to this mighty dilemma. What do you think I should do?"

"I think," I said, "that you should, without delay, inform Mr Rawle of the date and time on which Pepys will travel to France. I myself will provide you with that information. You should be aware, however, that as I am a mere woman, a blonde actress and French to boot, so I may well have misunderstood what I have been told. It is so easy to mistake the days of the week and, even, the dates of the month. If you would like me to give you that information now, I will say the journey will take place in three days' time. That, I think, will be Saturday. I anticipate that his coach will leave at approximately seven in the morning, which would allow him, with a clear road, to board the packet at two in the afternoon. In Calais, I suspect he will stay at the Hôtel de Bretagne, where he will be met by agents of the French King. In view of the timing it might be unnecessary for you to convey this intelligence before tomorrow evening. That, I think, is the best that I can do." I lowered my eyes towards my hands adopting an expression of demure idiocy. I heard Wilmot snort with laughter and, when I raised my head, saw that Pepys was mopping his eyes behind his spectacles.

"Oh dear," he said, "oh dear, Catherine, what have we done to you? In five days you have not only become a conspirator, you have mastered the art."

Wilmot rose, moved to the desk and made an elaborate display of lifting and dipping the quill. Taking a sheet of paper he applied himself to his writing.

"Now let me see," he said, "I must record this correctly. I am told by one of those close to Pepys himself, that the journey will start at, shall we say, seven on Saturday morning, which gives the earliest arrival in France at nine o'clock that night, even assuming a good road and a fair wind . . . There!" he said, waving the paper gently in the air, "What do we think of that? I will give this information to Rawle tomorrow evening. The little rodent will positively shit himself with delight. I hope he does not do it in a Hackney. He already has a terrible reputation with the drivers."

He carried the jug back to the fireplace and filled our cups, ignoring my feeble protestations. "Now," he said, "there is another matter. Rawle does not know the plans in detail but he believes he knows the identity of the man who will be entrusted with the ambush. Given the totally misleading information they will receive from me, there will be no ambush and you will be in Paris long before they have got to Calais. However, I think you should be aware of the name of the man charged with your death or downfall."

The mood had changed and, across the fireplace, we both watched him with rapt attention as he took a draught of wine and removed a small twist of paper from his cuff. He unrolled it and squinted at the crumbled surface. The name was strange and was connected to a French town I had not heard of. It looked like *Mornamont* . . .

Any further information was interrupted by a sudden crash as Pepys struck the table with his silver cup. The blow was sufficient to cause the wine, newly poured, to erupt from the brim. "Mornamont!" he exclaimed, "Seigneur de Mornamont, otherwise known as Scott."

"Scott, that is it," said Wilmot. "Exactly, Scott, that was his name. Colonel Scott!"

Pepys, now on his feet, pulled his spectacles from his face and thrust them into the air: "Colonel Scott. Not *Colonel* for many years. Not since his court martial at Navarre for extreme cowardice in the face of the enemy, which cost his regiment a hundred men. He was sentenced to a military garrison in the Americas. Five years later he appeared again with an American wife, whose money had bought his passage to England and then to France. There he shot her on the terrace of the house she had purchased, and blamed an entirely innocent servant who was, himself, hanged. No, Catherine, do not look at me with that staged disbelief. Every word of this is true. With his widow's money he came to England, which is where I had the misfortune to meet him. My friend, John Houblon, one of the finest and gentlest men in Europe was tricked into the purchase of a property in Petticoat Lane as a sanctuary for Huguenot refugees. Scott departed with three thousand pounds and was last seen boarding a boat to Calais. Houblon was near ruined. Not financially but his faith in humanity and his judgement was shattered."

He paused and I said, "*Mornamont* . . . I had never heard of Mornamont. Is this in France?"

"Mornamont does not exist. Mornamont is a fiction. Mornamont is the fictional estate used to defraud and debauch men and women, at least one of whom he has murdered. That is Colonel Scott. When he stole from Houblon I had him followed. I had the contacts and the power to do so. He was arrested in Bordeaux. It was not a formal arrest. It was done by my own agents. He escaped that night in a woman's dress, stolen from some poor tart he left beaten and tied in his room. Much of Houblon's money was recovered. Houblon himself will never do so." He paused, took up his cup, drained what was left and resumed his seat. When he spoke again his words were laced with irony. "That is the man that Lord Shaftesbury has selected. Lord

Shaftesbury, the pure and Puritan politician. It is so grotesque that few, I fear, will believe it.

The fury of the declaration left us silent until Wilmot spoke with an air of resignation. "Well, Samuel, I am pleased that my spying has been so fruitful. Now that you know the nature of the enemy and risks do you think it wise that you should make this journey? The King will forgive. There are, no doubt, other ways to cook this goose."

Pepys leant forward in his chair and his myopic stare moved steadily between us. "I will undertake this work. What you have told me makes me more, not less determined to do so. No one else has the trust or the knowledge to play this part, certainly not in the foreseeable future. Shaftesbury should not have his way, least of all in these circumstances. The course of history should not be in the hands of murderers or thugs. If I stayed here through fear of Colonel Scott, I would not betray the King, I would betray myself." He finished the wine in his cup and smiled. "Thanks to your intimate relationship with Roger Rawle we may ensure that Scott will attempt his ambush two days late. I will write to the King and suggest a second coach, identical to my own, and carrying three passengers. One may resemble a purblind civil servant but, in reality, all three will be the King's men. A second party may follow, apparently unconnected but able to provide assistance for the first. In Calais we can provide this information to our French friends who may arrange a reception for this counterfeit group. It is Scott who will walk into a trap. With good fortune, he will not walk out."

Placing his cup on the table, the Earl of Rochester raised both hands above his head and applauded with a slow rhythm.

"Sometimes Samuel, you come close to the devil they think you are. Now I have two tasks and I must be busy. The King is with Nell tonight at Aldgate. Don't ask me where, I cannot tell you but he will have the means to organise this little plan. So there is a neat symmetry: I must first lie to the sodomite Rawle and then interfere with the pleasures of a frigging royal. I feel moved to verse. I will compose it in a Hackney. Now, I almost forgot to ask, will Catherine be with you to face these dangers, which may be very unwise?"

I began the sentence which I had been composing for much of our conversation.

"I wish to . . ."

I was interrupted by Pepys. "No she will not. I have only Colonel Scott to deal with. She would have Scott and the worst of the French aristocracy. No, she will stay here, where the only danger is from her aunt. Now, before she can say another word I will see Johnny to a Hackney. We can find one on Mincing Lane . . ."

I made no further attempt to intervene. I had intended to announce my willingness to change my mind, to travel to France with Pepys or behind him but, in truth, I was relieved. The nagging guilt had returned but was, again, capable of rational absolution. Also, it was true, that I had no desire to add Colonel Scott to my formidable list of enemies. As we left the library Wilmot turned to me.

"So Catherine, Camille, it appears you will be alone in London for a week at the mercy of your aunt. You may need some protection or, at least, some company. I would be delighted to show you this great city now rising from the fire. I know it well. Perhaps we could take a ramble in St James's Park?"

I saw an expression of pain on Pepys's face before the inevitable removal and polishing of his spectacles. I smiled politely before I said, "I am most grateful to your Lordship. Such an opportunity can scarce be resisted by a woman of the stage left alone in such circumstances. But I am afraid I must decline. I have much writing to do, including the presentation of my own defence which will, one day, be advanced in the courts of France. Also, there are many papers here which require my attention if I am to be of use to my host."

During this exchange we had arrived at the street door. Wilmot took his cloak and gloves from the chest and inclined his head towards my ear.

"What a great pity, never mind, never mind. I will gently pine away with my poetry but if you change your mind Will Hewer knows where to find me at almost any hour."

Turning to Pepys, he said, "Bon voyage, *mon ami*. Those, I think, are *les mots justes*, which quite exhausts my knowledge of the *lingua Franca* apart from one or two Latin derivations, which occasionally prove useful. Don't come with me, Samuel, I am perfectly capable of finding a Hackney despite the deplorable amount of shit which appears to be flowing from your neighbour's house."

When the door shut Pepys turned to me and we held each other's eyes in silence until he said, "Thank you Catherine. Now let us take a little rest. Then we have pea soup, herring pie and Deborah will make us a syllabub. It is fine food for thought and then to the diary, which I think will be very short, before the instruments. I have discovered a little *aria amoroso* and a jolly song called 'Tomorrow The Fox Will Come To Town'. We can sing it in honour of the Earl of Rochester."

For what remained of the afternoon I lay on my bed, then sat at my desk and watched the London sky darkening from the west. What did I feel? A curious and unexpected sense of imminent bereavement. It was not comparable to the loss of Jacques Delaine but as the room darkened, a strange melancholy came over me. I contemplated the parapet outside my window and beyond it the drop to the street below. In the event of an attack on the house escape would not be possible. My mood led me to further imaginings. In the event of an attack it would be here in this room that I would make my final stand surrounded by what remained of my world, my clothes, my papers and my only gift from Jacques, the pebble, now balanced on the edge of the desk. With my index finger I gently rocked it and watched as it settled, still as stone. Why had he gone? Why had he left me, our estates, our life? In truth I knew full well. He could never have been the master of the Mas and my poor brother Robert. To him, the vast acres of the Périgord would have been a prison as deep as the Bastille. And when he freed himself, he freed me too. He gave me Paris, the theatre, the stage, Racine, Molière and now, by dire circumstance, Mr Samuel Pepys. I knew, had always known, that he left me because he loved me too well and had no choice. I rocked the pebble again and, above its tiny scratchings, I heard the sound of my own pulse. I felt a surge of freedom, absurd and, in the circumstances, incomprehensible but it was there and derived from different men, one a brilliant buccaneer, the other a spectacled civil servant; one a Republican dedicated to *psephos*, the vote, the other a man who did the royal will aimed at the dissolution of Parliament. One day, I thought, I would dissect and examine their similarities to explain the vagaries of my affections.

But not now. Soup and pie and syllabub awaited, followed by writing and music. I rose and stood in front of the mirror to adjust my English clothes. On an impulse I drew my sword and took guard against my own image. Pass, parry, feint, parry, thrust, touché. If this room witnessed my last defiance then I had seen it first. I sheathed the sword, crossed to the cubicle, splashed water on my face and deliberately adopted three different strides and gaits as I crossed the room and descended the stairs towards supper.

It was a convivial meal. Will had been to The Cock and Bull, where he had seen a troupe of dwarfs engaged in fantastic acrobatics. As a finale they leapt one upon each others' shoulders, five in all, to a height of ten feet, whereupon the top dwarf had disappeared into a first floor window causing much screaming from the lady profitably engaged inside. As we laughed and drank, I watched my employer examining his reflection in a silver plate. In order to do so he lowered his spectacles to within four inches of the surface before he lifted his eyes to mine. We both smiled over the wreckage of the syllabub in the centre of the table. He rose, filled our cups and indicated the ceiling above his head: "Diary," he said, "then harmony."

We climbed to the library, took up our positions. I had already sharpened two quills. I dipped the nib and held it expectantly above the page on which I had written *8 Mai 1670*. He began.

Up betimes and then to The Lamb with CB. We had a merry time and played well on bad instruments. CB sings perfectly in English which is pleasing for two reasons. First it sounds well and, second, no spy would guess her fugitive past. At home to find John Wilmot already in residence. He recites some new poems and fictions upon which he is engaged. I tell him of my plans for the coming week and he offers to guide CB through the perils of London. She declines although I suspect she may have wished otherwise.

Whilst still writing I allowed myself an expression of resigned disbelief which, as intended, he noticed.

She is, of course, well acquainted with the Earl of Rochester and his ramblings. Then to a good dinner of pie and syllabub and then to the diary. I look forward, as always, to the instruments.

After a pause I raised my head and saw that he was examining the contents of an open drawer.

"Is that all?" I said.

"Oh yes," he said. "Even in this room and between us our plans must remain in our heads. What you have written is true. Incomplete, yes, but true." He took his cup and walked to the fireplace where he stood examining the portrait of his wife. Without turning he said, "However, Catherine, if I were not to return from France, if this was the last page of my diary then it may warrant completion. Do not sign off the page yet or enter a further date. You are well acquainted with my style and will have no difficulty in completing our day's business. Take your time. This short diary will become your possession and when you are safe it may be given into secure hands, not, I suggest, the Earl of Rochester, who may yet end up in the Tower. I will provide a letter to my friend John Houblon. Will Hewer knows his address. So there it is, let us to the lute."

We played well, exceptionally so. At the end of a merry and spontaneous *rondo* he surprised me by announcing a wish to provide a solo rendition. With the barest use of the spinet, four chords at most, he sang a song of quite extraordinary beauty. When he finished we were silent until he touched another chord and said, "It is beautiful is it not? But it is not for me. It is not for a baritone, it is for the treble voice. Two weeks ago I heard a boy sing it in Westminster Hall. He was rehearsing and cast a spell over the entire building. He will sing it for the King's birthday. His name, I discovered, was Henry Purcell. I think we should remember that."

For both of us the music hovered in the air as we put aside the lutes and climbed to our rooms. As we came to my door, we stopped and faced each other scarce two feet apart. In the candlelight his magnified eyes softened and creased into the smallest smile. He raised both eyebrows before I said, "No, not now. I have made love to one man on the day before he left me. I do not wish to do it again. You will return and I will be here."

As I drifted into sleep, the precise words returned to my lips and I nodded with approval into the darkened room.

CHAPTER 17

When I woke it was barely dawn. I heard repeated banging on the street door below my window. I heard the door open and two male voices, Will Hewer and another I did not recognise. Then I heard a voice I had known all my life. It belonged to Marie-Claire Normande, who had nursed us since childhood and still had the daily care of my brother. I did not dress and in my nightshirt I rushed to the bedroom door and took the stairs at headlong pace. At the top of the first flight I met Will Hewer. Before he could speak I said, "Yes, Will, I know. I know the lady. I know who has arrived. Where is she?"

He did not speak but indicated the dining room. I leapt the remaining steps, flew across the hall and, still holding the door handle propelled myself into the room. She was standing by the window, dressed in black and holding a small valise. I crossed the room and embraced her as I had on many thousand mornings since my birth. The words, in French, fell from me without coherence: "Marie-Claire, oh my dear, how did you arrive? Where have you been? Oh my God, I have missed you so much. Now," I said and holding her at arms' length, "tell me what is the news? Robert? My parents? The estate? Tell me quickly, I have had no news at all from France."

She did not speak but her eyes held mine in silent fear and apprehension. Then suddenly I realised what had happened; what must have happened. The terrible, inevitable consequence of my flight broke upon me as though I was suddenly lifted from deep water into an intolerable light. I remember shaking my head silently from side to side and then swaying as though avoiding blows from a violent attack about to be launched. Moved by the same impulse I lifted both my arms and held them before me against any revelation. Still she said nothing and I began to repeat the words, "Not Robert, not Robert, no, no, no, tell me, not Robert?" Still she did not speak but began to cry then sank onto the seat below the window. As I recovered I was possessed of a strange stillness of mind. I was an actor. I was acting a play in which I had a part but which had no reality. I pulled out a dining room chair, sat upon it, took both her hands and said:

"Tell me, Marie-Claire, tell me what happened."

I remember her words as though they were spoken yesterday. I will not use them. She must have rehearsed her story many times but, with the telling, it became broken, subject to pause and punctuated by tears. I sat silent, without response. In part this was to assist her, in part it was the numb reaction to shock. It was the first account I received of my brother's murder. Since then others including my parents have provided detail of which she had no knowledge. Now, thirty years later as I write these *mémoires*, I can blend them into a single narrative, terrible but true.

My family had received news of my departure on the day that I left. Paul Challon, good to his word, had dispatched a messenger immediately carrying the short letter I had written. On a single horse he arrived at the Mas before nightfall. The letter, as I have recorded, told them little enough. There had been a terrible event. I was innocent of any wrongdoing but would leave Paris immediately. As I anticipated, my mother had recognised the code within the words "*tant d'horreur*" and concluded that my destination was my aunt's house in London. Many actions were discussed and rejected. Finally, it was decided that my parents would both travel to Paris the following morning. The presence of my mother was deemed advisable to provide support and, if necessary, some restraint on my father's actions. They had left at first light. No detailed explanation was given to Robert. He was told that they were visiting relatives and would be gone for several days. Had they told him their journey concerned me, he would have been seized with unspecified anxiety. He had never travelled beyond the Périgord and had little understanding of my employment. Above all he believed me to be happy and safe, which made him content. He read my weekly letters with concentrated care and limited comprehension but he knew I was well and knew I would return. Marie-Claire had been his nurse and his carer from birth. She was nearly fifty and unmarried, dedicated to her work and devoted to its purpose.

In my absence Robert had made the barn his daily home. Much of our life together had been spent within it and it was the scene of my theatrical rehearsals and performances, with or without Jacques. The rack of swords used for practice was still attached to the wall. On occasions, to the concern of Marie-Claire, he would take a rapier and swing it from side to side in a clumsy and awkward imitation of myself. The vernacular of fencing he had heard on many occasions and he would cry "en garde" or "touché" without reference to his own actions. It was, said Marie-Claire, a little dangerous but clearly provided a physical memory and connection with his absent sister.

On the second day after my parents' departure, they had come to the door. A small carriage, with two passengers, spare horses and three riders. At first they were denied entry at the lodge gates. Our keeper, in his seventies, had refused to draw the bolts until the passengers left the coach and one of them, a large and powerful man in a travelling cloak, advanced upon him, took him by the throat and forced him against the wall. The keeper was later to report the words the man had used. "Do you know," he said, "who the fuck I am? I am the Marquis de Pertaine. Édouard de Pertaine. I have come to see your miserable master. Now open the fucking gate." Of course, he had no choice and they passed through, cantering down the long drive, past the avenue of limes which framed the approaching Mas. Marie-Claire saw them approach from the window of the library. She was sitting with Robert playing chequers when her attention was taken by the sound of the carriage. On an immediate impulse she told Robert to leave the house by the kitchen door, from which he could pass unnoticed into the barn which stood thirty yards from the side of the house. She had time to place the chequers in their original positions before descending the stairs to answer the loud peremptory knocking on the door. All five men stood before her, two on the upper step, the remaining three on the gravel of the drive. There was no preamble or politesse. The one immediately before her she described as a huge brute of a man in a red travelling cloak. On the shoulder it bore an insignia, a coat of arms which she later noticed was also on the carriage doors.

"We have come for Robert Lefebre," he said. "If you get him immediately there will be no trouble." She replied, "Robert Lefebre is not here. The whole family have gone to Paris." Before he spoke he looked at each of his companions with shared smiles of disbelief. He turned to Marie-Claire, stopped smiling and stepped forward causing her to retreat into the house.

"Robert Lefebre is not in Paris. Robert Lefebre left Paris two days ago after he killed my brother. Before you ask, I am the Marquis de Pertaine, Édouard de Pertaine. Now, tell me where he is. If you do not do so in five seconds these gentlemen will have no trouble in beating it out of you." She answered with the truth. "Robert Lefebre has never been to Paris. Never. Robert Lefebre did not kill anybody. Robert Lefebre could not do so."

This amused them all. "Oh really? Robert Lefebre, the great actor, has never been to Paris and has never killed anybody. Let me tell you this, you fat whore, Robert Lefebre stuck his sword straight through my brother's throat. My brother was unarmed and was making a perfectly reasonable request."

"It is not true. He had never been to Paris until yesterday. There is no one in the house. You can search it if you will."

"Very well," he said, "Before they give you a good thrashing, we will have a look at your little Mas." All five pushed past her and within half an hour had searched every room. Every cupboard was torn open and all furniture was pulled from the walls to reveal hidden alcoves. In the process the contents of wardrobes were ripped apart. The destruction, she said, was terrible. In every fireplace they piled paper and clothing, which they lit, listening whilst the choking smoke roared into the chimneys and backwards into the rooms. When it was done they assembled once more at the front door. During the search she had been dragged from room to room. When they got to the main door she was propelled down the steps where she fell onto the gravel.

"No one here then?" Édouard de Pertaine stood above her. "No one here then, just like you said. I suppose you'll say we gave them no time to hide but we know we did. That is a very long drive. We will have it out of you but thrashing you now would simply waste time." To the others he said, "Search the barn, the stables, the outbuildings over there. Do it now, fast."

The four men dispersed and, within twenty minutes, had returned. Each said the same: "Nothing". One of them nodded towards the barn, "There may be something in there. It is huge and full of farmer's rubbish. It would take hours to search. There are only two entrances. I suggest we fire it. If he is there we will smoke him out."

The Marquis bent over Marie-Claire and closely examined her face. "Does that worry you, does it? Are you concerned? Are you worried that our little actor might be burnt alive? Well, we shall see."

No more was said but all five suddenly turned their faces to the barn door. From the interior came the unmistakable hissing noise of a sword passing through the air. The Marquis turned back towards Marie-Claire on the ground.

"Ho, ho. Ho, ho, ho, so what have we here? Someone has got a sword in there, haven't they? Someone is flashing it about. Could be an invitation, do you think?"

All five drew their swords before the Marquis said, "In a line, don't let him out and bring that whimpering tart with you."

The barn door was wide enough to admit two carriages and all five entered together, one thrusting Marie-Claire before him. In the centre of the barn Robert was standing, a rapier in his right hand, slashing awkwardly from side to side.

One of the men, to the right of the Marquis, said immediately, "That's him, that's him. No doubt about it, different clothes, no wig but that's him." A second joined in, "Oh yes, no doubt at all. That's the face alright, grinning like a jackass now isn't he but he wasn't then when I saw him stick Michel through the neck."

Marie-Claire had started to scream. "No, no, no, that is not him." The man holding her laid the blade of his rapier against her throat. "You shut up, alright? One more word and this will shut you up for good."

All five turned their attention to Robert. His expression changed. His mouth remained open but he frowned towards Marie-Claire. He gestured with the sword and said, "No, no. Stop."

"Right," said the Marquis, "we need to get this straight. We have a witness here. She may be a useless trollop but I don't fancy a basketful of bodies to explain. This must look right. Now we have all seen him waving his sword towards Patrice over there. Fine, I will now protect Patrice from attack and see what this little bum boy does in a fair duel."

He tossed aside his cloak and covered the ground in several strides. When a sword's length from Robert he stopped, balanced, and cut to the side of the face. By extraordinary chance Robert's harmlessly waving sword intercepted the blow, diverting the cut across the top of his head. Seeing the cut fail, the Marquis performed a classic feint and thrust at the left side. The sword passed clean through Robert's shoulder, causing him to scream. Withdrawing his blade, the Marquis slashed again at the sword arm opening a great tear through the shirt and Robert's rapier fell to the ground. The Marquis paused.

"Not grinning now, are you, you murderous little swine. Need a lesson do you? Here and here." Two further cuts struck Robert on both arms. He made no sound but stood mouth agape and eyes wide with astonished pain. The Marquis turned to those behind him.

"He's fucking useless. What's happened to him? You said he could use a sword. He's fucking useless."

The man holding Marie-Claire replied:

"He's probably drunk, that's why he can't close his fucking mouth. Anyway, he's finished now. What will we do with him?"

"What do you mean?" said Pertaine. "'What do we do with him?' We finish him like my brother." He spun and thrust in the same movement and the blade passed straight through Robert's throat. As it was withdrawn, he fell forward still without sound onto the stone flags.

There followed a prolonged silence broken by the man called Patrice: "Not much of a show was it, in the end. Just a useless cripple after all."

The Marquis was wiping his steel against Robert's back. He looked sharply upwards: "He got what he deserved, nothing more, nothing less."

Standing, he turned the body over and examined Robert's face. "Dead as hanging mutton, so we have work to do. Straight to the Magistrate in Ribérac and we will make our depositions. We were here to arrest Lefebre for murder. He launched a frenzied attack on Patrice who was restraining the hysterical maid. I intervened in time. There was a short, fair fight, death caused in necessary self-defence."

Crossing to Marie-Claire he placed the tip of his sword against her breast. "That's what happened. One word from you and you will end up in the box with him."

They departed as they had come. The lodge keeper arrived with others he had gathered from the fields. The surgeon was summoned. Robert's body, dressed and prepared, lay on the library table when my parents returned two days later from Paris. I will not rehearse the account I was given of their arrival or of the preparations that were made for his burial in the family grave. Before the Magistrate arrived there was time to consider reaction and revenge. Marie-Claire, of course, told my parents everything she told me in the same detail. My father's predicable reaction was vengeance. It was, he had said, rank murder. No one could mistake a disabled and crippled boy for the Robert Lefebre who had fought in the rue d'Essaye. It was murder and there would be revenge. He would avenge his son.

My mother, whose initial grief had been violent and terrible, now took control. There could be no vengeance outside the law. The power of the Duc de Pertaine could destroy the entire family and those that supported it within days. The truth of the rue d'Essaye was, of course, known to them. The account that I had given to Paul Challon had been recounted to them in all its details. In Paris they had decided upon immediate recourse to law. An appointment had been made with the Chief Magistrate in order to reveal the true facts. Before the appointment could be kept it was reported to Paul Challon by one of his clients that the Marquis de Pertaine had set out for the Périgord. The identity and location of my family had been revealed, as it had to be, by Paul Detain at the Théâtre du Marais. What he had not revealed was the true identity and gender of Robert Lefebre. My mother set out these facts in elaborate detail before my father and Marie-Claire sitting at the library table. She was, Marie-Claire reported, calm, rational and determined. This terrible thing has happened to us. It was none of our making and none of our fault but it has happened and our son is dead. Our actions may make it more terrible still. Michel de Pertaine is dead. That cannot change. Robert Lefebre was sought and Robert Lefebre is dead, that also cannot change. Camille Lefebre, for these purposes, does not exist. Camille Lefebre is sought by no one. The truth will kill her as surely as her brother.

In the event my mother prevailed. Marie-Claire did not contradict the depositions given to the Magistrate. She did not lie but claimed she had seen nothing. No charges were brought against Édouard de Pertaine and within days the book had been closed.

When she finished her account, Marie-Claire sat, her hands clasped, gazing at the rush matting of the dining room floor. I did not plan or prepare my reaction. It came from my body like a rising storm. I rose and, in doing so, smashed my hand into the surface of the table. "No, no, this cannot be. He was murdered in cold blood. No one who has ever touched a sword would think that poor boy could use a blade. He could barely hold it. A child could see that."

Marie-Claire had begun to cry. "I did not tell them. I could not tell them."

"It was not you. You did everything in your power and you did not tell them because you did not know. You did not know what happened in Paris but what you told them was the truth. Robert Lefebre could not commit murder. Robert Lefebre was no more capable of murder than of higher mathematics. No! This cannot be! This will not be!"

I had been screaming and behind me I heard the door open. Pepys appeared in the room: "Please," I said, "please not now."

He paused, hesitated, nodded and withdrew. Marie-Claire stopped crying and now stared me in the face. "There is one other thing. Your mother instructed me to say this precisely. She knew you would feel a terrible guilt for leaving Paris and leaving your brother exposed to this vengeance. She said two things. They know full well that you could not have contemplated what occurred. You must have assumed that your true gender and identity would be revealed. Second, you must understand that the loss can be put into context. You did not know, have never known, the extent of Robert's illness and disability. You were always shielded from it. His physical condition had worsened. At most he has been robbed of two years of life, probably only one. She says you must release yourself from any burden that you feel. You are safe in London and you must remain here for six months, perhaps a year." She finished speaking and I sat again facing her beside the table. My mother's words calmed me as they always had, but that was all. I was calm but I was not convinced.

"No," I said, "this cannot be. This will not be. My brother, whom I loved and whose very oxygen I stole, has been tortured and murdered by the family that would have murdered me. This cannot be left. This will not be left. That is my decision and it always will be."

Even as I spoke I had made a number of firm, irrevocable decisions. I rose and said, "Marie-Claire, you must remain here. You will be safe in this house until I return. I will not be long, a few weeks at most. You will be well cared for and word will reach my parents." I held out my hand against her protest. "From our childhood your care was beyond duty and beyond price. Our roles must be reversed. The time has come for me to care for you. Now, the time is near half seven and I must prepare. Stay there for the moment. You must be hungry, food will be brought and then you can be shown to my room which I will not need until my return."

When I left the dining room I found Pepys and Will Hewer standing at the foot of the stairs. Before I could speak, Pepys held up his hand.

"Catherine, we are aware of everything you have been told. Will and I have been listening. I told him you would not object and I hope you do not. You do not need us to tell you how we feel for you and for what has happened to your family. You are safe here and will be safe for as long as you wish to stay."

It was graciously said and I managed to smile. I had already rehearsed my words.

"I know," I said, "and I am deeply grateful for your past care and your future generosity. How long I will stay I do not know but that is in the future. Our carriage will arrive in half an hour and I have barely time to pack."

Pepys shook his head. "No, Catherine, I cannot allow this. I will not allow it. We have not known each other long but we have known each other very well. I know you are not coming to France to assist me, you are coming to France to avenge your brother. To kill the man who killed him. You will be in terrible danger and, in reality, without hope. I cannot allow that."

I smiled again and said, "You are quite wrong. I am coming to assist in your enterprise. In truth you cannot do without me.

These negotiations will be in French, a language at which you are very poor indeed. I know the plans, I have kept your diary. No one else could be informed in time so that is my decision. Anything I do for you will be done before I even consider the Marquis de Pertaine. Of that you may be assured. Furthermore you have no choice. You once accused me of planning possible blackmail and I told you I was incapable of it. Very well, I have now changed my mind. I will be on that coach at eight o'clock or else, by the end of the day, I will be in the company of the Earl of Rochester and, who knows, I may even be able to discuss France with the New Puritans. Please don't argue any more. I will be ready by eight if Will can carry my luggage."

He raised his eyebrows, returned my smile and otherwise said nothing.

I packed the majority of the belongings I had brought from France, left two hundred gold *livres* in the box beneath my bed and put fifty into my wallet. My rapier I wound into my travelling cloak which lay on my valise when Will came for my luggage. The coach arrived at eight. Two men, tall and taciturn, were already passengers and they assisted me and Pepys into the coach. The driver knew his directions and at eight-fifteen precisely we set out along the road I had travelled from France barely a week before.

CHAPTER 18

The weather had changed. Calm sunlight gave way to the first of the summer storms. Wind and rain battered against the sides and the roof of the coach. The roof leaked in several places, which restricted the available room on the benches. I found myself wedged between Pepys and the carriage window, uncomfortable but dry. On the bench opposite our two guardians fared worse. They were big men and it was impossible for them completely to avoid the increasing streams of water that fell from the canvas lining above their heads. Occasionally they grunted but otherwise maintained a polite and stoical silence. They were brothers, Ian and Thomas Alderson. They both wore the red button that marked them as soldiers who fought in the Royalist cause. Both had been with Charles when he escaped to France and had remained with him during his exile. They could speak some French and knew both Paris and the Palais Royal. It was for these reasons that they had been selected as our protectors.

At first I stared silently from the window and allowed myself to think of Robert. I experienced that curious detachment which I have observed, over many years, to be the first handmaiden of grief. The brain simply rejects reality and consigns knowledge to fiction. Since my childhood I had often imagined Robert's death from a variety of accidents and diseases. His vulnerable state made this inevitable. Now I felt myself taking refuge in these old imaginings. It did not last long.

Within hours reality asserted itself without mercy. My emotions came in three waves with a definite, uncontrolled pattern. First, pain unbearably reflected in images. I saw Robert in the rooms and grounds of the Mas. I heard his stammering and watched his struggles. His laughter, which I could so easily provoke, rang in my ears as the slate-grey English countryside passed before my eyes. Then came guilt, drowning and black. The fault was mine. I had run when I should have stood my ground. Had I stayed in the rue d'Essaye, surrounded by drunken brutal men I may have been injured or killed but, just as likely, *they* would have run, deprived of their leader and knowing of his assault. Had they not done so, those who arrived at the scene could not have failed to observe their drunken condition and their strength. The removal of my disguise would have revealed me to be a woman. The reputation of the Pertaine family was foul and no enquiry or magistrate could ignore it. Instead, I had fled to safety, the decision of a coward. In doing so I had killed my brother as though I had put my sword through his throat, an inevitable result I had wilfully failed to see. Over thirty years I have tried a thousand times to confront this guilt and rationalise my actions, taken, as they had been, in the heated aftermath of battle. In thirty years of a rich and tempestuous life, I have failed. It haunts me still. The third wave, driven by pain and guilt, was anger, uncontrollable and raw. There would be atonement and it would be at my hand. In the coming days the pattern did not change, it abated like a distant storm. I learnt to conduct myself in accordance with the necessities of normality. The events soon to unfold would leave no room for indulgence.

As a result of the weather we made slow progress. In places the road dissolved into thick mud and, on several occasions, it was necessary for us all to leave the coach while the coachmen and the Alderson brothers strained at the spokes of the wheels stuck in a cloying swamp. We all became soaked. There was no changing of clothes. We did not stop for the horses or for food and drink. Pepys decreed that we should press on to Dover in the fast-receding hope that packets would sail to France. We did not reach Dover until six in the evening. Here the gale appeared to be worse. From the slope above the town we could clearly see mountains of spray and spume rising above the harbour wall. Behind the wall the masts of boats on short anchor could be seen proscribing great arcs against the blackening sky. We reached the harbour and presented our papers to the Master. He informed us that no ships had sailed all day and he anticipated that no packets would run tomorrow. We found rooms in the newly renamed *Prince Rupert*, where I met Pepys for supper a little after seven. We had changed into dry clothes and the dining room was dry and warm. The mood remained sombre. We both carried the unspoken awareness that the delay for two days could have serious consequences. Our arrival in France would coincide precisely with the false information that had been given to Roger Rawle. That information could not have reached France any more than we could. However, it would certainly have reached Dover. We ate in uncomfortable silence both avoiding the inevitable subject of our future plans. The food and the wine were good and our spirits rose. When cheese and port arrived I posed the obvious question: "Do we continue with this journey as planned when the weather permits or return to London?"

Pepys shook his head. "Of course, I understand your concerns. If there is no boat tomorrow we will be travelling precisely in accordance with the false intelligence provided to Scott. We must proceed on the basis that the enemy knows where we are. What we do not know is what preparations have been made. Knowing Shaftesbury our journey will have been anticipated for days, perhaps weeks. Whatever reception they have for us, it would require only knowledge of our time of arrival and that they now have. That gives us two choices. If we continue now we can, at least, anticipate that they will ambush or intercept us. Since the enterprise has been entirely entrusted to Colonel Scott we must anticipate extreme measures. He, himself, is an arrant coward but he will, undoubtedly, have the funds to enlist others. The second choice is to abort this enterprise now and return to London. If we do so then it must be abandoned for the foreseeable future. Shaftesbury and Coventry have already accurately discovered the King's plans. The access to this information is unlikely to disappear. On the contrary, it is likely to strengthen. For our part we have our own spy in the Earl of Rochester but that will not survive the ludicrous infatuation of Mr Roger Rawle. If this plan is to continue it will never have a better chance of success, compromised though that now is. I shall certainly continue with the impressive brothers Alderson. You, of course, Catherine are free to return at any time and arrangements may easily be made for your safe transport to London."

I shook my head. "I have my own reasons to visit my own country and these have not been changed or affected by the odious Colonel Scott. I would have continued even if you had returned."

Pepys smiled for the first time in several hours and raised his cup.

"So we are joined at the hip, as they say. Let us dispense with the formal diary this evening. When you get to your escritoire you have my consent to use a little imagination. *'Up betimes, rotten journey, awful weather, leaking coach etc., etc.'* That is as close to reality as is wise. So that is enough for today. It is a pity that we do not have the instruments."

"On the contrary," I said. "As you are not wearing your spectacles you would not have noticed the alcove we passed close to the entrance. I saw a flageolet, a violin and the back of a spinet. They all looked rather worn and are unlikely to be tuned but we will not be playing to the Conservatoire."

He chased a further piece of Stilton across his plate, captured it, conveyed it to his mouth and followed it with the remains of his port. He rose, filled both our cups and said, "Let us make some merry music. I do not feel like a requiem."

The instruments were all surprisingly in tune and unaffected by the damp air, which now pervaded the lower rooms. We played well, sang a little and attracted a small crowd, which listened and applauded with satisfactory vigour. Several entered the inn for this express purpose and stood steaming and drinking beside the door. It was a happy assembly and, as we reached the end of our short repertoire, the perils of Paris had receded with the darkening daylight. The storm did not relent. My room overlooked the sea and the harbour wall and all night long it battered the windows and the walls. It came in massive irregular gusts, delivering great premeditated blows before sinking into a rumble of menace. I slept little. In the early hours the storm achieved its own personality. It became a manic nurse. The quiet intervals were a soothing lullaby followed by a massive shrieking punishment, unwelcome and undeserved. Despite the wind and the driving rain, the temperature remained mild. The heat from the fires lit in the grates below permeated the rooms above. My own chamber became fetid and, unable to open the windows against the storm, I found myself sweating beneath the linen sheets. My dreams mixed dread and familiar apprehension. I stood on the stage of the Marais as a beautiful Bérénice unable to deliver a single word. In my speechless dream I was mocked by a huge woman who I know immediately to be Colonel Scott, the master of Mornamont, grotesquely disguised.

The familiar thespian nightmare became mixed with my task for Pepys in France. If I could not remember my lines, how could I translate the language of international diplomacy? I was totally unprepared, had learnt nothing. I was a slattern, a wastrel. In my dream the disguised Colonel Scott thrust his face into mine. "You are an actor," he said. "Do not meddle in the real world." As I looked into his eyes he changed and became the Marquis de Pertaine, Édouard de Pertaine. He became reasonable, persuasive. "Go home," he said, "go home. You have lost a brother and so have I. Let us forgive each other."

The wind, the following morning, brought another storm. Denied any form of occupation, I paced and fretted in my room. From my window I could see beyond the harbour wall. Visibility was barely half a mile until the white sea merged into a black sky. Pepys was imprisoned by his spectacles. In the gale the light metal rims would not have survived five paces. Even if the spectacles had stayed on his nose the lenses, coated in sea-spray and rain, might just as well have been a sack over his head. At his request I made the short journey to the Harbour Master's office, where I arrived soaked to the skin. His clerk told me the obvious news that no sailings would take place that day. I asked if any forecasts were possible from those who studied the Channel weather. He shrugged his shoulders. He had lived in Dover for thirty years and had seen many summer storms. "This one could be gone by the evening or remain at full strength in a week's time." I carried this unhelpful information to Pepys, who was sitting disconsolate in front of a smoking fire. It was information for which he appeared singularly ungrateful. I suggested that we might pass some time at the keyboard. This he rejected with an irritated wave of his hand and I returned to my room carrying an increasing burden of resentment. I took to my bed, where I fell into a deep sleep. When I awoke at seven the storm had abated. The wind still rattled every window and beam in the house but, from my window, I could see a lightening sky and patches of azure blue on the far horizon. My spirits lifted but resentment remained. At dinner I was silent and Pepys was moved to apologise for his behaviour, and suggested a *rondo* to celebrate the improved atmosphere. It was my turn to refuse: I was, I said, exhausted and in no mood for light music unless he had a requiem mass in his luggage I was bound for my bed. He smiled gently at my obvious sulk, apologised again and said that we both needed our rest as tomorrow we would certainly be in France.

It was now possible to see the summer sun slanting across the Harbour and men and women could be seen boarding the ships with provisions and instruments for repair. Later, I climbed to my room and lay awake staring at a starlit sky. I am not a natural curmudgeon and I felt a familiar sense of guilt. I contemplated visiting Pepys's room to make my own apologies and to suggest some late music. There was, of course, a risk that my intentions would be misunderstood and I was not entirely sure of them myself. After a spirited internal debate I decided on sleep, which resolutely refused to come. I was restless and rose on a number of occasions to pace the room and check my luggage and the clothes I intended to wear for the morning passage. Both of my dresses, the under bodices and the petticoats, were still wet through. I was carrying one other set of female clothing that was dry but which I considered should be retained for any receptions or events that may take place upon our arrival in Paris. My male garments, the clothes of the false Robert Lefebre, were more robust and, having travelled in the bottom of my portmanteau, were dry. I decided that tomorrow I would travel in those clothes. It would surprise the brothers Alderson but could easily be explained as a necessary expedient, using borrowed clothes. The arrival at some resolution quietened my mind and I did my best to invoke some pleasurable anticipation at my return to my own country. The fact that it contained the Marquis de Pertaine and Colonel Scott represented imminent danger. In the interests of sleep and composure, I attempted to drive their images from my mind and replaced them with the Périgord. Behind my closed eyes I summoned the majestic sweep of its hillsides against the Dronne and the Dordogne. I settled upon the town of Bergerac. I saw its red roofs and parchment walls, apparently haphazard but forming a perfect symmetry set against the shade of the poplars and the sunlight reflecting from the silver river itself. It was an old trick but it worked and when I woke the sunlight told me that I was bound for France.

CHAPTER 19

I dressed as my dead brother, as Robert Lefebre. The boots, the breeches and the jacket still fitted well enough. The codpiece I rejected. It was now an unfashionable appendage and I had worn it only to add a measure of verisimilitude. I did not wear the rapier, which remained folded in my red travelling cloak. My hair fell to my shoulders but I gathered it behind in a single train and carried my wig. This I did in order to avoid too great a shock to our travelling companions. They arrived at nine shortly after our breakfast. When they saw me both raised their eyebrows in identical fashion and in perfect time: "Well," said Tom Alderson, "I now feel far better protected." It was the only observation and, insofar as I remember, their first joke.

Pepys's mood had much improved and we boarded the ten o'clock packet with far lighter spirits. He had prudently removed his glasses when he left the hotel but, on the quayside itself, this was scarcely necessary. The wind was still strong but the sun shone from a near cloudless sky. I checked and supervised the loading of our luggage and the packet sailed on time. Throughout the preparations Pepys had been scanning the crowds assembled on the quayside. For this purpose he had replaced his spectacles and I could see him squinting with concentration as his eyes moved systematically along the lines of passengers assembling behind notice boards indicating the identity of the ships. The port had been closed for two days and the packets would certainly be crowded to their utmost limit. Pepys I knew was searching for the first sign of the Seigneur de Mornamont or 'Colonel Scott'. He continued to do so until the gangplank was withdrawn and the boat, under limited sail, moved from the harbour wall. He glanced at me and shook his head with evident ironic disappointment. He joined me at the seaward side in an infectious and apprehensive good humour . . . As we cleared the harbour and put on more sail his demeanour rapidly changed.

The storm had passed but the wind remained close to a gale. We were running before it on full sail. The speed over the water was very great but the motion was erratic and wild. As the prow rose and plunged the boat itself twisted without rhythm or timing. Anticipating its direction was quite impossible and it plunged from left to right on a voracious and whimsical tide. Pepys was immediately sick and vomited consistently for the next four hours. At first he clung to the ship's rail and then, ill-advisedly, attempted to negotiate the ladder to the lower deck. Without his spectacles this would have been a considerable feat in flat calm. In the existing circumstances it was a disaster. He lost his footing, clutched at the hand rope and then swung helplessly beyond the reach of one of the crew clutching desperately at his ankles. I was, myself, by no means well. I descended the first three steps and grasped the swinging body by the collar. Exerting my not inconsiderable strength, I hauled him back to the ladder at precisely the moment when the boat pitched violently backwards causing the oak sidebar to strike him with great force between the open legs. The agonised scream was cut short by another headlong pitch of the boat, which drove his face straight into my corseted bosom. There it remained muttering muffled groans until the crewman, who now had him by the shoulders, hauled him back onto the deck. With that assistance and mine, he was returned to the boat's rail, where he hung helplessly retching into the roaring wind. The crewman's face appeared next to me and he shouted into my ear through a cupped hand: "You had better keep him there. Tell him to hold tight and bend his knees. For God's sake don't let him try that again and tell him," he added unnecessarily, "if he falls over the side we can't go back for him."

We were making quite startling speed and, within three hours, were within a league of the French coast. Here the wind abated and the deck ceased to heave and pitch under our feet. An hour later we were in calm water and approaching Calais under slackening sail. The harbour, like Dover, had been closed for two days and was now clear of boats released for their various journeys. The tide was friendly and the gangplank suitably short which enabled my employer to stagger down onto dry land. There he exhibited the curious lurching dance of those who have become used to the violent movement of a deck and are suddenly released onto firm ground. He found a convenient docker's bench and fell upon it to present a picture of abject misery. I saw our luggage unloaded and then, myself, descended, as a man, upon the very quayside which I had left as a woman travelling towards an uncertain future.

The far side of the quay was crowded with all manner of vehicles. They were divided according to type. Local carts – two- and four-wheel – were in the first bay. Next were the smaller and lighter carriages, requiring one horse for two passengers over a short journey. Next to these the larger carriages with two horses, already side-yoked, were available for three, occasionally, four passengers. A smaller number of yet larger coaches, drawn by four horses, could accommodate six to eight passengers. Some of these, apparently, did not contain their full quota. As a result their drivers stood on the roofs shouting their destinations. Because of the storm the vehicles had been waiting for several days and a pungent smell of manure mixed with the aroma of discarded fish from the landing stations by the harbour wall. This rich concoction was not improving the condition of Samuel Pepys who, I noticed, was leaning heavily to one side, one elbow propped against the bench, whilst the other hand was involved in the gentle massage of his genitals. It was not a happy sight. Together with the Alderson brothers I set about discovering our own transportation. One unmarked carriage was set aside from the larger coaches. Four good horses were in harness and two were tethered at the rear to be used in relay. One of the Alderson brothers nodded towards it and we walked to the quayside. As we approached the door of the coach opened. A man stepped to the ground and crossed to join us. Ian Alderson reached him first and they silently embraced. After the same greeting with Thomas, I was introduced: "François," said Ian in French, "this is Mademoiselle Camille Lefebre. No, do not look so surprised. All her clothes were soaked on the journey so she is forced to wear those uncomfortable garments. Beneath them is a quite normal young lady."

I held out my hand to François. "Enchantée."

He took my hand. "Camille Lefebre. I see."

"François," said Ian, "is a guard of the chamber in the Palais Royal. Indeed, he is the Captain of the guard of the chamber. We performed much the same function for Charles when he was there and so we know each other well. How is your family François?"

The Frenchman turned down his mouth. "Irritating as ever and even larger since your return to England, I told them you were coming and they have, as you say, 'baked a cake'." Turning to me he said, "I understood that I was to meet Monsieur Pepys."

"Indeed," I said, "he is over there. As you can see he is somewhat indisposed."

François stared at the reclining figure. "Indeed he is. Unsurprising I think, in this weather. Your journey must have been difficult. But why is he rubbing his private parts?"

"There was an accident. I am afraid that he damaged himself on a ladder."

"How very regrettable. Does he require a surgeon? I am afraid that we have a long and uncomfortable journey to Paris. The roads have been affected by two days of storms and it will take us, I fear, two days."

"I do not think he needs a surgeon but then I am hardly one to judge. Perhaps you could speak to him?"

We crossed the cobbles to the bench where Pepys was now sitting upright and adjusting his spectacles. Introductions took place during which Pepys rose with some apparent difficulty. François evidently had some English which, politely, he employed: "As you know I am a personal guardian for the French King. I have come with one of my colleagues to escort you to the Palais Royal. It will be a pleasure to start immediately but the journey is long and I understand you have hurt your genitals. I wonder if you would like a surgeon to manage them for you?"

Behind his spectacles Pepys's eyes widened before he said, "No, thank you. They are just sore and a little swollen. No doubt they will recover without being managed. I have already had my scrotum opened once to remove a stone. I do not wish it to happen again."

François nodded and his eyes softened with misunderstanding. "Ah so, I am sorry to hear that but we all have two, do we not, and they may function with independence."

Pepys pursed his lips. "When I say a stone I mean . . . well, never mind. Let us get started. We are all very dangerously late and, on that subject, may I ask if you are carrying any firearms?"

François shook his head. "We have firearms but they are not to hand. The use of a pistol from a moving coach is dangerous to many, not least the man who fires it. If we are to be a target for muskets on the road firearms will be of little assistance. We have four good swords and men who can use them."

We boarded the coach. Pepys walked with exaggerated care and, once through the door, sank into the rear seat with a stifled groan. Ian and Thomas Alderson took up their seats on the opposite bench and I heard our second guide, Alain, climb onto the rear of the carriage providing a constant view of the road behind us. Thus secured on all sides we set out on the road to Paris.

Before we left, the journey plans were discussed. That night we would break our journey at the town of Elbeuf, a mile from the Paris road . . . The area was known to Alain as one of his relatives, a cousin, lived in a nearby village called Mandolin. Its name, he said, derived from a tributary of the Seine, which flowed through the village over hard rock and provided a sound like the permanent plucking of strings. I sensed that this pleasant and homely tale was designed to increase our sense of security, which it did.

The journey was, indeed, rough. The storms that had raged on both sides of the Channel had done identical damage to the roads. Over hard ground we made good progress but on the softer parts nearer the river the carriage lurched and twisted in movements reminiscent of the boat we had left. As it did so Pepys groaned behind eyes tight shut.

As we drove further from the coast the roads became better and our journey smoother and faster. The land was flat and subject to intensive agriculture, which occasionally gave way to dense woodland. The last hour over gentle undulating turf provided a welcome relief and by the time we reached our hotel, the Maison Dannat, Pepys had fallen asleep. Indeed, on arrival he appeared much recovered and stepped smartly from the coach onto the forecourt, which was decorated with apple trees and overhung with jasmine. It was barely six o'clock and the early evening sun shed a flickering light through the yellow and purple shade. The Maison itself overlooked the main square on the far side of which, 200 yards distant, the second hotel, the Maison Lagrange, was shielded behind bushes of lavender and covered by wisteria in full bloom. The square itself, surrounded by lime trees, was almost deserted. In all it was peaceful and serene, as had been described. The rooms were simple and comfortable and, despite our many predicaments, I enjoyed a sense of secure wellbeing. In this frame of mind I descended to the dining room, where I found the brothers Alderson and François and Alain at the table, on which stood a pitcher of wine and two plates of olives. As I joined them bread was provided and a separate cup, which Ian filled following an enquiring eyebrow and an emphatic nod from my unwigged head. I had changed into my remaining, dry, female garments. In this male company I would have wished for a less revealing décolleté but I sensed in them an admirable chivalry and I was right.

It was half an hour before Pepys arrived and we enjoyed a jolly and convivial discourse on the regional variations of wine and olives. He joined us in the wine and the talk, although I sensed an air of disapproval. This, I thought, was related to my appearance and I was right. Soup was brought, followed by several different types of sausage and the fried corn peculiar to this area of Rouen. Cheese arrived with more bread and it was after eight before Pepys announced that it was time for the dictation of the diary. Our companions withdrew to the parlour and ten minutes later I heard their footsteps on the stairs to the bedrooms above. I had brought the blank diary sheets with me. I took a position across the table, replicating our positions at the library desk, and waited with an expectant smile. Despite his apparent good humour, I sensed an underlying irritation. I reminded myself that his journey had been difficult and painful. I decided that the maximum of tact and sympathy was required.

11 Mai 1670

After the storms the sea remains wild and the journey is very rough. The boat is very unstable and we are all much affected. I hold strongly to the ship's rail and by an effort of concentration and no little effort of will finally come to France in good order and prepared for the journey. We are met by two escorts from the French Court, which has provided a carriage and strong horses. The road is rough and testing but, by late evening, we have arrived at the town of Elbeuf. Here we have an excellent supper, soup, sausage and cheese with a strong wine and so to bed.

"That is it then for this evening. Are you alright, Catherine? You do not appear completely happy."

I deliberately paused then looked him straight in the eyes. "That," I said, "is not entirely accurate. Indeed, it is almost entirely inaccurate."

"In what way?"

"You did not 'come to France in good order'. Indeed, you came through very badly indeed. There was no effort of concentration and will, you were sick as a dog."

"That is a matter of individual interpretation."

"It is not a matter of individual interpretation. It is a matter of fact."

"They are not facts, Catherine, of any great importance. In short they concern the state of my stomach and not the state of the realm."

"In those circumstances why is it necessary to record them at all? Why bother the reader with the state of your health, good or bad, the exercise of your will or lack of it? And," I said feeling my colour rising, "who is the reader in any event? Who is going to be interested in the state of your health?" I observed immediately that I had struck a raw nerve.

"These diaries, Catherine, are for posterity. I do not know who will read them and I don't know why they will read them but, if they read them, they are entitled to all the facts. The facts about the Royal Navy and the facts about my guts and my health."

"If they are going to have the facts about your guts and your health then they ought to have the accurate facts. You did not bear it well, you bore it very badly. You were repeatedly sick and then, if you will excuse me for saying so, did little but complain about the state of your private parts."

"I did not complain about my genitals until it was suggested that I should have them cut off by a surgeon."

"No one suggested they should be cut off. It was a thoroughly reasonable enquiry based upon a misunderstanding."

There was a long pause before he said, in quieter and more measured terms: "You are a very spirited woman, Catherine. That is hardly surprising given your past and your profession but, as I have pointed out before, this is *my diary*."

"It may be *your* diary but *I* am writing it and, if it is for posterity, I do not wish to be part of a misleading and false account. And, for the record, I do not know what you mean by my past and my profession but if you mean that my independence is achieved by some form of moral deficit then you have lost your scribe and, on the basis of your behaviour, will be unlikely to find another one."

As we confronted each other across the table I sensed two immediate alternatives. Either we would part forever or would acknowledge immediately the absurdity of the position we had jointly reached. In the event neither occurred. Pepys rose and assumed a tone of formality.

"We are both very tired and I think it best that we go to our respective beds and reflect on what has just been said."

"Just so," I replied from my sitting position. The dignity of his exit was a little spoilt by the use of the wrong door which gave into the pantry. He recovered, however, and I heard him mount the stairs at a slow pace. For my part I was seized, immediately, with remorse. The argument, wholly unnecessary in content and tone, had been of my making. He was right. These details were, in truth, a matter of no consequence and if he wished to conceal the fact that he had been sick, fallen down a ladder and bruised his testicles it would matter little to the future study of the Restoration or its politics. I was at fault. It was, perhaps, hardly surprising considering the drink I had consumed and the dangers which we ran. These, I realised, I had deliberately pushed from the forefront of my mind but they remained, ready to reveal themselves in needless conflict with my friends, in truth, at this moment, my only friend. I was in the wrong and I knew it. In the morning I would apologise: a full, frank and unqualified apology. With a sense of resolution I rose from the table, gathered up the diary folder and its sheets of paper and, with an equally firm footstep (which I hoped was noticed) mounted the stairs to my room. My window looked onto the square, now lit by intermittent torches flickering between the trees. At the far end of the square the Maison Lagrange was still lit. The argument and the drink had made me restless and I thought I would benefit from some fresh air, a quiet brandy and perhaps a little music. It was barely nine o'clock. Half an hour would make no difference and would calm my mind still further. I took up my travelling cloak and contemplated for a moment carrying my rapier within it. This, I rejected. The town was quiet and as peaceful as any that could be imagined. I slipped on the cloak, softly descended the stairs, unlatched the door and stepped into the cool evening air. It was heavy with the scent of flowers. This increased my sense of calm purpose as I set out across the flagstones and gravel towards the Maison Lagrange, a location I would remember vividly for the rest of my life.

CHAPTER 20

As I crossed the walled courtyard a man stepped from the shadow of the trees. He stood slightly before me purposely to inspect my face or any other parts that mattered. I heard a soft whistle of surprise before he said: "Bonsoir Mademoiselle."

"Bonsoir Monsieur," I replied and passed through the door of the Maison. This gave directly onto the salon. It was similar in dimension to the Maison Dannat, rougher, less ordered but welcoming nonetheless. The salon was empty except for a young man who was packing a violin. I raised the tuning fingers of my left hand to invite further music but he smiled and shook his head. He left through the main door and I found myself a place at a small table set with two chairs. A game of backgammon was set out and I was moving the pieces when a fat, aproned man emerged from the dining room visible to my left. He appeared a little surprised to see me and made polite enquiries while I ordered my brandy. I told him that I lived nearby and that I was in the town staying with an aunt in rue Fabrique, a road I had noticed when we drove into the square. He nodded, smiled, and within five minutes reappeared with a large glass of cognac. Shortly behind him three men entered the dining room. They passed my table and all three observed me with unfeigned interest. I smiled and raised my brandy glass to my lips. The men chose an alcove eight feet from my chair. The man who had observed me in the courtyard then entered the salon and walked to their table. I saw him jerk his head in my direction while he said in accented English: "Came across through the trees – couldn't see from where."

One of the men replied in English: "I see, we must be careful. Let us explore this lady." He rose, left the alcove and stood above my table. He was large and muscular though running to fat. He wore good-quality travelling clothes, still dusty from a journey. This brought a recollection of four horses tethered on the house rail, steam still rising from their unsaddled backs. His face was large, handsome but coarsened by illness or excess. His mouth smiled and his eyes were cold as stone. He spoke softly: "Bonsoir Mademoiselle."

"Bonsoir Monsieur."

He changed abruptly to English. "Do you," he said, "speak any English?"

I half shook my head, not in answer but signifying total lack of understanding.

"Ah," he said, "vous êtes française."

"Oui."

"Et vous êtes d'où?"

"D'ici Monsieur, exactement, d'un petit village près d'ici, Mandolin."

He continued to smile, nodded then crossed to the innkeeper who was arranging glasses on a table in the dining room. I heard him speak in French: "Do you know the village of Mandolin?" The keeper nodded:

"Yes indeed. It is very close, barely half a mile."

"And do you know her?"

The innkeeper looked at me and shook his head. "No, I have

not seen her before but she is apparently visiting an aunt in the rue Fabrique."

"Do you know the aunt?"

"There are many aunts in this town Monsieur. If any of them look like her I am sorry that I do not know them better."

The large man smiled and walked back across the room. As he passed my table, he stopped quite suddenly. In a low voice he said in English: "Mademoiselle, I see that there is a scorpion immediately beside your right foot."

I was prepared for it. My eyes widened in response to the tone but otherwise I shook my head with blank incomprehension. I carefully avoided any movement of my feet although the impulse, I confess, was strong. "Ah," he said, "I see now that it is but a shadow."

His look now changed to one of undisguised carnality. He indicated my brandy glass, now half empty, and tapped his own employing the international code for offered liquor. I made a fine theatrical gesture which commenced with a demure shaking of the head then, as though observing the attractions of the offer, nodded with polite acceptance. He grunted, gave something close to a wink, and raised his voice to give his order in the direction of the dining room: "Deux grands cognac s'il vous plaît." He returned his gaze to mine, pointed towards his companions and held thumb and forefinger in a horizontal position to indicate but a short time before his return. He joined his friends in the alcove and barely lowered his voice in English to say, "No problem. Local French tart. Could be good sport when you have gone, so let us not delay."

He continued to speak English in a tone of careful authority:

"You know the purpose of our journey. Now here are the details of engagement. They arrived yesterday on the morning packet. This was expected from the intelligence that we had received. Jean Baptiste here had been at Calais for two days. His purpose was to enter the company of those who had been sent from Paris to meet them. He succeeded brilliantly. Got drunk with one called Alain, who said he was on a sensitive journey from Paris but anticipated being able to visit a relative when they stopped at the town of Elbeuf. That is why we are here and they are in the Maison Dannat 200 yards away."

I heard a low whistle before someone interrupted. "Are we not a bit too close?" The reply was peremptory: "No we are not. I am the only one who may be recognised and the only one who would recognise me is Pepys himself. He is as blind as a bat and has no reason to suppose that I am here. As for my time on the road I have taken certain precautions which I will mention. The place planned for the engagement is twenty miles to the east. There is a wood just before the town of Loisan. Louis Bretton is there with twenty men, several muskets, pistols and swords. He is a good man. I have used him before on difficult occasions. He is waiting for the message that you can now give him. Pepys and his party will leave at first light and will be there within two hours, say seven-thirty. The coach will be stopped by a herd of goats. These have been obtained for the purpose. We have employed goats before. A fallen tree is far too obvious. The men on the roof of the coach, including the talkative Alain, will be dispatched by musket. Those inside may have firearms, although I doubt it. Loaded pistols are rarely taken on coaches. They have often been known to kill the occupants themselves. The attack should be short, as there is overwhelming superiority in the numbers. These men know their business. What matters beyond all is that Pepys should be taken alive. This is an arrest and not an ambush. I carry Shaftesbury's commission for that very purpose. This arrest is to prevent and reveal an act of high treason and Shaftesbury requires both the traitor and his documents. These will certainly lead to the King, which brings me to my part. When you leave tonight, I will remain to watch our friends in the Maison Dannat. In addition to Pepys and the two men sent from Paris there are three other men. Two are Royalist soldiers and wear the red button. The other is younger, smaller, identity unknown. When they have left I will follow at a suitable distance. I will not be noticed but I have taken the added precaution of obtaining the travelling robes of a village priest. When we approach Loisan I will find a moment to pass them and be present at the moment of attack. Is that all clear?"

There was the murmuring of assent and then one questioning voice: "What of the road tonight?"

"The road tonight is easily passable on horseback. It is a clear night with a good moon. Should you require them I have arranged for torches and tinder which you will find by the tethering rail." The other voice continued in a tone of mocking praise:

"You've thought this one through, haven't you . . . Oh Christ, don't do that. That bloody hurt."

"I do not appreciate mockery Johnny. This is finely planned. It will go beautifully. Praise yes, mockery no. Now, there is one more thing, more important than anything else. Nothing, absolutely nothing, must happen until I have arrived. I carry the commission and the warrant. No one else may lawfully carry out this task. If it appears to be an ambush, a simple act of violence organised by Shaftesbury and whoever, then it will damn them and damn their cause. I have given this undertaking in blood. For that reason, although present, I will not take part in the actual engagement. Were I to fall then the rights of the business would fall with me. I must be there but I must be alive. Is that clearly understood? Good. Now let's about our business."

A third voice was raised. "Do we have time for another brandy? It is going to be cold on that road on a clear night."

"No, you do not have time for another brandy. I have a small conquest in mind and it must be completed. On the road you may think of me frigging and drinking and it may cheer you up. You are being paid well for this little job and you may have your own frigging and brandy when it is over."

During the whole of this discourse I had applied myself studiously to the backgammon, regularly moving the pieces, occasionally ensuring they fell against the table, conveying activity to the group concealed in the alcove. Now they rose and walked to the door. One, I noticed, was limping slightly. He glanced at me and shook his head with exaggerated sympathy. All four left the Maison but within minutes my large suitor had returned. He affected a smile of benign interest and occupied the seat opposite mine. We spoke French. He was surprisingly fluent and his accent not unattractive. He ordered two more brandies and I cautioned myself against consumption.

"Well now," he said. "Alone at last. Why don't you tell me your story?"

I swiftly wove a credible web of deceit. When the keeper brought the brandies I managed with inspired timing to mention the particular beauty of Mandolin and the reason for its name. The keeper smiled approvingly and said that he frequently visited the village and would be delighted to bring me some of his apples. I gave enthusiastic assent. I was, I said, a widow. My husband had been much older than myself, a wealthy wool trader in Rouen. I was unwillingly married to him by my family. I had no children as a result of his fumbling impotence. When he died, I had ample funds to return to Mandolin, where I had a small Mas overlooking the town. I was independent but occasionally lonely. I was, however, able to visit my aunt, who provided conversation but not company. On several occasions I had visited the Maison Dannat. This was the first time I had tried the brandy and the company at the Maison Lagrange. It was all very convincing and I did it well. The implications of my position were obvious but nicely understated. Whether, at this stage, I had a clear and coherent plan, I do not, in truth, recollect. During the overheard conversation I do know that I had made a number of clear calculations. If I revealed what I had heard to Pepys then, undoubtedly, the whole enterprise would have been aborted. There would be a rapid return to England. Any offensive action would be out of the question. We were heavily outnumbered and were, indeed, engaged on an enterprise that came close to treason, at least in the eyes of the New Puritans. Hasty retreat would be inevitable. As Pepys well knew, I had two reasons for my trip to Paris. The first was to assist his mission – a task which I would dutifully complete. The second concerned the Marquis de Pertaine and the murder of my brother. This could not be long delayed. My intention was firm but my skills with the rapier diminished every day through lack of practice. In view of the dangers of the road it might, nonetheless, become necessary to reveal what I knew. Before that necessity arose I was determined upon my own sabotage. What form that would take I had no idea but I knew I would find out soon enough.

As I sipped my brandy I held him with my most attentive stare.

That, I said, was my life story. Now I was entitled to know his. "Which," I said with an admiring blink, "would be far more interesting than my own."

He gave an elaborate and dismissive shrug. "I have," he said, "done things of passing interest." At heart he was a soldier. He had fought with the Earl of Essex in the Civil War and had been wounded twice. Thereafter, he had been engaged in the last Dutch War, receiving several medals and commendations ("all quite undeserved I am sure"). A further wound, now fortunately healed, had meant an end to his commission and he was honourably discharged as a full Colonel with a small pension. He had married a beautiful American wife (here he managed a slight tear, hastily dabbed away), who had been taken from him in a dreadful accident involving the gross negligence of an elderly retainer, whose family he had supported for years. Much of her wealth he had endowed on causes for the relief of poverty and disease. These charitable works and his military service against the Dutch released the gratitude of the French King. He had been granted substantial estates in France and a title to add to his decorations.

My thespian instincts told me that I was in danger of excessive adoration. I cast down my eyes as though baffled by such heroic philanthropy. When I raised my head I enquired as to the name of his estate and his title. "Mornamont," he said proudly, "and my title is Seigneur d'Ashford et de Mornamont."

Where, I asked breathlessly, was the estate of Mornamont?

He waved a hand in the air causing a small spillage of the cognac. It was, he said, close to the Pyrenees. In all truth he rarely visited the estate, finding it too grand and pretentious for a former soldier.

And where, I continued, was Ashford?

It was, he said, a large part of England in the vicinity of the Wash. It was unlikely that I would ever travel so far but if I did I would find it a place of haunting beauty, very different to the Pyrenees.

My reactions had now passed from excessive adoration to the very verge of uncontrolled laughter. Mixed, I confess, with a certain admiration. The two utterly fictitious accounts of our respective lives had both been delivered with consummate skill. I was a trained and fêted actor. He, I know, derived his skills from lechery, greed and a predilection for violence. Now, many years later, it may appear grotesquely unlikely that I should have been tempted to mirth. I was in grave danger and my life had been reduced to dark wreckage. It was, however, a darkness into which shafts of light occasionally appeared and this was one of them. I suppressed the laughter but the effort brought tears to my eyes, which he understandably and effortlessly misunderstood.

"My dear," he said, "I see I have moved you with my small saga. Let me comfort you. I am but a man like any man. I had my dreams and my aspirations but we are all mortal. As the great English bard once himself observed, 'we are but stuff that dreams are made of and this little world is rounded by a sleep.'"

This protestation brought further tears to my eyes which now ran helplessly down my cheeks and dropped into the brandy, from which I took another substantial gulp. Whether through the brandy or my state of unnatural levity, I had, by the merest whisker, avoided a terrible error in correcting the quotation.

"My dear," he said, "I have made you sad. I must atone." As he shouted for my cognac he moved his seat next to mine. He took my hand, observing as he did so, that it was a strong and beautiful thing then gazed into my tearful eyes with a look so profound and compassionate that my control nearly broke and my shoulders started to shake and pitch. It caused, I am sorry to say, my bosoms to rise and fall, to which he transferred his rapt attention: "I must make amends," he cried, rising from the table and receiving both brandy balloons from the delighted keeper. "I will make amends. I insist that you come with me to my chamber. I have several beautiful drawings and pictures of Ashford, which you will find a delight, and from which I will happily offer you a selection."

The moment of decision had come. Whether it was the brandy, the calculations or a natural and dangerous recklessness, I could not tell. I rose and walked behind him up the oak staircase carrying a glass of brandy in both my hands. I watched his gait with an expert's eye and concluded that he was very drunk. How much wine and brandy he had consumed before my arrival at the Maison I did not know. Certainly the effect was much increased by the four glasses he had drunk at my table. I had managed during the recital of his military exploits to decant nearly two of my glasses into an ornamental trough set against the wall. I was not sober but I was steady. We reached his room on the second floor. He pulled the latch with two fingers of his right hand and nudged it open. It was a handsome chamber, well-appointed and well-furnished.

Two oak pillars extended from floor to ceiling, indicating that it had once been two bedrooms of inferior size. Candles were already burning beside the bed and on the desk, which was placed below a wide window overlooking the square. From here it was possible to see the front of the Maison Dannat and was the perfect observation post. He made uneven progress across the floor to the desk, where he deposited both his glasses of brandy. When he turned I received the full salubrious smile of imminent seduction. He made his way slowly towards me, unbuttoning his jacket as he came. With both hands he relieved me of my glasses and turned again to place them on the desk. As he did so I scanned the room for potential weapons. There was little choice. At the foot of the bed was a washstand. On its marble top was a china basin and, in that, a substantial round water jug, somewhat over half full. Whilst his back was still towards me I gently raised it in my right hand. With an extended arm it took some effort and weighed probably four to five pounds. He turned from the desk, raised both hands and, with open arms, came steadily towards me.

I raised a weak defensive arm and dissembled, "The drawings and pictures of Ashford?" His reply was, at least, candid. "Fuck Ashford," he said, "you are not here to see fucking Ashford and I am not here to show it to you. We are here for some sport. The soldier and the widow, just as we should be."

Still I demurred and indicated a number of items prominently displayed on a chest beside the bed. He followed my gaze and smiled: "Ah those," he said, "yes, I thought you might be interested in those. Do you know what they are? They are army handcuffs and manacles. They are not for you. They are for a very important traitor who I have to return to England. And so are those." He indicated a coil of thin rope and a strong length of canvas already fashioned into a gag. "All for our Mr Pepys to make sure he gets home safe and sound and straight into the Tower. Won't mean anything to you, ma chérie." His eyes narrowed with thought as he fixed them on my cleavage. "Perhaps we might try them out. They can be made to fit most sizes. How do you think you would look in these?"

He picked up the handcuffs and held them under my nose, two hoops of iron joined by a single bar four inches long.

"How," I said, "do they work?"

"Easy, look. Remove the pin, tighten them on the rack, replace the pin."

I managed to look suitably impressed, although my determined state of élan was rapidly disappearing.

"Manacles," he said, picking them up. "Just the same mechanism, only longer. Clever isn't it? Then this, this is a ready gag. The ball here is sewn into the canvas and fits into the mouth. Then all you can do is gurgle. Now," he said removing his jacket, "shall we start with taking off before we think about putting on?" He approached me with both arms wide but again I raised my hands.

"I would rather do this myself. The clothes and underclothes are difficult. It is an embarrassing process. I can do it quickly but I would rather you looked away."

He shrugged. "The quicker the better, try twenty seconds." He turned to face the window and began a slow count. When he had deposited brandy glasses, he had also removed his wig, which now sat upon the desk. At the back of his head I could see a small bald patch and on this I concentrated my focus. I knew that I would get one blow and no more. There were no other apparent weapons. Doubtless he carried rapiers but they were not readily to be seen. If I missed there would be no time to search. I was strong and quick but I was a woman in a dress. If I missed I was dead and there was no other alternative. He had reached ten when I made an exaggerated rustle of my clothes to disguise the elevation of the water jug. When he reached fifteen I aimed and swung using the full length of my arm. He did not get to eighteen. The jug hit precisely the point and shattered. Water sprayed across the room, soaking the front of my own dress. He did not fall, he crumbled and lay quite still. I knelt beside him only to confirm that he was unconscious and alive, then I reached the door, unlocked it and listened for sounds of alarm. There were none. Either the crash was unnoticed or was assumed to be part of regular English coitus. I rolled him onto his back, pulled him to the first of the oak pillars and raised his arms on either side. It was close but they came together, allowing the handcuffs to be attached. I ensured that they were very tight. I knew this might cause injury but was unwilling to take risks. Next I took the gag, prised open his jaw and stuffed the ball into his mouth. A possibility occurred that he might choke on his own vomit. It was a risk, I decided grimly, that I was prepared to take on his behalf. His legs would not reach the second pillar by about two feet. I removed his boots and his breeches and attached the manacles as tightly as I was able. I secured the rope to the bars, passed it round the pillar and, using the pillar as a pulley extended him to full stretch. I passed the rope through the bars again, then round the post again and secured it tightly in a farmer's knot. I had been brought up an estate girl and I knew how to tether and hobble my stock. I stood back and surveyed the room. I decided on one further precaution. I pulled the mattress from the bed and with considerable effort stuffed it beneath the inert body. It was not an act of kindness, it was intended to muffle body blows to the floor which were, I calculated, his only existing means of communication. Some artifice was now necessary to discourage the view that my actions had a political motive. Beside the chest I found a leather bag secured with a brass hasp. I located the key in his waistcoat pocket, opened the bag and explored its contents. There was a quantity of coin, English and French. The French sum was considerable and was contained in two leather pouches. These, I presumed, were the wages for Monsieur Bretton. I could see no reason why they should end in such an unworthy pocket. I took the pouches, loosened my stays and suspended them beneath my dress. I briefly scanned the papers until I found the commission and the warrant for the arrest of Samuel Pepys. These I rolled and, inhaling deeply, thrust them beneath my corset. The smaller coin, still considerable in total, I took in hand before I left the room and locked the door. I deliberately made noisy passage down the stairs and, as a desired result, met the keeper on the way out. He raised an enquiring eyebrow and I gave my directions.

"The Seigneur d'Ashford et de Mornamont has gone to his room. I will be returning in a short while. He has asked me to say that we must not be disturbed. In particular, we do not wish to be disturbed in the morning, certainly not before midday."

I moved closer to him, extended my hand and placed the coins into his grasp.

"The Seigneur is very grateful to you and knows you will understand."

While he was nodding with complicity I added, "It may be that we will make some robust noises as we have only just met you understand." He nodded then smiled and winked in one facial gesture.

I crossed the square, allowed myself in through the main door, achieved my bedroom, completed my toilette, and took up station by my window. It was barely one o'clock and my duties were not over. The dawn came at five and by six I heard our carriage being prepared before a knock on my door summoned me to a communal breakfast. On the second floor of the Maison Lagrange, the curtains in Colonel Scott's room remained firmly drawn. I had closed them myself on the obvious assumption that if he had made an escape, his first action would have been to observe the Maison Dannat and its occupants. We assembled by the coach and I drew Alain to one side.

"Is it possible," I said, "to avoid the road for two miles this side of Loisan?"

His look questioned me before he said, "Yes, it is possible, inconvenient, but possible. Do you know this road?"

"Yes," I said, "I know it a little and also know it is dangerous. I do not think that anything will occur but, to be safe, I think we would be best to take an uncomfortable diversion."

And so we did. Pepys questioned the route and complained but, within an hour, we regained the Paris road and six hours later passed through the outskirts of the city itself. Pepys was in good spirits and, as we approached the Palais Royal, had observed that it had all been safer than our dire expectations. But it is always better, he said, indicating the brothers opposite, to take necessary precautions.

CHAPTER 21

I was awed by its magnificence. It is, quite simply, the greatest palace ever built. Some say otherwise, claims are made for Versailles, for the Alhambra, the Pitti, and even Hampton Court. Later, I was to visit them all and know that they are mere shadows of this great majestic work. Versailles is a monument to vulgarity, the Alhambra, a mighty ruin, has no purpose than to ornament itself, and Hampton Court is a red-brick frig house. None rival the majestic sweep of the Palais Royal. The strength of its central columns set against the elegant lightness of the screens. It is at once a royal statement of power and has a celestial quality appropriate to its founder and its first resident, Cardinal Richelieu, a man of God and a god of men who was, at his splendour, the most powerful man on earth. This was his residence, now reclaimed by the Kings of France. One of its many uses was an asylum for the exiled Royal families of Europe, growing in number with every passing decade. Here, for nine years, Charles learnt the ways of the French Court.

We had rooms in the north-east wing. The brothers Alderson occupied one, Alain and François another. Pepys and I had separate rooms and one was set aside for study and work related to the negotiations. These, we were told, would begin in two days' time. We were allowed, it seemed, one full day to recover from the journey. By contrast to the majestic grandeur of the Palais itself, the rooms were simple and sparsely furnished. I enquired as to the laundry and was told that clothes could be given to one of the maids who cleaned the rooms on a daily basis. They would be returned within the day. The majority of my clothes were still wet from the journey and were beginning to smell of mould. Prudently I retained the dress I had last worn at the Maison Dannat. The remainder of my clothes I entrusted to my maid, who stared wide-eyed at the shirt, breeches and jacket, which were the clothes of Robert Lefebre. I provided an unnecessary explanation that they were "theatrical", at which she nodded with brief incomprehension. Dinner was served to us in the communal room and we ate together at the long conference table. We now enjoyed the easy relationship of fellow travellers. There was much conversation as to the state of the roads and the relative benefits of the new means of suspensions employed in the modern carriage. The Alderson brothers and Alain and François exchanged news of their families. During the King's exile the brothers had been separated from wives and children for nine years. Both had experienced the strains of reunion with relative strangers. As they spoke I felt a surge of affection for these quiet and formidable men. We drank some wine and some brandy but Pepys, I noticed, had little. I followed his example. Our quarrel the night before had resulted, in part, from substantial imbibing and I wished to avoid a repetition. As this thought passed I reflected that the argument itself had produced the most benign result. Without it, indeed, we might all be dead or in chains. Such are the vicissitudes of quarrelling.

At the end of the meal we heard a commotion in the corridor. A knock on the door preceded the entry of a number of the Palais servants manoeuvring a spinet and carrying two lutes and a flageolet. Pepys, who was not wearing his spectacles, smiled happily in my general direction.

"I made this," he said, "an essential part of the negotiations. No music, no Navy."

I laughed, rose, and applied myself to exploring the keyboard. It was slightly out of tune but to a degree that would pass unnoticed by our companions. When I finished a small introductory trill they applauded with wholly inappropriate vigour. We were becoming friends. We now had a fair repertoire of songs, ballads and one or two short sonatas. We played happily enough, exchanging the keyboard and the lute to the further applause of our companions. At the end of a short rondo I was surprised when Tom Alderson asked if he might take his turn at the spinet.

"Of course," I said and made way immediately.

He was surprisingly good. He had a soldier's hands and occasionally produced a discord when adjacent keys were depressed. These flaws decreased with confidence and he began to sing a soldier's song dedicated, inevitably, to the girl who waited for his return from battle. His brother joined in the words and, taking the flageolet, produced a single note that nicely underpinned the melody. It was a sufficient cue. Alain and François sang, unaccompanied, a song dedicated apparently to the wines of the Loire. The melody was simple and the brothers Alderson began to play by ear. Pepys and I applauded with equal gusto. Pepys then picked up the other lute and sat expectant for the next song. I sensed that I was an inhibition. My male companionship consisted of four soldiers and a civil servant of doubtful reputation. I rose to make my excuses when Pepys said,

"Catherine, we must do a little for the diary. Perhaps you could give us half an hour of bawdy song and then we could begin. It should not take long. It has been an uneventful day."

I managed a smile, which contained no irony, and crossed the corridor to my room. I needed some time alone. From my window I could see the rooftops of Paris, dark against the light sky. I was uncertain of direction but I imagined that I was looking at the roofs of the rue d'Essaye and the Théâtre du Marais. I was back with my own business to finish. I had taken, on a regular basis, to searching my resolve. I was bent upon a revenge which, in all probability, would result in my death. My brother was already dead and his poor life had been shortened by only a matter of months, a few years at most. I observed myself with interest as though testing a difficult child. Had my resolution dimmed? Was the "pale hue" of thought now tending towards thoughts of a rational withdrawal? I could return, in peace, to the Périgord and to my parents. They, I knew, would beg me to do so. I heard their arguments in my head. "We have lost a son. We need a daughter." In my mind I returned to the Périgord, embraced them at the door of the Mas and walked with them through the farms and the woods, greeted by the many friends and guardians of my childhood. Then I opened the door of the barn. I stepped in and closed it behind me. The vast open space where I had duelled, exercised, studied, acted and fallen in love, yawned before me empty and now full of menace. I saw the rack of rapiers. I approached it and selected a blade and began the passes: thrust, cut, parry, feint, slash, parry. Against whom was I fighting? I saw a brute of a man. His face twisted with cruelty, his grinning acolytes waiting for the sport. I heard Marie-Claire sobbing in the corner. I was ready, I was poised. My balance was sure, my eyes were sharp, the wrist and sinews of my right arm felt strong, supple and taut. Then, unwillingly, I re-entered the barn. I saw a poor boy, near crippled by the accident of his birth. I saw a poor boy with a sword he could barely lift. I saw his vacant smile betraying the trust of a long, sheltered and loving childhood. I saw puzzlement in his eyes as the man I had confronted and his pack of followers closed for the protracted and sadistic kill. Tears rushed to my eyes and I thrust open the window. The cool Paris air carried the sounds and smells of a massed humanity. I remember clenching my jaw until my face shook. Then, I said into the Paris night: "This is not revenge. This is justice. This is human justice. This was foul murder. It cannot be allowed to stand."

I crossed to my travelling cloak hanging against the door. Behind it I found my rapier, which I drew from the scabbard. I did not go through the passes. I did not fight an imaginary duel or inflict an imaginary death. I looked at the blade, in which I could see my miniature distorted reflection. I knew that my resolution would not change. I knew that I would revisit this scene time and again until the very conclusion of the course that I had to run. I smiled to myself. *We* had taken our decision. The difficult child was no more.

Beyond my door I heard the last of a number of jolly choruses marked by a final flourish on the spinet and then the lute. I recognised Pepys's signature and I smiled again. Was this love? Was this the beginning of a requited passion? If so, it could be short indeed. Édouard de Pertaine stood in its way.

When I entered the room, they all cheered. I affected surprise and gave them the full pirouette and curtsey. They cheered again. Alain was on his feet.

"Camille," he called, "come, let us do one more round. We have four instruments. I will turn this table into a drum and Ian can lead with his English baritone. Then you can get to your writing." I took to the keyboard and we embarked on a ballad that Pepys and I had played many times before. Everyone joined in and, in truth, it was awful. No one else appeared to notice and we finished with a suitable crescendo.

"Excellent," said Pepys, at which they all laughed. "Now we must to the diary and then to bed."

Our four companions left us. I had brought the folder, paper, ink and pen with me. We took up our now familiar positions on either side of a wide table. I carefully wrote the date *12 Mai 1670*, then looked up to see him regarding me with such unfeigned affection I felt myself blush. Unexplained sensations ran across my back. I made an obvious and determined attempt to address the white paper with the poised nib.

Up betimes. I wake with a feeling of regret and remorse which I had taken with me to my bed. Last night I quarrelled with CB over this dear diary and, in particular, the descriptions of my own behaviour. Her criticisms were entirely justified and my defence inadequate and unworthy. I resolved that a fulsome apology was necessary which I will provide.

He paused long enough for me to raise my head and he said: "There, will that do or would you like to hear it from me direct?"

"Of course it will do. I also had decided upon a full apology. The fault was entirely mine. On reflection I was completely wrong. Facts, it is true, were not accurately recorded. You did vomit, fall down the ladder and cause painful injury to your private parts but injuries to your private parts are of no consequence to history, painful though they may be for you. The apology should be mine and, although I cannot record it in your diary, I give it freely and without reservation."

By the time I had finished we were both laughing with something approaching relief.

"Thank you Catherine, that is kind but, in truth, I think you are wrong. History is not a monolith. It needs to be set against the small pains and vicissitudes, lusts, and loves of those who passed through it. What will they learn from a correction of my facts? That the Channel can be appallingly rough? That ships, of whatever size, will be subject to battering, which will increase the misery of their passengers? That ships' ladders can be dangerous for purblind men and that injuries to the genitals are initially more painful than most? There is no reason to suppose that any of this will change but recording it will bring, I hope, a sense of comfort to those who read it in hundreds of years' time. Comfort will be derived from precisely the fact that it *does not* change. The fact that their lives, however sophisticated or scientific they may become, are linked to us not by an unfolding history of war and treaty but by trivial, often sordid and disagreeable, lusts and discomforts of no consequence whatsoever."

There was a pause in which we regarded each other, knowing that our relationship had moved to another, perhaps more dangerous place.

"Do you wish me," I said smiling, "to record all this or to correct yesterday's facts?"

"No," said Pepys decisively, "that would only, I think, confuse the reader. I have always tried to keep it simple, inaccurate at times, but simple nonetheless so let us continue from Elbeuf this morning."

The carriage leaves early and the journey to Paris is without event. We took one uncomfortable and, apparently, unnecessary detour but otherwise the damage done by the recent storms appears to have been repaired. Once at the Palais Royal it is possible to reflect on our concerns as to the safety of the journey. These were, apparently, entirely misconceived. I always regarded them as fanciful and, in particular, the information relating to Colonel Scott. On reflection it is inconceivable that Shaftesbury or Coventry would have resorted to the services of this disgusting brute of a man. I confess that I was concerned but, thinking on it, that concern was, in reality, for the safety of CB. Scott is a licentious and violent beast. Had she been exposed to his advances and his pleasure it would have been a tragedy beyond contemplation. Now that we have attained the Palais Royal we may place these matters behind us. After the negotiations we will travel without papers or commissions and will therefore be of no use to Shaftesbury and his friends.

He paused, waiting for my customary attention when he did so. I continued to stare fixedly at the paper: "That will do Catherine, won't it? I think it is fair." He must have observed my pursed lips for he added: "You don't appear entirely happy with that?"

I mastered the feelings within me, smiled and looked at him across the table.

"No, no. I think that is very fairly and beautifully put. If I may add, away from the diary itself, I am, of course, immensely grateful for your concerns and your guardianship on this journey."

"Well said," he observed with a smile of satisfaction. "Well said. Now the final paragraphs."

We all enjoyed together a fine supper, soup, rabbit stew and a good yellow cheese. Then to the instruments which I had obtained. It appears that our companions are all, more or less, proficient at the instruments or with the voice. We pass a jolly and musical time. CB plays exceedingly well and is much applauded by our friends. And so to bed. Tomorrow is set for preparation and full negotiations the day after.

I powdered the page, waved it gently in the air and placed it in the folder which I closed with a robust snap.

"Catherine," he said, "you still appear a little upset. Have I been guilty of other inaccuracies? If so, please tell me. We have much to do together and I would not wish us to quarrel."

"No," I said, "it is nothing. Considering your exaggerated fears it occurs to me that this Colonel Scott, this Seigneur d'Ashford et de Mornamont is but a figment of your imagination. So foul a brute would surely, by now, have been revealed, punished and probably hanged."

Pepys, suddenly serious, leant across the table. "Oh no, Catherine. You must not think that. This man exists and he is everything that I say he is. If ever there was a man to be avoided by your sex, it is Scott. The thought of you in his company is sufficient to stop my breath. But, one thing is sure, the danger, if there was such a thing, is now over and you are safe and well. For that, who knows, we may have to thank our stalwart friends from the armies of England and France. Who knows?"

"Who knows indeed?" I echoed, gathering the diary to my bosom. "And now to bed."

We passed into the corridor and paused outside my own room. Pepys removed his spectacles and the expression in his eyes carried unmistakable request and invitation. I smiled and placed a hand against his lips.

"Not now," I said. "There are many dangers to be faced despite the fact that none have so far occurred. Let us wait until they are behind us, then, perhaps, who knows?"

CHAPTER 22

The following day we kept to our rooms. Wandering within the Palais (or, indeed, Paris itself) was firmly and positively discouraged. I was allowed one exception. After several entreaties I was taken, under escort, to the Théâtre du Palais Royal in the west wing. A rehearsal of Molière was in progress, which I watched from the darkness of the empty stalls. Some of the actors were well known to me and I carefully kept beyond their sight. Whilst I was there the rehearsal came to an end and the cast departed towards the rue Saint-Honoré. I waited until they had all gone and then, despite the protestations of the maid who had been sent as my guardian, walked onto the empty stage. To the dark auditorium I delivered a speech from *Bérénice* and curtseyed into the silence. Joy and sorrow came in alternate waves as I joined my maid, an agreeable and pretty young woman called Roxanne, who escorted me back to the west wing. We passed many wonders. The breathtaking scale of the rooms was matched by the size, quantity and quality of the art that hung on their walls. Furniture, polished to reflection, or painted in meticulous detail, stood on Ottoman carpets produced by the slavery of thousands. The size of the doorways imparted, as was intended, a sense of insignificant mortality. Richelieu, himself, must have been daunted on occasions by his own creation. Only a man who believed in his own deification could have created such an excessive paradise.

When we reached our rooms I thanked Roxanne, who smiled and said, "You were really quite good on the stage. You should give it a try."

That was my only journey; otherwise Pepys and I sat at the table revisiting the French inventory that I had already considered in so much detail. Meticulously we discussed the detail and answers that would be necessary, including the non-committal. It was arduous and dull. When we took necessary breaks I paced the room, reeled out snatches on the spinet and performed delicate fingering on the lute. I felt a desperate need for action. The room became oppressive and I began, inevitably, to resent the careful and diligent presence of my companion. Once, when he asked for a particularly simple and obvious translation, I hissed between my teeth and shook my head.

"Catherine," he said. "You must restrain yourself. I know where you have been. To visit the Théâtre Royal and the stage on which you could well be playing to vast acclaim. It must be a torture to you but it will come. You will return. You can, I think, play Shakespeare in any language, Molière or Racine too for that matter."

I was totally mollified and a little guilty. He possessed a gentle percipience of my mood, my frustrations and my intentions. It did not extend to my meeting with Colonel Scott but then those facts were beyond his knowledge or, I suspect, his imagination. I smiled and tapped my finger on the copious notes we had taken.

"I do not think this will take very long," I said. "Half of it we know already, the remainder is factual, accurate and easily explained."

"I would not be so sure. The French negotiators are both military men. Fine soldiers, no doubt, but civil service detail may well be beyond them. We may have to repeat information more than once. That is to say *you* have to repeat it more than once, which is why I thank God you are here."

I smiled. "If there is a God minding this particular journey then I think we have much to thank him for and I will happily continue to do so, sceptical though I am."

Pepys looked at me sharply. "You do not believe in the Almighty?"

"I believe that there is a profound impulse that drives us towards improvement despite the weaknesses and temptations which we have, some of us, in abundance. It is an unhappy fact that those who wish to grasp life with the greatest joy are capable of the greatest selfishness and harm. That is subject to the impulse I have referred to. It is obviously related to guilt."

Pepys laughed. "Profound indeed and worthy of a thespian. We will discuss this more in the future. I am widely thought to be a Catholic and that view is based upon my own wish to grasp life. It is an interesting and flawed logic as you say."

During that day I can remember no other conversation worthy of record until we assembled for our evening meal. Alain had spent the day in Paris and he arrived in a joyful mood. He had, he said, the most interesting tale to tell about the town of Elbeuf and our stay in the Maison Dannat but it would wait, he said, until we had completed the meal. It was not suitable meat for valets.

When the meal was over and the cheese and wine left on the table, he made an expansive gesture and settled to his story.

"My relative from Elbeuf," he said, "came to Paris this afternoon. On a good horse it was possible to complete the journey in two hours which he did. He came expressly to see me and to give me this news which he thought might amuse me. We met at the Hôtel de Montreuil, where I often spend the afternoon in Paris. It was fortunate that we met because I was about to leave. We ordered some more wine and then he gave me this news. Apparently there has been an Englishman staying in the Maison Lagrange which, you may remember, is immediately opposite the Maison Dannat on the far side of the square. During the evening of our stay this Englishman apparently imported a French woman of, he said, dubious appearance and substantial visible bosoms. They had drunk a good deal of wine and brandy and then disappeared to his room. It became clear, my friend told me, that this man practiced the most appalling acts of sexual deviance including bondage and the use of handcuffs, manacles, gags and oranges."

"Anyway," Alain continued. "The following morning, yesterday, nothing could be heard from his room save for muffled bangings and grunts. The staff had been warned by the woman in question that their activities might be a little noisy so they took no action. By two o'clock in the afternoon the noises had become more intermittent but when they did recommence they were of extraordinary violence. Finally it appeared that the bangings were actually on the floor itself. This caused some alarm and attempts were made to enter the room. The key was nowhere to be found. One of the staff was able to look through the keyhole and, so my relative was told, recoiled in absolute horror. The decision was made to break the door which was difficult as it was of sturdy oak with a good lock. Finally, when they entered the room, they found the Englishman chained to the oak beams, gagged, without his trousers and with . . ." Alain glanced at me with a look of apology, "an orange pressed between the cheeks of his buttocks."

Unhappily, at this stage, and hearing the total fiction, I could not restrain a *sotto voce* exclamation: "That's not right!" I said.

Only Pepys heard me and he looked sharply in my direction: "What did you say?"

I said: "That cannot possibly be right. It is too awful."

Pepys nodded but I noticed that, from time to time, he glanced at me, the eyes, behind his spectacles, narrowed with interrogation. Alain had continued: "Well, they removed the gag, the handcuffs, the manacles and the orange and demanded an explanation both for his presence and the circumstances in which he had been found. He was, my relative told me, quite unable to provide one, attempted to leave and became quite violent when he was restrained. Constables were called. The handcuffs were reapplied and he was taken post-haste to the Magistrate at Rouen. This story had spread like wildfire and the court, held this morning, was full to overflowing. When he was brought before the court (my relative had attended to see the spectacle) he positively snarled at the Magistrate and said what he did was his own business. The Magistrate then read out a series of edicts, national and municipal, which expressly forbade sexual activity of this kind. He then, apparently, shouted from the dock in English, 'I don't give a fuck about your edicts. The King will hear of this.' Whether he referred to Charles or Louis was unclear. The case was adjourned for an hour, during which he calmed down and was given the service of an interpreter with some knowledge of the law. Apparently a kind of deal was done. He was released on his undertaking that he would leave immediately on an accompanied coach to Calais, then to be placed on a packet to England. There was a condition that he should return immediately to his home which, my relative told me, is somewhere called d'Ashford."

I saw Pepys start on the other side of the table. "Ashford?" he said.

"Well, if that is your pronunciation, as you wish, but Ashford or d'Ashford it certainly was."

I now felt Pepys's eyes boring into my lowered head.

"So," said Alain. "What a fine story. I thought you would enjoy it."

General discussion then followed, suitably censored by my presence, as to the sexual predilections of the English and particularly those that came from d'Ashford. Tom Alderson expressed the view, surprising for a soldier, that love was the greatest aphrodisiac, much to be preferred to chains and manacles. It was obviously a repeated sentiment and his brother slapped him playfully on the shoulder and observed that love came with its chains and manacles, likely to endure far longer than rusting metal. We did not pursue this family confidence and brought the conversation to a close. Alain suggested that we might take a turn on the instruments but Pepys declined.

"Tomorrow," he said, "will be a busy and important day, though not for you gentlemen, who have Paris at your disposal. Also we have a brief diary page to complete and there is one matter that I wish to discuss with Catherine."

When they had left I stared at him across the table, my face a picture of total innocence. After a prolonged silence, he said: "Did you leave the Maison Dannat after we retired to bed?"

"Certainly not," I replied. "And after what we have just heard I am pleased indeed that I did not do so. Who would have thought that such things could occur in such a town?"

Pepys's eyes narrowed to near slits. "The man that was arrested was undoubtedly Colonel Scott."

I widened my eyes in amazement. "Scott? How do you know? Of all the brutality you have described, it did not include behaviour of this kind."

"He is perfectly capable of anything, although," he added reflectively, "I doubt that it would involve *himself* being the subject of bondage."

"Well, there you are then," I said, "totally out of character for our man."

Pepys continued to muse while creating an obvious effect. "But what if he was disabled first? What if someone, the woman for instance, had tricked him or rendered him unconscious, then it could well be 'in character' as you say."

I gave a protracted sigh. "I have never known," I said, "a woman who would be capable of such things. You are older than I am, have you met such a person?"

His mood had changed and he was now openly smiling from behind his spectacles: "No," he said, "I certainly have not. Indeed, in all my imaginings, I would not have thought that such a person existed. Let us hope that she has survived her ordeal, whatever that may have been, and is even now enjoying the company and affection of her friends."

"Just so," I said and raised my brandy glass to which he reciprocated. A little unwillingly he indicated the folder on the table and we prepared to recommence.

13 Mai 1670
Up betimes. A day spent in the dull preparation of statistics
and ordnance. We are now well prepared for the negotiations
tomorrow and may sleep easily as a result. After supper Alain
brings extraordinary news of vile events which took place in Elbeuf
during our stay at the Maison Dannat. Apparently an Englishman
from Ashford engaged in acts of appalling depravity which involved
being manacled and gagged with an orange inserted between his
buttocks.

Pepys paused and, inevitably, I lifted my head.

"Do you think we ought to put that bit in about the orange?"
His eyes were dancing with laughter. "If you think it goes a bit
far then we can leave it out. I mentioned that particularly in view
of your desire for factual accuracy."

"Oh," I said, "I see no reason to remove it. What effect it has
one can only conjecture."

"Just so," he said on the verge of outright laughter. "So let us
leave the orange where it is and continue the account."

We are told that the matter was resolved by the Magistrate at Rouen
requiring the Englishman to return to England. He apparently lives
at Ashford or, as the Magistrate understood it, d'Ashford. Whether
such activities take place in this delightful town in Kent must be
debatable. Certain it is that their elected representatives should
be informed. It is a matter of passing interest that the villain
Scott purports to be this Seigneur d'Ashford et de Mornamont.
Coincidence can be an extraordinary thing.

"That, I think, concludes for the day, Catherine." As I looked up I saw that his shoulders were still shaking with repressed laughter. I affected not to notice but enquired in a voice full of innocence.

"Is Ashford in Kent? I thought that it was by the Wash?"

"Quite different. Ashford is set in beautiful countryside in the Garden of England. The Wash is the most gloomy and horrible place, full of Fens and fever. You really would thoroughly dislike it. I have some pictures of it somewhere that I would be delighted to show you."

"That would be very nice," I said, gathering up the folder. "Let us do that when we return to London." We both walked side by side down the passage to my room. As we parted he said:

"I make it a matter of principle never to change anything in my diary. Sometimes I correct an impression in the later entries. However, I am concerned about the passage regarding your own safety and my concerns for it. Do you think we might add how completely unwarranted they were?"

I smiled and touched his lips with my finger, a gesture which was now becoming a regularity. "Oh, I don't think so," I said, "I should leave it exactly as it was and I think that your concerns were indeed well noted, perhaps even more than you know."

He smiled, raised his candle in salutation, and disappeared towards his own room.

CHAPTER 23

The following day we attended, as directed, the chamber used for negotiation of affairs of state. It was grand enough but otherwise resembled a small courtroom similar to the regional court in Ribérac, where my father received petitions for the King. Around the walls two rows of benches were available for observers or advisers as required. In the centre was a table, eight-foot square. Around it were a number of chairs, high-backed and straight to encourage concentration. Immediately adjacent to this table was a second smaller table. When we arrived this was already occupied by two scribes, before whom were piles of vellum, inkwells and a number of sharpened quills. We were immediately preceded by the French negotiators and we stood by the table and made our own introductions. When I was introduced by Pepys both of our counterparts raised their eyebrows with perceptible surprise. Both the French team were, as Pepys had predicted, military men, although neither wore uniform. The first held the highest rank in the French army, Marshal, and had been commander of a cavalry regiment whose name I did not retain. His name was Guillaume Defos. The second, representing the French Navy, had been an Admiral of the Fleet but was now retired. His task, he told us, was to implement Navy reform and to attempt the reconstruction of the Fleet. As such, his work bore similarities to that of Samuel Pepys. When we were seated Pepys drew breath but was silenced by a peremptory finger raised by the Marshal.

The reason immediately became apparent when a black coated figure entered the chamber and walked to the centre table. As he did so he waved his right hand and spoke in French.

"Do not get up gentlemen, do not get up. I see that you have already made yourself comfortable." He stopped by the table and briefly inspected its four occupants. As with the French negotiators his eyebrows raised when I came under his scrutiny. He continued: "For those that may not know me, may I introduce myself? My name is Robert Rolain. I work in the office of the Monsieur Colbert, the principal adviser to the King of France. I am here to set out the background and the scope of these early negotiations. Before I do so, may I enquire as to the identity of this young lady and her rank in the British Government? I know who you are Mr Pepys and no such enquiry is necessary."

Pepys replied. "This is Camille Lefebre. She holds no rank in the British Government and, indeed, could not do so, as she is French. She is my principal adviser, assistant and amanuensis."

"Oh really?" said Monsieur Rolain. "Oh really?" He had a long hairless neck and was obviously bald, a fact not disguised by his periwig. For these reasons he resembled a reptile, improbably adorned with false hair. "Oh really," he repeated again. "I am afraid that this is most irregular. Only those holding a direct commission should attend negotiations of this kind."

Pepys had now arisen from his seat as a matter of respect. It also gave him equality of height, essential for such a confrontation. "Monsieur Rolain, Camille Lefebre enjoys my total and complete confidence, both as to her abilities and to her discretion. I should say that this confidence is also shared by the King of England before whom she was presented barely four days ago. She does not hold her own commission but she is named in mine. If you wish, I can have it produced. I would simply add that, in addition to many skills, she is fluent in both English and French to an extent well beyond those who occupy this table. These negotiations are complex, requiring an understanding of direct speech and nuance. It is simply impossible for us to proceed without her."

There was a pause as Colbert's man turned to the members of the French team. One of them, Defos, gave a small, barely perceptible nod. "Very well," said Rolain. "Irregular it may be but if it is necessary, that is that. If she is indeed French then the matter is improved." Turning to me he suddenly spoke sharply in French. "Tell me Mademoiselle, what is the identity of the French King's mother?"

I did not deliberately dissemble for effect (as Pepys suggested later). The speed of the question had literally emptied my mind. There was a moment's pause whilst I was regarded with both concern and scepticism. Finally, I said: "Queen Anne of Austria, daughter of Philip the Third. Louis was born at the Château de Saint Germain-en-Laye. My grandfather was one of those invited to attend at the birth."

The courtier gave a smile as cold as fish. "Yes, I see. Well, that will do." Addressing Pepys he said: "I do hope you know which side she is on?" Without waiting for a reply he reached into a leather satchel and retrieved a written script, which he unfolded and read with clipped precision: "We are aware that the King of England requires substantial sums of money in order to govern the country to which he has been restored. The King of France is well disposed to provide such money but he cannot do so as personal charity. The sums involved are huge and there must be some real and perceived benefit to France and to the French people. The first benefit which lies within the hands of the English King is the toleration of the Catholic faith. That is not the subject of these negotiations. King Charles has already agreed to pass an Act of Toleration which would enable the practice of Catholicism without fear. The other benefit is more complex. The power of the Dutch increases every day. They threaten French and British interests in Europe and abroad. The French King and the government wish to eliminate this threat and to protect our vital interests. In protecting those interests we also, as we perceive it, protect the interests of Britain. We do not doubt that the French Army can master the Dutch in the field." He paused and on cue, Marshal Defos provided an energetic nod. "We have less trust in the ability of our Navy. Indeed, it would be fair to say that we have no trust or confidence at all in their ability to match the Dutch at sea." Again, on cue, the Admiral slowly nodded his head. "We require the assistance of the British Navy. If they can contain the Dutch in their ports, destroy them where necessary at sea and deny them the movement of men and supplies, then victory is assured. In those circumstances the financial benefits to France will be huge. They will far outweigh the assistance which is to be given to the King of England to pursue his noble ambitions in government. That is the simple logic of these politics and these negotiations. For the present, these must remain secret negotiations and if there is to be a treaty it must be a secret treaty. Funds themselves may be provided through numerous and trusted sources. The reasons for secrecy are the religious divisions within England and the conduct of negotiations unknown to its Parliament. Whether that provokes another Civil War is something that we, in France, cannot assess but it is certainly possible. So secret this must be."

Concluding his recital he folded the script, replaced it in his satchel and continued, "Now, to the matter in hand. We understand, Mr Pepys, the claims that are made for the power and the reach of the British Navy. We do not distrust those claims but we would be foolish indeed if we did not assure ourselves that they could be met and met in detail. That is why you gentlemen are here. It is not simply a question of the size of the Navy, it is the extent of its capabilities when operating alongside an army from France. All of these things are complex and are set out in the document we have already provided and which I see, Mr Pepys, you have on the desk before you. It effectively seeks assurances through detail. No one is better qualified, gentlemen, than you to carry out this exercise and I will now leave it in your capable hands."

So saying, he turned his heel and left the chamber silently through one of its four doors. We fell to the business. How it will be recorded by history is still unknown. Whether it was wise, tolerant governance by a monarch frustrated at every turn by those who would ultimately have had his head on the block or whether it was rank treason will, no doubt, form fertile argument for centuries to come. As we sat there on the 14th of May 1670, I had neither the knowledge nor the political experience to judge. I realised, however, that I had come to trust the instincts and the motivation of the man for whom I worked. I knew that he also was subject to conflicting forces, which were the inevitable product of the time.

We set to our task with diligence and skill. Long, tedious and time-consuming it certainly was. Pepys knew full well he was providing answers in a vacuum ignorant of the overall strategy to which they related.

"How quickly can you provide a blockade of Amsterdam? Do you have the logistics and supply chains to maintain such a position? You say that is the case but if you look at the answers you gave in relation to supply vessels it seems improbable?"

Whether the French military strategy would, in fact, require the blockade of Amsterdam or whether this was simply an exercise based on hypothesis we did not know and could not speculate. And so it continued. The scribes completed neat piles of vellum and my own notes extended over several pages. I knew I could not remove them from the chamber but found them essential for the order of the mind. Every hour we rose for five minutes to take some exercise and to allow the scribes some rest. From time to time one of the four doors into the chamber would open and unidentified visitors would occupy the backbenches for indeterminate periods of time. What did I contribute? Everything and nothing. Skilled in neither politics nor military science I could provide neither advice nor answers. For Pepys and, I think, for the French, my translation was invaluable. The capabilities of any organization, be it an army or a theatre, may be stated partly in fact, partly in statistics, and partly in hope. All of these are dangerous without knowing the subtle shades of meaning. The translation of statistics and capabilities into the realization of hope requires shades of meaning that may be lost in translations or unknown to the translator. In this regard I possessed a considerable gift bequeathed to me by my mother. I could think in both languages simultaneously, my mind working like an abacus along precise alternatives, near-indistinguishable, but essential in context.

"Camille, what exactly does that mean in French? No, I mean exactly. Ah, I see."

And so we progressed. By two o'clock we were exhausted and, by general agreement, parted for an hour. Pepys and I repeatedly crossed and recrossed an inner courtyard to which we had now been admitted. Food was available to us but neither felt the need for anything other than water and, in my case, lemonade. I estimated that we had barely completed a third of the agenda represented by the original French document. We were moving faster but days of detailed tedium lay before us.

The next session was, if anything, slower. The French Admiral was far from his youth. He was seventy at least by estimate and had, I suspect, sustained himself with some of the excellent brandy available from the palace cellars. His eyes began to glaze and, on occasions, resembled Pepys's own myopic stare. His was the detailed brief, and questions were repeated, answers misunderstood. At four o'clock I was, with hindsight, aware of the opening and closing of one of the doors and the occupation of three seats at the edge of my vision. Our visitors remained there for an hour, unusual in the circumstances. At the end of this time one of them rose and, followed at a distance by the others, approached our table. He came from behind Pepys and the Marshal noticed him first. Immediately he sprang to his feet and bowed from the waist.

"Your Majesty," he said, "we were not aware of your presence."

At the same signal, we all rose and instinctively followed the obeisance. The King of France smiled in response and gently waved his right hand: "Do not concern yourselves, gentlemen, Mademoiselle. My subtle entrance was entirely calculated. I wished to hear how my money is to be donated to my cousin Charles. It is so difficult to get the details without a measure of subterfuge. I now have the broad picture and I think I may save you some time."

With a wave of his other hand he indicated one of the remaining chairs, which was provided for him. He sat, arranged his elbows on the table, and smiled directly at me: "I have been listening with interest to your translation, if that is the right word. I should say interpretation was more accurate." I inclined my head and said nothing. "I see I am right. That is what is important. We need to understand each other's motives and each other's hopes and each other's expectations. These are far more important than statistical analysis. We have some clever statisticians in France including an exiled gentleman called Leibniz. None of them will win any battles, let alone any wars. They are won by hope and expectation and, above all, by the understanding of each other's hopes and expectations. We are all very grateful to you."

As he spoke I was able to examine his face. He was thirty-two at the time but appeared much older. Lines extended from his eyes as though someone had drawn a medical diagram to explain muscular contraction. He had a long aquiline nose, the hallmark of the Bourbon, but a wide and generous mouth permanently moving from smile to laconic disbelief. It was a face of weary humour and, I thought, no little wisdom. His movements indicated an economy of effort which contributed a sense of irony to a carefully considered delivery. "Mr Pepys," he said, "let me have some news of my cousin. We correspond, of course, but I do not entirely trust his assessment of his own wellbeing. His view is necessarily coloured. So, how is he? Does he fare well? How is Miss Gwynne? He sends me an interminable number of small paintings. They all look the same to me but obviously not to him."

"He is well, Sire, and his Court is well attended. He is popular with the people and still cheered wherever he goes. Miss Gwynne does not attend Court but I think he sees her often enough. It is a Court based on toleration."

"So I have heard and so it would appear. Your Great Fire has brought him fine craftsmen and architects, many of them from our own city. We could do with them back. The Royal Society flourishes I am told. When he was here he spoke repeatedly of the desire to blend the arts and modern sciences. It appears that he is succeeding."

No reply was required and Pepys remained silent. Louis scanned the back of his left hand. "And poets too, I gather. Poets and writers are kept in his Court. He is proud of them. He sent me some verses last month. They were apparently written by an aristocrat. I found them most peculiar. One was called 'A Ramble in St Charles's Park'. Have you read it?"

"I think, Sire, you will find that the title is 'A Ramble in St James's Park'."

"Ah, that was it: 'St James's Park'. It is a strange thing. I counted ten references to the pudenda in forty lines. My cousin told me that it was art. He said that it reflected the Spirit of the Restoration. I do hope that is not true. I have nothing against the word myself, properly employed, but it should not come to represent the spirit of an age. If that is indeed the Spirit of the Restoration I wonder why we spent so much time and money achieving it. Still, if it makes him happy. I suspect that the real problem is that he does not have enough to fill his time." The question was quietly delivered but obviously significant. The royal eyes were staring directly at Pepys's spectacles before he removed them and began to polish them on his cuff.

"Your Majesty, I fear, is right. He cannot govern because he does not have the money to do so. For that reason he is frustrated. He is supposed to rule but he cannot do so. I fear that this is deliberate. It is designed to provoke him."

"Do you think it will?"

"He has learnt the lessons of half a century as well as any. He has no wish to follow his father to the block but, more than that, he has no wish to plunge his country into another war from which it may never recover."

"Well said, Mr Pepys, well said." He turned his gaze to the ornate cornice. The question he asked was direct but invited reflection. "If he could govern, what would he do, do you suppose? I know a little of government and I have much practice. He has very little practice although it appears he has fine counsel. What would he do, Mr Pepys? What would he do?"

"Your Majesty asks a wide question."

"So I do, Mr Pepys, so I do," said the King, returning his gaze. "I ask a wide question and I invite a wide answer. I do not ask for municipal details, the mending of roads, the cleaning of streets. What will he do to ensure that his country is wealthy, happy and at peace with itself?"

"I do not speak with his authority but I am aware of his aspirations. First, I think he desires tolerance. That may be a condition of any grant that is made to him but he wills it in any event. He has seen intolerance at work and so have I. He sees religious toleration in the same stable as science and the arts, literature and poetry. The poems of the Earl of Rochester may not be to everybody's taste. They are not, incidentally, to mine, but they are free. They cause affront and offence but they are free. That is their value. Like hope, this cannot be easily calculated with statistics but it is an important part of his government. The second priority is, I think, linked to the first. The Commonwealth left many parts of Britain in a sad and deplorable state. Our great parks have fallen into decay. According to the Puritan Government they were places of licentiousness and sin. Perhaps there was some licentiousness and sin but for the majority of our people they were places of joy and recreation. They need repair, sustenance and stewardship. That, I know, is close to the King's heart. Finally, he is absorbed by education. The Commonwealth regarded this as a religious commodity and many of our classrooms taught the science of theology and not the theology of science. We urgently need reform. Teachers who will be trained and will embrace the true spirit of the age, the true spirit of the Restoration. That, I think, Sire, is how he would govern. I have spared you the municipal details as you asked. That is the broad brush he would apply to England if he were able to paint it."

There was silence for a while before Louis said: "You are an advocate Mr Pepys. You may not have been authorised to say what you have said, nor have you been briefed to do so but you have said it well nonetheless. Your King would be proud of you. You have rebuilt his Navy and now you may have gone some way to rebuilding his fortunes. If ever you tire of London, Deptford and Chatham, you would be welcome to assist in my endeavours. You may not get on with Colbert, very few people do, but, for all his cleverness he cannot run a Navy and sometimes, I think, he lacks . . ." We all attended upon the royal pause. "He lacks *vision*." He waved a hand as though pushing aside unwanted reflections and then pointed to the table. "So let us forget these facts and figures and all the frail hopes upon which they are based. Tell me, Mr Pepys, and I ask the question simply, can your Navy beat the Dutch?"

"I will give you, Sire, the answer I gave to my own King. The Navy can beat the Dutch if our commanders are good enough to do so. It is my belief that they are. We have bred a new strain. Our dukes and barons no longer leave their estates to command a battleship in the hope of prize and booty. Our captains are there for the duration and they are there for the Navy that they serve. That is my belief. It will be tested in any future conflict and my hopes, like my statistics, may appear pious. I do not think so and that is my honest assessment."

"Very well, Mr Pepys, tell your King he can have his money. The exact methods by which it will be transferred and then, no doubt, dissipated and concealed will be the work of Colbert and whomever you appoint for the purpose. That, I anticipate, will not be yourself. Your energies and your duties and your abilities will be required elsewhere. As I say, if you are attracted to Paris then we can arrange for your employment with the minimum of tuition in the *lingua franca* and, on that subject," he said, turning towards me, "may I return to the question which I posed to myself some time ago. Who are you and why do you have such mastery of our neighbouring tongues?"

The time elapsed had allowed me to compose my thoughts and my answer: "My name is Camille Lefebre. My father is French but my mother English. They met in England when she was acting on the stage."

"Really, how romantic. And I suspect she spoke English to you from birth?" When I nodded, he said: "The same attempts were made with me. My mother attempted to bring me up to rule the Austrian Empire. She failed I'm afraid but, your name, Lefebre, Lefebre? One of my Prefects is called Lefebre. Jean Lefebre."

"Your Majesty is entirely correct. My father is a Prefect and our district is Périgord."

"Périgord? How beautiful. The hillsides, the rivers, it is incomparable. I dare say such scenery exists in Britain but I doubt that it can be surpassed. Jean Lefebre, Jean Lefebre? Yes, I think I can picture him. He is a big man, yes? Strong?"

"Your Majesty has the right man." As I agreed the King had begun to frown.

"Lefebre? There is something else, something recent. Was there not a death? Your brother?"

"There was, Sire, barely a week ago."

The King was looking directly into my eyes and his own narrowed with concentration and thought. "Yes, now I remember." He turned away and said, "That, I think, concludes your business gentlemen. You must be grateful to me for relieving this tedium but I am grateful to you for the monumental efforts you have made." He rose and we all stood with him. Before he turned to go, he lightly took my arm. "Mademoiselle Lefebre, a word if I may." We walked some paces towards the benches at the wall. We did not sit but he lowered his face close to mine. "News of your brother's death has reached us. That is not surprising. Your father is one of our most respected Prefects. He was killed, was he not, by Édouard de Pertaine?"

I could not meet his eyes but stared at the cushions on the bench when I said: "He was, Sire, yes, he was killed at our own house."

"So I have heard. An act of revenge of some kind?"

Without shifting my gaze, I said: "So it is said."

"Camille." The surprise at hearing my given name caused me immediately to meet his eyes. "Camille Lefebre, let me give you some advice in return for the work you have done today. The family de Pertaine is as powerful and dangerous as any in France. Your brother's death disturbed me, not because I knew him or knew the background or wider justice of the case. It disturbs me that those who possess that power may use it with impunity. I am the most powerful monarch in Europe but, in truth, the control of families such as those tests my power to breaking. It concerns me that any of my subjects should be beyond the reach of the law, imperfect though that law undoubtedly is. Please ask your family to bear that in mind. Édouard de Pertaine is a dangerous brute. His father is little better. Weigh that well in considering any further action that you may take. I understand that Michel de Pertaine was killed in Paris. Pertaine has lost a son and so has your father. It would distress me to think that you or your fine family should suffer any further loss. Your father is valuable to me and to France.

From what I have seen today you may well become so. That is as far as I can go."

He turned abruptly and signalled to his two attendants and left the chamber. Behind him there was an almost universal exhalation of breath. The French Marshal, a soldier to his boots, lent forward to Pepys and said audibly in French: "Thank fuck that is over."

Pepys smiled. "D'accord," he said, "d'accord."

CHAPTER 24

We returned to our rooms and took our customary places across the table. We sat in silence. Anti-climax drained us both. Finally Pepys said: "Did we really succeed?"

I shook my head: "*You* succeeded. You were brilliant."

"No, what Louis said was right. I provided the facts, the raw material. You provided the interpretation. Without that we would have had nothing."

We both smiled and I replied: "Let us say *we* succeeded and have done with it." He nodded towards the diary folder which lay on the table before me. "Shall we complete that first? There is not much to say."

I laughed, opened the folder, dipped the nib and waited.

14 Mai 1670

Up betimes and to the negotiations with CB. France is represented by the Army, the Navy and a man from Colbert who could be neither. The process is long, tedious and factual. CB provides translation which adds meaning and purpose. The afternoon brings first tedium and then a shock. None of us observed the royal presence in the chamber. Le Roy Français surprised us all. There was much talk of Charles and of government. The strength of the Fleet was reduced to one question. Can the Navy beat the Dutch? I gave the answer I had already given to Le Roy Anglais. With good command and good luck we certainly can. I was asked to describe the nature of a future government if funds were provided. I set out my own priorities. In truth they are hope not expectation but they sounded well enough: the English countryside, toleration and education. These things pleased him and he wanted to know more. A treaty will follow and the money will follow the treaty. Secrecy is essential. There will be no record apart from this diary page which will remain, for the present, in France.

I raised my head and an eyebrow, which caused him to smile: "The pages will be safe here in the care of Alain and François. After the treaty is signed they may be brought to London. Let us conclude."

By way of diversion I have been offered employment in France. So has CB. I will not accept it and neither, I hope, will she.

He observed my head nodding above the page and let out a small sigh of relief.

After the business was over, Le Roy had some private discussion with CB. I have not been made privy to its contents and perhaps I never will.

He paused in expectation and I obliged. "He repeated his earlier phrase. He said you were a master of your craft and he approved your priorities for government particularly education. He repeated that several times."

Pepys smiled. "It is easily promised by those who seek power and money. Delivery is another matter."

And so, finally, tonight we will celebrate with the instruments and the bottle. We have achieved the means for a great government and that, for now, is enough.

Yes, it was emotional. We ate goose and figs for supper and consumed a great deal of wine. After the meal we took up the instruments and we sang, not well, but *con brio*. I was permitted to stay for the soldiers' songs and even joined in the choruses, to the evident delight of my friends. As we parted to our rooms we were all more than a little drunk but I stopped Alain before he reached his door.

"My friend," I said, "I need to speak to you tomorrow before you disappear into Paris. I know that we have two more days in these rooms but I have business that must be started tomorrow and I need your help."

He smiled with obvious enquiry but nodded his head. "I will wait for you in there," he said indicating our communal room. "I am curious indeed."

Pepys made no further overtures, for which I was grateful. I needed no distractions. Tomorrow, I thought, the final test will come.

To my surprise I slept well and late. By the time I left my room at eight o'clock Alain was waiting for me, seated at the table, drumming the surface with mild impatience. I apologised and he said: "It is nothing. I need some air that is all." I poured some water for us both and sat beside him: "Alain," I said, "I need to find Édouard de Pertaine." His face registered surprise and some alarm.

"Édouard de Pertaine! Do you know this man?"

"I do not know him but I know of him well enough."

"Do you know his reputation?"

"I think so. I think I know it very well."

"Then take what you know and magnify it to the end of your imagination. He is as bad as he is powerful. You do not want to meet this man, Camille. You do not want to come anywhere near his presence."

"I am afraid it is inevitable."

"Inevitable? Why? Why do you wish to meet Édouard de Pertaine?"

I took a deep breath and told the truth. "I am going to kill him."

"No!" Alain struck the table with his open hand. "No, Camille, you are not going to kill him. He will kill you. Several men have tried to kill Édouard de Pertaine, men far bigger, stronger and more powerful than you. They are all dead. Some dispatched slowly and in great pain. Of course he would be better dead and many would rejoice but why do *you* want to kill him?"

Again I told the truth. "He murdered my brother."

Alain's eyes widened and his mouth opened speechless before he said: "How? How did he murder your brother?"

"He beat him with a sword and then put a rapier through his throat."

"My God, you are serious. This is true?"

"As true as anything I know." He was silent for a while looking intently into my face.

"Camille, you must hear what I say. This is a brute of a man in every way. There may be better swordsmen in France but it would be difficult to find them. In duels he does not fight, he tortures.

278

He is widely detested but universally feared. Camille, he may have killed your brother but do not allow him to kill you too."

I remained quite calm and my voice was steady when I said: "Alain, I have no choice."

He shook his head violently from side to side. "No, Camille. I will not do this. I will not assist you to bring on your own death. We have become friends. I love and admire you, we all do. I will not be a part of this madness."

I leaned forward and took his hand still resting on the table. "Alain, I will find him. I will find him if I have to search every house in Paris. I will find him but that will take time, perhaps a long time. Inevitably he will learn that I seek him. When he does, then he will come looking for me. That, I wish to avoid. I have few advantages, surprise is one of them."

He was silent, shaking his head as though in pain. Finally he raised his eyes and said:

"Very well. I will discover where he is and where he may be found. This will not be difficult and, as you say, he would find you anyway. I will do this but only if you make this promise. You will spend the day considering what I have said. It contains nothing which is false or exaggerated. You will kill yourself as soon as falling from a bridge over the Seine with a block around your neck."

"Thank you, Alain. I will happily make that promise and I will keep it. If I change my mind then your enquiries will be wasted and you will be the happier for that."

"Bien sûr," he said.

We spent the day, Pepys and I, walking the gardens of the palace. Rose bushes mingled with peach trees and lilac. Great lavender bushes gave a heavy scent and a thousand bees clung to their purple stems. We found a small hill that supported a pillared alcove, a folly and a refuge. We lay on the bank and both drifted asleep to an insect lullaby. I dreamed of the Théâtre du Marais. I sat in a darkened box, the box where Michel de Pertaine had spent his last evening. I watched myself on the stage. I was anxious that my memory for the lines would fail. Unprompted I would stand silent waiting for ridicule and mockery. I wanted to cry out, to save myself from inevitable failure and disgrace. Suddenly, I drew a sword from beneath a cloak, which had fallen on me. I turned a full pirouette and thrust the sword at the box. Then, slowly, I advanced across the stage, which, impossibly, extended and rose towards the edge of the box where I sat. When the rapier came within feet of my face I attempted to turn, to run. I was held by a form of paralysis unable to move and unable to speak. I confronted myself and waited for the inevitable thrust. I closed my eyes and when I opened them I saw the pillars of the folly rising above my head against a clear, blue Paris sky. I had survived. The attempt to kill myself had failed. I did not change my position. The sound of the bees had now been joined by a steady insistent snoring coming from Pepys, lying content, mouth open, three feet to my left. The sounds compelled me back to sleep, dreamless as I now remember. When I next woke the sky was darkening into evening. Pepys had gone but I rose and saw him peering without his spectacles at a small plaque bearing the name of a flowering bush. As I watched him, he reached for his spectacles and, without putting them to his face, used a lens to examine the Latin script. He grunted and gave a nod of confirmation.

He was right and happy to be so. He heard me approaching behind him.

"It is a form of azalea. Rare but very beautiful in the spring. I had one but it died. I must replace it."

I did not pause and, on an impulse, kissed him lightly on the lips. It was not anticipated and, without his spectacles, he was unprepared. He stood back and he stared at my face with an expression of utter, simple happiness. Conflicting emotions battled within me. As he moved towards me I took his hand and said: "If you are not going to wear your spectacles, I will have to lead you from the gardens or you will be here for weeks." He let me do precisely that and when we reached our rooms, we stopped beside my door. His expression was unaltered when he said:

"Is it time?"

I shook my head: "Nearly. There is a matter to which I must attend. It is heavy on my mind. Pleasure and passion must wait."

He nodded slightly and asked: "Can I assist?"

"No, you have made enough conquests for one day. You do not need more."

I entered my room, and looked at the Paris skyline, now red with the falling sun. I heard a soft knocking on my door and when I pulled it open, Alain stood before me.

"Have you," he said, "kept your promise?"

I smiled. "Yes indeed, I have. I have thought of little else. You are a wise and a good man, Alain, but I have a purpose that cannot be avoided. Do you have the information I need?"

He sighed deeply before he said: "I have it. I am unwilling to provide it, as unwilling as I have ever been to provide anything. It

is information that I hope, even now, you will ignore and forget."
As I still waited he sighed again and said: "He dines tonight at
the Société Bleue. It is . . ."

"I know where it is. I have been invited there before. Perhaps
I should have gone."

"Think on what I have said Camille. Think long and hard. Life
is a beautiful and precious thing and yours more than most."

He turned on his heels and, seconds later, I heard his door
close. The time was barely seven and I had no appetite for food.
I opened the portmanteau and laid out the clothes of Robert
Lefebre. Beside them, on the bed, I set the rapier attached to
my leather belt. I returned to the window which I opened. I
took one long deep breath of the Paris air and set about my task.
I dressed slowly and methodically. I had a short mirror in my
room which I visited regularly during the process. I would be a
better, more convincing man than I had ever been. The codpiece
I rejected. Bravado I did not require. I listened at my door and, at
eight o'clock, I heard Pepys and the others assembling for dinner.
I heard the lute begin, playing his unmistakable signature.
I gathered the rapier to my side, slipped through my door and
then, unnoticed and unheard, into the streets of Paris. The last
time I had walked these streets as Robert Lefebre I had killed a
man. Now I went in pursuit of his brother.

CHAPTER 25

The journey was not far but I deliberately chose a circuitous route. This took me past the Théâtre du Marais. A performance of *Bérénice* was in progress. Who was playing the lead I deliberately did not ascertain. Tonight I needed no regrets. I walked the rue d'Essaye to the point at which Michel de Pertaine had died. Twenty minutes later I turned into the rue des Singars; the Société Bleue was distinguished only by the colour of the door. I found a bell pull beside it and heard the summons in the building. The upper panel of the door contained a grille and a hatch which opened almost immediately. Dark eyes peered through the metal and a voice demanded to know my name.

"De Pertaine," I said loudly. After a short pause the voice replied, "The Marquis is here."

"I am not the Marquis de Pertaine," I said. "I am his brother."

The pause lengthened before he said: "Michel de Pertaine is dead."

"I am not Michel de Pertaine. I am his youngest brother Pierre. How much longer are you proposing to keep me standing on this step?"

Two weeks had passed since my conversation with Michel de Pertaine in the rue d'Essaye but in my mind it could have been spoken within minutes. I had no difficulty in employing precisely the same accent and precisely the same intonation. I assumed it was a voice well known to the doorman at the Société

Bleue and I was right. I heard bolts being withdrawn. The door was opened and I strode through. The doorman, a big loutish man, stared at me, residual suspicion in his eyes: "You sound like your brother alright but you don't look like him. I thought you refused to come here."

"Not anymore," I said. "I have moved to Paris and I intend to join the Société at the first opportunity. Now where is my brother?"

"He is in the salon on the first floor. You can't take that with you." He indicated the rapier hanging from my belt and I nodded in agreement. I freed the hooks and he placed it upon a rack which contained several similar weapons. I had no cloak and was now free to mount the stairs to a landing from which two matching doors stood slightly ajar. Beyond them I could hear the sound of male voices and, as I stood there, combined laughter and the clapping of hands. I pushed open the door and entered the room. I would have known him without introduction. He was, indeed, a brute of a man, thickset and heavy-jowelled. A handsome face was distorted by a mouth permanently twisted in derision. He was seated facing the door with one of his companions. The other three sat opposite, their backs to me as I entered. Otherwise the room appeared deserted. It contained a number of leather chairs and sofas, two card tables and a fireplace in which logs were burning. At the sound of my entry the Marquis glanced up and then looked away and suddenly back to bring me into focus.

"My God," he said, "who the fuck is this?"

The man beside him looked straight at me and the other three turned for the same purpose. Of the four the reaction of two was identical. On their exclamations all five rose to face me. One of them exhaled loudly between open lips. Then he said: "I don't fucking believe it. It is Robert fucking Lefebre but he is dead."

Behind him the Marquis stepped forward and inclined his head: "Of course he is fucking dead. I put my blade straight through his throat. This man hasn't a mark on him. That is not Robert Lefebre so who the fuck are you?"

I felt an extraordinary sense of calm, a sensation that had occurred before in the Maison Legrange. I was watching myself on a stage speaking lines I had rehearsed on many occasions: "I am Robert Lefebre," I said in a steady voice, which caused a gasp from the one who stood closest to me. I repeated: "I am Robert Lefebre, son of Jean Lefebre, the Prefect of Périgord."

The Marquis moved forward, pushing one of them aside.

"If you are Robert Lefebre . . .?"

"Who did you kill? You killed my brother, sometimes called Robert Lefebre but christened Jean after our father."

The Marquis shook his head. "No, no, that cannot be."

"Oh, it is. Yes, it is. The boy you killed was my brother. He never left the Mas. He had nothing to do with the death of Michel. He was a poor, crippled boy, disabled from birth. He was barely able to hold a sword, let alone use it. You must have known that as you whipped and prodded him and thrust your sword into his throat. I killed your brother. I had no choice and your friends know it. They were there."

The face of the Marquis twisted with disbelief: "No," he said. "No, that cannot be."

"It is. You had no difficulty whipping and killing that poor boy. It was the kind of duel I hear you enjoy."

It was an obvious taunt calculated to provoke and I was ready for the rage I had seen in his brother. It did not come. My words were followed by a long silence. Deliberately he placed his glass on the table and tilted his head until he looked at me along his nose through hooded eyes. The lips smiled. It was a facial gesture of calculated, contemptuous cruelty from one about to enjoy the careful infliction of pain: "You know," he said softly, "that you are going to die?" When I did not reply he continued. "And do not expect me to make it easy for you as I did for your brother." Still I said nothing. I held his gaze as he slowly lowered his eyes. The smile disappeared before he said, "Name your time and your place."

I stared back, controlling my voice as if to an audience hushed in anticipation: "There is no need for delay. Tomorrow, six o'clock. The place you may choose as your brother did."

The smile returned: "Pas de Marche, Bois de Boulogne, six o'clock." He indicated the men on either side of him. "Pierre Rabonne, Patrice Moulin, my seconds and who are yours?"

This I had not expected. The etiquette of the duel was unknown to me. I dissembled.

"I will provide those . . ."

He interrupted. "No, that is contrary to law and custom. You must name your seconds at the time of challenge."

I was lost. Five pairs of eyes looked directly into mine. Before I could speak I heard an interruption from my right.

"We will act as his seconds," said a voice. "There is no need for introductions. If necessary you can take our names from the Société's register."

Two men had risen from the high-backed leather chairs that

stood before the fire. Both held glasses of brandy. They were both old. I assumed them to be well into their seventies and, as it transpired, I was right. They were of an age but there the similarities ended. One was very large. He now stooped with a slight deformity of the back but, in his youth, must have been a giant. The other, by contrast, was less than average height, slim and poised to the point of affectation. The face of the larger was raddled with lines that spoke of good humour and good living. The features of the other displayed careful maintenance. He had an unfashionable moustache and a small beard, neatly trimmed to a point. The Marquis eyed them with an obvious malevolence. But there was something else: if not fear, at least a wary respect. "This boy," he said, pointing directly at my face, "how is he known to you?" The larger one stepped forward, closing the distance between them to little more than three feet. Beside him, the size of the Marquis reduced before my eyes:

"That, I think," he said, "is our business and nothing to do with you or the little toads behind you. Now one of us has got to leave and I suggest it is you. We have some business to discuss and I wouldn't want you confused."

The Marquis squared his shoulders. "You old fart. Who do you think you are talking to? Don't answer that because you've probably forgotten and we were going anyway. If we had seen you in those chairs, we would have gone a long time ago. It is hot in here and we don't need smelly old dogs lounging round the fire." He nodded to his companions and they, with studied ill-grace, left the salon.

As he passed me the Marquis thrust his face into mine. "You be there . . ."

When they had gone I suddenly, desperately, needed a chair. As I swayed, the taller of my new friends placed one behind me and I sat heavily on the padded seat. "Thank you," I said. "Thank you very much." The older one spoke and, as he did so, held a glass of brandy under my nose.

"Here, take this. It is a pleasure. We do not like Édouard de Pertaine and he knows it. Anything that gets up his fat nose is good by us. Now, we have some duties to perform. First, is that your real name, Robert Lefebre or was it, indeed, your brother?"

"It is me," I said. "I am Robert Lefebre. It is as I said. My twin brother was a crippled boy. He never left our Mas."

"I see. And why did our disgusting Marquis wish to kill him or you?"

I told the truth. "I killed his brother Michel."

The smaller man let out a whistle of surprise. "So it was you? We have heard a little about this although the family did their best to keep it quiet. He attacked you in the rue d'Essaye, am I right?"

"You are absolutely right. I had no choice."

"Well," said my larger companion, "it appears that you may be tougher meat than you look. I was going to offer you a little training but, at my age, that might be very dangerous. Now, tomorrow, our carriage will be available to you and we will meet you in good time. Where are you lodging?"

"In the rue Saint-Honoré. I can be outside the palace at five-thirty."

"Let us make a quarter past. We will bring a surgeon. We should not rely upon theirs."

At the mention of a surgeon, for the first time I felt my nerve begin to crack. This was observed and the smaller man said: "The surgeon is there to heal you, not bury you. Pertaine is a pig of a fighter but he is getting old and fat. You look fit and if you can finish his brother, you can finish him. You will have done the world a double favour."

"Thank you," I said. "I am much in your debt. But now, may I have your names?"

They exchanged glances before the larger one said: "Let us keep this as formal as possible. We will do our job but then we will leave Paris. We meet here only once a year. It is a type of reunion."

"I see. Is it a celebration?"

"A celebration of a kind. We have shared memories. There were four of us but one, unhappily, is dead and another in a monastery, which is probably worse. If you need to refer to us I am Monsieur A. and this big fellow is Monsieur P. I think that will be sufficient for our purposes. When this game is over we will disappear back to our homes, which are far away. When you speak of us it will be as a fiction." He smiled as we all drank the remains of our brandy. We descended the stairs together. I obtained my sword from the rack and immediately inspected it for possible damage. Noticing my action, P nodded with approval: "Very wise. You are older than you look."

They remained talking to the doorman. I stepped into the rue des Singars and made my way back to the Palais Royal. I did not anticipate ambush or foul play. The identity of my seconds remained unknown but they were witnesses and, I already sensed, as valuable witnesses as a man or woman could wish for.

When I reached the Palais Royal I was admitted by the porter to whom I had already identified myself as a colleague of Mr Pepys. I climbed to our rooms. The corridor was dark. I found two candles burning as I closed my own door. There was no message and I was relieved. My mind was set. Any affection would bring weakness, and weakness I could not afford.

CHAPTER 26

They were early. As I stepped from the door of the palace I saw their carriage at the corner of the rue Saint-Honoré. My progress was watched from the rear window and as I approached the door opened and Monsieur A. descended to the street. He smiled, nodded and stood aside for my entry. Monsieur P. sat at the far side of the coach at the rear. On the bench opposite I saw our surgeon, a stern, bespectacled man with the inevitable leather bag. We were introduced and I sat beside Monsieur P. facing the front of the carriage. Monsieur A. resumed his seat, tapped smartly on the partition behind him and the carriage moved forward into the deserted Paris streets. As we travelled my companions rehearsed the elementary rules of duel and challenge.

"The boundaries will be marked," said Monsieur A. "But that is of little consequence on this terrain. Generally the extent is fifty yards so you will have much room to manoeuvre. The length of the duel is indeterminate and there are no formal courses. That only occurs when more than one weapon is used. That does not apply in the present case. The initial positions which you adopt may, if required, be decided by the toss of a coin. Otherwise it may be settled by agreement. Before the duel we will meet with his seconds to agree any specific limitations. If either party attains a position of total dominance, they may offer mercy and terms. That, I think, will not apply in this case. The Marquis de Pertaine has never been known to do so. If one party is completely helpless and overwhelmed they may seek quarter. That again, I suspect, has no relevance in this case. Only the duellists or seconds are permitted in the proscribed area. Surgeons may approach with the agreement of both. Weapons will be inspected at the outset. Following the duel, the seconds will meet to prepare a report. It should state that the contest was fair and in accordance with the law and the rules of amity. That is all, I think."

He turned to Monsieur P. who nodded and said, "I have nothing to add as to the law. I can tell you something about the ground itself. I know the Pas de Marche, although I have never seen it used for this purpose. In this weather the ground will be firm and the grass will be short. Until recently it has been grazed by sheep and is used for horses and recreation. We could have insisted on firmer ground. There are streets in Paris where it is still possible to arrange such contests. In my view the softer ground will be to your advantage. He is strong but you are lighter and, I expect, faster on your feet. On this ground he is likely to tire. You should make him do so. He has a fearsome temper. If he tires he will lose it. If he becomes wild you have a large enough area within which to manoeuvre. That is my contribution."

"I should add," said Monsieur A., "that the rules forbid the turning of the back for more than five paces. In other words, to put it bluntly, you cannot run away. I do not, for one minute, suggest that you might."

We relapsed into silence and, from the coach window, I watched Paris passing before me. The sky was a light slate blue. Against it, the russet roofs, the increasing trees – plane, lime and oak – set out their own contrasts. The air was cool and rich with familiarity. I thought I had never seen anything more beautiful. I had never felt more intensely alive. After twenty minutes we passed the early woodlands of the Bois de Boulogne and ten minutes later, turned onto a wide track. This led to a clearing and, beyond it, a handsome wide avenue cut through the trees extending the near horizon in the east. The Pas de Marche. The coach stopped and we all stepped onto the hard ground. I scuffed the grass with my boots. The grip was firm and I shifted my balance, rocking on both feet and then bracing my knees.

They had arrived already. A table with one chair had been set out fifty yards to the east. A court had been marked with white flags, in all some fifty yards square. Enough space to die in, or to live. One of de Pertaine's seconds raised an arm, which Monsieur P. acknowledged. Our own table was unloaded, together with a chair for the surgeon and, if necessary, for the reception of the disabled. Monsieur A. consulted a fob: "It is a quarter of the hour. Let us get this done." The two of them walked towards the de Pertaine party and, as they did so, his seconds walked to meet them. They met in the middle ground and a conversation took place. Immediately it concluded they split and each accompanied a member of the opposing side. Monsieur A. returned to us with the man known as Patrice Moulin.

"Inspection of the weapon," he said, indicating the rapier which I had placed on the table. This was drawn and given to Moulin, who grasped the hilt, ran his eye along the metal and then his finger along the edge. He stepped to one side and drew the blade through the air in three practiced cuts. He then moved forward at the thrust, focusing as he did so along his gloved arm. He grunted with satisfaction and handed it to Monsieur A., who placed it on the table in full view. He then left us and walked the distance to his own table passing, as he did so, Monsieur P. striding back to our position.

He was noticeably moving uphill. I had been surprised from the outset to notice that the position that my opponent had selected was lower on the slope. It provided for me an advantage, not important but significant. In particular the difference in height was diminished. I did not mention this to my companions. If positions could be by agreement then my agreement was assured. Monsieur A. handed me the rapier and said, "Some details. You should fight bare headed. The wigs provide no advantage for either side. You may choose whether to retain your jacket. He will retain his but you may do as you please."

"I will keep it," I said with emphasis. The morning chill was still evident and my body needed to be warm. Also, removal of the jacket risked revealing the corsetry essential for the shape of my male body.

Monsieur A. continued. "In accordance with the rules I must ask whether you are content with the court and the arrangements that have been made."

I nodded. "I am content."

"If you fall we need to know the identity of those who should be immediately informed."

I drew a deep breath. "Samuel Pepys," I said. "You will find him staying at the Palais Royal. He will then pass the news to those that need it."

There was nothing more to be said. I clasped the hands of both my seconds who smiled into my eyes. Whether they believed I would survive I could not tell, nor did they attempt to give the slightest indication. As we walked towards the middle ground, Monsieur P. muttered in my ear, "Make him move, you have the space. Make him move."

We met, more or less, precisely at the centre point. His mouth was twisted, as I had anticipated, in malevolent disdain. Even with the sloping ground he was a head taller and his bulk was increased by the wearing of the loose fencing jacket. The rapier was already in his right hand and he moved it in swift jerks, not the full cut but sufficient for the blade to sing through the morning air. I remained entirely still and met his gaze with as much composure as I could maintain. It was a pretence. Under my corsetry I felt my heart beat. Sensations of alarm ran down my back as though applied by a cold hand. My eyes remained fixed and my gloved hand, I was relieved to see, remained steady in the grip of my sword. I pictured Jacques before me, the best swordsman of his regiment. I had beaten him and I had beaten this man's brother. I could do it again.

Patrice Moulin was speaking into the air between us: "I will raise this handkerchief above my head and let it fall. During that time you will remain on guard. When it reaches the ground and not before, you may commence. The rules of mercy and quarter are known to you both and they will be observed." He raised his arm, paused and, from his extended fingers, the lace handkerchief floated slowly to the grass. We stood, on guard, ten feet apart, able at that distance to observe each other and the handkerchief as it fell. It struck the grass between us and we began.

At first we did not engage. Our bodies and blades moved through programmes of feint and gesture, calculated to observe the nature and speed of reaction. From this I could tell that he was very quick. His eyes moved continually and rapidly between my sword, my legs, my upper body and my face. Never still, they kept my entire movements in play. As I employed precisely the same process we tested each other without contact or attack. As we moved I was surprised that he made no attempt to alter our positions relative to the marked space. He held the lower ground. In his position I would have instinctively have moved to left or right to equalise the advantage. He did not do so and, for a full minute, we maintained our relative positions.

Then he came. It was sudden and fast. It began with a feint that he had made on several occasions. Unusually he began straight with the lunge, relatively easy to avoid. Then, as he closed, he began a series of cuts of increasing and substantial force. He was, as I had anticipated, using his much superior strength to exhaust my arm and wrist with repeated parry. It was anticipated and I retreated to achieve deflection. It is done with the smallest movements of the wrist. If done well it absorbs the attack without sustaining repeated shocks through the violent meeting of the blades. It also tires the attacker; the movement of the sword is increased rather than blocked. It strains the whole arm and, in particular, the shoulder. He persisted over a long and sustained assault. Thirty or forty times he cut and slashed and, as many times, I deflected the blow. I was moving steadily backwards but I had space in plenty. Finally, he paused. In the clear morning light I could see that he was red from exertion and anger. To increase the latter I raised an eyebrow in ironic enquiry. What, I was saying, are you going to do now?

Despite the danger and the fear, my own blood had begun to course. I saw his face twist with rage and he came again, slower, harder and with sustained control. This was more difficult. I found myself having to parry, sometimes at the upper end of the blade. If repeated often enough the effect can numb the muscles of the lower arm. I was now forced back close to the end of my ground and I needed to change my response. I dropped my body to the left side, managed a deflection of the answering thrust and then, with a sudden burst of energy, made my own attack. He did not expect it. He failed to anticipate a backward cut aimed at the head and was forced backwards, stumbling as he went. I followed, working the sword at the greatest speed that I was able. Lunge, cut, parry, lunge, feint and lunge again. His facial expression changed. It was not yet alarmed but had intense concentration.

This was a contest and now he knew it. From his face I believed that he also sensed something else. He saw in me the unshakeable, implacable, emphatic desire for total victory. I was my brother as he should have been. He knew this and I could see it in his eyes. Slowly I forced him back, beyond the middle ground. Again, to my surprise, he made no attempt to deviate from the centre line. I maintained the advantage of the slope, both balance and momentum. But I was also tiring. I had not practiced for many weeks. My arm was beginning to ache and my grip was beginning to fail. As we paused, staring at each other in the growing light, I realised that I could not win if the duel continued in this pattern. The repeated impact had taught me what I had been told. He was immensely strong and at least as good a swordsman as Jacques, the best I had known. As the contest continued, my advantages would become less when set against his clear superiority.

But I had my plan. It had worked well against the best and I trusted in it now. I set up the position. I feinted, deliberately mistimed a cut and allowed him to come forward, his rapier extended for the full sweep. I established my balance, felt the firm ground beneath the balls of my feet and swung in a full pirouette. As I did so I exchanged the hilt between my hands and faced him again ready at the thrust using my empty right hand.

As I turned I was instantly blinded. It happened very suddenly and was totally unexpected. In that split second, when I turned again to face my opponent, the top of the morning sun, huge and positioned precisely in the line of the Pas de Marche erupted into my sight. Momentarily I was quite blind. Instinctively I raised my right hand to protect my eyes and with that movement lost my balance. The thrust of my sword against an unseen target dissolved into thin air.

I immediately felt a stab of acute pain in my right shoulder. The cut that he had delivered inflicted a long wound above the muscle, from which I felt blood flow down my arm. The right arm was now instantly, completely, numb and I let it fall to my side. Without it I was looking again straight at the rising sun.

Purblind I turned to see him preparing another assault. He moved to his right, which caused me, again, to look directly to the east. I did not see the thrust coming but felt a sudden intense pain, adjacent to the armpit and through my right breast. I heard a grunt of exertion as he pulled his blade clear. As he stepped back, I saw it was red and dripping for half its length. He stood back and I saw that he had begun to smile. He raised his left arm and made a beckoning gesture with his gloved hand. He waved his rapier, unmistakably drawing me down towards the inevitable thrust. I remained stationary and he raised his eyebrows and shook his head with exaggerated sadness. "Not coming on then, eh?" he said softly. "Not coming on? Just like your brother, fucking useless."

I realised that he was playing with me in more than words. With his back to the sun he could see exactly where his shadow passed. If he stood before me, it fell on my face and I was able to see. If he moved aside, I was again blinded. My right arm would not move to provide a shield and my left still gripped the sword: "Can't see, can we then? See about this then?" He moved to his left, exposed the sun and, in the same second, I felt a searing pain in my left leg. I dropped my head to see his rapier being ripped back from the front of my leather breeches. A gout of blood followed its process. I knew, immediately, that I could not move. Any attempt to use my leg would simply result in my falling to the ground, a position even worse than my present helpless state: "There," he said, "I expect that hurt, didn't it? Well, try this." The forward cut flashed through the air and struck the upper part of my left arm. It was a savage blow but ill-timed. His enjoyable cruelty had made him reckless. It struck the leather, which braced the shoulders and the pain it caused could, for the moment, be endured.

But I had nothing left. Unable to move, to shield myself or barely lift my sword, I was, I knew, completely finished. I kept my eyes on his face. I thought, even then, that I would not give him the satisfaction of bowing my head and falling to my knees. His expression changed. The disdain returned and he drew his right arm back from his shoulder. The point of the sword was now aimed directly at my face and I waited for the end.

I then saw a flash of light across his face. It was quite sudden and intensely bright. As it struck his eyes he delivered an immediate curse and instinctively raised his left hand to shield them against the blinding effect. After a second he removed his hand but the flash came again, straight into his eyes, which blinked before he, again, lifted spread fingers in front of his face. I had but one moment. My left arm could still function and with a massive concentrated effort I withdrew it at the shoulder, took aim, and thrust at the base of his glove. My blade passed clean through the leather. That resistance made it impossible to tell whether it struck any other surface or passed into space beyond. That was all I had. My hand fell from the hilt and dropped to my side. My rapier remained where it was left, apparently suspended in mid-air, the wrist piece of the glove remained impaled half-way along its length. I closed my eyes for a second. When I opened them I saw his left hand fall to his side. As it did so the glove remained skewered and suspended before his face. Slowly, the weight of the finger parts caused it to rotate. As it turned I saw that my rapier had passed clean through the glove and into his throat. His eyes were open and his lips were drawn back from his teeth. His sword remained in his right hand and I saw his arm jerk with the effort to lift it. It rose barely two inches before it fell from his grasp. I watched his eyes close and then with gathering speed he fell forward onto the grass at my feet. As the hilt of my sword hit the ground the blade was driven upwards, projecting near full length from the back of his neck. A fountain of blood rose up and fell back.

I felt my senses leaving me but I heard voices before me and saw his seconds approaching: "Alright," one of them said, "let's have him then."

I heard another voice at my left shoulder: "Oh, I don't think so," said Monsieur A. "I don't think so at all. The duel was fairly fought and your man lost. That is the end of it."

They stopped directly before me. The man called Pierre Rabonne raised his voice: "It was not fair. He was blinded. I saw it. He was blinded by that fellow there." I turned, with difficulty, to follow his pointing arm. Behind me Samuel Pepys was standing ten yards distant. His head was bowed and he was engaged in the energetic polishing of his spectacles. Pierre Rabonne continued, "He's got a mirror. I told you, he's got a mirror."

Monsieur P. stepped forward. "He has not got a mirror, you fool. He was wearing spectacles. If you want to come with me I will show you." I watched them both cross to confront Pepys and saw him hand the spectacles directly to Rabonne. He looked at them with exaggerated care and held them up against the sun. As he did so, I saw the reflected flash dance against the green of the trees. Rabonne handed them back and joined his companion.

"He's right, spectacles, that's all they are."

"And," observed Monsieur A., "speaking of the use of the sun, I do not think that there is much that you can say. It may have been strictly lawful but it was trickery nonetheless."

Four men glared at each other but Monsieur A. continued: "We have no further business here. You must get rid of your body and we must care for our man. He is about to fall and I would not want him impaled on his own blade. We will meet you gentlemen at twelve in the salon of the Société Bleue. We have a report to make for all our sakes."

When he finished speaking I felt consciousness begin to leave me but I did not fully pass out. Strong hands took hold of me and

I saw that Alain had also joined our group. I was carried to the coach, laid out on a bench and the surgeon took charge: "At the end," he said, "I counted four inflicted wounds. Two slashes to the upper arms, a thrust through the right chest and one through the left leg. Does that accord with your view gentlemen? I do not wish to be searching for non-existent injury."

Monsieur P. nodded. "That is what I recollect."

"Good. Then let us to business. We may still be too late to save him." The surgeon withdrew a knife and I felt the jacket being cut from me. The shirt was then ripped away revealing both the wounds and my corsetry. I heard the surgeon's intake of breath: "My God. Do you see that? This is a woman!"

Above him I heard Monsieur P. speaking quietly across the carriage, "Yes, we suspected as much. Something in the voice and the unreasonable persistence."

"Help me," said the surgeon, "release this thing."

He examined all three injuries to the upper body, concentrating on the thrust through my right breast and into the base of the arm. "This is deep," he said, "and may be serious. The others may be painful but are not dangerous. I will apply what medicaments I can and bind it. There is little else I can do. It must be kept clean and that arm must be immobile. Now let us look at the leg."

I felt the breeches being cut from me and a further exhalation of breath. I was now in a sitting position and with some regained consciousness. I was able by only the movement of my eyes to inspect my own wound. It was a ragged gash and blood pulsed from it as though boiling below the surface. The surgeon raised his head.

"It looks bad but it is not as dangerous as the other. I think it has only just passed through the muscle. Again I will pack it with medicament and bind it. There is little more that can be done. As with the chest it must be kept clean and should not be moved for at least two days."

I remember I felt a deep and sudden fatigue. I was empty; there was no joy, elation, fear or trepidation. I closed my eyes and knew nothing more.

CHAPTER 27

When I awoke I was in bed in my room at the Palais Royal. My chest and leg were tightly bound with linen bandage. A strong smell of mixed medication filled the room. The wounds, themselves, caused little direct discomfort until I began to move. I lay still and listened for sounds of my companions. When they came, they came all at once. I heard them in the corridor through my closed door and awaited their arrival. I had no clock but the view from my window and the temperature told me that it was evening. As they approached my door I heard muffled conversation, *sotto voce* and whispered, before the door was silently opened and François' head peered round it, scanning the room, before he located my bed.

"Ah," he said. The head disappeared and I heard him speak to others. "Alive and, I think, ready to receive her guests." The door opened and they all came in: François, Alain, the Alderson brothers, Pepys, Monsieur A. and Monsieur P. I had three chairs, occupied in seniority by Pepys, A. and P. I indicated the end of my bed, on which François and Alain settled. The Aldersons, they said, preferred to stand. One of them briefly left and reappeared with a bottle of brandy and a stack of cups.

"This," he said, "is the only liquor you are allowed. Fortunately we have a lot of it. The King, himself, apparently sent a case this morning. It is the Bourbon's best and we ought to drink it." Cups were poured and the inevitable toast was drunk.

"Camille Lefebre," said François.

"No," I said, intervening to their surprise. "Robert Lefebre."

"Ah, yes," said Monsieur P. "Robert, Robert Lefebre." We all drank and the cups were refilled whilst I was given the necessary news.

First this came from Monsieur A. "We have been to the Société Bleue. We met Rabonne and Moulin as arranged at twelve o'clock. By this time they had become surprisingly agreeable. Indeed the atmosphere in the Société Bleue resembled a national celebration. It was getting quite out of hand so our business was conducted in one of the bedrooms. They had decided that there was no complaint and our joint report recorded a fair duel resulting in the death of one participant and serious injury to the other. The duellists were identified as the Marquis de Pertaine and, then, I am afraid, there was a problem. His adversary was identified as Robert Lefebre and accepted to be so. The problem was that Robert Lefebre is dead. Moulin and Rabonne knew this full well because one of them, Rabonne, had been present when he was killed. Enquiries at the Société, among its members, revealed the fact that Robert Lefebre had been buried at Ribérac and that his father, the Prefect of the Périgord, had spoken the eulogy. It was suggested, of course, that this was a brother. But those that knew the family indicated that there was no brother. There was a sister, thought to be an actress, who was in London in order to follow her profession free from the irritating edicts of the Paris Municipality. What were we to do? The report had to be presented to the Magistrate in order to ensure that there was no inquiry and no prosecution. Some of those drinking at the Société suggested, unhelpfully, that this was some kind of spirit, a vengeful ghoul adopting the guise of the deceased, Robert Lefebre. It was pointed out that whereas those from the spirit world may be quite capable of inflicting death or injury, it is unlikely that they would allow themselves to be stabbed and lashed in the process."

The general laughter that followed was interrupted by my own gasp of pain. I immediately waved away concern: "It is nothing. Laughing is difficult but don't stop."

Monsieur P. took up the account. "We settled on the phrase 'one said to be Robert Lefebre but thought to be otherwise'. By the time we got to the Magistrate he was, of course, well aware of the death, indeed, there is scarce an attic in Paris that is not vibrating with the news. He was far more anxious about possible public disturbance than ascertaining the identity of the man who had rid us of a serious, persistent and exceedingly powerful criminal. The report was accepted and that is the end for the law. Whether the Duc de Pertaine will prove as accommodating remains to be seen. With that, I am afraid, we cannot assist. We would like to do so but our age denies us the ability to engage in such adventures. I think that our work is now done. We have paid the surgeon and," he said, lifting a hand before protestation, "are delighted to do so. We both enjoy swordplay and, in our youth, thought ourselves mighty proficient at it. To that extent it was a pleasure to watch the duel, although a great sadness to see the wounds inflicted on our young friend. While you were unconscious," he continued addressing me directly, "the surgeon was able to take certain . . . 'liberties' with your person and has explored your wounds in detail. He is confident that you will recover. They must be regularly cleaned and you must rest for two days. I understand that your time in the Palais has been extended and there is a young lady, an aspiring maid called Roxanne, who says she will be delighted to dress your injuries on a daily basis. She says you are a talented actor, although where she receives this information is unknown."

He turned to Monsieur P. with an enquiring glance, drained his brandy and they both nodded in unison. "Our work, I think, is now done. We will spend the night at the Société, which should be enjoyable if the present celebrations continue. I have no doubt that the health of Robert Lefebre will be drunk even more enthusiastically than it has been in this room. Tomorrow we will return to the country." He raised his arm again in order to stop my interjection. "Please do not thank us now nor attempt to discover our whereabouts in order to do so. We are," he said, talking directly to Pepys, "as your famous playwright would say, 'such things as dreams are made on'. We will leave now and it will be as though we had never been."

As they reached the door I called out, "I will thank you messieurs whether you wish it or not and I would wish you to stay but as you can see I have good friends and I am in good hands."

"Ah," said Monsieur P. "How do we put it? Let me think . . . 'All for one' I think. That's it, 'All for one.'"

As the door closed behind them there was silence broken by the sound of the brandy bottle being applied by Ian Alderson.

"Extraordinary," said Pepys. "That they should simply have appeared in that way when they were desperately needed." I nodded, sipped my brandy and turned to my employer.

"How did you . . . ?"

"How did we know where you were fighting your duel? At dinner last night Alain told me that you were going to the Société Bleue to confront Édouard de Pertaine. I came after you but by the time I arrived you had left. The doorman was an irritating and difficult man but one gold *livre* was enough to elicit the time and the place of your confrontation. He had overheard the exchange in the salon. Indeed, I think, it was known to most of the Société. When we got back last night you were already in bed. We had a meeting. We decided that we could not possibly stop you and that any attempt to do so would simply weaken your position and your resolution. It was decided that Alain and myself should follow you to the Pas de Marche. Our coachman took the wrong turning and we were later than anticipated. We arrived barely in time to see the final stages of your fight."

With a slight grimace of pain, I turned to face him directly. "Did you . . .?"

"Did I deliberately blind Édouard de Pertaine? That is not entirely easy to answer. Watching the duel I realised that you had lost and I also realised the reason why. The rising sun was a torment for my weak eyes. For that reason I removed the spectacles and noticed immediately the reflected light. I would like to say that it was a skilful device but it would be difficult to do so. Without my spectacles I am quite blind and could scarcely see where you were standing, let alone the face of Édouard de Pertaine. I think I did my best and the rest was good fortune. Like our departed friends, I ask and deserve no thanks."

"And," I said, raising my cup to him, "as with them, you cannot avoid it."

A silence fell until I said to François, "Is it correct that we have our rooms for two days?" He smiled. "Yes, indeed, I have that authority from the King himself. I am due to return to my duties with his guard and I spoke to him on that subject. He was already aware of the main news. Colbert has many spies. Some of them no doubt disguised as trees in the Bois de Boulogne. It was then that the King ordered the brandy that we have been drinking. He has asked me specifically to send you his best wishes and to thank you for ignoring his advice."

I smiled. "This is becoming something very close to a conspiracy. I think it is better not recorded." I saw Pepys nodding as I struggled to lift my right arm from the bed. "I can do nothing with this for some days. I can fence and drink with my left but, I am afraid, cannot hold a quill."

He laughed. "My own day was barely eventful. Certainly it need not trouble posterity and it is, after all, *my* diary."

Supper was brought to my bed but Roxanne fussed about me, rearranging my pillows and my blankets. "You should be on the stage," she said. "Not fighting in the woods, then you wouldn't get into this state. I will be back to wash those after your supper."

Whether she came that night I do not know. I barely touched my food, finished my brandy and returned to a deep sleep. I remained in my bed for two further days. My friends and my visitors came and went. The spinet was moved into my room and, when I finally left my bed, I managed a passable duet using my left hand. By the third day I could walk with some difficulty and held my right arm firmly strapped in a sling. I sat at the table with Pepys after a good lunch and discussed the future.

"I have made arrangements," he said, "for you to travel to the Périgord. Your parents were hellbent on a journey to Paris but I sent word that you would, inevitably, wish to spend some time at your home, not least to visit the grave of your brother. Their journey will, therefore, be superfluous. It will take two days to reach Périgord. In your condition the coach cannot travel at any speed. You are to meet them at Saint-Étienne. Rooms have been booked in the Hôtel de France. You may then continue your recovery. I hope that I anticipate your next question and I will answer it immediately. The answer is 'No.' I will not come with you, much though I would like to meet your parents and to see your estate. I wish to spend some time in Paris in the office of Jean-Baptiste Colbert. The French Civil Service is an infinitely better machine than our own and I want to find out why. He is making France a prosperous and industrious country despite his master's predilection for war. There are secrets here that I wish to discover. If I have time I would like also to visit Fontainebleau and Versailles. That is a personal odyssey and it is better done alone. I will return to Paris and, on the 27th of May, will leave for London." He paused and stared fixedly at the window. "I would, of course, wish you to be with me for a number of reasons all of which you know."

I waited until he had transferred his gaze and said, "I will be in your coach to London. I will bring all of my possessions except for the clothes of Robert Lefebre and his rapier, which will remain wherever it has now been discarded. I will also be somewhat poorer. I will return much of my gold coin to the Théâtre du Marais. I have never provided the services for which it was paid." The happiness I read in his face caused me to catch my breath and I rose abruptly from the table, wincing as the weight fell on my left leg.

"So, let us about our business. When does my coach depart for Saint-Étienne?"

"Tomorrow at dawn, if you agree."

He rose and crossed to the spinet, now returned to its rightful room. His fingers flew over the keyboard and *Vertes Manches* filled the room. I could not play but I could still sing and we sang it together before I returned to my room to pack my belongings. Before I did so I said, "There is one journey that I must make before I leave Paris. It is, of course, to the theatre. Alain will, I am sure, go with me in our coach; otherwise I think I will go alone."

He nodded. "I am, myself, invited to Colbert's table. Miserable, thrifty experience I am told that it is but I must go. We will say goodbye to each other tomorrow morning. Your coach leaves at six. You have a long and slow journey."

At four o'clock, Alain and I made the short journey to the Théâtre du Marais. I had not told them of my arrival. I limped through the foyer, waving to the surprised doorman who smiled and touched his cap. I walked through the passage behind the boxes and found the office of Paul Detain. He was sitting at his desk. When I entered he cried out, raced across the small room and seized me in both his arms. Only when he heard me yelp in pain did he notice the sling below my light cloak: "Camille, you are injured?"

"Yes, Paul, I am injured but I am alive and I am well and I am safe and I am happy beyond measure to see you. Is it only two weeks since we drank together that first night?"

"Two weeks and one day," he said gently leading me to a seat. "Camille, I know much of what has happened. The day after you left, the de Pertaine family came to the theatre. They came in strength looking for Robert Lefebre. By then I was aware of the fight in the rue d'Essaye. They said it was murder but, of course, absolutely nobody believed it. I did not tell them your true identity. I thought it best at the time. I simply said that you had been playing the female lead, that you had given your notice. They asked for the address of your lodgings. I gave them the wrong address knowing that they would return. They did and I directed them to the rue Feuillette knowing that, by then, you would have made your escape. I have been in agony since as to whether I took the right action."

I smiled, lent forward and placed my left hand over his. "What you did was exactly right and, yes, you gave me time to get to England. I am very grateful. None of us could have foreseen that they would pursue my poor brother or that anyone could possibly take their revenge on him. The man who killed him is now dead which you will learn if it has not already reached you."

He lowered his eyes and nodded his head. "Yes, yes. It has. Paris is full of speculation but I think it will remain just that. I hope it will." He then looked at me urgently across the desk. "Camille," he said. "Camille, come back. Please come back. The edict has been rescinded. You may return as Camille Lefebre, the great actress that you are. Robert Lefebre is dead but your renaissance is desperately needed for this theatre, for Paris and by Molière himself, who groans about your absence every day that I see him."

I kept my hand over his and said: "Paul, I cannot, not now. Perhaps one day but it will be a little time."

"Have you work in London that you need to finish?"

I nodded. "Yes, in a way, I have. How long it will keep me I do not know but I know that I must return to England."

He shook his head. "It is a terrible pity Camille, a terrible pity. We have auditioned for the first Molière play and all the parts were filled. However, the end of the edict has meant that we must audition again. That is for female parts. The male parts are already filled. We audition again in two weeks' time. Camille, it is your part. He *wrote it for you.*"

Again I shook my head. "You are making this difficult for me Paul but I will not change, *cannot* change."

He made an exaggerated gesture of acceptance. "Well, so be it but if you go, do not go for long."

"One other thing," I said, withdrawing my hand. "I have gold coin which belongs to you and the theatre. Much of it I have with me here in Paris and it will be returned to you tomorrow morning. The remainder I will send from London. I had to take it with me. If it had remained at my lodgings it could have increased the wealth of the Marquis de Pertaine."

He waved his hands in exasperated refusal. "Keep it, keep it. I know you are not here but the reputation of the theatre has been immeasurably improved. Molière would not have written for us without you. He would still be churning out plays at Versailles or the Palais Royal. Also, I hope, it will bring a deep sense of guilt. We want you back and I want you to feel guilty until you return."

I smiled. "Paul, I will have none of this, good though it is to hear. I have a new security in London and it is a great security indeed. The money will be returned whether you like it or not. If you do not accept it I can think of several institutions that will. They are dedicated to impoverished thespians of which there are thousands." I rose and he followed me.

"Oh very well. Send it if you must but keep what you need. Do what you have to and then come back." Before I opened the door, he said: "This will be a very good production. We have cast the male leads and we have some fine, fine players."

I raised an eyebrow. "Anyone new?"

"One or two but most of all we have a great return. He has not played on the Paris stage since he was caught frigging Dubarry's wife blacked up as Othello, a fine theatrical moment but it cost us a great talent. Anyway, Dubarry is no more and he is back."

I was stock still and staring at Detain. "Do you mean," I said, "Jacques Delaine?"

"Of course I do. Jacques Delaine. Do you know he is even better than he was? Resting for ten years does wonders for the artistic temperament."

Half to myself, I said: "Jacques Delaine has been here, has auditioned in this theatre?"

"No, has been here and is here still. He is rehearsing on the stage. Molière has just left and gave him some new lines with stage directions. He is working on them now."

"Now?" I said. "On the main stage?"

"Yes, yes he is. Camille? Are you alright? Do you know him?"

"Would you mind, Paul," I said, "if I was to sit in one of the boxes? Perhaps the one nearest the stage, from which they threw the chicken. I would like to see this great actor."

"Of course Camille. I will come with you."

"No Paul. I will go alone. I know the way to the box and I assume it is unlocked?"

"It is indeed," he said. "Leave when you wish but not for long."

I felt weaker than I had since I waited for my death in the Pas de Marche. I limped along the passage to the boxes, silently opened the door of that nearest the stage and sat in the very seat where, I suspect, Michel de Pertaine had sat the night I killed him. Jacques Delaine stood on the centre of the stage. He had changed little and his movements, once known to me so well, were precisely the same. He was working a range of facial expressions, reading *sotto voce* from a manuscript. I pressed myself towards the back of the box, beyond his sight lines but able, myself, to watch his performance. As I watched he went into full declamation. He recited the lines, a short soliloquy, with comic gusto. His timing, even without an audience, was exact and precise. He employed imaginary props, no doubt signified in the stage directions. One, a bucket I think, he raised above his head, majestically revolved and threw into the wings. "Fin," he said smiling towards an empty auditorium. From the back of the box I started a slow and emphatic applause. It was difficult. My right hand was still caught in the sling but I managed nonetheless. He gave an exaggerated start of surprise, then called to the empty boxes, "Merci, merci mon ami. Qui êtes vous?" I walked from the back of the box and stood facing the stage. He remained frozen in theatrical gesture. "Camille," he said. "Camille, is that you?"

"Yes Jacques, it is, it is me. Now what are you doing in my play?"

He did not reply but ran to the far side of the stage where temporary steps led down to the auditorium. He ran across the front of the seats, leapt onto one and jumped the six feet to the edge of the box. His arms locked over the velvet ledge and he hauled himself up and beside me. I had not moved and we stood inspecting each other's faces from a distance of barely six inches. He spoke first: "Camille, I have . . ."

"Yes, you have a part. I know. I have been speaking to Paul. You have returned to the Paris stage and I am very glad. And now you can tell me why you left my life."

He sat heavily on one of the front chairs and spoke lines which I suspect he had rehearsed for years.

"There was no choice. After we loved each other you spoke of my stewardship of the Mas. That was impossible. I have neither the ability nor the aptitude nor the desire to own and manage land. It would have been a disaster. Also it would have dispossessed your brother. It would have guaranteed great love and abject unhappiness. When you left that evening I did not sleep. It was not until the morning that I made my decision. I travelled with little enough and departure was physically simple. In every other way it was a torture beyond telling."

I stood above him, anger in my voice. "Why no letter? Why no note? No word in seven years!"

"Would it have helped? No, it would not. What could I say? 'I love you to distraction and that is the reason I must leave? I wish desperately to live my life with you but cannot live where you live?' I am an actor, Camille, and a little of a politician, that is my vocation and my calling. I could never be a master of a Mas and you must know it now. Had I told you then you would

316

have come with me and I could not have stopped you. You would have come with me to Paris, to anywhere I could work and you could work with me and that would have destroyed your life, your parents' life and the life of your brother. None of this could be. So what could I write? I started. In the hours before dawn I started twenty letters, all utterly inadequate. Best, by far, that you should think of me as a rogue, a debaucher, a carnal villain. Better that you should hate the memory and then forget it."

"My God," I said, laughing despite myself. "You are an actor aren't you? I think you'll do very well here. Paul Detain thinks you are pretty good. If you can keep your hands off Mademoiselle Dubarry you might even join Paris society."

He was smiling as well. "Are you recovered from me, Camille? Before you answer that let me tell you that I am in no way recovered from you. Not a week, not a day has passed without my mind recording those last days as though I was Molière writing and rewriting the final scenes which I have here." He waved his papers in the air. "He can do it. These characters, brilliant as they are, belong to him. Their lives he can change, bend, alter. Their loves and their proclivities can be reworked, fine-tuned for his pleasure and our delight. I have done it with us a thousand times. The last act has been changed, rewritten, revisited. The words have been changed, mauled, omitted altogether in the search of some new ending, some new dénouement where we lived side-by-side, had children and grew old. I am creating a theatre, a comedy, a tragedy. None of it is real, only what happened is real."

"Did you ever wonder . . .?"

"Whether you had become pregnant? Yes, indeed, I did. I knew you had not."

My eyes widened. "How did you know?"

"Your mother told me. Yes, don't look so startled. I was in contact with your mother. She knew what I did and what I was doing. She did not entirely approve but she did not disapprove either. She knew very well that if you were pregnant I would return. We have corresponded regularly, three, four times a year. I know what has happened to you Camille until, that is, your departure from this very theatre. Now, may I ask, why is your arm in a sling? Have you fallen from a balcony ordering your Roméos to climb over your balustrade?"

I smiled. "No, I have not fallen from a balcony. I have been repeatedly stabbed with a rapier by a man whom I subsequently killed."

Now, years later, I have to confess that it gives me great pleasure to record those words and to recall the shock on his face: "What did you say?"

"Do not worry Jacques. I am perfectly safe and nothing will come of it but I should tell you that what you taught me has undoubtedly saved my life. Ruined and saved by the same man. I think that has happened before in a thousand theatres."

He was silent for a long while before he said, "Camille, come back. Come back to the stage, to this theatre. They need you and have been waiting for you. Paul and Molière talk of it every day. I knew it was a possibility when I auditioned and I auditioned in part because of that very possibility . . . no, not in part, entirely because of that possibility. Come back. Let us act together."

For the second time in half-an-hour and for the same reason I held out my left hand to end the entreaty. "No Jacques. I have already told Paul. I will return to London where I am safe and where I am needed."

"You are needed here."

"No Jacques, I am not needed here. Certainly I am wanted. Need is too big a word. Now, my dear, I am going to leave you. This has been painful but I feel better about you than I have for seven years. You were right. You left me after you loved me, which has its callous side. However, if you ask me whether I would have rejected you knowing that you would go the following day, the answer is no. Not then and not now. Don't get up. I do not want a long and difficult goodbye. Besides that my leg hurts and I need to get back to my coach. Oh yes, that too was a rapier thrust. You didn't teach me quite enough to avoid them." I kept my hand on his shoulder to ensure that he did not rise then turned, left the box and limped as fast as I could to the coach, where Alain was waiting.

CHAPTER 28

I met my parents as arranged in the salon of the Hôtel de France at Saint-Étienne. The meeting was, as you would expect it to be. A joy. At first we spoke little, as though by common consent the events of the past two weeks were placed in abeyance, postponed until ephemeral matters had established our old perspectives. The proprietor of the hotel was known to my father and we dined well. Perfectly devilled eggs were followed by braised duck, the local specialty served with oranges and sweated leeks, a syllabub and then a fine, strong cheese. We drank champagne and two bottles of the local wine. My parents drank brandy after the meal. I had consumed enough of the Bourbon cognac and declined. Unbidden, the proprietor opened a further bottle of champagne and it was well gone midnight before we climbed to our rooms.

Over the meal I told them everything as I have recorded. I stopped short of my visit to the Théâtre du Marais. I did not want to be pressed on questions for which I had no answer. My mother revealed that she had not corresponded with her sister in London for several years but was still shocked by the zealous adoption of the Puritan cause.

I had feared that the death of Robert would be a dark shadow between us. I was wrong. The extent of his illness and his likely expectation of life had been unknown to me. For my parents it was a mitigation. The death of the Marquis de Pertaine was an expiation. My father spoke his mind: "Had I known of your intentions I would have done everything in my power to stop you. Now I delight at the result."

I told my father, in particular, of the conversation with the King. When I came to his own reputation and the royal regard in which he was held, he shook his head in disbelief but coloured with pleasure. My father had consumed too much brandy and was the first to his bed. I sat alone with my mother drinking wine. I put the question directly without preamble: "Why," I said, "did you not tell me that you have been in correspondence with Jacques?"

"Ah," she said. "So you know. I thought you would find out and I would have told you soon enough. He was a fine young man and what he did was entirely right. To be tied to the Mas would have killed him. You are well aware of my desire for you to marry but not if it kills the husband you obtain. When we get to the Mas I will show you his letters. They all concern you and your wellbeing. There is normally a detailed questionnaire as to your happiness and achievements. That is the past, now what for the future? This Samuel Pepys, is he a prospect for . . .?"

"Marriage? I don't know. I have no doubt that he wishes me for a wife."

"And you?"

"In truth, I don't know."

"Do you love him?"

"In a way, yes. Do I admire him? Yes, even more. Do I desire him? I think so. Has he the substance to care for my family? Certainly, at present, I would say so."

My mother looked at me, her eyes creased with shrewd analysis: "That is a pretty comprehensive list of ambivalence."

"It is. And there is one other thing. He saved my life. That is no small thing. It can forge strong bonds."

My mother nodded. "Yes, well, I see that but he is a man of substance?"

"In every way. Setting wealth aside, he is now one of the most powerful men in England. As with most powerful men in England he lives permanently on the verge of death and disgrace."

My mother said nothing else on the subject. In truth there was nothing more to be said.

* * *

It was now summer. As we passed along the great River Dronne, the hills unfolded beyond it, majestic and full with vast trees heavy as though sleeping under their folded blankets of grey and green. My wounds still ached but it was a slow, receding manageable pain as though cured by the very landscape through which we passed. We came to Bergerac and stopped in the square. My father had some small commercial business to attend and I wandered through the market, happy as a child in her model farmyard of pigs, ducks, hens and tethered sheep. We reached the Mas in the early evening. Marie-Claire was there with hot bread, cheese, chutneys and tears of welcome. It was sufficient food. I drank a little wine, walked through the libraries and came to my mother's spinet. Gently I removed the sling and held my right hand above the keyboard. I fingered a short round and added a chord and another. It was awkward and slow but it was accurate enough. I added the left hand and created something approaching harmony. I turned to see my mother watching from the door. She was carrying a package wrapped in paper and tied by ribbon. "You will play well enough," she said. "Do you want to read these now or wait until the morning?

I took them to my bed, lit three candles and read my lover's letters twice over until gone midnight. There were forty-three of them, spread over seven years. They were written from many cities of Europe. Paris, London, Madrid, Rome, Florence, Vienna, St Petersburg, Amsterdam. They came from many directions but they possessed the same theme: my welfare, my wellbeing and my happiness, my education, my music, my care for Robert, for the land, for those who served our house. Had I been sick? Was I safe from the recent plague? Did I still walk in the woods, play in the barn, practice my dancing, my drama, my sword craft? Did I still play the lute? Had I taken to the violin? For seven years, in thirty cities of Europe, my name had been repeatedly inscribed, my presence and being repeatedly invoked. Of course I cried. In part the tears were anger at this monumental secret, kept from me for year on year. But I understood why. I know myself and my personality well enough. Had I known of their existence I would have followed their author. I would have become a traveller, a follower, stateless and landless in love. I bundled them together, left my chamber overlooking the park and went to my childhood bedroom.

The bed itself was now too small for me and stood awaiting future children. There was a cupboard and loose boarding which had once formed part of a shelf. It concealed a small, dry void unknown to anyone but myself. In my childhood this had been a place of secrets. Only those things which had special significance and warmth – toys, writings, ephemera gathered from the woods – were placed in this small hide. It was empty, cleared and dispersed by me long ago. I took the parcel, placed it carefully behind the board and tapped it into place. One day they would be found. Meanwhile they would be safe, dry, warm and secure as my dreams. I returned to my bed and, despite the nagging of my injuries, fell into a deep and contented sleep.

In the morning a messenger arrived. He was from the Duc de Pertaine. The Duc wished to meet my father to discuss "our family business". It was his request and he would travel. Assuming my father's agreement he was already, observing the date, on the road to the Périgord. He would stay at the Hôtel d'Aubille and would be prepared to meet my father on this neutral ground on the 20th of May at ten o'clock. "Tomorrow," said my father, passing the documents to my mother. She looked at him across our table. "Will you go?"

"Of course. If I do not go he will come here. I want no more of his family at my door."

I spent the day walking the estate, through the woods and fields and along the streams and rivers. My mother came with me and we talked, as we always had, on a vast and eclectic range of subjects, profound and ephemeral side-by-side. She did not mention the letters or ask for their return. We took food with us, eggs, bread, wine, which we consumed overlooking a bend in the river. We lay together and slept in the shade of an ancient willow. We woke together as the first cool breeze touched our faces. We walked, sometimes hand in hand, back to the Mas where I left her. I had a pilgrimage to make. She knew it and so did I. I opened the door of the barn and stepped into its vast interior. Evening light fell through the vents and windows, forming pillars of gently dancing dust. The bales and boards, my imaginary stage, still stood twenty paces distant, theatrically framed in the falling light as was intended. For the next object of search I moved along the wall unsure of memory. My father's voice came from the door: "It is gone, *ma chérie*, gone for good." He was framed in the doorway and did not move to enter.

"And the swords?" I said.

"All gone. Burnt and buried to rust."

I nodded my head. "Mine too. It was not retrieved and I will not see it again."

We walked together to the kitchen door by which Robert had left, bidden by Marie-Claire, to conceal himself in the barn. As we entered the door my father said: "I am going to Ribérac tomorrow to see de Pertaine as you know. Robert's grave is close to the hotel. Would you like to come?"

I shook my head. "No." I tapped my forehead. "It is here in my imaginings and I do not want it disturbed. His grave is here and I have seen it." He grunted, I thought, with approval and we spoke no more of it. We were early to our beds and, at eight o'clock the following morning, I heard my father's carriage leave the front of the house. It left at speed, its metal wheels tearing against the gravel. I ate with my mother in near silence and we parted for the remainder of the morning. I read a little and practised my finger work at the lute. The sling was now permanently discarded and my arm loose and supple at the shoulder. It was wasted and every hour I methodically clenched my fist to drive weight and strength into the upper muscles. A little after one, my father returned. Lunch was set out in the dining room and we ate quickly before he spoke. On this report concentration was essential. When the meal was finished my father poured some water and some wine, both of which I declined. He then gave us his account.

"I met him at the hotel. He had commandeered the salon. There were others with him but we were left alone. He began: 'Let me tell you what I know. You are a Prefect of the Périgord. You have an estate and a Mas that bears your name. You have two children, a girl and a boy, Camille and Robert. They are twins. Your daughter was an actor working at a theatre in Paris. She dressed as a man. This, I understand, was made necessary by some foolery of the municipal government. On her way home, as *him*, she killed my son, Michel'." On a number of occasions I wished to intervene but he simply held up his hand indicating that I should listen until the end, which I did. "'She killed my son. The circumstances of his death I have investigated. My older son, Édouard, was told that it was a coward's attack, a stabbing in the dark. The main architect of this fiction was a man called Rabonne. He was a leech on my son Michel and I never liked him. I had his story tested. He was put to the hot iron and the test did not last long. The duel, if it may be so called, was the fault of Michel. He was not the worst of my sons but I had no illusions. He was an opinionated drunken fool. Whether he would have matured differently we will never know. I think not but, for the comfort of his mother, I will assume otherwise. Édouard believed the story, partly because he was told no other and partly because he wanted to believe it. That was his nature. Vengeance was his stock-in-trade; vengeance for anything, insult, woman, imagined theft. He was a walking fire ship ready to destroy anything against which he drifted, by circumstance or planning. I could not control him. As I say, Monsieur Lefebre, I entertain no illusions as to my children. From my enquiries I understand you to be the same. Édouard believed your son Robert was the actual killer. This was a genuine belief and it is a mitigation. How that belief survived the confrontation is impossible to comprehend. I have made my enquiries. Your son Robert was a reclusive cripple. He resembled his sister, I know that. But no one who had ever touched a sword could believe he was the genuine article. The mitigation, therefore, is slight. Édouard is now dead, killed by your daughter. I believe that the duel was fair although there is some rumour about a mirror. I discount it. Édouard had many, many faults but he was a fine swordsman and a powerful bully. Your daughter was, as she is, an actress. If he was temporarily blinded then it would even the score. From what I have said you may guess my conclusion. I wish an end to this matter, a final conclusion. I have lost two sons and I have no wish to lose a third. Pierre is the only one I now possess. He is a different boy. I have often wished that he, rather than Édouard, would inherit the title and the estates. Now that wish, at least, is granted in circumstances which I would not have chosen. So these are my proposals. As of this moment we give each other our word, our solemn word, that there will be no more vengeance on either side. Publicly I will never speak ill of your children or make allegations against them. I ask the same of you although I understand it will be more difficult in your case. If your daughter wishes to resume her career in Paris, she may do so free of fear at least from my family. Her fellow actors may be another matter. That is it. It is simple and it is what I have come to say'."

"There was, in truth, little I could add. It is over. The price is a small one. History will not record the truth but justice of a kind has been done. I simply said: 'I accept everything that you suggest and, where necessary, you have my word as a gentleman.' I was surprised when he suddenly smiled. His reputation is well known: powerful, ruthless and, when he wishes, cruel. He has another side. He continued. 'Thank you, Monsieur Lefebre. That concludes our business and I have asked that some wine should be ready when I signal.' He raised his hands towards the door and, silently bidden, a servant entered with champagne and two glasses. 'If you prefer brandy, please say so. At my age I find this better for the health. It is important that I live as long as I can. My family is running out of men, old or young.' The glasses were poured and he raised his towards me. 'There is one other matter. The Théâtre du Marais. I have been there myself on a number of occasions. I admire its productions and I am an admirer of Molière who, I understand, now writes for them. This "incident" has caused them much damage. They have lost their principal actress. Their performances have been curtailed. All that is the fault of my family. There can never be adequate recompense. Art cannot be measured in money. However, my family name is at stake. I have arranged for ten thousand *livres*, gold coin to be deposited at the theatre. It should already have been done. I wish for no thanks and no acknowledgement. I wish them well in their endeavours.'"

My father finished and turned to me. "Would you like some of that wine now? I see that you would. Let us drink brandy, it is better for us."

I stayed five further days at the Mas and I was now near fully recovered. It was serene and necessary but I had become restless.

On the 26th I packed my portmanteau, took leave of my family and went to my old lodgings in the rue Feuillette. I dined happily with Paul Challon and his family, recounting, yet again, the much-edited facts of my travels. The following day I was due to leave with Pepys for London. He had sent details of his address and I replied with my own message. I asked that his coach should collect me from the Théâtre du Marais at ten o'clock. I was anxious to see Paul Detain and to ensure that the money promised by the Duc had safely arrived. It would be, I hoped, a pleasant task.

I slept well and Paul Challon arranged for my portmanteau and my valise to be transported to the theatre and left in its foyer. I travelled in the same coach and, by nine-fifteen, was in Detain's office. His eyes were wide with enthusiasm and news: "Camille," he said, "I am so pleased you came to say goodbye. Let me tell you the news but first let me say you must not, on any account, return the money that you were given. There is a reason for that which I will now tell you. Yesterday a man arrived in the full uniform and livery of the Duc de Pertaine. You can imagine the consternation that it caused. Some of the cast, I hear, were attempting to hide under the stage furniture. That was just the men. Most actors will never make soldiers, I fear, except in the wings with a spear. He was brought straight to my office and declined the offer of a chair or refreshment. He carried two leather bags, which he placed on my desk. They are over there on the floor. 'This,' he said, 'is from the Duc de Pertaine. He requires neither thanks nor acknowledgement and, indeed, would be displeased if this was public knowledge. He wishes me to convey his personal regrets and his best wishes for your future productions. He particularly asked to have his compliments paid to Monsieur Molière, whom he greatly admires.' He then left. Pertaine has a terrible reputation and booby traps were thought more than likely. Nobody touched the bags until Jacques Delaine arrived at the theatre and cheerfully pulled them both open at the clasp." He lowered his voice to a near whisper. "Camille, in those bags there are ten thousand *livres*, gold coin."

I opened my eyes as wide as I could and allowed my mouth to fall with theatrical flourish.

"Just think. The boxes can be refurbished. New drapes! New scenery that does not sway in the wind. Even a mechanical revolve that rises to stage level as though from Hell. All of these things are now possible. It has been suggested that we rename the theatre Le Pertaine but that has been overruled. No doubt there are many artistic venues that have been named after mass murderers. Caligula must have had a few but, for the moment, the Marais will stand."

"Paul," I said, "I am simply overjoyed. I will go to London a very happy woman."

He stood and moved round the desk. "I am sorry you are going but I know you will return. This theatre is always open for you, that you know."

"You do not need me, Paul. You now have the money to assemble a fine cast."

"And I have one. They have just finished their rehearsals. If you hurry you might see the end."

I paused and said: "They are rehearsing at nine in the morning?"

"Yes. I am afraid our new leads themselves demand perfection. Your Jacques Delaine combines rare talents: brilliance and hard work."

"He is here?"

"Probably still on the stage. He works later than most. Irritating for some of the cast but an inspiration."

The clock that hung in his room told me it was nine-thirty. "I have time," I said. "I will see if there is anything to watch." I went to the back of the auditorium and looked at the stage, empty save for the presence of Jacques Delaine, in costume and pacing the boards.

The scenery behind him portrayed a country house. Large doors stood at ground level and, above his head was a balcony with open windows, now deserted. I had an inspiration. I hastened through the corridors behind the boxes, opened the door to the wings and, in near darkness, felt my way along the back of the scenery. There was, as I hoped, a roughly constructed staircase leading to the windows I had seen from the auditorium. The stairs were as dangerous as most created for the use of actors and, in my haste, I was close to falling before I arrived at balcony level and stepped into the set. I had hoped that the balcony was intended as part of the stage and not simply as decoration otherwise I would have plunged downwards adding immediately to the injuries I already carried. It was solid enough and I found myself standing six feet above the head of Jacques Delaine, still pacing and still muttering from an invisible script. I leaned across the balcony, filled my lungs and shouted into the empty stage:

"Hé! Roméo, où es tu? Monte toute de suite! Dépêche toi!" His head snapped upwards and he regarded me with wild disbelief. It did not last long. He was a thespian, trained for surprises.

"Hé, Juliette," he cried. "Attends! J'arrive!"

I did not think he would do it but with his first leap he caught the bottom of the balustrade. From my side I could see that it had been nailed together from the flimsiest of materials and I saw the wood split as it took his full weight. By good fortune his other hand had seized the only part of substance. He had always possessed considerable strength and now, as the first handhold gave away, he swung and placed both hands on the second part of the balustrade. With a grunt of pain he hauled himself upwards, executed an athletic movement, swung his feet above the rail and stood facing me, breathless but otherwise unhurt: "Eh bien, Juliette, que veux tu?"

I dissolved into laughter, which he shared. Before I could resist he held me in his arms and I inhaled the familiar smell of stage makeup, wax and chalk. We stood and kissed with a forgotten passion until I pulled away and placed one hand upon his chest.

"No," I said. "This was a mistake."

"Camille," he said. "You have come back."

"No," I said. "I have not come back. I came to see Paul about the money. I knew it was coming and I wanted to make sure it had arrived. That was wise. This is a mistake."

Despite my hand he reached out and held my shoulders: "Camille, you cannot, you must not go."

I felt tears in my eyes and I answered: "Jacques, Jacques, my darling, my darling Jacques, I must go. You know that and there is no argument. I have a debt of honour and I must pay it."

"To whom Camille, to whom? To this servant of a king?"

"He is not a servant. He is his own man. He makes kings. He does not serve them. He seeks good government for the people and, in doing so, lives a life as full as any I have seen. That is the man."

"Very well Camille. Very well. I know he is a great man. I have heard his reputation but you will live with him for years. Do you love him?"

I was now crying real non-theatrical tears. "Yes, in a way I do. Jacques, my darling, I do not love him as I love you. I will never love anyone as I love you. In my heart there is no course of action that I would rather take than to stay on this balcony and act with you for the rest of our lives. But this cannot be and that is the end of it. I have a debt of honour and I must pay it."

"What is this debt?"

"He took me into his house. He protected me when I was in the greatest danger and, more recently, he has saved my life. That is a debt which must be paid. He needs me and I will not fail him."

Delaine's head fell but he spoke with kindness. "I understand. Go you must. I am sure that Detain has just said this to you. When you return, we will be here."

"Jacques, my darling," I said. "I know that and, and now that I have read your letters I know that very well"

I made my exit through the balcony doors, safely negotiated the stairs, passed through the wings and into the corridor behind the boxes. I noticed as I did so that the door of the box nearest the stage, the box in which Michel de Pertaine had spent his last evening, was standing open. I had nearly a quarter of an hour to compose myself before my carriage arrived. As I hastened along the corridor Paul Detain came out of his room.

"Camille," he said, "you have found your friend?"

It was a question I immediately misunderstood. "I found Jacques Delaine and he is certainly my friend."

"No Camille. Not Jacques, the man in black with the spectacles."

"Pepys?" I said. "He is here already?"

"Yes, he has been here for ten minutes at least. He asked where you were and I said that you were in the auditorium watching a rehearsal. He asked if he could join you and I showed him to the first box to get the best view."

"Paul," I said, "he has been in the first box?"

"Yes, yes. He has been there for ten minutes, perhaps more."

I stated the obvious for no real reason. "He would have heard everything that was said on the stage?"

"Of course. That is why I showed him to the best box. The acoustics are wonderful."

I began to run along the corridor and into the foyer. Apart from the doorman it was deserted. My portmanteau and my valise still stood by the door. As I crossed the foyer he held out a piece of paper.

"Camille," he said. "Are you looking for the gentleman with spectacles?"

"Yes," I said. "Yes. Where is he?"

"He has left. He asked me to give you this." It was a slip of paper, the back of a theatre bill. On it was written three words in English: the timeless actors' exhortation. I ran into the street. There was little traffic and, to the right, the only carriage was moving steadily away, fifty yards distant. It was slowly gathering speed and any pursuit on foot would have been futile. In the rear window of the carriage I saw that I was observed and I caught a flash of glass in the morning sun, spectacles beyond doubt. As I watched, an arm extended from the window of the coach. In the hand was a black folder. The knowledge of its contents was shared by two people who now watched each other disappearing in a Paris street.

I had no option. I executed a full pirouette and sunk in a full curtsey onto the cobbles below me. When I raised my head I saw the carriage turn to the right. The hand with the folder made one gesture of unmistakable joy as it disappeared from view.

1. The secret Treaty of Dover was signed on the 1st of June 1670. Until the discovery of these diary fragments the process of negotiation was unknown. The Treaty did not become public knowledge till 1771.

2. The third Dutch War began on the 27th of March 1672. England and France declared war on Holland. For England, it was a disaster and ended with the Treaty of Westminster in 1674.

3. In 1672, Charles II issued a Declaration of Indulgence relaxing penal laws against Roman Catholics. When reconvened, Parliament declared the Declaration to be illegal and declined to vote funding until it was withdrawn. It was withdrawn later that year.

4. Pepys's Parliamentary enemies continued to work against him. In 1678, he was accused of "Piracy, Popery and Treachery" and committed to the Tower. Colonel Scott appeared as a witness against him. The case collapsed. (Camille's aunt was lying to her. Pepys had not been committed to the Tower before 1670.)

5. Pepys died in 1703 in William Hewer's house in Clapham, shortly after he had sent the diary entries to Camille. Hewer

himself had become Clerk to the Navy Board, MP for Yarmouth and Judge Advocate General of the Navy.

6. The sums advanced by Louis as a result of the Treaty are unknown. They were insufficient to enable the dissolution of Parliament.

7. John Wilmot, 2nd Earl of Rochester, died of syphilis in 1680 aged thirty-three. He is widely regarded (certainly by the author) as the most seriously neglected of English poets. His portrait hangs in the National Portrait Gallery next to that of Samuel Pepys (and above that of John Dryden).

8. The first official record of women appearing as professional actors on the English Stage is immediately post Restoration. The first recorded performance is that of Margaret Hughes, as Desdemona at the Vere Theatre in 1660. However, it is inconceivable that women did not, with the minimum of artifice, play on the stage during the great Renaissance of English Theatre, which took place at the beginning of the seventeenth century until it was eclipsed by the Commonwealth in 1642. Indeed, the Puritan aversion to the Theatre may well have been stimulated by the growing and tolerated popularity of women playing female leads.

9. Duelling in France was forbidden in 1626 by Louis XIII. The edict was widely ignored. Between 1686 and 1716, 10,000 duels were fought by French Army officers alone, resulting in 400 deaths. Judicial pardons were routine where the duel was fair and in accordance with the rules of swordsmanship.

• ACKNOWLEDGEMENTS •

I am much indebted to:

Catherine Mew (nee Poinso) for her tireless work,
infinite good humour and patience in dealing with
my appalling Franglais.

Jill Fennel, my own wonderful amanuensis.

Isadore Kaplan, with whom many years ago, I discussed the
Treaty of Dover and who suggested, over a bottle of Mar,
that SP was behind it.

John Bond, Annabel Wright and whitefox,
who believed in Camille.